The Thousand Days of Disbelief

- Book Two of 'The Thrice-Cursed Godly Glories' Trilogy -

Jim McPherson

I0548735

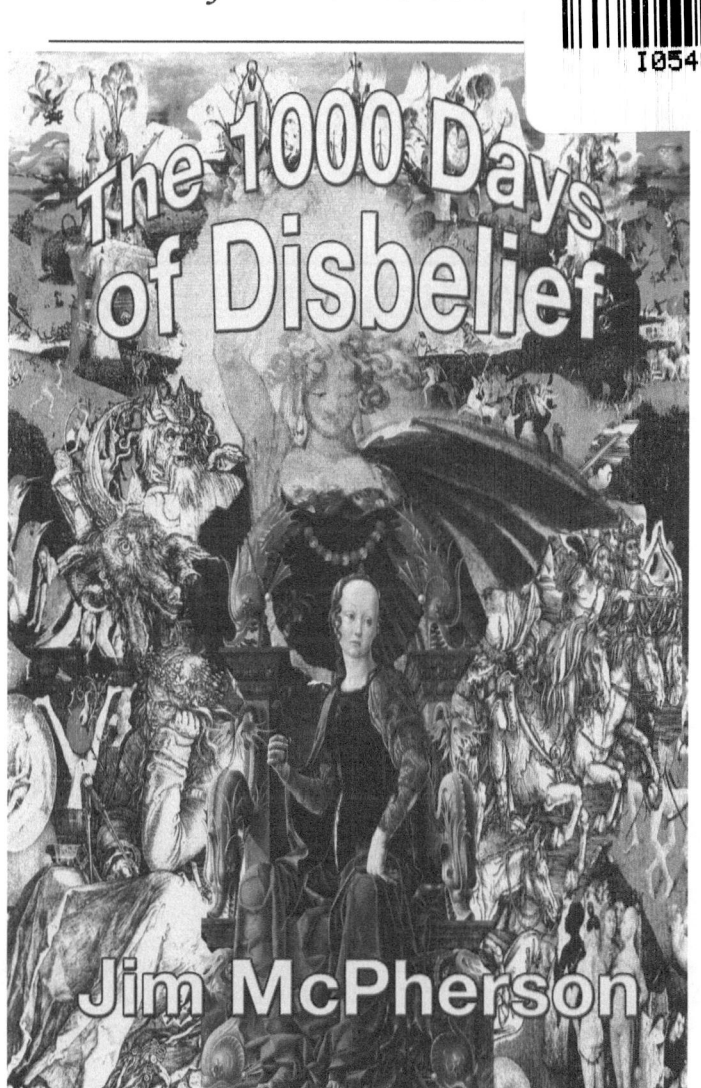

A ***PHANTACEA* Mythos** Mosaic Novel

published by James H McPherson

ISBN 978-0-9781342-1-1

CONTAGION COLLECTORS

A *PHANTACEA* MYTHOS PRINT PUBLICATION

www.phantacea.com

Conceived, written and produced by Jim McPherson
Cover and interior collages prepared by Jim McPherson

James H McPherson, Publisher
74689 Kitsilano RPO
2768 West Broadway
Vancouver BC
V6K 4P4 Canada

MEANWHILE, ON THE OUTER EARTH

His parents feared for his life. He didn't know the meaning of fear. Truth told, at age 4 he barely knew the meaning of much of anything. He did know his fifth birthday was coming up in May, when it would be warm again; that the snow frosting his window meant it was cold outside; and that his dog was somewhere out there barking loudly.

He'd heard mention of Nuremberg. He hadn't connected it with the name of the long ago officially proclaimed free city wherein he lived. He certainly knew what a bed was – he was lying in his. He didn't know his parents worried it might be his deathbed because he'd never experienced death, not that he could remember anyhow: hence also his failure to fear it. He didn't realize how sick he was; only that he didn't feel very well.

He wouldn't have heard that his surname meant *'door'* or *'door-maker'* in English because he only spoke German. He did know the door to his bedroom gaped invitingly. Plus, he could still hear Drang raising cacophonous Cain, as his father might alliterate, albeit in his own language. But it was already sounding much fainter than it did when it woke him up.

Ergo, his ever faithful, but clearly dumb as they come hound must be dutifully chasing some bogie or another farther and farther away from their familial sanctuary. Dumb as they come wasn't an insult either. Drang had to be at least that dumb because he'd somehow missed the bogie in his bedroom.

The podgy putto, as demonologists identified his aberrant species, looked a lot younger than he did. If it weren't for the spiffy, embroidered outfit, dinky shoulder-wings and receding hairline, what almost contrarily made him look nearly as old as the boy's Hungarian-born goldsmith of a father, he'd have thought he was a baby angel.

"Get dressed, kiddo," the green-eyed, no doubt ne'er-do-well bird-brat demanded, as he passed him his stuff. "Your fiddlehead doctors may diagnose your condition dire, but it sniffs to me that you'll get better soon. That means we've got to hurry. Otherwise we'll waste all that good contagion."

"Can I fly too?"

"Don't see why not. Faerie farts like me don't infect easily."

Print publications featuring

Jim McPherson's

PHANTACEA Mythos

- ### *PHANTACEA* One to Six
(A series of comic books with artwork by various artists)

- ### Forever & 40 Days – The Genesis of *PHANTACEA*
(A graphic novel with artwork by Ian Fry as well as background material and a short story featuring the Damnation Brigade, the Death Dodgers & Signal System)

Feeling Theocidal
(Book One of *'The Thrice-Cursed Godly Glories'* Trilogy)

- ### The War of the Apocalyptics
(The first entry in the *'Launch 1980'* story cycle)

- ### The Death's Head Hellion
(A mini-novel derived from *'The 1000 Days of Disbelief'*)

- ### Contagion Collectors
(A mini-novel derived from *'The 1000 Days of Disbelief'*)

In one form or another, all are available for ordering through:
www.phantacea.com

Send inquiries, certified cheques and/or money orders care of:

James H McPherson, Publisher
74689 Kitsilano RPO
2768 West Broadway
Vancouver BC
V6K 4P4 Canada

Auctorial Preamble

"The Thousand Days of Disbelief", Book Two of *'The Thrice-Cursed Godly Glories'* trilogy, consists of three distinct mini-novels. Although comprising a whole, each segment is complete unto itself. At some point in time they may come out in one volume. That point is, for now, in the future.

Many of the characters featured in the mini-novels are immortal or seemingly immortal. Their influence is thus felt throughout the ages covered by the overall trilogy. Indeed, some of those listed on the reference pages counted with Roman numerals hardly ever appear in the mini-novel at hand, whereas a few others are only mentioned in it.

"Contagion Collectors" commences on page 1. The first chapter of the next mini-novel chronologically, "Janna Fangfingers", is provided as a bonus. It begins on page 145.

========

Sedon Plague 5456-5476
– "CONTAGION COLLECTORS" –

(Extracted from a capsulated character companion for *'The Thrice-Cursed Godly Glories'* Trilogy)

Index

1. Myrionymous Devils – An Ease-of-Identification Key

2. Shining Ones: First, Second and Third Generation Devils

- The Moloch Sedon
- The Six Great Gods and Goddesses (Thrygragos Lazareme, Thrygragos Byron, Thrygragos Varuna Mithras, and the often three-in-one Trigregos Sisters: Demeter the Body, Devaura the Soul or Spirit & Sapiendev the Mind)
- Master Devas
  - The Firstborn Unities of Lazareme (Balance, Chaos & Order)
  - Significant Additional Lazaremists (Dame Chance, the Skinless Rasp, Vladuca Fangfingers)
  - Significant Mithradites (Sinistral Lust, Gravedigger, Sinistral Envy)
  - Moderately Significant Byronics (APM All-Eyes, Djerrid Ruin)
  - More Lazaremists (Rumour, Librarian, Krepusyl Evenstar, Irisiel Mercherm)
  - More Byronics (Chimaera Glimmenmare, Pyçonja Volant, Camorva

Freeflight, Yati, Vanthysces)
- More Mithradites (Pyrame Silverstar, Thanatoid Death Gods, King Harvest, Nergal Vetala, Tammuz, Osiraq, Reptilians, various Apocalyptics)

3. Deviants, Demons, Faeries and a Mandroid Mother Machine

- Definite Deviants (various Legendarians, Pusan Wanderlust, Morgan Abyss, Quidnunc Tethys, Quibble Tethys, Quoits Tethys, Squiggly Tethys, Zalman Somata & the Terrible Twins, Sraddha and Janna Somata)
- Definite Demons (Primeval Lilith, Daemonicus)
- Mandroids (All of Incain, Magnus Minus)
- Herta Heartthrob
- Tomcat Tattletail

4. Mortal Descendants of Original Extraterrestrials

- Utopians of Weir on Earth
- Illuminaries
- Biomages
- Scientocrats
- Trinondevs
- Imbeciles
- Cabalarkon, the Undying Utopian, Cabby the Daddy
- Melina born Tethys become Somata

5. Norman & Norma Notables

- John Barleycorn
- Dire
- Drang the Dog
- Twisted Tommy
- Bosco

========

1. Myrionymous Devils

Devils (meaning big and little gods) within the **PHANTACEA** Mythos have a variety of talents, titles and given names. With the exception of the first and second generations of devazurkind as well as, perhaps strangely, Pyrame Silverstar (qv), devils did not start receiving individual names until roughly a thousand years after they started to become individually solid deities circa 2000 Year of the Dome (YD).

Even then, the names they received came from their sworn as well as mortal enemies, the Utopians of Weir on Earth. Before that they were mostly known by their attributes. Indeed, throughout the Years of the Dome 5456 to 5476 devils still tend to call each other by their titles or attributes.

What follows immediately is an ease-of-identification key to the most common terms used during "Contagion Collectors" to refer to some of the more prominent devils in the mini-novel.

- Ahriman – see the **VAM** Entity
- Aphropsyche Morningstar – see **APM** All-Eyes
- Balance – see **Harmony**
- Bodiless Byron – see **Byron**
- Datong Harmonia – see **Harmony**
- Eye-Mouth in the Sky – see **Sedon**
- Lightning Lord Yajur – see **Order**
- Miss Mist – see **Krepusyl**
- Miss Myth – see **Methandra**
- Mr Myth – see Varuna **Mithras**

- Odour, Ordure – see **Order**
- Providence – see **Pyrame**
- Smiler, the Smiling Fiend – see the **VAM** Entity
- Sparky – see **Order**
- Thunder and Lightning – see **Order**
- Uncle Abe, Uncle Abe Chaos – see **Chaos**
- Undying One – see **Lazareme**
- Unholy One, Unholy Abaddon – see **Chaos**
- Unmoving One – see **Byron**
- Yajur – see **Order**

========

2. Shining Ones: First, Second and Third Generation Devils

- The Moloch Sedon
  - the seemingly immortal, but nowhere-near-almighty, All-Father of Devazurkind; the Devil Himself, capitalized;
  - solitary member of the first generation of devazurkind; acknowledged king of chthonic or earthborn daemons or demons since Ragnarok, circa 234 PD (Pre-Dome);
  - grown or developed, more so than engendered let alone created, by the Male and Female Entities on the Trigon Asteroid, part of the First Weir System, in the dim recesses of the time-space continuum;
  - the Entities started the process that resulted in the Moloch by using the right eye of Cabalarkon, a then wholly alive Utopian biogeneticist, for raw material; consequently Sedon still regards the now undying Utopian as his father, hence Cabby the Daddy;
  - in the Year of the Dome (YD) Zero (4000 BCE), Sedon used his essence to form the Cathonic Zone or Dome (consequently also the Sedon Sphere) in order to separate the consequential Outer Earth from the thereafter Inner Earth of Sedon's Head;
  - the mighty Eye-Mouth in the Sky, as depicted on the back cover of "The War of the Apocalyptics" (the predecessor in terms of **PHANTACEA** print publications to 1000-Daze), is Star Sedon; details of his origin appeared in "Forever & 40 Days – The Genesis of **PHANTACEA**", a graphic novel published in 1990; somewhat atypically in term of the **PHANTACEA** Mythos,

Sedon deigns to make a personal appearance in "The Death's Head Hellion";
- the bulk of the "Contagion Collector" mini-novel takes place between YD 5456 and YD 5476 (AD 1456-1476), by which time Sedon has been using an additional part of his essence to protect the Weirdom of Cabalarkon from the Ghostlands' still rampant radioactivity for in excess of 600 years.

- • The Six Great Gods and Goddesses
  - the Thrygragos Brothers and Trigregos Sisters comprise the entirety of the second generation of devakind;
  - the Three Great Gods are Thrygragos **Lazareme** (aka sometimes the Lackland Libertine, but most commonly Thrygragos Everyman), Thrygragos **Byron** (aka both Bodiless Byron and the Unmoving One due to that fact that he's all head, with his facial features frozen in the same expression, not because he can't transport himself wherever he wants on the Inner Earth), and Thrygragos Varuna **Mithras**;
  - neither Byron nor Mithras appear in the mini-novel; however, there is more than mere mention of a eminently forgettable, but possibly not apocryphal, individual known as the **VAM** Entity – Thrygragos Varuna Ahriman Mithras (the reference harkens back to passages of "Feeling Theocidal", Book One of *'The Thrice-Cursed Godly Glories'*);
  - the ostensible 'A' in the VAM Entity has too many fingers on his hands and they in turn have too many joints or knuckles per digit;
  - he also plays a mean panpipe and goes by any number of names; they include Smiler, the Smiling Fiend, the Judge, Judge Druj (meaning *'the Lie'*), Bad Rhad and Rhadamanthys;
  - Pyrame (Providence) is among those who believe this Rhadamanthys was actually the Moloch Sedon during the 500-year-long, so-called man-hating, mad goddesses' Middle Sea matriarchate that lasted from roughly 2000 to 1500 BCE on the Outer Earth (YD 2000-2500);
  - Smiler considers himself the rightful Demon King; apparently Sinistral Envy concurs, which strongly suggests the panpipe-playing fiend might actually be the Moloch Sedon slumming, something the then Legendarian suspected when he came close to encountering one or the other (unless they really are the same) in Feel Theo;
  - because they must have worshippers in order to flourish, Great Gods, like their offspring, are not allowed to kill lesser beings;
  - if they do, Sedon will cathonitize, catasterize, or ill-star them (i.e., fuse their spirit selves or essences, often along with their power foci, with his such that they thereafter shine out of the night's sky above the Hidden Headworld);
  - the Three Great Goddesses are Trigregos **Devaura** (the Spirit or Soul), Trigregos **Demeter** (the Body), and Trigregos **Sapiendev** (the Mind); they do not appear in the mini-novel;
  - their terrible talismans do, however; hence why "Contagion Collectors" is an integral part of *'The Thrice-Cursed Godly Glories'* Trilogy.

- Master Devas
  - dictionaries often define *'devas'* or *'daevas'* as *'the shining ones'*; hence also the English word *'devils'*, meaning *'little gods'*;
  - Master Devas compose the third generation of devazurkind; the Trigregos Sisters always bore them simultaneously, in threesomes;
  - they believe their fathers are one or another of the Thrygragos Brothers; hence why it's accepted that there are only three devic tribes: the Lazaremists, the Byronics and the Mithradites;
  - when Sedon, Great Gods and/or Master Devas possess sentient beings for procreative purposes, their resultant offspring are often long-lived and, once in a while, unnaturally gifted mortals known as deviants.

  - The Firstborn Unities of Lazareme
    — **Harmony**, called Datong Harmonia by bygone Illuminaries of Weir on Earth; the Unity of Balance as well as Panharmonium (her pet project, a planetary panacea for beneficial devils and their worshipful multitudes alike);
    - reputedly, by a matter of a few seconds, the first Master Deva ever born; beauty incarnate as well as loveliness personified;
    - her power focus or Tvasitar talisman is a golden torc, the so-called Necklace of, as you might expect, Harmony; from it she conjures her golden, chain-mail gowns and the broken chains often manifested manacled to her wrists; from them she sometimes shoots, what else?, chain lightning;
    - her fortunately rarely manifested alter ego is the nihilistic Nemesis, a relentless avenger along the lines of the Classical Furies.
    — **Chaos**, called Unholy Abaddon by bygone Illuminaries of Weir (after the Biblical Angel of Apollyon, the Bottomless Pit); the Unity of just that, Chaos;
    - his power focus or Tvasitar talisman is the Chaos Blade, which he keeps forever-sheathed out of fear of causing a chain reaction that would bring irreversible carnage to the world, if not the cosmos;
    — **Order**, called Thunder and Lightning Lord Yajur, or variations thereof, by bygone Illuminaries of Weir; the Unity of just that, Order;
    - from his power focus or Tvasitar talisman he shoots vajra bolts – white lightning of the non-alcoholic variety;
    - goes by Sparky when he's in altogether human form;
    - Chaos and Order hate each other passionately; they'd seek to annihilate each other, and all that stands between them, if Harmony didn't always do just that, stand between them mollifyingly.

- Significant Additional Lazaremists
    — **Chance**, called Wintry Moira by bygone Illuminaries of Weir; a fifth-born also known variously as Lazareme's Luck, Fata Fortuna and, most commonly among devils, Dame Chance;
    - because of her dangerously unpredictable attribute, coupled with her nevertheless undeniable attractiveness, some refer to her as the luscious Lady Luck;
    - sometimes regarded as the Legendarian's charming devic stalker since she

seems to seek him out for purposes procreative wherever he recurs;

- as such, the devic half-mother of many eventual Legendarians (Jordan *'Q for Quill'* Tethys, a recurring deviant sometimes recalled as the legendary 30-Year Man or Woman, as well as 30-Beers);

- the half-mother, for example, of Master Morgan Abyss, aka the Death's Head Hellion, who is often mentioned in the mini-novel;

- her azuras are called Fatazurs;

- her power focus or Tvasitar talisman is the 3-spoke wheel of fortune traditionally known as the Triskelion.

— **Skinless**, the Skinless Rasp, or variations thereof; a comparatively lowborn Lazaremist called by bygone Illuminaries Rastha Aragon;

- a White Godling flagellant with a flail for a power focus;

- seems to have a strangely loving relationship with Fangfingers (Faustus Vladuca);

- chosen (in 5474) by the Unities and the Terrible Twins' parents, Zalman and Melina, to *'occupy'* Janna Somata when she gets married and whenever she conceives and bears children;

- since her deviant offspring would be as unimpressive as her, the choice is a deliberate slap in the face to the Mithradites, who are scheduled to resume governorship of the Weirdom of Kanin City come 5500 YD (AD 1500).

— **Fangfingers**, a comparatively lowborn Lazaremist called by bygone Illuminaries Faustus Vladuca after a combination of Dacian, Carpathian, Gothic and/or Slavonic deities, folk legends or heroes;

- devils tend to refer to him as the Fop because he fancies himself something of a fashion plate, one with a penchant for wearing a black opera cape with red lining;

- has, for a power focus, a Brainrock glove with fangs rather than claws on its fingertips;

- a Black Godling with an unsavoury reputation for sadism in that he welcomes animal sacrifice;

- seems to have a strangely loving relationship with the Skinless Rasp (Rastha Aragon);

- chosen (in 5474) by the Unities and the Terrible Twins' parents, Zalman and Melina, to *'occupy'* Sraddha Somata when he gets married and whenever he fathers children;

- since his deviant offspring would be as unimpressive as him, the choice is a deliberate slap in the face to the Mithradites, who are scheduled to resume governorship of the Weirdom of Kanin City come 5500 YD (AD 1500).

• Significant Mithradites

— **Belialma**, Sinistral Lust of Satanwyck (Hell on Earth, Pandemonium, Sedon's Temple on a map of the Hidden Headworld); Hell's Belle, also sometimes called the luscious or lascivious Lady Lust as well as Bouncing, Beguiling or Bedazzling Belialma and variations thereof;

- a second-born Mithradite whose power focus or Tvasitar talisman is the Ruby Red Apple of Concupiscence; like her fellow Apple Goddesses, Concord and Discord, she carries it as the pupil of her third eye;

- always an object of desire, her reciprocal interests cross tribal boundaries to include not just Unholy Abaddon, the Unity of Chaos, and his brood brother, Lord Order, but their father, Thrygragos Lazareme;

- Bouncing Belle resides in her bastion of bliss overlooking Pandemonium, the capital of Satanwyck (Hell on Earth), where she entertains her paramours, who also number Zuvem *'Gravedigger'* Nergalis and, centuries earlier, King Cold (Tantal Thanatos) and Cruel Plathon, the Bull of Mithras, neither of whom appear in the mini-novel;

- wants to *'occupy'* Janna Somata when the latter gets married and whenever she conceives and bears children; that way her deviant offspring would be as impressive as Hell's Belle is and always has been;

- Mithradites are scheduled to resume governorship of the Weirdom of Kanin City come 5500 YD (AD 1500); Belle, who's bored of being the vice-regent or surrogate ruler of Hell on Earth, reckons she'd rather run the Mastery of Marutia through Janna when that day arrives.

— **Gravedigger**, a fourth-born called Zuvem Nergalis by bygone Illuminaries of Weir; generally manifests himself black-skinned, like a male Utopian of Weir;

- name in part derives from his power focus or Tvasitar talisman, which is a Brainrock spade with a razor-sharp edge, and in part because he's sometimes called the Nergalids' Planter even though he actually alternates planting duties (of Vetala-Fecundity) with King Harvest;

- among his other love interests include bedazzling Belialma (Hell's Belle, still Sinistral Lust of Satanwyck in 5476);

- figures he should *'occupy'* Sraddha Somata when the latter gets married and whenever he fathers children; that way his deviant offspring would be as impressive as Zuvem is and always has been, at least in his mind;

- Mithradites are scheduled to resume governorship of the Weirdom of Kanin City come 5500 YD (AD 1500); Gravedigger reckons he deserves to rule the Mastery of Marutia through Sraddha when that day arrives.

— Sinistral **Envy**, a lower-born called Bobby Badboy or, less frequently, Robin Goodfellow by bygone Illuminaries of Weir; generally manifests himself as a cupid or putto, which is why devils, somewhat incorrectly, tend to refer to him as Cupidity;

- realizes his much higher born sister, Bouncing Belle, is bored of acting as Sedon's viceroy, the surrogate ruler of Satanwyck (Sedon's Temple, Hell on Earth), and figures he's in line to succeed her when she moves to take over the Mastery of Marutia;

- like virtually everyone else, possibly including Sedon himself, he has no recollection that someone else has a greater claim to the throne of Hell until he manifests himself visually in front of him; that someone else is a certain myrionymous, always smiling fiend with too many fingers on his hands and they with too many knuckles.

- Moderately Significant Byronics
    — **APM** All-Eyes, lone daughter born in Bodiless Byron's third brood; as such a member of his secondary Nucleus (along with her triplet brothers, Damon Goldenrod and Nevair Neverknight, who don't appear in the mini-novel);
    - a love goddess, Byron's Venus, bygone Illuminaries of Weir named her Aphropsyche Morningstar, hence APM;
    - likes to appear as if composed entirely of eyes, hence All-Eyes;
    - her flutter-eyes (winged eyeballs, which she can externalize and sometimes uses as spies) are also called *'little angels'*; it seems they have the capacity to retain what they see as well as just long-distance-transmit what they're seeing or have seen to APM;
    - her witch-followers, who aren't just confined to the Byronics' territory of Aka Godbad at the time of the mini-novel, are known as love-loving Afrites.
    — **Djerrid Ruin**, Byron's Bowman, one of Byron's autumnal Zodiacals, as such associated with Sagittarius the Archer;
    - called his Green Man due to his proclivity for assuming the form of a 3-eyed, vegetative human somewhat reminiscent of the work of the famous Milanese painter Giuseppe Arcimboldo (1527-1593);
    - his power focus or Tvasitar talisman is a bow and quiver full of arrows.

- More Lazaremists
    — **Rumour** of Lazareme: devic half-father of the first Legendarian;
    - probably does not appear in "Contagion Collectors", but is mentioned in it fairly frequently because his power focus or Tvasitar talisman, a multipurpose Brainrock quill, transfers to the Legendarian, a recurring deviant who, whenever he returns to life, does so in his dying son or daughter, grandson or granddaughter;
    - Rumour was supposedly eaten by faeries circa 4000 YD in the Land of Daybreak (nowadays Crepuscule, the Land of Twilight);
    - his putative son, the recurring Legendarian, seems to think (possibly wrongly) that he became Tomcat Tattletail sometime after they ate him;
    - the Legendarian also thinks that Tomcat was the legendary Pied Piper of Hamelin; in this he is probably correct; (Tomcat is the panpipe-playing faerie trickster who often takes on the guise of Thrygragos Lazareme and thereby both seduces and bedevils Harmony; evidently he's done this frequently over the centuries leading up to "Contagion Collectors");
    - many devils, however, suspect that the Legendarian is what became of Rumour of Lazareme after he committed devic suicide by cutting out his third eye after the collapse of Phantast and Strife's Crimson Conspiracy on the Outer Earth circa 4000 YD (Year Zero AD); in other words, they don't believe the Legendarian is a deviant.
    — **Librarian**, Biblio Drek, sometimes called Specks due to the fact that his power focus or Tvasitar talisman is a pair of three-lens eyeglasses (as depicted in "Forever & 40 Days – The Genesis of ***PHANTACEA***", a graphic novel

published in 1990 that he in part narrates);
- Lazaremist ambassador to the rededicated Weirdom of Kanin City since roughly 4825 YD.

— **Krepusyl** Evenstar, second-born sometimes called Miss Mist or the Grey Lady; reputedly Harmony's closest and perhaps only female friend;
- primary devic over-ruler of faeries-friendly Crepuscule, the Land of Twi-light (Sedon's Outer Nose on a map of the Hidden Headworld);
- conceivably Lazareme's Venus since her power focus or Tvasitar talisman, a Holy Water Sprinkler, is also called a Morgenstern (morning star, a barbed ball on a short, chain-link cable or cord);
- formerly Mariamne Dawnstar, she once of the Land of Daybreak on the other side of the Hidden Headworld.

— **Tvasitar** Smithmonger, a third-born called Vulcanian, Anvil or Anvil the Artificer by his fellow devils; resides in the Prometheum atop Sedon's Peak, in the centre of the Cattail Peninsula (Sedon's Ponytail on a map of the Hidden Headworld);
- since sometime a few decades before 2000 YD, he has been using molten Brainrock or Gypsium, the miraculous Godstuff bubbling out of the Peak's lava lake, to forge devils their power foci or talismans, hence Tvasitar talis-mans and why he's often thought of as the devic Prometheus;
- his talisman is an anvil, hence Anvil the Artificer;
- mentioned but does not appear in the mini-novel.

— **Irisiel** Mercherm, Lazareme's preferred Heliodromus or sun-runner; called Speedy by devils for reasons obvious.

• More Byronics
— **Chimaera** Glimmenmare, ever-changing second-born Nucleoid often thought of as Byron's stallion even though he changes sex almost as often as he shifts shape;
- like his fellow Primary Nucleoids, he once frequented Iraxas (the Penile Peninsula, Sedon's Mutton Chop on a map of the Hidden Headworld), where Nergal Vetala has been ruling since the expanding empire of Lathakra drove Byronics back to the Godbadian subcontinent in the 48th Century of the Dome;
- centaurs worship him; evidently he can also control pterippi psychopomps (winged horses such as Attis's Pegasus in "Feeling Theocidal", Book One of *'The Thrice-Cursed Godly Glories'* trilogy; ones with the ability to travel be-tween-space);
- along with triplet siblings, Sedona Spellbinder and Devil Wind (the Whirl-ing Deva, aka Vayu Maelstrom), featured in "The War of the Apocalyptics"; only appears briefly near the end of "Contagion Collectors".

— **Pyçonja** Volant, called Fish Face by many devils on account of she some-times looks like an anthropomorphic shark, albeit one with legs, arms and wings (hence her surname) rather than fins;
- her power focus or Tvasitar talisman is a fisherman or fisherwoman's barbed

gaffing hook;

- worshipped by humanoid amphibians in the Gulf of Aka, which suggests the Death's Head Hellion (Morgan Abyss) may have been brought up praying to her;

- devic half-mother of Fisherwoman (aka Scylla Nereid, a major character in "The Trigregos Gambit", Book Three of *'The Thrice-Cursed Godly Glories'* trilogy).

— **Camorva** Freeflight, lepidopterous or moth-like Byronic whose elongated body is also somewhat dachshund-like; perhaps best envisioned as a hollow, vermicular tube with moth-like wings;

— **Yati**, Byron's Dragon (beware his burps);

- a highborn Byronic first depicted in "Forever & 40 Days – The Genesis of *PHANTACEA*", a graphic novel published in 1990, but only appears briefly in "Contagion Collectors";

- in his human form goes by Hiyati Samarand, after his unofficial protectorate (Samarand, once Sedon's Tongue, now lies on the occipital side of Hidden Continent of Sedon's Head);

- as such appeared during the *PHANTACEA* comic book series.

— **Vanthysces**, called Scarecrow by devils, once the Byronic Grim Reaper as well as the main devic overseer of Iraxas (Sedon's Mutton Chop on a map of the Hidden Headworld);

- King Harvest (Yama Nergal) fused his scythe with his own pickaxe just before he (Vanthysces) was cathonitized in the Dome's 48th Century;

- other than as a fairly bright star in the night's sky (the Sedon Sphere) above Iraxas, Scarecrow (Vanthysces) hasn't been seen since.

- More Mithradites

— **Methandra** Thanatos, a firstborn Mithradite known variously as Mithras's Virgin, the Scarlet Empress, Seeress or Sorceress, the Crimson Queen to Tantal's King Cold, and Miss Myth, after Mythland (the Jewel in Sedon's Crown on a map of the Hidden Continent of Sedon's Head;

- does not appear in "Contagion Collectors" but is mentioned occasionally.

— **Tantal** Thanatos, a firstborn Mithradite most commonly known as King Cold;

- the Frozen Isle of Lathakra (off the Cattail Peninsula on a map of the Hidden Headworld), once Sedon's Horn then Sedon's Lens, Monocle or Cataract (off Sedon's Human Eye, the Gulf of Corona), is his devic protectorate;

- does not appear in "Contagion Collectors" but is mentioned occasionally.

— **Phantast** Thanatos, the third of the firstborn Thanatoid Death Gods; called Dream or Dreamweaver by devils;

- cathonitized circa 4000 YD for masterminding the Crimson Conspiracy on the Outer Earth along with Strife (Mithras's Ewe for Aries, aka Kore-Eris, Discord, Kanin Marut, Fitna Marutia, among many other names);

- does not appear in "Contagion Collectors" but is mentioned occasionally.

— **Pyrame** Silverstar, the Pauper Priestess, the fabulously female (adult) Perpetual Presence; sometimes called Providence, among many another name or title;

- unless programmed otherwise, All of Incain obeys her; hence why she can often be found occupying the She-Sphinx on the Prison Beach of Incain, at the bottom of the Cattail Peninsula (Sedon's Ponytail on a map of the Hidden Headworld), about as far south as one can go on the Head without having to swim or ride in a boat;

- does not appear very often in "Contagion Collectors".

— **King Harvest**, Underlord Yama Nergal, a fifth-born, so-called Earthling (his brood sister, Shal Ereshkigal, and his brood brother, Gibran Nimiki, being the other two);

- when the Lathakran Empire conquered the Penile Peninsula (better known as Iraxas, Sedon's Mutton Chop on a map of the Hidden Headworld), he helped cathonitize Vanthysces, the Byronics' Grim Reaper;

- he thereafter fused the latter's power focus, a scythe, with his own, a miner's pickaxe; thereby cemented his position as the Nergalids' Reaper even though he shares fecundating duties of Vetala with Gravedigger;

- unchallenged devic ruler of the radioactive Ghostlands since circa 4825 YD;

- more so than the Thanatoids of Lathakra, he's considered the devils' primary Death God.

— **Vetala**, Nergal Vetala, more commonly addressed as Fecundity by her fellow Master Devas; also called the Nergalids' Grower;

- though only a twelfth-born Mithradite, she's a Moon Goddess like Lunar Uma, a Byronic firstborn; her power focus or Tvasitar talisman is considered a moon-sickle in that its blade is shaped like a crescent moon;

- Vetala becomes pregnant by one or the other male Nergalid come the New Moon and gives birth every Full Moon;

- her azuras, who number in the thousands – more like tens of thousands – are called Vetalazurs or Nergalazurs, albeit only if their fathers were either Zuvem or Yama;

- Vetalazurs seem to be only good for animating Dead Things, thus in effect rendering them zombies;

- when the Lathakran Empire conquered the Penile Peninsula (better known, once again, as Iraxas, Sedon's Mutton Chop on a map of the Hidden Headworld), thus displacing the Byronics who'd ruled it for millennia previously, she stayed behind to oversee its affairs on their behalf;

- despite commonly having vaguely greenish skin, blood-red lips and too-sharp teeth, when not pregnant, considered something of a mouth-wateringly beautiful temptress;

- by tradition vetalas (lower case) manifest themselves with their hands on the wrong wrists; Vetala, though, seldom remembers to appear this way;

- Vetala resides in the former Weirdom of Manoa, called the Gleaming City due to its golden walls, at the start of "Contagion Collectors";

- only appears briefly in the mini-novel.

— **Tammuz** and **Osiraq**, Mithras's onetime torchbearers; sometimes depicted in Mithraea on the Outer Earth, where they're commonly referred to as

Cautes and Cautopates;
- not just devils nowadays think of them as either the Idiot or Atomic Twins after their part in rendering the Ghostlands radioactive in 4825 YD;
- only mentioned in the mini-novel.
— various **Apocalyptics** are mentioned but only the Primary Four (War, Death, Plague and Catastrophe – the ones featured in "The War of the Apocalyptics") show up, albeit off-camera.
— the same is true of the two surviving **Reptilians** from Mithras's Eighth: Klizarod Rex and the Emperor Chameleon.

========

3. Deviants, Demons, Faeries and Mandroid Monstrosities

- Deviants
  - When Great Gods and/or Master Devas possess sentient beings for procreative purposes, their resultant offspring are often long-lived and occasionally unnaturally gifted mortals known as deviants;
  - in many respects, the action in "Contagion Collectors" is deviant-driven.
    — the **Legendarian**, aka always Jordan *'Q for Quill'* Tethys, the legendary 30-Year Man or Woman, as well as 30-Beers;
    - a multitalented musician, painter and recurring tail- as well as taleteller who, whenever he returns to life, does so in his son or daughter, grandson or granddaughter, albeit not until they're irrecoverably dying, whereupon they recover, though now as him, not them despite looking nearly identical;
    - depicted in "Forever & 40 Days – The Genesis of *PHANTACEA*", which he in part narrates);
    - all Legendarians develop a telltale scar in the middle of their forehead, about where a devil would have his or her third eye; it's about the only physical difference between what they looked like before he took them over;
    - when he comes back he keeps the memories of whomever he was previously but additionally brings with him his own memories, which date back to his first incarnation circa 4000 YD;
    - can read tee-tee tails, which only Illuminaries of Weir, some witches and very few other non-devils can;
    - even as a woman, he suffers from a procreative imperative (the compulsive need to reproduce such that he can succeed himself or herself, quite literally, lifetime after lifetime); as such, he may be the natural father of Morgan Abyss, the Death's Head Hellion;
    - most crucially, Rumour's quill, what Tethys sometimes calls his power pen as opposed to power focus, follows him from lifetime to lifetime;
    - among many other purposes he uses it to draw himself and others betweenspace (the Weird, the dark-grey universal substance of Samsara, mundane reality), provided they've previously given him permission to do so;
    - he can draw on anything, even the air itself, but generally draws on a pad of paper or parchment that he splotches out of the nib of his quill; he naturally calls it his splotch pad;
    - Rumour's quill being Brainrock, its ink is too; as such it never runs out;
    - anyone can use his quill while he's dancing the legless limbo between lives

but it always comes back to him whenever and wherever he reincarnates; as described in both FEEL THEO and "The Death's Head Hellion", this can cause whoever is using it when he recurs considerable inconvenience, to put it mildly.

— **Morgan Abyss**, Melusine Master of the Weirdom of Cabalarkon in 4824/5, called the Death's Head Hellion;

- (probably) does not appear in the mini-novel but is often mentioned due not just to what became of the Upper Head in 4825 YD.

— **Pusan Wanderlust**, a self-psychopomp or Wayfarer in the Wild Weird (between-space, the dark-grey universal substance of Samsara);

- in this respect she's like garudas, mutated ravendeer, pterippi flying horses such as Attis's Pegasus, Kore's hellhounds, All of Incain and virtually any devil who has a power focus;

- also known as Trailblazer because she can supposedly track anyone between-space (aka the Weird or the Grey); most often called Goat, which she considers complimentary;

- a resolutely female faun or fauna (a female satyr) who's been around perhaps 1,500 to 2,000 years longer than Quill Tethys (the Legendarian); fauns famously have a voracious appetite for sex;

- unlike Quill, Pusan can only recur in her daughters or granddaughters (when they're on the verge of dying);

- deviant father was Taurus Chrysaor Attis whereas her devic half-mother was most likely Amal-Althea, Lazareme's female healer;

- a pedum or shepherd's crook that once belonged to Goatfish, one of Byron's female Zodiacals (Capricorn), who vanished during the heyday of the Outer Earth's Goddess Culture circa 2000 to 2500 YD, automatically returns to her whenever she comes back to life;

- non-devic acquaintance, friend or occasional companion of both Harmony and the Grey Lady (Krepusyl Evenstar);

- can often be found working at the Dinq, Doinq, Danq Cavern Tavern in the foothills at the far, north-western corner of the Diluvia Mountain Range, where it hasn't stopped raining since the Genesea or Great Flood of Genesis.

— Jordan *'Quidnunc'* Tethys, black-skinned son of Quill Tethys (the Legendarian), who wasn't black-skinned;

- devic half-mother, Dame Chance, often visited while he was growing up;

- at the insistence of his mother, who was black-skinned, grew up as an abstemious teetotaller;

- also at her insistence, he became a cadet then a member of the Marutian military;

- such a fabulous swordsman many believed either the Unity of Order or the Unity of Chaos possessed him when he won innumerable fencing contests during his late teens and early twenties.

— Jordan *'Squiggly'* Tethys, son of Quidnunc; as such had black skin;

- a fine artist and trained cartographer brought up alongside the Terrible Twins, Sraddha and Janna Somata, both of whom love him;

- Zalman and Melina, the twins' parents, agreed that Janna could marry

Squiggly when she came of age.

— Jordan *'Quibble'* Tethys, originally a white-skinned grandson of Quill Tethys (the Legendarian); other Q-names may include *'Quit Quill'*, *'Squab'* and *'Squib'*.

— Jordan *'Quoits'* Tethys, originally a (very white-skinned) hybrid-Utopian daughter or granddaughter of Quill Tethys (the Legendarian);

- a millennial child, meaning she was born in the Year of the Dome 5000;

- chances are Dame Chance (the Master Deva bygone Illuminaries named Wintry Moira) is her devic half-mother, which at least partially accounts for her extremely long life even for a Utopian;

- has faithfully served an unspecified number of Masters of the Weirdom of Cabalarkon over the centuries;

- given Jordan for a first name, her initial Q-name was Queer; gave herself the Q-name of Quoits when she rediscovered ringots in the Weirdom of Cabalarkon;

- Melina nee Tethys Somata, the High Illuminary of the Weirdom of Kanin City throughout most of "Contagion Collectors", calls her Granny Jordy even though many generations separate them.

— **Zalman** Somata, black-skinned, very popular Master of the Weirdom of Kanin City throughout most of "Contagion Collectors";

- an acknowledged deviant whose devic half-father was Thunder and Lightning Lord Yajur, the Unity of Order;

- (possibly) possessed by Thrygragos Lazareme when he impregnated wife Melina (possessed by Harmony, the Unity of Balance as well as Panharmonium) with result being the Terrible Twins, Sraddha and Janna Somata.

— **Sraddha** Somata, deviant son of Zalman (possibly possessed by Thrygragos Lazareme) and Melina nee Tethys Somata (possessed by Harmony, the Unity of Balance as well as Panharmonium), respectively the Master and High Illuminary of the Weirdom of Kanin City, when conceived;

- half of the Terrible Twins, on their 18th birthdays their parents and the Unities of Lazareme agreed that he would be occupied by Fangfingers (Faustus Vladuca) when he married and conceived children;

- had black skin like his father; best friend of Squiggly Tethys, son of Quidnunc, who also had black skin.

— **Janna** Somata, deviant daughter of Zalman (possibly possessed by Thrygragos Lazareme) and Melina nee Tethys Somata (possessed by Harmony, the Unity of Balance as well as Panharmonium), respectively the Master and High Illuminary of the Weirdom of Kanin City, when conceived;

- half of the Terrible Twins, on their 18th birthdays their parents and the Unities of Lazareme agreed that she would be occupied by the Skinless Rasp (Rastha Aragon) when she married and conceived children;

- had white skin like her mother and silver hair like her ancestor, the Valkyrie Ute Tethys (who featured in Feel Theo); beloved of Squiggly Tethys, son of Quidnunc.

— **Herta Heartthrob**, constructed by Magnus Minus (qv) during the latter days of Morgan Abyss's mass-murderous reign as Master of the Weirdom of

Cabalarkon;

- first name a jumble of letters making up the word *'earth'*, indicating she's earthborn; antique goddesses Hera and Rhea have same letters, albeit minus a *'t'*, and the Norse, Teutonic or Germanic Erda isn't faraway;

- initially based on Harmony, the ever-exquisite Unity of Balance; the self-proclaimed mighty Minotaurus of Minius (after himself) made Herta as a drunken favour for Unholy Abaddon (the Unity of Chaos);

- remains rediscovered and reactivated by Tomcat Tattletail and Quoits Tethys at an unspecified date during the Dome's 13th or 14th Centuries;

- no longer just based on Harmony, Herta is ameliorated by residue Harmony leaves behind when she steps on Brainrock hearthstones as she goes through the Cathonic Zone from Tholos to Tholos in pursuit of trillion-timing Tommy (see Tattletail);

- seems to be slowly acquiring snippets of Harmony's memories as a result;

- reputedly, along with Tomcat Tattletail (qv), has given birth to a number of putto-type cupids, apparently a form of daemon, or demon, who seem able to detect highly communicable disease in Outer Earthlings;

- as such, a major contagion collector working for Quoits Tethys.

—— **Tomcat Tattletail**, a faerie trickster evidently reconstructed by Utopian Biomages on the instructions of Quoits Tethys and an unnamed Master of the Weirdom of Cabalarkon at an unspecified time presumably circa the mid 13th Century of the Dome;

- a metamorph or shape-shifter; when on the Inner Earth, often affects the guise of Thrygragos Lazareme as Harmony most commonly sees him – as a blue-skinned, golden-haired pretty boy, albeit with only two sea-green eyes;

- one theory is his first incarnation was what had become of Rumour of Lazareme after faeries ate him circa 4000 YD;

- another theory is that, after his reconstruction, Quoits reanimated him with the spirit of an unnamed and probably eminently forgettable devil she found trapped in a ringot left over from the days of the Death's Head Hellion (Master Morgan Abyss) who loved an earlier version of Tomcat, one with a Q-Name;

- Harmony calls him trillion-timing Tommy, on account of he's loved her and left her many times over the centuries; Lazareme calls him cat-crap;

- a master musician whose favourite instrument is, highly suggestively, a syrinx or panpipe.

• Definite Demons

—— **Primeval Lilith**, Demon Queen of the Night; the thought-immortal queen of chthonic or earthborn daemons or demons;

- fused with Pyrame Silverstar, then unnamed, sometime after All of Incain, when she was Ginny the Gynosphinx, ate the latter circa 725 PD.

—— **Daemonicus**, Dusted Daemonicus; reputedly indestructible, pre-Sedon king of chthonic or earthborn daemons or demons possibly connected to

Smiler (see the VAM Entity).

- Mandroids
    — **All** the (self-proclaimed) Invincible She-Sphinx of Incain; once Ginny the Gynosphinx; Mandroid Mother Machine as well as occasional monster maker;
    - more often than not huge and winged; a therefore perhaps surprisingly mobile psychopomp – meaning she can travel at will through the Weird (between-space, the dark-grey universal substance of Samsara, mundane reality), though always leaves a root of herself behind on the Prison Beach of Incain;
    - used by devils, especially Unmoving Byron and the Unities of Lazareme, as both a temporary holding cell or as a long-term prison for their transgressing fellows;
    - in addition to highborn devils, though not to the Moloch Sedon, whom she's designed to eat, All tends to be responsive to Pyrame Silverstar;
    - although possessed of a modicum of sentience, if not much in the way of actual intelligence, still a machine; can be turned off and on as well as reprogrammed.
    — **Magnus Minus**, origin unspecified, might be a demon but, just as likely, might be a mandroid; may have been a monster made by All of Incain, the Dual Entities or even Pyrame, through All, since she seems to know a lot about him – including how to revive him after howsoever many centuries of moribundity;
    - self-proclaimed as well as self-named mighty Minotaurus of Minius (Absudyl, the Subterranean Realm of the Mandroids);
    - regardless of whether he's more mandroid than demon, he's a daemonic demiurge, one who fancies himself a latter day Daemonicus in that he's a demon king lacking subjects but completely capable of fashioning them;
    - as such, he fashioned the future Herta Heartthrob during the reign of the Death's Head Hellion upstairs in the Weirdom of Cabalarkon (Sedon's Devic Eye-Land on a map of the Hidden Continent of Sedon's Head).

========

4. Mortal Descendants of Original Extraterrestrials

- Utopians of Weir on Earth
    - **Utopians** living in the Weirdom of Cabalarkon are brought up to hate the Moloch Sedon and his devic progeny;
    - oddly, as if to prove their non-Earth heritage, pureblood Utopian men are always black whereas Utopian women are invariably white;
    - the be-all and end-all of Utopians stuck on the Whole Earth (either beneath the Cathonic Dome or due only in part to an absence of functional spacecraft beyond it) remains the destruction of their ancient enemies.
    - **Illuminaries** of Weir, Utopian polymaths, supposedly learned in a wide variety of not-necessarily-related matters; the highest educated class in Cabalarkon;
    - often act as advisors to the reigning Master, who's usually elevated from their

rank; very seldom are they not pure U-bloods.

- **Scientocrats** of Weir, still nominally scientists but long more like functionaries charged with keeping Weir's archaic, First and Second Weirworld machinery operating as well as it can;
- even though they're highly educated, most scientocrats are specialists in their chosen fields; they can't match Illuminaries when it comes to sheer breadth of knowledge.
- **Biomages** of Weir, scientocrats specializing in the design and manufacture of life forms;
- as such, they might be considered biogeneticists, the same as Cabalarkon, the undying Utopian (Sedon's Daddy Cabby), was when he was altogether alive and living on, or travelling off of, the first Weirworld;
- considered mages, which implies facility with magic, because they concentrate on making life forms out of subtle matter Solidium or Stopstone, the stuff of mandroids and suchlike earthborn or chthonic creatures as demons and faeries;
- indeed, it's said of them that they make demons and faeries to order;
- at the time of "Contagion Collectors", they work or have worked for the Master of Cabalarkon's Weirdom under the supervision of Quoits Tethys, a very long-lived millennial child;
- much of what they do suggests they have access to the discredited, as well as nowadays generally despised, science of Old Eden, the Ice Age civilization that preceded the so-called Golden Age of Humankind.
- **Imbeciles** of Weir, also the idiots of Weir; inbred and therefore very much low functioning Utopians; almost always purebloods, hence the inbreeding.
- **Trinondevs** of Weir, Weir's Warrior Elite, almost always purebloods who manage to overcome their inbreeding in order to function as soldiers;
- their main weapons operate by willpower;
- eyeorbs placed atop eye-staves double as prison pods in that they can suck devic and azura spirit being out of the shells they're occupying and into them, thus incarcerating them;
- once an eyeorb is full it ceases to function as anything except a prison pod; if it's not replaced, the eye-stave becomes useless;
- eye-staves, like all their other anti-devil weaponry, haven't functioned in the Weirdom of Kanin City for over a thousand years by the time of "Contagion Collectors".
  — **Cabalarkon**, Cabby the Daddy, the Undying Utopian; a biogeneticist when he lived and worked on, or travelled off of, the First Weirworld;
- when he was a wholly alive Utopian scientocrat the Dual Entities used his right eye to jumpstart the process that resulted in the Moloch Sedon, hence Cabby the Daddy;
- currently subsists in a tub of life-preserving but animation-suspending Cathonic Fluid beneath the Citadel of the Thinkers in Cabalarkon City;
- it, like the rest of the territory composing the Weirdom of Cabalarkon (Sedon's Devic Eye-Land on a map of the Hidden Continent of Sedon's Head),

is named after him.

— **Melina** nee Tethys Somata, the High Illuminary of the Weirdom of Kanin City throughout most of "Contagion Collectors";

- her parents were distantly related to the same Jordan Q Tethys who fathered or mothered the eventual Quoits Tethys (or one of Quoits' parents); both claimed they could trace their ancestry back to George Masterson and Ute Tethys, both of whom featured in Feel Theo;

- at least one of their parents or grandparents was the Tethys who fled the Weirdom of Cabalarkon some centuries earlier and eventually settled in the rededicated Weirdom of Kanin City;

- probably not a deviant, Melina's skin is so white that many consider her a throwback to pure U-bloods such as the Sarpedon underclass and the Imbeciles of Weir;

- be that as it may, she's still a hybrid Utopian, one possessed by Harmony, the Unity of Balance as well as Panharmonium, when she and Zalman conceived the Terrible Twins, Janna and Sraddha Somata.

========

5. Norman & Norma Notables

- Inner Earthlings

— John **Barleycorn**, known as *'JB'*, a bartender at the DDD (the Dinq, Doinq, Danq Cavern Tavern) in the foothills at the far, north-western corner of the Diluvia Mountain Range, where it hasn't stopped raining since the Genesea or Great Flood of Genesis.

- Outer Earthlings

— **Dire**, a self-named, sickly, hence valuable, child brought through the Dome by Herta Heartthrob and her latest putto (the cherubic demon that swallowed an ever-envious Master Deva, thus rendering the devil, as the putto puts it, an *'internal infernal'*).

— **Drang the Dog**, Dire's dog, a hound that Herta and her putto brings beneath the Dome to keep the child company.

— **Twisted Tommy**, a Black Friar Dominican (sometimes thought of as *'Domini canes'* or *'Hound of the Lord'*, albeit in Latin, for the order's lead role in spearheading the terrifying Spanish Inquisition of the day); brought through the Dome by Tomcat Tattletail in his role as a contagion collector.

— **Bosco**, at the time a still-struggling painter ostensibly of religious warnings in the Burgundian-cum-Hapsburg Netherlands; brought through the Cathonic Zone (Dome) by Herta Heartthrob from his hometown of 's-Hertogenbosch, which he refers to as Den Bosch.

****

Contagion Collectors

- Years of the Dome 5456 to 5476 -

Jim McPherson

A **_PHANTACEA_ Mythos** Mini-Novel
Published by James H McPherson, Publisher

ISBN 978-0-9781342-6-6

1: Quotidian Quidnunc

Up to 5456 YD – The Mastery of Marutia

"In the year of 1284, on the day of Saints John and Paul, the 26th of June, 130 children born in Hamelin were seduced by a piper, dressed in all kinds of colours, and lost at the calvary near the koppen."

These words, translated into the Universal Tongue spoken throughout the Hidden Continent of Sedon's Head, are recorded in a localized, Outer Earth language on the walls of the so-called 'Rattenfängerhaus', or House of the Piper, in the German town of Hamelin. The Legendarian knew this because he did the translation.

========

A decade or two after the events thus recorded, bereaved locals paid an itinerant, yet highly talented craftsman to prepare a stained-glass window commemorating the tragedy in the town's Market Church. (Obviously having learned their lesson, they paid him properly too, without quibbling.) The artist scratched his name into the bottom right hand corner of the window once he finished it. The name he scratched into it? Jordan Q Tethys of course.

Tethys's window depicted the piper dressed in multicoloured clothes leading a crowd of kids dressed in white towards the dark, vaguely skull-shaped entrance to a cave within a nearby hill. He reckoned that, even though it was shaped more like a Tholos or beehive than a human head, the word *Koppen*, meaning just that, head, must refer to that hill whereas the word *Calvary*, place of the skull, probably referred to the cave's mouth. Hamelin's townspeople clearly had an even more vivid imagination than he did.

Although it was now twenty years shy of two centuries after the events he depicted in stained glass, chances were the hill, and the cave within it, still existed. While, at a stretch, the word Koppen might refer to the Head, capitalized, by the time he visited Hamelin it definitely didn't contain a link to the Hidden Headworld. That it had in 1284 (5284 on the Head) was pretty much a given, he reckoned.

He reckoned as much because he was almost as certain the Pied Piper had a name he never gave to the townspeople. That name wasn't Tethys. It was Tomcat Tattletail.

========

Star Sedon disappeared from the night's sky on the 25th of Tantalar, 4824 Year of the Dome. It had long been back upstairs some 30-plus years in excess of six centuries later.

========

Jordan Q Tethys was a half-black who looked all-black. These days that might mean he had Utopian relatives. Just as likely it might not. In contrast to his ever-wayward father, who wasn't the black forbearer, he did not have a scar in the lower part of his forehead. Nor did his middle initial stand for *'Quill'*. If the woman who was his black forbearer could be believed, it stood for *'Quidnunc'*.

'That's your father's idea of a joke,' she often told him while he was growing up in southwestern Marutia, Sedon's Cheek Land.

A quidnunc was a busybody. Then again, in Marutia a jordan, small case, was a chamber pot. While it might be argued that one was no better than the other, there were hundreds of Jordans, upper and lower case, in Sedon's Cheek. By comparison, as far as he'd heard anyhow, he was the only Quidnunc, capitalized. Since neither name appealed to him very much, he came to prefer Quid.

Even though he was named after him, his mother didn't approve of his father. For his part, young Quid couldn't recall ever meeting him. He did learn, once he became a star cadet in the Marutian military and was allowed to go to bars – though, at the risk of homelessness, never to drink alcohol – that joining the army in general, and not drinking beer in particular, were two of the last things his father would have done.

Those who knew Jordan *'Quill'* Tethys held that he'd never have done either/or unless he'd first committed suicide, been resurrected as a Born Again zombie, and then conscripted into one of the armies of the Inglorious Dead's booze-free divisions. Which did exist, they further assured him straight-faced.

(As did Fata Fortuna, the highborn Lazaremist who'd possessed his birthmother when she conceived him – though the decidedly naughty nanny, aka Lady Luck, Dame Chance or sometimes *'Damn Her 3-Eyes Anyhow'*, was more of a straight-laced sort, albeit only when it came to her bodice. Quid knew this because, while he was growing up, she popped physically by to visit he and his mother once in a while, ostensibly just to see how he was doing in these pox-stricken times.)

His birthmother's unbending antipathy to his fertilizing father explained why she brought him up as an abstemious teetotaller. It further explained why she insisted he become a soldier. That he also became a rakish, thoroughgoing sexual predator, what less charitably inclined Marutian progressives condemned as a throwback to the age of manly barbarism, well, nature was stronger than nurture. It certainly was when it came to the slew of incurable illnesses then plaguing Sedon's Cheek like a lifelong outbreak of far worse-than-unsightly pimples. It was all the more so, in some respects oppositely so, when it came to penile swords.

Despite his paternal heritage, he took to the blade like a sculptor to a chisel or a wizard to a wand. In a way, that was understandable. The Utopian Mastery of Marutia had been at peace within itself for so many centuries that fighting-and-dying soldiering was less a thing of the past than approaching the stage of becoming an oxymoron. It being the Age of Panharmonium, there were more prospects of fighting and dying in a Kanin City playground than on a Marutian battlefield.

Sure, many pockets of inviolate devic protectorates endured within, and on the boundaries of, the Cheeks proper. Since disputatious Mithradite Master Devas controlled most of them, they remained dangerous, even tumultuous territories both inwardly and outwardly.

However, few true Utopians dared venture into devic protectorates because fewer survived long enough to venture out of them. Unless as members of a large battalion, they especially didn't venture into them armed with eye-staves. They did so singly or in small groups, odds were even or poorer they'd ever be seen again.

Devils hadn't considered true Utopians lesser beings since the time of the mass murderous Death's Head Hellion. As a result, their more overenthusiastic supporters considered them sport to be hunted down and shot. If they weren't shot dead right away, well, sport could be had in many a mostly unmentionable manner. Typically, though, release came in the form of death and not as a result of ransom or escape.

Rather, it had. Other than in terms of flashing steel, Quidnunc was no bright light. But even he must have realized that, by the 55th Century of the Dome, the only purebloods left beneath the Dome lived far to the north of Marutia, in the next-to-unreachable Weirdom of Cabalarkon, Sedon's Devic Eye-Land – next-to-unreachable since the waning months of Morgan Abyss's hellacious Mastery, as it happened.

No matter how dilute their bloodline had become, Utopians of Marutia, chiefly those in its armed services, nonetheless retained one maxim above any other: *'You lose your edge, you risk losing your life on the edges.'* When it came to staying out of devic protectorates, Quid was no different than his fellow soldiers. Where he was different, by a considerable measure, was in the practise yard and showground.

He was such a splendid swordsman that, in his teens, he emerged victorious in verging on countless fencing contests throughout the Cheek's hinterlands. He won so many tournaments that many neutrals, and more than few of his adversaries, sour-griped he had to be devil-possessed as well as at least a quarter devil-conceived.

More specifically, they maintained Unholy Abaddon, the Unity of Chaos, who had a well-deserved reputation for upsetting the status quo purely for the sake of disruption, possessed him. Which, while possible, wasn't very probable since Abe Chaos claimed he never intentionally possessed anyone. And devils couldn't lie.

Be that as it may, in due course Quid found himself in Kanin City, just below the Gregarian Fields (to not just devils aka Sedon's Mole). There, in the Mastery's megalithic as well as antediluvian capital, the lad challenged for possibly the supreme accolade available during the cyclopean city's annual Midsummer Games: namely, the Five Blades Championship of Weir.

Shockingly, Quid won that too, the Utopians' highest honour for individual swordsmanship. Doubly shockingly, at 21 he was the youngest recorded winner ever. Trebly shockingly, he won it with Abe Chaos, flanked by his two fellow Unities of Lazareme, Order and Harmony, watching his every bout. Significantly, despite what their frothing-at-the-mouth flock of fanatical followers may believe, even first-born devils can't be in two places at once.

Only the mighty Moloch could do that, and then only debatably. It could be his Sedon Sphere – aka Cathonia, the Cathonic Zone or Dome – did not need to retain any measure of his presence in order to remain in place whenever he ventured downstairs, on either side of it. Which he occasionally did for purposes courtly, procreative and/or much more devilishly sinister.

As everyone beneath it knew, Sedon raised Cathonia out of his own essence to prevent the Genesea – or Great Flood of Genesis – washing over the then archipelago of Pacifica, thusly referred to, accurately or inaccurately, as the Places of Peace during the Golden Age of Humankind and its Edenite precursor. Give or take howsoever many days, weeks or months the Dome had, for the most part, kept the Outer Earth separate from the Inner Earth throughout the intervening 5,456 years.

Star Sedon had vanished from the night's sky many times during the course of its multi-millennial existence. Although only devils and a couple of recurring deviants had memories that went back to 4824/5 YD, at least one of his absences lasted many moons. Nevertheless, no one who persisted in, on, below or above his Hidden Headworld ever had to build an ark, sprout gills or learn to swim underwater against his or her will.

In this regard, many living beyond the Dome came to believe Sedon – albeit as Satan, hellfire's capitalized Devil – shunned water. In their faiths he did so because he feared liquid extinguishment, hence both regular baptism and Holy Water. Such-like twaddle was of course understandable. In the absence of visible gods to physically hold their hands, Outer Earthlings hatched oceans of exceptionally nonsensical notions.

Inner Earthlings sometimes did too. One of the most enduring was that Piscines, who generally worshipped the Byronic Zodiacal known as Pyçonja Volant, hatched out of eggs laid by their mothers in Akadan, the Head's interior ocean. The truth of that was Piscines hatched out of eggs laid by their mothers in any of the Head's four oceans.

Then again, in a manner of speaking anyhow, each and every animal, including humans, did as well. And they did it anywhere they could. It was called gestation.

========

Quid Tethys also didn't win the Five Blades Championship of Weir purely by luck. Devic half-mom Fata Fortuna was another god-devil visibly in attendance.

========

Azky 21, 5456 YD – The Weirdom of Kanin City

With skin nearly as black as midnight on a cloud-covered, moonless night, Zalman Somata was the unassailable Master of Marutia in 5456 YD. In deference to the over 5,000 years of originally extraterrestrial Utopians who'd preceded him as Masters of the Weirdom of Kanin City, he continued to proclaim himself Kanin's Master of Weir.

Amongst themselves, his adoring, non-devic public referred to him as Zal. His popularity only partially explained why his position remained so incontrovertible. While they may not adore him, nor even like him, Master Devas from any of the three tribes knew better than to mess with him. You messed with Zalman Somata; you chanced messing with his patrons. You did that, you're a devil, and you might be up top with Grandfather Sedon, shining down on Marutia before you could say sorry.

Quidnunc stood proudly as the Master came to pin the Five Blades' medal on his chest. Zal had a big grin on his face. So did Zal's patrons: the same three firstborn Lazaremists who'd watched his every bout. So too did Zal's very pregnant wife, whose first name was Melina but whose maiden name just happened to be Tethys. And, because Sed was hardly the only one back in relative action, equally temporarily, on the 21st of Azky, 5456 YD, so did the Somatas' court chronicler.

That would be none other than Quidnunc's conceptive father, Jordan *'Quill'* Tethys.

========

From the looks of her, Zal's Mel may be something of a regenerative mutant. But she couldn't possibly be a pureblood Utopian. For one thing, she was no in-bred imbecile like the majority of Cabalarkon's purebloods. For another, her grace-fully aging parents lived with her in Kanin City at the Masters Palace.

While they could trace their ancestry back much more than a thousand years, to the borderline legendary pair of George Masterson and Ute also born Tethys, they weren't purebloods either. Indeed, Mel's Daddy Tethys was more white-skinned than black-skinned whereas Mommy Tethys was the reverse, exactly the opposite to the usual state of affairs in most Weirdoms, Kanin's included.

Finally, she wouldn't have been allowed to marry Zalman if she was a pureblood for the lone qualifying reason that devil-gods – third generational Mas-ter Devas – could not possess purebloods. You didn't need to be a tale-telling court chronicler like Quill Tethys, an Illuminary of Weir like both Zal and Mel, or even a deliberately kept barely educated, howsoever-superior swordsman like Quidnunc Tethys, to know that was the secret behind the roughly 600-year success story of the Mastery of Marutia.

Its Masters, to a one, were deviants. The fact of the matter was one of the three immortal devils advancing towards Quidnunc behind the current Master was Zal's half-father. Like so many of their fellow Lazaremists Abe Chaos was a complete anarchist. Unlike most of them, though, he never possessed anyone. Consequently Zal's half-father had to be Order.

He and his immediate siblings were often misidentified with the Outer Earth's Hindu Trimurti: the post-Vedic, Indian Lords delineated Brahma the Cre-ator, Vishnu the Preserver and Shiva the Destroyer. Be that as it may, Order was the only one of the three Unities who, on a daily basis, made a point of looking as if he was from the Indian subcontinent. As therefore per usual brown-skinned, with shockingly electric, sparking hair, antique Illuminaries named him Lord Yajur.

They called him thus after the vajra thunderbolts he generated, Vishnu-like, from his Tvasitar Talisman, his Lightning Blade, when it was unsheathed (which it wasn't), and he'd mentally triggered it (which he hadn't). It, in its sheath, was strapped to Yajur's back. Although his faux-feathery drawing tool, Rumour of Laz-areme's Tvasitar Talisman (which Tethys sometimes referred to, faux-facetiously, as his power pen), was many times mightier than most swords, Yajur's Lightning Blade was, approximately, inconceivably mightier than Quill's quill.

So too was Unholy Abaddon's Chaos Blade. It was sheathed as well; in what most people erroneously thought was his power focus, his Shiva-like trident. Al-though devils could vanish their power foci as easily as they could transmute them, he held his, with his left hand, in full view of everybody attending the medals ceremony.

Other than his left-handedness and refusal to possess anyone, Abe Chaos was normally consistent solely in terms of inconsistency. He'd go to sleep as a whatever. He'd stick with howsoever or whomsoever he awakened as until he changed his mind, which he sometimes did on an hourly basis, if not less.

This hour dressed in a cobalt-coloured robe, he affected the glamour of a clean-shaven, humanoid demon, albeit one without a serpentine tail or leathern wings. Sporting splotchy, blood red skin, he had jet black hair flowing down his back to his waist and eight unlit, glisteningly silvery, trident-like prong spikes haloing his face and head.

By contrast, their triplet sister, the Unity of Harmony as well as Panharmonium, had much in common with their father. Somehow or other, whoever was looking at that Great God perceived him as his or her ideal of godhood; hence why even devils often referred to Lackland Lazareme as Thrygragos Everyman. While in her case every man and every woman, of any sentient species, saw her exactly as she wanted them to see her, they invariably considered her incomparably gorgeous.

Her universally admired attractiveness combined with an overstated capacity for compassion – overstated due to her seldom seen and therefore thought-fabulous, as well as ill-natured, Nemesis persona – helped to make the Unity the most popular devil-goddess of the time, if not necessarily all-time. Trimurti-worshippers said much the same about Brahma the Creator of course. However, as good-looking as he reputedly was good-hearted, Lord Brahma was, resolutely, never Lady Brahma.

Today Datong Harmonia, the name uninspired Illuminaries of yore accorded her, appeared entirely human. Which is to say as entirely human as a manifestation of unrivalled womanhood with three eyes could appear. With long, richly dark and crinkly hair as well as butterscotch skin, she affected a similar look to Lord Yajur's in that she might pass for a native of the Outer Earth's Indian subcontinent.

Rather, put in terms appreciable by most of the non-devils there, she could pass as a native of the Inner Earth's occipital region of Ophir-Moorset. In addition to open-toed sandals, scales-of-justice earrings, bracelets, anklets and a bellybutton bauble shaped like an almond, she even wore a midriff-baring sari with a green top and yellow wrap.

About her neck was her Tvasitar Talisman, presumably the same golden torc that inspired the Outer Earth's possibly not altogether baseless myth of a malignant Necklace of Harmony. Because everything about her glimmered with the telltale glows of Brainrock-Gypsium, there were those who claimed her clothing and, indeed, her entire body-beautiful depended from her power focus. That may be as well, because very few devils were more of a consistently possessive Spirit Being than her.

Perhaps she did it so much in order to make up for her conscientiously inconsistent brood brother's refusal to possess anyone. Then again, unlike every other known Master Deva, most likely including her immediate siblings, perhaps a de-brained demon didn't individually solidify her. Perhaps her body was all-devic, like that of a Great God or Sedon Himself.

She, the as yet only potentially half-birthmother of his twins-to-be, the very same devil who'd been occupying Missus Master when they were conceived, tapped Zal on the shoulder. She wanted to pin the medallion of swordsmanship excellence on Quidnunc Tethys herself. With a smile that was as bright as the sun and far brighter than the moon, men refused her only at risk to their sanity. Zalman Somata was exceptionally sane, if more than just seemingly shocked by her request.

Harmony couldn't help herself laughing as she did so. "And to think, young Jordy, your forefathers avoided the military like death itself."

========

That Harmony didn't just pin the Weirdom's medallion of swordsmanship excellence on Jordan 'Quidnunc' Tethys's chest-covering; that she actually poked it into said mightily masculine chest; that too could be disputed. What could not be disputed was that, milliseconds thereafter, the masterful, much honoured and well-laid, young swordsman clutched his chest more so than his medal, collapsed in a heap, jerked a few times, and promptly expired.

Not so certain was which one of the Terrible Twins, Janna or Sraddha, chose that precise moment to begin a-birthing.

========

Simultaneously, if nowhere near so heart-attack-abruptly, Melina born Tethys screamed then went down herself, albeit in the throes of parturition. Wasting nary a second's concern on freshly falling Quidnunc, Harmony flew quite literally inside of Zal's Mel. Her immediate siblings, Chaos and Order, spared just as much of nothing on the stricken swordsman. Instead they exchanged hate-laden glares at each other. The singular slurp of a collective sucking-in-of-breath suddenly superseded the inane nattering of the awards ceremony onlookers.

What had, effectively, been the Age of Panharmonium for so many centuries began as an almost afterthought-addendum to what was still nominally the Age of Lazareme. Third generational devils were genetically as incapable of disobeying their fathers as their fathers were of disobeying the Moloch Sedon. However, the three Unities' father, besides spending most of his time asleep on the Isle of the Undying One, was a notoriously laissez-faire libertine.

Fortunately for mortals, Thrygragos Everyman was the live-and-let-live kind of Great God. The two male Unities had, unfortunately, earned their reputations as very much the unkind, live-and-let-die sort. Presumably painful, premature circumstances having forced Harmony to occupy Mistress Melina and thereby help her out in the birth-giving department, the assembled gawkers responded with a terrified hush less of alarm for the well-being of the Mastery's High Illuminary, let alone the fate of today's just-dropped-dead hero of the Championship, as for their own hide.

Given the two male Unities' allegedly opposite attributes, everyone understood Unholy Abaddon reviled Lord Yajur beyond any extremes of conventional irrationality. The feeling was mutual. Even the cousinly hatreds wrought by interdenominational schisms, such as those tearing apart so many of the previously superbly organized, patriarchal religions of the day, and not just those practised principally on the Outer Earth, paled by comparison.

With or without the Moloch Sedon's tacit approval, if Harmony much more so than their father hadn't been around to balance off her brood brothers, her Age – and by extension Lazareme's with it – never would have flourished as fruitfully as it had to date. In truth, her two immediate brothers were so surpassingly powerful many feared not even Sedon had the clout required to cathonitize them should their rage reach the point where they went at each other unrestrained.

That happened, the Hidden Headworld itself might be terminally endangered. That apprehended, the mere fact they were seen togethcr in Kaɴin City, let alone seen smiling amidst the same company, was an occurrence noteworthy for its close-to-unprecedented matchlessness. It must have struck the crowd gathered as a pure wonderment they could look at each other without drawing weapons and spilling blood.

Yet, significantly, not to mention retrospectively suspiciously, as if the day's startling events had been prearranged, ever so callously, to the detriment of Quid-nunc much more so than anyone else, heads didn't instantly fly off shoulders. Not only that, Harmony being otherwise occupied, they did it again. Then they smiled at each other.

As if in unspoken, telepathic concord, Chaos went to assist Quill Tethys and his lower-born, variously named Lazaremist of a sister, Dame Chance – Quill's, as well as Quid's, devic half-mother – with their poison-pricked son, who had sadly ceased convulsing. Hesitating no longer, Order did a ditto with Zal and Mel, their immediate sister still inside the latter, adding her shrieks to the Master's beloved.

The collective whoosh of relief must have seemed, if not necessarily sounded, cyclonic.

========

Quidnunc Tethys died on the 22ⁿᵈ of Azky, Year of the Dome 5456.

========

"It's about time you came to, Quill," said the Jordan sitting beside the bed in Kanin City's ancient, yet kept sparkling clean, hospital.

"A Quit-Quill," marvelled the Jordan lying in bed. A young, extremely fit-looking fellow, he had a scar – which he never had before – in the lower part of his forehead, about where his eyebrows would have met if they'd kept growing. No one would have noticed that he'd just had a heart attack. Then again, he hadn't, had he. Quidnunc had, hadn't he.

"Congratulations," he said to the other Jordan, the one in the chair. "Um, … grandson, wasn't it?"

"Grandson it was, granddad, though my notes indicate we aren't that rare." Bodily nearing sixty, but looking older, the speaker was so flushed, podgy and thoroughly out of shape a casual observer might have wondered why he wasn't in the bed instead of the very much former, oft-times-champion swordsman.

"Notes? Oh, right. I've all your memories."

"Only those of your pre-me incarnations. I can recall most of mine, and that includes pre- and post-you. Still a bit fuzzy, I see."

"I usually am. Quidnunc isn't as strong as you were, though. I seem to remem-ber you fought me tooth and mental nail after you died."

"I fell off a horse. I was only fading away when you revivified me. Assuming for the sake of argument you didn't have the heart attack you looked like you had, that was awfully fast acting venom Harmony jabbed into you. It wouldn't surprise me to find out an Athenan War Witch or a Hecate Hellion concocted it.

"Hell's Teeth, maybe Mel did it herself. She's a highly skilled witch and, believe me, until today she hasn't had any kids, let alone a daughter she can trade to the life-loving Anthean Sisterhood for any of their tiptop, though usually non-lethal, training. Of course that doesn't mean she hasn't been trained by any other craft, even one of the killer Sisterhoods."

"Got your facts wrong there, descendent. Neither Zal nor Mel jabbed anything into Quidnunc pre-me. Murder isn't like us. It isn't even like Tethyses who don't become me. Were you that desperate to become a Quit-Quill? Is Harmony that confident her Grandfather Sedon won't cathonitize her?"

"You're not a lesser being so devils don't count killing you as murder."

"Wrong again. It wasn't me she killed. Quidnunc was just an ordinary Joe, even if he was a Jordy, Jordy. Or should I call you Jordy?"

"Tell you what, since we're both Jordan Q Tethyses, maybe we better stick with the q-names."

"That'd make me Quill and you Quit-Quill. Funnily enough, Quidnunc's mother always said your middle name should have been *'Quitter'* not *'Quill'*. Where is it by the way?"

"Call me Squab."

"That isn't a q-name."

"It's got a *'q'* in it so that's good enough."

"Why Squab?"

"Hey, if it walks like a duck and talks like a duck then it's a duck. Me, I'm short and fat so I'm a squab."

"Quibble, that was it, your original q-name – Jordan *'Quibble'* Tethys. Got an answer?"

"As to whether you had a natural heart attack or an induced one? I'm sure Harmony would insist the excitement just got the better of ex-him, now-you. Tragic, really, especially for one so young. Plus, she'd also insist you were only dying, not dead, when Quill took you over, so technically she didn't kill anyone. Patience has never been one of his – your – stacks of knacks so, if someone has to be punished, maybe it's you?"

"Not much of a flagellant either, am I."

"No. Besides, I left my scourge at home. I brought your cap, though."

Sitting up and stretching out, the Quill once Quidnunc reached out to take it with his right hand. It had six fingers. "Oh, there it is."

"Guess that's the answer you're looking for then."

With his five-fingered left hand, ex-Quidnunc pulled out the extra finger of his right hand – thereby rendering himself no longer a polydactyl poltroon, as he'd have had it should he be tale-telling and fay-saying simultaneously, which he usually did. It instantly transformed into his faux-feathery Brainrock quill, what along with the scar tissue in his forehead automatically transferred to him from one lifetime to the next.

As if a family heirloom being rightfully passed on, which in a way it was, the latest Legendarian accepted his predecessor's peaked tweed cap. "I was afraid you were trying to pull a fast one, Squab," he said, about to stick Rumour's power focus into a well worn hole in the cap beside the real feathers of a variety of plucked birdies, including that of a Garuda, who were, technically, avian-human birdmen. "You recall the story about the Steg who killed a bunch of Quill Tethyses trying to make it her own?"

"Can't say I do but, speaking of stories, you want these? I'm afraid I've already forgotten how to read them." He was referring to the dozens of tee-tee tails attached to his shaved-bald pate by their own ichors.

"Might as well, though I've still got a full head of hair."

"Splotch them in then."

"I will."

So long as you had the requisite willpower – they being primarily composed of Brainrock-Gypsium – you too could secrete stuff between-space within devic power foci. Most witches, in most sisterhoods, could do a ditto with their bottomless bags, called kibises, or even via their similarly ensorcelled stepping-stones.

Touching tip to tail, Quid-Quill proceeded to vanish the tee-tee tails one by one into the Weird. It doing so instantly reminded Quit-Quill-Squab of a hungry kid slurping noodles down his throat. He couldn't help but be figuratively bowled over at the ease with which a physical youngster, one barely into his twenties, was picking up on the Legendarian's bags of bric-a-brac bents and idiosyncrasies.

It'd certainly take some getting used to not being able to do anything like that anymore. He just hoped he could still remember how to actually draw something with an ordinary quill and non-Brainrock ink.

"Death came calling," said Quit-Quill, as if by way of conversation.

"And I arrived," said Quill, thinking an explanation was belatedly forthcoming.

"I didn't mean Quidnunc. I meant Death came calling for Mistress Mel's twins."

"Twins, eh? Wasn't that a bit premature? Sure, I'll grant you stillborn births and infant mortality are shamefully commonplace these days, but her twins have to be deviants. They'll be tougher stuff. We wouldn't be here if deviants were pansies."

"Actually Mel was spot on her time. But I take your point and I guess, now that I think about it, so did he. Deviants do tend to live much longer than your everyday average sentient being. Plus, both Zal and Mel still have some U-type blood inside them. Even nowadays, Utopian hybrids consistently outlive humans two or three years to one."

"From the looks of her Mel has a lot more than just some Utopian inside her."

"I'm with you on that, and I'm not the only one. Her twins were proper Utopians. The boy's more black than white and the girl's the other way around, though I grant you it's still too early to tell how starkly black and how starkly white they'll turn out to be. Allow me to rephrase: Death came calling for them later. In other words, he served notice they belong to his tribe and not to the Lazaremists. He wasn't alone either. The other two Nergalids were with him."

"Ah, that Death. I didn't think the Thanatoids would be awake so soon. And I'd forgotten how close it's coming to the half-millennial date of transference. What happened?"

"What do you think happened? The Unities drove them away. Even if the Thanatoids of Lathakra were awake and fighting alongside them, thirty Mithradites couldn't handle the three of them acting together. Besides, it's 44-years till the Lazaremists have to turn over Kanin City's half-Mastery to Mithradites."

"That's 14 more than I'll be 30-Years."

"I'd give up the sword if you hope to make it that far."

"I'll do that, too. Fact is I think I'll have a beer. In a manner of speaking, it'll be Quidnunc's first."

"Splotch out two, will you, Quill? It's too early to start working on becoming a Squib."

========

Thus began a beautiful, if perverse, as in reverse, relationship.
****

2: Love Deeds

As he desired, short and pudgy Squab died a short and skinny Squib. As he also desired he got a sealed tomb, not a burial site, for his last resting place. It was either that or cremation. Minus the Legendarian Jordy inside him, Squib shared a common Marutian superstition with regard to graves.

He didn't want his corpse exhumed, then consumed, by cacodemons.

========

Squib's funeral was held in Kanin City, arguably the most ancient, continuously populated metropolis on either side of the Cathonic Dome. The date was the 22nd of Azky, Year of the Dome 5474. Ironically, though hardly intentionally, it was the 18th anniversary of the day the Quidnunc, meaning *'Busybody'*, Jordan Tethys died.

Nonetheless, Quid bodily attended it. So did about 2-dozen of born-Quibble's spermatic sons and daughters. As a measure of his popularity, so did that many or more Master Devas. At least two of these last were Mithradites.

"We claim Mole-Rules, Balance. Planter and I are here to pay tribute to Squab Tethys. He was a fine Jordy, a finer artist and a friend to all three tribes." The speaker wore a red, floor length gown that displayed scandalous heaps of eye-catching cleavage. Her two horns and third eye weren't all that identified her as a devil, however.

Not just her gown was red. So was her hair and so was her skin. As for her third eye, its pupil didn't just look like a ruby red apple. It was a ruby red apple. It was also her power focus. Any devil could subsume his or her Tvasitar Talisman, but only her and her two immediate siblings – one of whom vanished, never to be seen again, some 1500 years earlier – kept theirs in the form of their devic eyeball.

"You are like hell, Belle," this Balance responded. "You're Mithradite spies, plain and simple. I bet you never even met Squab, by that name or as either Quibble or Squib. If it weren't for the fact you're such highborn spies, I'd toss you both into All of Incain for sheer temerity."

The responder outshone her companion in every way imaginable. In her case it wasn't a matter of beauty being in the eye of the beholder. There wasn't a beholder alive – and probably none that were dead – who didn't consider her incomparably gorgeous. That included her companion. Then again her companion was no more known for choosiness than she was for having preferences when it came to the sex of her partners.

"And the Pauper would release us immediately, for sheer seniority."

"I suppose Pyrame would have to do as you say, wouldn't she? Unlike you I don't have any older siblings I have to obey, so sometimes suchlike subtleties slip my mind."

"You've still got a father, though. We don't."

"Fuck you anyhow."

"At least it's me they fuck, not me in a shell like you."

"That's crap and you know it."

"I meant proportionately. When was the last time you fucked anyone not in a shell?"

"Last night."

"Who?"

"I'm not telling."

"You don't remember, do you?"

"What aren't you telling me?"

"That I don't remember either. I've a sense he had a nice smile, though."

"Very well, Belle. Mole-Rules it is – but only because I already conceded them to APM and her Baby Byronics. Even if I was, and I am, I wouldn't want to be called anti-Mithradite. No chicanery, though. Be as young, as fleshy and as flashily dressed as you like. Just make sure you show yourselves off as normal, 2-eyed humanoids.

"I don't care what skin colouration you pick, so long as it's natural-looking, but I want your inviolable word you'll both stay in full view at all times. No possessing anyone, understood?" The devil nodded solemnly then altered her glamour accordingly. No more horns and red skin, but the dress and the cleavage stayed the same. Knowing her as well as she did, however, her counterpart still wasn't altogether satisfied.

"Not so fast, Belle. Those are the same conditions the Byronics agreed to, yes, but just because you're you, there's a few other things you have to do for me: Keep your clothes on, your legs crossed and your mouth shut – primarily with respect to our now-concluded conversation, but also in the sense I'm sure we both understand without going into any succulent details. Chaos and Order are here and they don't need any gratuitous stimuli. They're cranky enough as is."

"I got you. They'd hate to hear you're sleeping around again, especially when it isn't with either of them. Since I'm not here in an official capacity, consider it done."

When anyone talked about Lady Lust – let alone talked to her, as Harmony was doing within the Masters Palace at that moment – Hell's Belle became an unavoidable juxtaposition. The bedazzling beauty, Bouncing Belle or Beguiling Belialma, as antique Illuminaries equally had the Mithradite second-born, one of Mithras's three simultaneously born Apple Goddesses, was then again currently the Prime Sinistral of Satanwyck, Sedon's Temple.

As such, as Sinistral Lust, she rarely appeared clothed in public.

========

On the Summer Solstice of 5474, the day the Somata Twins attained their 18th year and could be officially betrothed, Kanin City was one of the last Weirdoms left on the Hidden Continent still occupied by a majority of Utopians. Although long no longer purebloods – otherwise devils couldn't possess them – their genetic integrity stayed strong. That is to say they were still more Utopian than human or, for that matter, any of the Headworld's myriad other sentient species.

Which is also to say they lacked the mental wherewithal to abide, let alone encourage, unforced devic worship. As for how a Weirdom full of Hate-Sedon Utopian hybrids not only survived but thrived in the midst of the Mithradites' Marutia, Sedon's Cheek, that was no mystery. Mostly it had to do with Kanin's millennium-old tradition of allowing devils to occupy the ruling couples and thereby parent successive Masters.

Mole-Rules referred to Sedon's Mole, perhaps better known amongst non-devils as the Gregarian Fields. Almost precisely 1100 years earlier, the terrible Theomachy that effectively ushered in the Age of Lazareme occurred in the Mole. He was so devastated at what befell his favourite son, Thrygragos Varuna Mithras, on Thrygragon – as Mithras himself had named the day – that the Moloch Sedon nearly submerged his own Head in fury.

Which proves that you don't want to piss off the Devil because he'll just piss all over you in return. And he'll do so for 40 days and 40 nights at the minimum.

Once he dried up, as it were, and allowed the land below him to at least begin to dry out, which it eventually did, the mighty Eye-Mouth in the sky above rededicated the Gregarian Fields, once again declaring them places of perpetual peace. Since Kanin City had the distinction of being the only populous metropolis in their vicinity, he further vowed not to obliterate it so long as its Masters agreed to help preserve the Fields as such.

Sedon's Mole thus became the sole area on the entire Inner Earth where neither devils, for fear of instant cathonitization, nor anyone else, initially for fear of sometimes unduly severe consequences, were allowed to assault each other physically. As inconceivable as it was for many on the Head to fathom, for non-devils caught in breach of its pastoral stillness by Kanin's Utopians there were, indeed, arguably worse things than death.

What might be construed as capital punishment only resulted when the person responsible for disturbing the peace sought to kill a hybrid attempting to apprehend him or her and, as a matter of self-defence, the hybrid killed him or her on the spot. Thankfully, the immobilizing aspects of the most common devices used by Utopians, namely their eye-staves, rendered terminal encounters rare occasions. It was how they dealt with those they captured that, for devils especially, constituted undue severity.

The Utopians applied their extraterrestrial technologies to recondition the perpetrators such that repeat violations of the Mole's sanctity were even more infrequent events than deaths in combat. However, what they euphemistically termed rehabilitative brainwork, others said amounted to nothing less than outright mind-reaming immediately followed by thought-replacement therapy.

Liberty-loving Lazaremists were particularly appalled. But no devil was happy because, as part of the reconditioning process, Utopians in effect rewired the offenders' synapses such that they could no longer willingly worship devils. Good intentions can no more render *'initially'* into *'perpetually'* than the Devil can, however.

Put another way, harsh reality pays heed to no man, not even to long-lived Utopian hybrids.

The ninth-born Pauper Priestess was All of Incain's devic mistress as much by default as anything else. The first, third generational devil to gain individual solidity, Illuminaries began calling her Pyrame Silverstar over three thousand years before they started assigning names to any other devazur. For reasons approaching innumerable, the most renowned Mithradite in the entire history of the Hidden Continent, Pyrame occupied the earliest Master of Weir charged with maintaining the Fields as Sedon required.

Time passed. That Master Deva moved on when that Master inexplicably expired. Kanin City being in the midst of Marutia, other Mithradites took over her successors. One of their earliest, as well as most important, acts was to negate the effectiveness of the Utopians' eye-staves. They did so by the simple expedient of sealing the removable eyeorbs atop them with Solidium-Stopstone, Gypsium-Brainrock's chthonic countermeasure. In that way they thus caused them to become useless as devic prison pods.

That done (and they having no Great God Father left to moderate their innately distrustful tendencies), nastily over-compensatory, tit-for-tat aggression incorporating less detrimental-to-devils, yet still extraterrestrial technology ensued. After most of a century of aggravation, Harmony intervened and – backed not by her Lazareme-lazy father, whose Age it nominally was, but by her two frighteningly tough, direct siblings – negotiated an accommodation acceptable to a number of highborn devils.

These included the extant Apple Goddesses (Kore-Concord and Lady Lust), their two elders (the nowadays long asleep Thanatoids, Heat and Cold), and Bodiless Byron's firstborn Silverclouds (Savage Storm and Gravity). Although the Mithradites did so more as a matter of mutual self-preservation, at the Unity's insistence the highborns reached their oath-binding agreements as amendments to her pet project, the Panharmonium Accord itself.

Consequently, as of 4500 YD much more level-headed Byronics gained the right to possess Kanin's Masters for fully five hundred years. Although this worked reasonably well at first, worse ultimately followed. Again for wholly selfish motives, certain Master Devas from all three tribes began withholding worship properly due their two enduring fathers and solitary grandfather. Worship withheld in short order became worship retained for self-aggrandizement purposes exclusively their own.

Toward the end of the Dome's 47th Century, the Moloch Sedon responded as only he could. He literally excavated huge landmasses, their peoples and places still intact and attached to them. He then re-deposited them elsewhere on his Head-world. Outbreaks of monomaniacal devotions-hoarding subsided immeasurably after that, albeit only for a few more decades.

Empire building, primarily, at least initially, in the Upper Head, dominated the 48th Century. By far the biggest empire to begin building was that of one of the displaced landmasses, the Thanatoids' perilously volcanic, Icicle Isle of Lathakra, which by then lay off the east coast of the Cattail Peninsula, Sedon's Ponytail.

At its peak the Empire covered close to ¾ of the Head – the principal exceptions being Byron's Godbad, great swaths of Yajur's occipital regions and the westernmost expanse of Sedon's Forehead. It additionally attracted devils from all three tribes. Among the most impressive tally three of the Thanatoids' fellow firstborns from the other two devic tribes, Lazareme's Abe Chaos and Byron's Silverclouds.

Once Sedon's Horn, then Sedon's Monocle, Lens or Cataract, and finally, as it remained to this day, *'Sedon's Frozen Flake of Dandruff'* – to quote the Legendarian's incarnations also to this day – the Empire of Lathakra's rise took 95 years whereas its 4825 downfall took, by some calculations, less than 95 minutes. Vast territories in Sedon's Forehead, the Heaven-on-Earth paradises for many Mithradite pantheons, that rapidly reduced to the radioactively uninhabitable Ghostlands resulted in unheard of multitudes of refugees flooding Marutia.

Throughout these decades of turmoil the Byronics steadfastly held onto the Mastery of Kanin City. They also oversaw its spreading out over the Cheek Lands into what thereby became the Sedon-approved, Cheeks-stabilizing Mastery of Marutia. On top of that, equally to their credit, the Gregarian Fields remained unscathed.

They were places of peace when the Byronics left Kanin City and the Lazaremists took it over in 5000 YD, the year traditionally associated with the dawning of the Age of Panharmonium. They remained thusly pristine today. As for whether they would continue unaffected come 5500, when the ever-disputatious Mithradites were scheduled to take over its Masterly successions again, that of course remained to be seen.

Prevailing opinion was overwhelmingly in the negative. Acrimony amongst Mithradites stayed as irresolvable as ever – as did the unquenchable yearning of the two male Unities to massacre each other. Not just devils felt like that either. Sadly for many, what didn't remain to be seen was any sign that Kanin's at first extraterrestrial weaponry continued to be viable in any way, shape or form.

Sooth said, unless you valued artefacts as museum pieces, they had long ago ceased to serve any exceptional purpose. Even their fabled power grid – the obelisks topped with firestones that absorbed and channelled stellar as well solar energy throughout the megalithic, antediluvian city – had gone as black as its future looked bleak.

Utopians interbreeding with humans and other compatible species, no matter how insignificantly slowly they did so, had been going on unabated since long before the reign of Helena Somata, the Weirdom's Master at the time of Thrygragon. The purity of the hybrids' bloodline had become so dilute their ludicrous insistence on continuing to call themselves Utopians transcended the risible. It amounted to nothing more than pusillanimous pomposity. Kanin's elite had become akin to musclemen incapable of lifting a mussel without a hand-cranked crane.

Due to an admittedly difficult to fathom, psychical link between the sturdiness of their bloodline and the functionality of their technology, time had correspondingly eroded their unique capacity to act as the Mole's non-devic guardians, or guarantors, of its non-violent tranquility. Metaphorically speaking, time had done much more than that. It had eroded their uniqueness unto the ordinariness of sand for its hourglass.

Most tellingly, the Stopstone-sealed eyeorbs that nonetheless allowed their eyestaves to stay so very useful, in so many ways, went the equivalent of brain-dead.

That cut the applications eye-staves had down to those of plain poles; brittle and easily broken ones at that. As a result, the burden of keeping the Gregarian Fields safe places for everyone venturing inside them – be they expecting sanctuary or just some degree of worry-free passage – fell to devils alone.

Rather, their father being a dissolute libertine and her direct siblings being such pig-headed proponents of their way or, just as contentedly to them, no way, its preservation had pretty much fallen to one devil exclusively. Could her age last forever? She thought so. Why would anyone think otherwise? More to the perpetual point, why would anyone want to risk ending it by seeking to harm her?

Besides, other than maybe – just maybe – Chaos and/or Order, who could harm Datong Harmonia, the Unity of Panharmonium as well as Balance?

=========

Throughout the Hidden Continent of Sedon's Head, many regarded the summer solstice as a day of unmitigated wretchedness. It being the last of the long days and the start of the long nights, it marked the end of hope and the beginning of despair.

Jordan 'Quill' Tethys didn't see it that way. He reckoned it another opportunity to down at least a decent portion of his maximum allowable allotment of 30 beers, maybe tell some tall tales for his daily bread or, failing that, play some terpsichorean tunes for dot-ditto. If he got lucky, he might even bed-bag a dancer or two.

Heaven forefend pleasure. For him it'd be purely for the self-perpetuating purposes of his inbred, procreative imperative. Squib-Squab-Quibble would approve.

=========

"I still say that's rude, Jordy. Calling it *'The All-Eyes Contraption'* isn't very respectful."

"You didn't object when I first did it, APM."

"As I recall I was doing a stretch in All of Incain when you did."

"Ah, yes. 700-odd years ago your Daddy Unmoving didn't approve of you siding with the Thanatoids as they marched through the Pastures of Plenty."

"I merely recognized reality. And it wasn't really the Thanatoids that concerned me then. It was my Daddy Unmoving, to use your term, thinking areas of the Cattail Peninsula bordering on Akadan rightfully belonged to us. They didn't."

"They belonged to Abe Chaos. More like they belonged to anyone he approved of in terms of belonging to no one, including him."

"All right, so it was really Chaos that concerned me. 700-odd years later he still does. So does Lord Order. Thank Sedon for Harmony's my last word on that subject. Daddy Unmoving still thinks the Head's Interior Ocean is our own private bathtub, though. He also thinks Iraxas should still be ours. Except, while it too might have been ours once, it certainly isn't anymore. Not even Great Byron can force adulation and Iraches adore Fecundity."

"Ask me your Daddy Unmoving will be lucky to hold onto Godbad. What with this plague or pox or whatever it is ravaging the Head these days, folks are rapidly losing faith in devils. Look what happened to Thrygragos Varuna Mithras when that happened to him specifically. And let me tell you another thing for free. It doesn't help when someone as massively powerful as Lord Yajur denies any of it is devil-doings; that it's just the natural order of things."

"What do you expect he'd say? He is the Unity of Order."

"And Chaos is Chaos, but it isn't his doing either. Whoever or whatever is to blame, it stinks. Of course it also doesn't help that devils and seemingly most deviants are immune to whatever it is. Do you know how many of my offspring or my offspring's offspring are here in Kanin? A couple of dozen, Fortuna tells me."

Fata Fortuna, she of the tri-spoke wheel of same – Wintry Moira as Illuminaries named her – was elsewhere in Kanin City, being possessive at not just Harmony's insistence. Aka the Luscious Lady Luck, albeit mostly by him, Tethys reckoned she was his Guardian Angel. Others reckoned her his charming stalker.

Speculation persisted she was the devic half-mother of every Quill Tethys after the first one, the one born circa 4000 YD. Of course speculation just as much so persisted he was a devic suicide; that Quill Tethys was merely a series of 2-eyed versions of Luck's once and forever beau, Rumour of Lazareme.

"Do you know how many of their non-deviant parents came with them? Zip, zilch, nary a unit. They're all dead. Combined with age and too much good or bad booze in his pre Quit-Quill years, it killed Squib. Straight up it killed Mistress Melina's parents and Quidnunc's mother; no loss there I shouldn't say. It would have killed a lot more Normie and Norma Normals if Zal hadn't had his physicians or Mel's Alt-nurses scratch dried-up pox scabs into everyone under fifty's mitts a few years ago."

Alts were Althean Witch Healers. Generally speaking they revered goatish Amal-Althea, Lazareme's female healer. Mostly male physicians revered her older brother, Azkeecyoos the Surgeon. Regardless of how ineffective their technology had become, Kanin's Utopians for the most part remained secular. Nonetheless, their Illuminaries could still read books, papyri or cuneiform-engraved clay tablets, some of which they'd had for millennia and some of which Legendarian Tethyses copied beyond the Dome and brought back.

Asiatic Outer Earthlings recognized the value of inoculations against diseases such as smallpox thousands of years earlier. Furthermore, the Utopians' insistence on cleanliness kept rats and their plague-carrying fleas at bay. Frustratingly though, all this applied knowledge only combined to make countering the mysterious malady – more like maladies – then currently ravaging the Cheeks more maddening.

It was almost as if the Inner Earth's inhabitants were being scourged for the unpardonable transgression of not worshipping their devil-gods fervently enough.

True, even if they discovered what they were up against, they couldn't manufacture vaccines and antibiotics anymore, but they knew what they were. They also knew where they could be produced – namely, in the same place they could get replacement eyeorbs, cosmicars and parts for their power grid, assuming anyone there could remember how to install them.

It was just a difficult, if perhaps not insurmountable, matter of logistics to get there. Once they were there for a while, however, how to get back would presumably prove a much easier question to answer. They'd fly back; some of the more mindful maybe even under their own steam, as in willpower focused by eye-staves topped by eyeorbs.

"I can see I opened a can of worms. And I don't mean the ones sticking out from under your cap. What do you think she's up to?"

"Morgan Abyss? Funnily enough I saw a picture of her the last time I was on the Outer Earth. I've heard it called '*An Allegory of Spring*' but I spoke to the artist, an Italian fellow by the name of Cosimo Tura, and he said it was of Calliope, the Muse of Epic Poetry. He'd been commissioned to do a bunch of paintings of the Nine Muses and said Calliope's quill was standard for images of her."

"As well as images of you."

"Too true. Anyhow, what wasn't standard was Calliope's throne, all those toothy dolphins, or whatever they are. Master Morgan had a throne just like that; one she'd had handmade by her own fish-folks, Melusine craftsmen the lot." She gave him one of those looks of hers – a very unsettling look given how many eyes she could manifest. "Or craftswomen of course." This seemed to satisfy her so he felt free to carry on.

"Even weirder, it looks to me like he copied his Calliope from one of my own paintings, one that still hangs in Cabalarkon. Don't ask me how he learned of it. He claimed it came to him in a dream, which might be the weirdest thing yet. And you don't have to take my word for it either. Unless he bit the big one in the last few months, he's still alive. Maybe you could get more out of him. I'm no devil."

"So you keep insisting. But what're the chances of any of us even bothering? We don't visit Italy when we're out there; isn't in our bailiwick. Besides, that isn't what I asked."

"No, you asked me to what I think Morg's up to in that painting. Except it isn't a matter of thinking is it. It's a matter of historical record. She's riding the Battle Beetle, what she also called her lady-buggy. That's the Master's Mace she's holding up, the oldest eye-stave in this world and possibly any other world. All those eyeballs sticking out of it like so many ommatophorous antennae are actually half-opened prison pods on pipes.

"That's Sedon coming out of them, though, like a lone genie out of a bundle of bottles. You can tell by the red skin, knobbly horns, goatee and pitchfork, hence the forked lightning in the background. The Atomic Twins had just set themselves off, causing the unprecedented chain reaction that ruined the Forehead Lands possibly forevermore, and Master Morgan …"

"… Is trying to hold onto Grandfather at the same time she's partially releasing him in hopes of shielding her Weirdom. You've told me and probably many another – no doubt including a few of my sibs here – the her-story of the Death's Head Hellion before. Cacodemons deployed, Grand Elysium booby-trapped, her threatening Great-Granddaddy Cabby, pre-Earth sibs and cousins ejected, Cathonia endangered, etcetera, etcetera, including how she died and who was responsible."

"Sed never admitted it; at least not to me, he didn't. Then again we're not exactly prone to having mutual, give-and-take conversations."

"No one is anymore, not even Pyrame I'm told – by her too. And, yes, chain lightning is suggestive of, um, others. But it's not something anyone really wants to know."

"Curiosity and the cat."

"I tell you; I'd have to kill you. Or, in our case, cat as in cathonitize. Precisely. Be that as it may, you're how we found out Cabalarkon – the Weirdom, not the Undying Utopian – avoided the Ghosts' irradiation. That's not what I'm asking, though. What I'm asking is what you think Harmony's up to by bequeathing as well as half-betrothing a couple of lowborn Lazaremists to the Master's twins?"

"Hey, conditionally anyhow, one of their future shells could be me."

"Sraddha's best buddy Squiggly, right? I got that too. Only, if I understand your deviancy correctly, he can't become you until you're dead, yet again, and even then not unless he's already turned a minimum of 20. How about you with an answer?"

"And how about you wearing peacock feathers? They may have peashooter pricks but they're peabrain males and you're all woman as well as all eyes."

"What can I tell you? You're me; you're All-Eyes; you want all eyes upon you. The only way you can do that when Harmony's around, and wants you to look humanoid, is to wear them."

========

Kanin City's Great Hall was a domed, circular enclosure akin to a Tholos or Beehive Ghost or Guest House. A *'megaron'*, in that respect it was virtually indistinguishable from any other great hall in any other Weirdom. What made it only *'virtually'* identical to its cousins elsewhere on Sed's Head was most Weirdoms usually had just the lone great hall.

Elements of the Headworld-wide-despised, and thoroughly discredited, millennia-antediluvian, Ice Age civilization of Old Eden began the mosaic they were regarding. They'd done so shortly after founding Kanin City. That made it an ongoing work-in-progress from at least two thousand years prior to extraterrestrial Utopians definitely arriving on the Whole Earth a decade before Xuthros Hor caused the Great Flood of Genesis.

The mosaic's beginnings now lay beneath the cyclopean immensity of the Masters Palace. In artificially bolstered, and thereby preserved, tunnels or caverns reminiscent of catacombs, they could still be accessed. They could therefore still be appreciated firsthand for the works of fine, not to mention irreplaceable, heritage-art that they were in Whole Earth terms.

Like the honeycombed hives of halls composing the Masters Palace, they and their add-ons continued to testify to the egocentric indulgencies of approaching uncountable generations of rulers who chose to build onto rather than build over-top the mosaic. In the multi-millennia of its existence, it had grown so huge and winding – call it coiling – some fantasists extolled it as the engraved skin shed by an ever-enlarging, divine snake akin to the Outer Earth's Quetzalcoatl or some other variant of its World Serpent.

Quill Tethys favoured the apiarian analogy. Marutians, he said, must have been keeping bees for far longer than there'd been a Hidden Continent, let alone a nominal Marutia. Plus, as distasteful as he personally found the bilge water, mead was Zal and Mel's preferred poison. And didn't members of a royal family always eat royal jelly? Funny guy that he purported to be, for those reasons and more he often referred to Kanin City as Honey Heaven.

Joking aside, he had to admit bees buzzing beat the scrunching sounds made by overfed buzzards, carrion crows, flesh-eating vermin, scavenging jackals and rot-frenzied black flies heard wherever you ventured in the vast plains of Marutia these days. The twitch-tickling, lips-blistering, pock-marking contagion presently besetting the Cheeks went far beyond any Godling's gloomiest prophecy of impending doom.

It was so horrible even Tethys didn't dare pun on the word *'apocalyptic'*.

========

The dome and walls of this particular hump had been constructed and then decorated fine artwork-wise, not to mention irreplaceable artwork-wise, during the quintuple centuries of the Byronic Mastery. That Great God's Venus, APM All-Eyes, hadn't wasted all that time held on the Prison Beach of Incain by the pre-Flood Gynosphinx, All the Invincible, either.

Once the Unmoving One got around to releasing her, if almost surely not forgiving her, she moved up to Kanin City. There she did a penitential stint as the honoured half-mother of one of Zal's predecessors, the self-proclaimed Dragon Master. He declared himself accordingly because his devic half-father was none other than Yati, Byron's Dragon.

Besides avoiding an anti-devil riot, Yati being in Kanin City had a lot to do with why Harmony insisted non-Lazaremist Master Devas there for the twins' bequeathal-cum-betrothal and/or Squab's funeral appear humanoid. As might be expected, his preferred form breathed fire. A terrible tippler, for a Byronic, she feared the damage he might do if he burped.

Byronics outnumbered Mithradites in Kanin City by at least five to one. In the perhaps significant absence of their domineering, notoriously uncompromising father and his second-born enforcers – his Primary Nucleoids: Sedona Spellbinder, Vayu Maelstrom and Chimaera Glimmenmare – APM, a third-born, Yati, a fourth-born, Djerrid Ruin, a Zodiacal, and some of their much more lower-born siblings were doing just that, tippling.

They were doing so in the mostly deserted megaron completed during the final century of Bodiless Byron's hegemony. They were doing ditto humanoid and in public. No vows were being broken; not that devils could break their vows any more than they could disobey their fathers or senior siblings. No glasses were being broken either.

Primarily that was because they were on vacation and didn't want to attract attention. Attract a crowd of curious cretins and they might decide the Byronics were having far too much fun. They did, they might start a riot solely for their fun. As likely, fair being fair in the Age of Panharmonium, they might feel they should be getting some of what the Byronics were getting as if out of thin air – be it in a glass, a mug or a hollowed-out horn – and demand equality.

When you've a pen-pal named Jordy, someone that can draw up whatever tipple you fancy, chilled as desired, plus refills, it was more convenient than bringing your own. The barkeep in the faraway Dinq, Doinq, Danq Cavern Tavern, who was long-distance-filling their orders, credited Tethys's account there rather generously, and one of many other reliable things about devils was that they always paid their debts, usually with interest.

Yati did burp. Tethys cringed reflexively. Long ago pre-Flood, meaning long ago pre-Dome – in the year 516 PD, to be precise – Yati was occupying a dragon docilely binging with the Biblical Enosh, whose actual name was Enolon Su. He deliberately caused the infernal beast to burp. So much for Golden Age of Humanity's third patriarch, a grandson of Alorus Ptah and Trishtar Thrae, the Biblical Adam and Eve (Pair #2, for scholars keeping count).

"You do have an answer, don't you, Jordy?" he, in his fiery red, black and yellow, silken kimono, asked Tethys. Transmogrified devic dragons no longer counted blazing belches among their traits. "You always have an answer. Sedon's Teeth – and I dwelt between them! – I've even known you to be right once in a while."

His effective protectorate, Samarand, the easternmost jut of the Head's backskull or occipital regions, was another of the displaced landmasses. As he liked to remind folks, it'd been Sedon's Tongue until closing in on a thousand years ago.

"What Harmony's up to by promising Janna and Sraddha Somata to a Black Godling and a White Godling? You're the genius, Yati, but I should think it obvious. Unless one of them gets me, eventually, she's ensuring there won't be anything special about their offspring. What I'm more concerned about is what the Mithradites will do about it."

"What can they do about it?" asked APM. "And what's all the hue and eye-spy-cry about Godlings anyhow? They don't impart sterility, do they?"

She was channelling China Doll; had green eyes, epicanthic eyelids, dark hair and powdered porcelain skin. Her feathery, brilliantly colourful outfit was so stunning it was a wonderment peahens weren't flocking her direction through the Masters Palace. Then again, maybe they were; maybe they just hadn't arrived as yet. It was a big place.

"What with Harmony and Sedon knows who – maybe her father – being their half-parents, and Order for sure being their paternal half-grandfather, the twins are the special ones. Assuming they last that long, come 5500 they'll be in their forties. I realize they're deviants but that's liable to make them too old to have any worthwhile children, again assuming they have any at all. The Mithradites designated, or destined, to hook up with them probably wouldn't even bother trying to establish a dynasty around late-life lowbrows like that."

"I'd have said huge hue and eye-spy-cry myself," Tethys said, "But thanks for the eye-try. It was a fay-fairly-worthy attempt."

"Screw you too, Jordy," APM snarled, disliking criticism.

"Don't I just wish." He smiled before finally volunteering a response: "Well, as to that other matter, um, as far as I know Godlings are no more infertile than any other god-devil. By themselves, with each other, all they have are azuras. By themselves, with any non-devils, they only have sex. Deviants like me have kids. Devils like ye and thee, ye have to possess these like me or they – non-deviants, I mean – for you to half-parent our whole kids."

"More fay-saying, Jordy?" queried Djerrid Ruin. "You sure you aren't Rumour of Lazareme?"

"Rumour got eaten by fays way back when the Land of Twilight was the Land of Daybreak, bowman. Me, I party-hearty with them."

"Hear, hear," chorused the Baby Byronics, who seemed inordinately fond of hard liquor such as whisky, vodka and/or tequila, clinking together glasses, mugs and hollowed horns.

The 30-Year Man had earned his 30-Beers reputation so that's what he stuck to tipping, stein-wise, more so than tippling, stein-wisely. Byron's eldest Zodiacal, his Bowman – that Great God's Green Man, whom Illuminaries did indeed have as Djerrid Ruin for their own obscure reasons – threw back the Danq's specialty swill, entheogenic mushroom wine, as if it was going out of season. Which, being midsummer, it probably was.

Yati naturally preferred sake whereas APM called whatever she drank an eye-opener. Right now it was a sparkling bubbly mixed with carrot juice. She hated blurry vision. For his part Tethys hated to disappoint an enthusiastic audience, all the more so when they were paying. Encouraged by their response, he carried on in background mode, as if he was about to embark upon a tale-telling – or, as was almost as likely, a tee-tee-tail reading.

Who knew? Maybe tonight he would get lucky with APM All-Eyes, albeit altogether in the flesh and, preferably, with no out-of-place eyeballs, thank you very much. There was probably nothing more off-putting than being stared down at by a cyclopean navel.

"The white ones are puritanical to a fun-free fault and the black ones are just as tedious, though they're more morbid than anything else. *'Repent for the end is near'* kind of thing. *'And, oh yes, a penny for the preaching, please – who needs money where you're going? Want to buy a whip?'* Thunder and Lightning Lord's their protector, so that fits. Even when you start out as one, never trust a teetotaller."

"Jug-a-lord-in-a-gourd," the Baby Byronics chanted boisterously, obligingly chug-a-lugging what they had left.

A few reached out as if about to request more but APM frowned, scrunching her two visible eyes disapprovingly. They must have seen, or at least sensed, her array of invisible ones scrunching too, because they retracted their reached-out containers. APM did form one-third of Great Byron's Secondary Nucleus, his third-born threesome of sometime enforcers.

"I know what bygone Illuminaries named them," Tethys continued, noticing – but without remarking upon – APM's somewhat uncharacteristic, yet unmistakeable, display of authority over her sibs: "Rastha Aragon and Faustus Vladuca. But I've never bothered to find out why, which gives you an idea as to how inconsequential even their fellow Lazaremists regard them.

"I can tell you Rastha's power focus is a flail – she's a flagellant – whereas Vlad's is, get this, a prissy glove, not a proper bash-your-face-in-gauntlet at all. Except, to be fair, his glove comes with its own Brainrock fingernails. They're nicely dirty, talon-thick and curvy claw-like, too. Because of that, Harmony and Yajur both call him *'Fangfingers'*.

"Abe Chaos doesn't think much of him so he calls him the *'Fop'*, on account of he always dresses formally, like he's about to attend some hoity-toity theatre or snooty sit-down concert. Or a funeral, for that matter: Which, now that I think about it, might explain why he looked so happy at Squab's this morning. Then again, knowingly being about to be betrothed to a silver-haired, Pyrame of a beauty like Janna Somata would definitely make me happy."

Although he'd never say it to either his long time half-lover, Lady Luck, or to his devic half-mother, Titanic Metis, Pyrame Silverstar – whom many devils, including most Byronics, called Sedon's Whore – was one of Tethys's two embodiments of ideal womanhood. The other was Datong Harmonia (both words of which, in different Outer Earth languages, meant *'harmony'*).

Hardly a surprise that: the Harmony Unity was everyone's personification of female perfection. As for Pyrame, independent of Sedon she'd saved the Head so many times everyone who loved the Hidden Continent should love her as much as they did her grandfather. In truth, many more loved her than did Sedon. Even though he in effect created as well as preserved his Headworld, the Devil just wasn't the lovable sort.

Despite their promising beginnings as a pair of proper Utopians, Sraddha – Shreds to his friends – turned out to be nowhere near as night-skinned as his father whereas Janna grew up not even remotely close to being as light-skinned as her mother. Indeed, except for her amazingly silvery hair, they looked very much like similarly easily tanned, interracial twins found throughout the Cheeks.

"With respect to her, I'm told she likes *'Rasp'*, which I suppose explains the Illuminaries' Rastha, if not their Aragon, whatever that is. But, well, you've seen her. There's a reason Lazaremists calls her *'Skinless'*. Ugly options the pair of them, I'd say."

"Best we do somethihg about it then, Jordy."

========

The phantasmal figure stepping out of the Weird was a presumably deliberately kept ill-defined wobble of darkness. Only his pink face and pink hands presented perceptibly amidst the 3-eyed devil's muck of murk. Oddly, these last two seemingly had too many fingers on each one. More oddly, the too many digits the therefore polydactyl devil did have were too long by a joint each on average. Most oddly, nobody recognized him right away.

The newcomer did have a very bright smile, though.

****

3: Kill Quill

Jordan 'Squiggly' Tethys did not carry a quill filled with Brainrock ink like his father did. He didn't carry a quill period. Nor did he pack a sword. Since guzzling upwards to thirty beers a day eliminated the possibility of winning duels, though not the probability of provoking them, neither did his dad.

As was then fashionable for ancillary members of the Mastery of Marutia's upper crust elite, Squiggly did, however, carry a slender blade strapped to his side in a sheath.

========

Squiggles, as some of his friends had him when they didn't have him as Squigs, was one of a number of *'trophy'* sons, daughters too, that the pre-Legendarian Jordan *'Quidnunc'* Tethys engendered after winning actual trophies, for a different kind of swordsmanship, during his teens and very early twenties. (He'd never had a heart attack while doing so either. The man was a stud, unless he was a stallion.)

So long as he didn't drink alcoholic beverages or rape anyone, his late, personally unlamented mother didn't object to sexual triumphs. In Marutia, heroes were expected to spread their heroic qualities around liberally. She'd been the result of one such post-victory liaison herself, sooth said.

Jordan *'Quill'* Tethys called Lazareme's Fata Fortuna the luscious Lady Luck. Bygone Illuminaries named her Wintry Moira. Plenty of others had her as Dame Chance. Devils tended to stick to Chance. Howsoever she was addressed, his charming devic stalker brought Squiggly to Kanin City shortly after his birthmother tragically died having him.

Nearly everybody who didn't know better believed Quidnunc had indeed died of a heart attack. Quill having recently transferred into Quid's consequentially vacant body, both Zalman and Melina nee Tethys Somata insisted the latest 30-Beers stay on as their court's chronicler. As an arguable result of whomever's murderous manipulations to keep a Quill in Kanin City, the boy received an unavoidably advantaged upbringing alongside Sraddha and Janna.

Best buddy of the former, he was the spouse most sought after by the latter. As of the Summer Solstice of 5474 all three were 18. Puppy love was past tense. It was present tense for firsthand experience. Which was why the twins' perceptive parents, Kanin's Master and its High Illuminary, acceded to their daughter's plea that, whomsoever the three Unities chose to occupy them for half-parenting purposes, she be allowed to bodily marry Squiggly.

As plans went, it wasn't a bad one.

========

Warily walking through the residential quarters of the Masters Palace – where privileged god-devils sometimes stayed as guests of the Family Somata – Squiggly heard passionate panting coming from his just-today-declared fiancée's private sitting room.

Fearing the worst, he burst into it dagger drawn.

========

Everyone knew it was Janna and Sraddha's 18th birthdays. Similarly everyone knew the traditions that went with 18th birthdays throughout Marutia. Their oaths being binding, Harmony trusted the two Mithradites self-declared there not to possess anyone. However, she also shared the Legendarian's oft-expressed concerns as to what they or their siblings' would do once the Lazaremists announced their nominees for the twins' devic darlings.

Perhaps quite correctly, therefore, she further suspected Sinistral Lust and the Planter – Belle's principal consort of recent centuries, whom Illuminaries had as Zuvem Nergalis – were in reality just the only devils belonging to their tribe in Kanin City openly. Anticipating that many another subterfuge-prone Mithradite might be there covertly, she got Wintry Moira to possess Janna while, at the same time, she had Ursine Bardol possess Sraddha such that the Rasp and the Fop could bodily appear beside the twins at their bequeathal-cum-betrothal ceremony.

In addition, realizing her always headstrong, and already smitten, half-daughter professed to love Squiggly as much or more than she did her twin or either of their birthparents, Harmony assigned him to the Librarian, Biblio Drek. Those who knew Drek could say whatever they wanted about the studious highborn, but no one would ever mistake his bookishness for boorishness. He'd keep Squiggly squarely in line.

It likely never occurred to her that someone else might seek to jump that line, jump Janna too. It certainly never occurred to her that she'd slept with that same someone the night before. How could it when, other than a vague sense of a big smile, she could never remember who he was unless he was right there in front of her?

Then again, like the Legendarian, she too thought the Pied Piper of Hamelin was Tomcat Tattletail, a long recurring faerie lover she could never forget.

========

Uncle Abe Chaos hadn't had black skin earlier in the day but whoever was having his way with his betrothed did. Reflexively reacting – rather than pausing to reflect on the possible outcome of his actions – Squiggly Tethys plunged his blade into the man's back. The man screamed. So did Janna, except it didn't sound like her voice.

Evidently unaffected by young Tethys sticking a knife into his back, the man whirled as his couch mate continued to writhe beneath him. Despite having three eyes and a positively evil grin, a horrified Squiggly recognized the devil possessing the man immediately. Regardless of whether the recognition was mutual, said possessed man smashed the hapless teenager almost effortlessly across the room into a wall. Then he let the lad have the full brunt of his eyefire

Devic eyefire can burn anything except, as Squiggly could have told him, another devil.

========

In 20-20-20 hindsight, for devils, part of the problem had to be the abundance of Love Gods and Love Goddesses in and around the Masters Palace that day. Aphropsyche Morningstar was Byron's Venus. Save for her self-indulgent promiscuity, Bouncing Belle was APM's closest Mithradite equivalent. Lazareme had a Venus of his own and it wasn't Harmony. She, once Mariamne Dawnstar of Daybreak, by then Krepusyl Evenstar of Twilight, was there, though. So too was Holy Hetaera, Lazareme's Sacred Whore (as opposed to Pyrame Silverstar, Sedon's Whore, who wasn't there – at least she wasn't there visibly.)

Tally among the always ready-to-roll, devic studs or non-horsy stallions in attendance the Nergalids' priapic Planter, Byron's Bowman, the other two Unities and a gaggle of their younger brothers, who, so long as they stayed clothed, Harmony allowed to strut around 3-eyes shining. Satanwyck – which the bedazzling, serial bed-bouncer co-ruled alongside her coal-black escort, whose power focus was a spade – even had an Eros-like, potential Sinistral-in-the-waiting.

Devils addressed him as Cupidity, and not just because of his commonest appearance. He being in Kanin City clandestinely might account for what transpired. Not to draw too fine a distinction between it, cupidity or covetousness, but most agreed his foremost attribute was Envy. Still, the fact remained that no matter what their best-known individual aspects were, it was a rare Master Deva who didn't do double or treble duty as a deity of fertility.

Besides, Everyman's Rumour and his Lady Luck had been forever lovers, so it might have been as simple as that.

========

As deleterious as both Utopians and monotheists believed devic possession to be, much more often it was quite the opposite. It could also be much more than just beneficial. It could be life preserving. A dagger in the back – big whoop that. Eyefire roasted? Not Squiggle's nut-balls. Yajur's rage? That almost certainly did what the dagger couldn't, but it definitely did more than that. It vaporized Jannu Somata.

Except …

========

The official pomp and ceremonies of the day done, Squiggly Tethys had joined the elder Somatas in the Weirdom's cabinet room on the uppermost floor of the Lazaremists' latest and probably last extension of Kanin's Masters Palace – last extension for the next millennium-plus anyhow. Zal's half-father and Mel's occasional occupant, the Unities of Order and Balance respectively, were already there in the daemonic flesh.

"Where's Chaos?" Squiggly wanted to know before he sat down and they got to business. Rather, since he had a 3rd eye and a different voice, that's what Biblio Drek wanted to know.

When you're a librarian not even bookworms worship you. Or, if they do, it's probably infrequently. You do, however, sometimes get appreciated. Both Master Zalman and Mistress Melina were trained Illuminaries: a former High Illuminary in Zal's case, a current High Illuminary in Mel's case. They appreciated Biblio Drek so much so they happily invited him to their council sessions more regularly than they did any other devil or hybrid Utopian.

Indeed, if it could be said that devils, of any tribe, had an official ambassador to the Somatas' court – versus an official chronicler, who was actually a self-proclaimed deviant in any event – it was Drek. The Somatas were hardly the only ones who appreciated his advice. Their predecessors did; the three Unities of Lazareme did, and so too did their father.

Unlike they or any other devil – nor any Lazaremist-descended deviant for that matter – Drek had been living in Kanin City for virtually the entirety of their nearly 500-year occupancy of its Masters. In that respect, it could almost be said he was Thrygragos Everyman's personal representative to the Weirdom, a position he'd held, officially, during Byronic times as well.

"I imagine he is wherever we don't him want to be as usual," Yajur responded.

"Or he's asleep in bed," said Harmony, ignoring Order's jibe. "You mind going to get him, Squiggles? We've a lot to discuss and, no offense, but we'd prefer to do it unencumbered by any howsoever occluded guest like yourself."

"Is that wise, sister?" asked Drek, again speaking through his host.

"I'll do it, Specks," volunteered his eldest brother there.

Thunder and Lightning Lord thereupon obligingly changed places with Librarian. So it was Squiggly came in with one 3rd eye and went out with a different 3rd eye.

Biblio Drek should have repeated himself.

========

Vaporization left vapour in its wake.

As it cleared, Janna Somata arose from the couch as if waking up. Appealingly wrapping herself in a bed-blanket – and for all he could see nothing else – she asked her puppy love boyfriend, as well as today-declared fiancé, why he was standing over his father's corpse.

His response consisted exclusively of one word: "Huh?"

========

Squiggly came back to the council room with just two eyes. Tears spilt from them both.

"Now what?" Zal demanded.

"You promised Janna to me," Squiggly gurgled, evidently choked up to an inconsolably emotional extreme. "Not to my father."

"What happened?" Mel demanded.

"I killed him."

"You killed him?" Harmony differentiated, perhaps not as shocked by Squiggle's admission as she should have been. The absence of a devic eye must have switched something on in her cerebral synapses. Perhaps it was hope. "Or Yajur killed him through you?"

"Does it matter?"

"What about Janna?"

"That's the damndest thing of all. She seems completely unharmed."

"Is there a new star in the night's sky?" asked the Librarian dubiously. He didn't trust the Mithradites any more than his eldest sister did.

They – Squiggly (still separate from the Librarian), Biblio Drek, Harmony and the two elder Somatas – went out onto the palace's highest balcony above the cyclopean city and looked. There was. It was in the Lazaremist Quadrant, too.

"Extraordinary," muttered the Librarian. "Dark Sedon always punishes Master Devas who cause the death of anyone's worshipper or potential worshipper the same way. It's almost as if starring ourselves is pre-bred into us. But if Janna's perfectly fine then what's that doing there? Killing a Quill shouldn't count as a killing. Even if he's been denying it since cutting out his third eye after the Crimson Conspiracy failed and Dream at least in part blamed that on Rumour for blabbing about it to whomever, the Legendarian's a suicide, one of our own."

"That's not me, Specks," said Yajur, materializing beside them out of the Weird, "Though what it's doing down there instead of up there, I have no idea."

Harmony rounded on him. Instantaneous multiplications of Brainrock chain links clacked off her bracelet manacles. For a second it looked as if she was going to haul off and try to thrash him with them. Then something he said must have finally clicked because she held off, if only for the moment.

"Wait a minute! What's *'down there'* supposed to mean? And aren't new stars supposed to be *'up there'*? Where else would they be? Oh no!"

========

To no one's surprise, Lord Yajur never blamed any of what happened that evening on the presence of so many Love Gods and Goddesses in Kanin City. He blamed it on Abe Chaos. He would of course. Order was as much Order as Chaos was Chaos. If ever the twain did meet, needs be it would result in the unrelenting slaughter of damn near everyone else.

Nonetheless, notwithstanding the Unity of Harmony seemingly spending so much of her thus far endless existence, both literally and figuratively, standing between her brood brothers, she never once suffered the same doom-for-devils Fata Fortuna did on Midsummer's Day 5474. Rather, touch wooden head as well as never saying never, she hadn't thus far.

========

"Far-sight it, Harmony," Drek demanded, suddenly realizing the how of the matter, if not the why of it. His power focus, a set of 3-rim and 3-lens spectacles, hence *'Specks'*, was somewhat similar to that of his sister, Fata Fortuna's 3-spoke wheel thereof. "That's Chance's Triskelion. Sedon curse you to Belle's Hell, Order, you catasterized Lady Luck!"

"Impossible," Yajur objected indignantly, albeit already with a perceptible tinge of resignation. "I cathonitized Planter. That's why I said it should be up there, directly above us, not down there, to the southeast, in our Quadrant."

(Not just popular imagination divided Cathonia – the part of it that made up the Sedon Sphere's sky, put more accurately – into four sectors. Because they were so troublesome, most of its internal stars were in the Mithradite Quadrant, to the northeast, above Sedon's Cheek and Temple. Byron's Quadrant was to the southwest, above the subcontinent of Aka Godbad, whereas Lazareme's was above the Gypsium Wall and Cattail Peninsula. Star Sedon usually shone by itself in the northwest, above his Forehead and Devic Eye-Land.)

"Far-sight that instead," shouted Melina Somata, pointing to the northwest.

"What is it, Mistress?" said Squiggly. "I don't see anything."

"Precisely, you little peckerhead!" Lord Yajur was by now positively incandescent with outrage. He didn't know the who or the how of it, but he felt played the fool and no one, not their father, nor even their grandfather, played him for a fool. Someone besides Dame Chance would pay for trifling with him.

Devils couldn't occupy anyone already occupied by another devil, which was why Harmony had felt confident no Mithradite – nor any other devil-god, from any other tribe – could take over the twins any more than they could Squiggly. As per usual as well thought-out as her precautions were, however, Balance was no more infallible than her Grandfather Sedon.

Comparatively speaking, their lack of omniscience matched their lack of omnipresence and omnipotence in every respect except the degree to which they lacked suchlike absolutes. Truth told, the difference between mighty and almighty was why Utopians of Weir and Outer Earth monotheists never capitalized 'godlike' when referring to devil-gods.

They did capitalize 'devil' when referring to the mighty Moloch most often in the sky above them, though. They did so because what really differentiated the Devil Sedon from nearly every other god-devil was his absolute lack of a conscience. Nonetheless, Fata Fortuna hadn't murdered anyone. Consequently, no one would have thought it odd if Sed had released her straightaway.

That he hadn't might not have had anything to do with his lack of conscience, however. Star Sedon had gone completely dark. Likely he was down below, on whichever side of the Dome, half-siring more Cathonia-preserving Sed-sons with perpetual half-mom Pyrame, aka the Pauper Priestess or, more previously than presently, Providence. Much less likely, virtually to the verge of impossibly, thinking he was running the Planter through, Yajur had somehow managed to cathonitize two devils simultaneously: one of who already was Cathonia.

Could that be why the Nergalid had been smiling so broadly when Thunder and Lightning intentionally took him out of the Legendarian – thus shamefully robbing the 30-Year Man of yet another complete 30-year lifespan – while, at the same time, he accidentally took Chance out of Janna Somata? Might he not have been the Planter at all? Could he have been Grandfather Sedon having the last laugh?

Already memory of the travesty was fading.

========

Lady Lust gazed upwards. "Look there, Abe: A new star in the night's sky. I don't know whose it is or whoever it killed but, henceforth, that's got to be our lucky star."

"Let's hope so, Belle. Because that's not just any star, that's Lady Luck."

"Who'd be stupid enough to cathonitize her?"

"Someone who wanted really, really bad luck, I'd imagine."

=======

Sometime afterwards, Anno Domini

"You there, friend friar," a scruffy, yet undeniably strikingly handsome drifter called out, successfully catching the attention of an ordained Dominican.

The black-clad holy man, out for a stroll one pleasant afternoon in sunny Segovia, on the Outer Earth's Iberian peninsula, where he had been serving as prior of the Monastery of Santa Cruz for a number of years, eye-balled the caller curiously.

Although the man sounded like he spoke the local dialect impeccably, he'd never seen him before.

The stranger was leaning against a centuries old, mostly ruined, but still noticeably round chapel. A decade or maybe more ago, the priest recalled, the area's indigenous peasantry started complaining that the ancient chapel was haunted. Responsively, if only to shut them up, one of his older confreres in the Order dutifully exorcised then re-consecrated it.

"Come over here a minute," the wanderer haled again, this time waving an inviting hand. There was something about the contrary character that drew the priest toward him; something verging on irresistible. An odd phrase, *'angels with dirty faces'*, came to him unbidden. Was he having a visitation? If he was, well, he was certainly worthy of one.

Perhaps unconvincingly feigning nonchalance, the black friar – as some referred to Dominicans – sauntered across the sward borderline obediently. "What can I do for you, ruffian?"

The drifter sniffed the air rudely, then smiled. "You've been poorly of late."

"Not me," the priest answered, still not altogether sure why he was bothering with this masculinely attractive wanderer. "Some years ago many of those I was preaching to started to fall ill. I, however, did not; not for long at any rate. Neither did those I prayed for most especial," he added almost despite himself. He did manage to withhold the identity of the most special one, however. It wouldn't do to name the Infanta Ysabel, as her loyal Castilians spelt Isabella.

"Thought as much. Good on you, friend; doubly good on me. Take my hand, this is both of ours lucky day."

"I will do no such thing."

"Of course you will. You're a hound. I'm a cat. Hounds always chase cats don't they."

The priest did not approve of puns. He did not approve of much. Yet he approved of this one – and for a very sensible reason. Some wag (of the non-tail-wagging variety) once noted that Dominican sounded much like *'Domini canes'*. In Latin that meant *'Hound of the Lord'*.

In any tongue, Tomas de Torquemada was definitely that – a Hound of the Lord, capitalized.

=======

Some months more so than years later, someone else got lucky. His name was Jerome. Hers was Herta. He was tempted. She was temptress.

They consummated their relationship over a bowlful of ripe, succulent fruit.

****

4: Two to the Garden

Until the Spring of 5476

Janna and Sraddha Somata's upbringing proceeded normally until their 18th birthdays. Jordan 'Squiggly' Tethys's did too. Had he not killed his father, Jordan 'Quill' Tethys, the Quidnunc 30-Beers, on Midsummer's Night in 5474, all three might have continued to live relatively normal lives for upper echelon Marutians.

He did, they didn't, and a second onetime Legendarian, one who never got a chance to become a Quit-Quill, ended up ensconced in the same tomb as his father and predecessor.

========

Despite Lord Yajur's initial protestations to the effect that extenuating circumstances contributed to the Quidnunc Jordy's second death, he'd forgotten what they were long before dawn came calling. Seemingly so had everyone who'd heard them, let alone anyone who'd been there, notably Squiggly himself. As for their darling Janna swearing her beloved fiancé caught the Legendarian raping her, that rang wrong, defamatorily wrong.

No Jordy would ever rape, nor attempt to rape, anyone. He might be a perfidious philanderer but he was always a gentleman, or gentlewoman, when it came to pursuing his or her procreative imperative. Consequently, Squiggly was immediately placed under guard and confined to his quarters within the Masters Palace. Although officially he was only being held pending the outcome of a full investigation into all that occurred that terrible night, his effective arrest was just the start of his problems.

Months passed. If only because of the high regard their very popular Master and his nearly equally popular wife, Kanin City's latest High Illuminary, held the Legendarian, Quid's and Squib's final resting place quickly became a hugely popular shrine. Compounding Squiggly's problems, having lost their benefactor his near multitude of half-brothers and half-sisters – as well as the offspring of the far more prodigious Squib-Squab-Quibble Tethys, who kept on siring children well into his sixties – thereupon began to stir up even more hysteria.

No matter how much his ever-loyal son and increasingly desperate daughter pleaded with him, public indignation grew so heated Zalman Somata simply couldn't let Squiggly's thoughtless act of spontaneous patricide go unpunished.

Capital punishment having been outlawed for practically as long as there had been a Hidden Headworld – devils did not approve of potential worshippers being executed, especially by Hate-Sedon hybrid-Utopians – the Master of Marutia felt he had no other option.

He banished him.

========

Even if Jordy knew who, or what, got into him the night he got into Janna – Lady Ultimately Unlucky occupying her at Harmony's insistence – no one could ask him. The legendary 30-Year Man hadn't recurred or, if he had, no one knew where. Moreover, not even the firstborn of the firstborn, the three Unities of Lazareme, and therefore the tiptop threesome of third generational Master Devas, could locate his quill.

Since it went wherever he went – unless she'd recurred somewhere of course, in which case it went wherever she went – that strongly suggested he or she had recurred somewhere. Too bad the one individual that might be able to help them, because she might have been his or her devic half-mom, was now a star shining out of the night's sky.

Dame Chance was stuck there too, because the one individual who might have released her wasn't a star in the therefore non-Sedon-Sphere. Or, if he was, he wasn't a discernible star in the consequentially continuing Sed-Sphere. And the one individual who might know what had become of heavenly him, Pyrame Silverstar, denied having any idea as to his whereabouts.

Aka the Pauper Priestess, because she had no protectorate to call her home, and no worshippers to call her own, she should do more than might know. She should know for sure. He may be the devils' solitary grandfather but she'd been the half-mother of their Sed-sons – or sedons, small case – in terms mortal, for almost as long as there'd been a Hidden Continent of Sedon's Head.

As most undeniably knew for a fact, yet virtually no one, including him-Sedon or her-Pyrame, could explain satisfactorily to anyone else, the existence of Sed-sons at least partially accounted for the persistence of the Sedon Sphere. Its halcyon, though uncertain, and oft-times experimental, early days proved sedons had to be born, one at a time, every human generation or so. Said evidentiary early days further indicated their half-mother had to be her, Pyrame, hence also Providence, her earliest nickname. As a result he, Sed-him, came to collect her fairly regularly, in terms immortal.

He hadn't lately, the Pauper informed Harmony the day the latter popped down to the Prison Beach of Incain, at the bottom of the Cattail Peninsula, in order to make inquiries of the former. From Pyrame's perspective that might merely mean they already had plenty of sedons born and yet breathing on either side of the Dome.

"Luck be a lady tonight," she observed astronomically. "And you're a firstborn. So, if you're that concerned about Jordy, why don't you just leap upstairs and ask her yourself?"

"By becoming a star in Cathonia? No thanks. I'm not that cat-curious."

========

"I'm hardly the one to ask," stated the priapic Planter, Zuvem Nergalis, once Lord Yajur found and confronted him in the Gleaming City of Manoa, a former Weirdom just north of the Circumcision Canal in what not just jesters like Tethys, when he was around to jest, called the Penile Peninsula (aka old Iraxas or, as commonly, Sedon's Mutton Chop). "But I'd be happy to help you contact the unlucky lady who might know. Then you can ask her directly."

"You haven't the power to ill-star the likes of me, Nergalid," Order responded.

"He never said he did, Sparky," countered the other Nergalid there. Illuminaries named the Mithradite Moon Goddess, one of a few, Nergal Vetala after a deceptively beautiful Outer Earth ghoul best known for having her hands on backwards, a conceit she seldom remembered to emulate. That did not mean she wasn't conceited of course, far from it.

"But Iraches love me. That makes Iraxas-Krachla my protectorate. You're standing in Manoa, its biggest and most populous city in terms of both the Living and the Ambulatory Dead. So guess who could? Me!"

========

"You could go ask her," Lady Lust said to Abe Chaos in her bastion of bliss overlooking Pandemonium, the sometimes cross-Satanwyck capital of Hell on Earth, if not precisely the abode of all demons anymore.

"And you could go fuck yourself," he replied, inappropriately for anyone except her.

"That'd be boring."

"Then change your splendour and I'll do it for you."

"Who to?"

"How about Janna Somata? I'm starting to fancy her."

"Are you really? Hmm."

========

As had more often than not been the case since she (arguably) contributed to the near instantaneous collapse of the Lathakran empire in 4825 YD, Pyrame was sheltering in All, Incain's self-proclaimed Invincible She-Sphinx, for her own personal protection, when Harmony asked her about Sedon's present circumstances.

All in all then, all agreed it was a right royal mess.

========

Largely due to public education, superior medical knowledge and facilities, obsessive hygiene, flush toilets, running water and suchlike sensible appendages to a civilized society, Kanin City remained far less afflicted by whatever was sickening so many in the vast plains of Marutia. Consequently, as the situation beyond its cyclopean walls continued to deteriorate so distressingly, Wintry Moira had brought more and more of Quidnunc's thus orphaned, trophy children, many of Jordan *'Squib-Squab-Quibble'* Tethys's pre-Quill offspring, and most of his known Quill-kids to the capital.

After he became a Quit-Quill, the Somatas granted Squib a small apartment-cum-studio within the Masters Palace. At the same time, his Jordy of a successor, Jordan *'Quidnunc'* Tethys, retained Quill's suite and position as their court chronicler. Quidnunc being Quill, not to mention Quill being Quill, Squib ended up taking responsibility for raising his effective grandchildren.

In order to help him do so without privation, the Somatas further granted Squib unlimited access to an isolated, but fully staffed and pristine, lakeside estate in what most Marutians called the Gregarian Fields (and most devils called Sedon's Mole). Since its villa doubled as the Somatas' home away from home, that was where and how Squiggly grew up so close to the Terrible Twins. It was also there that Squib taught him to draw, paint, sculpt and, indeed, do all things visually as well as musically artistic.

For purely practical purposes, he also taught him how to perform proper surveys and prepare high quality maps. Because of that, and other than his youth, there was no compelling argument either Zal or Mel could make to dissuade their son from appointing Squiggly his chief cartographer. That he additionally appointed him his lieutenant and consequential chronicler, that came about because, annoyingly to Specks, who would have loved the job, Shreds wanted Squiggles, not the Librarian, not even just possessively, as his companion.

True, unlike pre-Quill Quid, Squiggly wasn't much of a swordsman, let alone a soldier, but chroniclers and cartographers in particular didn't need to be fighters. As a result of Squib's tutoring he had the necessary qualifications, they were best pals, both loved Janna and Janna loved them. Plus, Zal-Dad wouldn't be Kanin's Master forever, would he, Mel-Mom?

No, she promised Janna.

========

For the first nearly 4,400 years of the Dome there were no devic protectorates.

========

Each of the three Great Gods had his own sphere of influence and the multifarious sentient inhabitants that went with them. Provided they transferred an obligatory third share of the worship thus accrued to their father Sedon, they could divvy them up as they pleased amongst their offspring.

Roughly speaking, the territories the Thrygragos Brothers could call home lay below the corresponding four quadrants bearing their names. However, because Mithradites made up half, if not more, of the 500 or so Master Devas who survived the Genesea, the mighty Moloch usually in the sky allotted much of what could be construed as his to them.

For some six centuries longer that his Hidden Headworld even existed, the only sizable area Dark Sedon retained for himself was Grand Elysium and its magnificent pyramid. Unreachable as it now was for anybody except devils, demons, and reanimated Dead Things, it may not have been the world's first pyramid. However, it likely remained the largest ever built upon the Whole Earth.

Until Thrygragon devils simply had to make do with picking up devotees catch as catch can. While that basically remained true for Byronics and Lazaremists, the price Mithradites exacted under the Panharmonium Accord for betraying their father was receipt of his, her or their own inviolable domains. Most devils couldn't do much to prevent anyone entering his, her or their protectorate but he, she or they could usually rely upon members of his, her or their more militant and/or most fanatical flocks to drive unbelievers and therefore undesirables away.

The partially Pyrame-provoked debacle of 4825 had many long-lasting repercussions. Few were predictable. Its final act may have resulted in the nigh-onunrecoverable ruination of Sedon's official cult-centre since long pre-Dome times. But it also forced Master Morgan Abyss to free him from the dozens of pre-Earth prison pods she'd slyly suckered, as well as slurped, him inside of such that he could save Cabalarkon – his Devic Eye-Land if not, at that precise moment, the Undying Utopian of the same name he regarded, with some justification, as his father-creator.

Unless it was Harmony, her immediate brothers or their Lazareme of a father, Thrygragos Everyman, Sedon promptly rewarded the so-called Death's Head Hellion for letting him loose just as irrevocably. The Devil being the Devil, he did so by providing her with a swift trip to hell (as in the Hell-Well of the World, which lay directly below the Weirdom of Cabalarkon), via a chain lightning railroad, she no doubt screaming and smoking all the dying way.

After shielding it from radioactive fallout precipitated by the Idiot Twins going Novadev-nuclear on the Upper Head, he further responded by in effect adopting the Weirdom to replace Grand Elysium as his personal fiefdom. He did so, accordingly perversely, knowing full well the only thing that obsessed Hate-Sedon Utopians more than trying to destroy him and his was them, independently and collectively, staying alive long enough to succeed.

Their focus hadn't changed for tens of thousands of Earth and pre-Earth years. Sooth said, without denying the existence of their immortal souls, Utopians of Weir had virtually always striven toward achieving individual as well as what boiled down to racial immortality. Indeed, in what had to be one of the most monumental examples of irony ever recorded, the Utopians' quest for unending life, and unending self-awareness to go with it, led Cabalarkon, a geneticist by profession, to co-create Sedon in the first Weirsystem at what might as well have been the beginning of time.

It thus followed logically that maintaining the capacity for breathing, of any and all of their number, for as long as possible, remained their species' paramount concern. However, Master Morg had been an outsider. She'd brazenly sworn to delink *'Undying'* from *'Utopian'* with reference to the geneticist. And, the vast majority of Daddy Cabby's fellow Utopians being inbred imbeciles, nobody except the miserable Moloch had the inclination, let alone the wherewithal, to try and stop her.

Although the Lazaremists, arguably as a result of a complete fluke, managed to rescue Cabby the Daddy from Absudyl-Minius (the fore-noted aspect of the Hell-Well wherein the Melusine Hellion had secreted him, he in his leak-proof sepulchre), they held onto him until such time as Sedon, released, demanded and received Cabby's return.

Had the Lazaremists done as Pyrame Silverstar wanted all those centuries ago, had they sent Cabalarkon the Undying Utopian back to Cabalarkon the City shortly after they got hold of him, most likely the Thanatoids would never have dared attack Cabalarkon the Weirdom. Had they not, in fact, been about to attack, Pyrame never would have conscripted the Idiot Twins to go Novadev-nuclear on the Lathakrans. And, had that been the case, Morg might never have released Dark Sedon in order to save her adopted homeland, ultimately at the cost of her life.

(In 20-20-20 hindsight therefore, maybe the Lazaremists, their father and the indescribable Harmony foremost, knew exactly what they were doing all along.)

In part no doubt fearing another potentially mortifying threat made against what remained of his precious thought-father, Sedon strongly discouraged visitors to the Weirdom. He didn't do so forcefully, though unlike most other devils he probably could have. The starlight-masticating Eye-Mouth, when mainly in the heavens, would no more deny anyone entry into Cabalarkon than he would rely on anyone else to drive those he didn't approve of away again. He just made it damned difficult for anyone to get there. And that included through between-space.

Presumably because it suited him, another thing he didn't do was to prevent recurrences of the Legendarian long-distance drawing what was going on there. That was how second and third generational devils like the Unities and their father found out the borderline-antediluvian metropolis and its delightfully verdant, splendidly productive, surrounding landscape avoided becoming irradiated like the rest of Sedon's Forehead – nowadays the Ghostlands – had.

As a general, but breakable rule, Sedon did stop the 30-Year Man drawing himself, or anyone else, to Cabalarkon against his wishes. Once in a very long while, though, he enjoyed his company. So did his thought-father. Naturally, what Cabby really enjoyed was 30-Beers pricking his finger and dripping nevertheless invigorating, deviant blood into his tub of life-preserving, yet animation-suspending, Cathonic Fluid, thereby temporarily reviving him.

Tethys seldom stayed up north long. Sometimes Sedon gave him the boot. Sometimes the reigning Master did, usually for seeking to sate his procreative imperative with an inappropriate person or, even more offensively, persons. Conversely, having become pregnant by the reigning Master of the day, only to have said Master confiscate her quill in hopes of averting her leaving him, a fabulously female Tethys of comparatively recent history went so far as to stow away on a Krachlan trader returning to Apple Isle in order to escape the place.

That time, as was the case most times, what drove him or her south was the inability of the Weirdom's remnant of First Weirworld's Mother Machine to program into itself simple, earthly instructions. Even though Utopians boasted beer, ale and suchlike suds resulted from their originally otherworldly recipes, it spewed out piss-poor pilsners, emphasis on spew.

Fortunately there was a way to correct that. Unfortunately a different Tethys had long felt obligated to keep it – make that them – secret. She couldn't resist changing her Q-name, though.

========

Sometime in early 1476, Anno Domini

His parents feared for his life.

========

He didn't know the meaning of fear. Truth told, at age 4 he barely knew the meaning of much of anything. He did know his fifth birthday was coming up in May, when it would be warm again; that the snow frosting his window meant it was cold outside; and that his dog was somewhere out there barking loudly.

He'd heard mention of Nuremberg. He hadn't connected it with the name of the long ago officially proclaimed free city wherein he lived, however. He certainly knew what a bed was – he was lying in his. He didn't know his parents worried it might be his deathbed because he'd never experienced death, not that he could remember anyhow: hence also his failure to fear it. He didn't realize how sick he was; only that he didn't feel very well.

He wouldn't have heard that his surname meant *'doormaker'* in English because he only spoke German. He did know the door to his bedroom gaped invitingly. Plus, he could still hear Drang raising cacophonous Cain, as his father might alliterate, albeit in his own language. But it was already sounding much fainter than it did when it woke him up.

Ergo, his ever faithful, but clearly dumb as they come hound must be dutifully chasing some bogie or another farther and farther away from their familial sanctuary. Dumb as they come wasn't an insult either. Drang had to be at least that dumb because he'd somehow missed the bogie in his bedroom.

He couldn't figure out how come he couldn't see through the spirit. Weren't spooks always supposed to be transparent? That's what his dad claimed and his dad never lied, not even when he was making things up for story time. Then again, how was the boy to know there was nothing of the spirit world about the evidently non-nightmarish creature flitting about his room fetching his boots and warmest clothing, the one who'd been sitting on his chest sucking in his breath when the increasingly distant barking first roused him?

His sort were earthborn; hence mainly earthen if not precisely earth-made. They didn't have souls; which strictly speaking was a prerequisite for being a spirit. He did have a mind, though – unless, being soulless, he was more correctly referred to as *'it'*. Regardless of semantics, if the word *'spirit'* could be defined as the melding of a mind with a soul, then having a mind was the other requirement. A mind and, a body to go with it, definitely made him, at the minimum, possibly chthonic. A pair of wings contributed to make him specifically chthonic.

The podgy putto, as demonologists identified his aberrant species, looked a lot younger than he did. If it weren't for the spiffy, embroidered outfit, dinky shoulder-wings and receding hairline, what almost contrarily made him look nearly as old as the boy's Hungarian-born goldsmith of a father, he'd have thought he was a baby angel.

"Get dressed, kiddo," the green-eyed, no doubt ne'er-do-well bird-brat demanded, as he passed him his stuff. "Your fiddlehead doctors may diagnose your condition dire, but it sniffs to me that you'll get better soon. That means we've got to hurry. Otherwise we'll waste all that good contagion."

"Can I fly too?"

"Don't see why not. Faerie farts like me don't infect easily."

As soon as he was dressed, and had on his thickest coat, the puerile scamp gave him an additional coating – he, the chubby cherub himself. Thus winged, though technically not possessed since chthonic critters couldn't possess anyone (not internally, in the same way cathonic ones like devils could anyhow), the absolutely delighted, until then bed-ridden boy flew through the wide-open doorway from his bedroom.

Putto-predictably, he attempted to physically pull up short as he neared the next one. It being so freezing cold where he wanted to go, outside after Drang – meaning *'stress'*, dad said, because, especially for a hound, he was exceedingly high-strung – mom had shut tight the kitchen door. Even as young and feverous as he was he could appreciate wings weren't hands.

"Nay problem," the bird-brat imparted to his undercoating, forcefully fluttering forward despite the lad's countervailing resistance. "We're subtle matter; we are. Our only barrier's our imagination, or lack thereof. That's why we've genuinely genius genies to think things through for us before we're allowed to fling much of anything. Doors, though, we don't need hands or handles to get through them."

Notwithstanding that assurance, the 4-year-old shut his eyes. Relinquishing reflexive reluctance – to fay-say some, as the cupid was plainly prawn-prone to do, as he'd putto-put it – he let his cherubic coverall do the work for them both unhindered. Looking back, once he reopened them, he apprehended they'd already travelled a fair distance beyond his home since before birth, as his stunningly attractive mother might say, patting her baby belly.

Even more astonishingly, he found himself flapping away as energetically as he was involuntarily. Not that the boy realized it as yet but putti were comparatively pea-brained worldly wights. Nonetheless, they were still better brained than any sickly kid scared thankfully thus far shitless.

He didn't realize what traversing the wild Weird, let alone between-space, meant either. If asked, all he'd be able to say for sure was that, somehow or other, they were rapidly skirring off uphill, in the direction of the Luginsland tower, the newest and most prominent feature of the imperial city's stonework fortifications

His dog was no longer barking when they, two as one, winged their way into the circular, open-walled, garden gazebo situated deep within the publicly accessible area of the Kaiser's otherwise exclusive parkland. He knew where he was now: on the south side of the great hall, not far from the Sinwell Tower, its original keep. ('*Sinwell*' meant round or around in High German, not sin well, let alone good, in any other language including Sedon Speak.)

Some years ago Friedrich III chose this spot to lay out a '*hanging garden*' supported on pillars and planted with vines, flowers and small fruit trees. Of course the little boy didn't know much about any of that either; no more than he knew about the castle's only occasional occupant, the current Kaiser or Holy Roman Emperor, and his fascination with the possibly legendary Babylonian or, more correctly, Assyrian Queen Semiramis. His mother used to push him here: he in his perambulator, when the weather was pleasant and he was too tired to walk this far uphill himself. That much he did know.

Needless to fay-say, that was pre-flight facility.

Drang looked tuckered, altogether barked-out. He lay complacently half-asleep at the feet of a much bigger-winged, much better-looking angel. One other term he did know, mostly from his dad's bedtime storytelling, was fairy godmother. However, his understanding of them matched words dad frequently used for suchlike folkloric fancies: evocative words along the lines of kindly, matronly, basically dumpy and tending towards elderly.

This heavenly phantasm given flesh didn't fit any of those descriptions. If, presumably invisibly, he hadn't spotted his maybe 20-year-old, if that, very much alive mother toiling at the table, cracking bones and chopping up flavourful roots as condiments for their nightly soup, he would have sworn she was sitting there, howsoever melancholically, awaiting their arrival. The consequently not quite incomparable, very much youthful-looking vision was that beautiful.

So, not a fairy godmother; something else – one of these genie geniuses the earthborn delinquent made mention of in his bedroom, perhaps. Since, to be fair to the boy, words like eidolon or simulacrum, both of which were closer to the truth of what she was, were hardly familiar to anyone, in any language, let alone used anywhere with any regularity, genie would do nicely. It certainly beat '*scum demon*', which was what she was specifically.

"You look sad," said the putto after disgorging the child, who went immediately to Drang for hugs and returned licks, "Even sadder than usual – more like a Herta Heartache than a Herta Heartthrob."

"She's been here before," the borderline habitually, down-in-the-dumps lovely answered. "Or somewhere like it."

"Babylon," provided the putto in a knowing, ancient, though never exactly old voice, one accompanied by the momentary flare of a third eye, also green. "She took human form, lived human lives, howsoever briefly, many times in the past. She'd have been there, in Babylon, what, two thousand years ago now, probably more."

"She got about, didn't she?"

"Still does," the putto confirmed, in its regular, still not quite childish voice. "A lot more than my internal infernal did, that's for Satanwyck-sure. I still think it's weird – the itsy-Betsy bits of scunge the Utopian hag's biomages scrape off the hearthstones Harmony used to traverse the Weird when she went outside."

"They're not all that make me up."

"Maybe not, but their scrapes contain scraps of her memories, and that's what makes weird the right word."

"Weirder than daddy feeding a demon a devil?"

"That wasn't weird. That was punishment. My internal infernal aspired to the throne Lust hated. How was he to know it wasn't hers to hate and therefore not his to covet?"

The, to put it impolitely, scum demon shrugged her shoulders in typical fashion, for her, and changed the subject. "Who have you got there, baby?" she asked the putto, who was indeed her baby; at least he was externally, and in the same sense that someone's offspring was always his or her baby. "He a bad one?"

"So bad he's among the best so far, ma."

"Good! Let's get going then. I've an itch to scratch."

"Better an itch than a twitch, dad always said."

"Don't you mean twit?"

"Dad's back from nostalgia land?"

"Bad is back, put better. Yet again!"

"Bad Dad's back again?"

"So Quoits tells me," acknowledged the genie, "Hence the itch. And, also according to her, Hamelin's in Saxony, northwest of here, not nostalgia land."

"My reference is to where it all started, back in 5284."

"Whatever."

The boy had perked up the moment he heard her say Hamelin. Having always reckoned it a make-believe place he didn't realize it was northwest of where he lived. Nevertheless, he had no problem recognizing the name. Hamelin was where dad set one his favourite bedtime stories, the Pied Piper of just that.

His attention off his animal as a result, the sad-eyed angel addressed him directly: "You belong to the mutt, child?"

"Drang's no mutt. He's my friend. You're pretty."

"She's pretty. I'm Herta, sort of like the word '*earth*' jumbled up but mostly like the condition of '*hurt a lot*'. You got a name?"

"How about Dire, after my own condition? Can I take Drang? He's a hound."

"So long as he isn't a hellhound. They've mixed loyalties."

=========

Hellhounds, particularly Keres Hellhounds, were earthborn demons. Remarkably often 3-headed – Hades' Cerberus (the Ker or cur of Erebus or Darkness) being the most classically renowned in that regard – the ones on the Head mostly lived on Apple Isle, the pupil of Sedon's Human Eye, speaking cartographically.

Although Thrygragos Varuna Mithras ruled there for thousands of years, nowadays his onetime Boss Cow for Taurus, Lady Lust's fellow, second-born Apple Goddess, Myrionymous Kore, was its primary deity. As such this Kore, Divine Coueranna as Illuminaries named her, commanded the hellhounds' loyalty.

While that explained the scum demon's reluctance to take Drang, Quoits, the not-quite-pureblood crone who commanded hers and the putto's loyalty, wouldn't have hesitated. The Hellion hag claimed that when it came to contagious communicants, the happier they are the more social they become. The more social they are the more sickness they inadvertently spread.

And that's a decidedly good thing, speaking Mother Earth centrically.

****

5: Happy Hundredth

Antheal 5476 – The Weirdom of Kanin City

Life-loving Ant Nightingales had much better than decent training. So too did Hate-Sedon High Illuminaries of Weir. Melina nee Tethys Somata was both. She also had a stunningly ancient, even by Utopian standards, though generations removed, Granny Jordy. It was thanks mainly to her – a 'Q' Tethys though never a Quill Tethys – that that gorgeous, if melancholic, genie and her fellow recruiters had somewhere pleasant to take the outsiders they'd handpicked, albeit only after first nose-smelling them for transmissive utility.

They called it the Garden of Earthy Delights. After crossing Marutia in near-record time – its unique-to-the-Headworld Time Quakes being fortuitously somnolent – Sraddha Somata, with Squiggly Tethys as his chronicler-cum-mapmaker, stumbled upon it during the latter part of the Byronic Ternary in 5474 YD.

They and the rest of those with them, all of whom had been handpicked by Zalman Somata for their lumberjack, carpentry and/or shipbuilding talents, had been busy there ever since.

========

A sucker if ever there was one, Mommy Melina wasn't just Daddy Zalman's successor as Kanin City's High Illuminary. Having Janna qualified her to receive her second seven years of training. Having completed it without once breathing hard, she became a full-fledged, as well as fully pledged, life-loving Anthean witch.

Recognizing her innate brilliancy, Mel's superiors encouraged her to continue training such that she could become one of them, a bona fide Ant Nightingale, a Sister Superior in the Superior Sisterhood of Flowery Anthea. Having turned fifty a month ago, Ants of all ages now could and did address her, publicly, as just that, Superior.

Being a superior entitled her to much more than mere respect. It also entitled her to do much more than train then assign those underlings she did train. Given that Nightingales would never do anything that might amount to life negating, like every other Superior her authority extended to any and every Ant. And any and every Ant who had the witchcraft's full 14 years of training could use Anthean Agates to step between-space.

One of her first acts, as an official Ant Nightingale, was to send some of those she could assign to deviant son Sraddha's super-secret mission westward. Some months after just as deviant daughter Janna, increasingly despondent after Squiggly's banishment, started having what amounted to safe sex with Unholy Abaddon, some of mom's Ants stepped through the Weird carrying a satchel of correspondence from both son and still wannabe son-in-law.

Thick envelopes – separately labelled for Janna's eyes alone – composed the bulk of the dispatches. Although exclusively Squiggly's work, Sraddha wrote that, while he hadn't seen them himself, his pal had gone a tad strange of late. He therefore recommended his parents decide for themselves if Janna should be allowed to view what they contained.

Perusing the rest of his missives – which pretty much read *'mission accomplished, dad, awaiting your arrival'* – it became apparent Sraddha knew zilch of his twin's scandalous affair with their Uncle Abe Chaos. Nonetheless, as the blinkered protector of her soiled virtue, Zalman was glad that, prior to passing them onto to his daughter, which he definitely wouldn't do now, he'd opened and subsequently scoped the contents of Squiggly's envelopes.

They held sheets of hand-drawn, and then coloured, erotic sketches. Many of them featured group sex involving naked but, curiously for heterogeneous Marutia, predominantly white men and women. Far more curiously, and not just for Marutia, not quite so many featured mass orgies in which their participants performed indecent acts with oversized, and thus grossly distorted, ruby red fruit such as ripened apples, tomatoes and various berries.

Some of the renderings were so disgustingly explicit that, once they saw them, most agreed the boy had to have taken to drugs. In his accompanying letters, Sraddha confirmed that to be the case. Squiggly called them entheogens, which made them akin to the Dinq, Doinq, Danq Cavern Tavern's much celebrated, even amongst devazurkind, mushroom wine. Evidently he and some of his pals took to them fairly frequently too.

As Shreds explained – without confessing it, yet doubtlessly having sampled some himself – entheogens were hallucinogens that supposedly induced visions of godhood where no one else there saw much of anything special. Even more worryingly, he reported, the form of godhood Squigs most commonly envisaged wasn't 3-eyed devilish.

It was 2-eyed him: Sraddha Somata himself!

========

Dispassionately digesting Sraddha's information, bespectacled Biblio Drek – who didn't just read and study, he retained what he read and studied – speculated that these entheogens may have been intentional extractions from a form of fungus that infected many cereals and grasses throughout not just the vast plains of Marutia, Sedon's Bread Basket.

The word he used, ergot, meant little to those there. However, when he said this ergot produced a shiny sticky liquid called honeydew, that immediately brought to mind Quill Tethys referring to Kanin City as Honey Haven. With a disapproving grunt, he assured them that beehive-honey may well be heavenly but ergot-honeydew was pure poison, albeit not necessarily instantly fatal to mortals such as Shreds, Squiggles and/or anyone else tempted to sample the stomach-churning stuff.

The Librarian further remarked that, even allowing for deliberate distortions, there was something somehow familiar about the sketches. By that, though some of those depicted were recognizably members of Sraddha's expedition, he didn't mean a few of the figures either. The drawings had, as he non-jokingly termed it, a seminal significance. After searching what passed for his mental reference library, he had it.

Decades ago now, the Squib-Squab-Quibble 30-Beers came back from one of his, at the minimum, once a lifetime jaunts to the Outer Earth. Upon his return, Legendarian told Librarian about an oddball sect of hedonistic monotheists. To understate it somewhat, their interpretations of the outside world's so-called Bible, the Book of Byblos, were highly unusual for the priest-plagued, religiosity-repressed times in what many of those beyond the Dome called Europe.

"Adamites?" queried Zal. "Surely you mean Xuthrodites."

"We call them Horrites," provided Unholy Abaddon pseudo-informatively.

"Adamites, Abe," Drek reiterated, whereupon he swung into professorial mode. "As those of us who were around in those desperate days for not just devils can attest, Xuthros Hor was the real name of the Biblical Noah. However, the Outer Earth Europeans that Jordy told me about were, and from the looks of things still are, howsoever-heretical Christians. In other words they know nil multiplied by millions of noughts about the actual Golden Age of Humanity and/or its founder and principal patriarch, Alorus Ptah, the Biblical Adam.

"Mind you, to be fair, I've read that certain admirably fearless scholars out there claim there are in point of contention two distinct Adams described in this Bible of theirs; that, presumably, the Xuthrodite Brotherhood, whom we devils do indeed demean as Horrites, deleted virtually all of its allusions to our Adam, Prime Patriarch Ptah.

"If they're to be believed then it seems Hor and his wife – the first and, for Il-luminaries, inspirational Anthea – along with their fellow survivors of the Genesea, didn't want it bandied about that Alorus Ptah established the Golden Age only after he intentionally, not to mention mass-murderously, brought about the sinking and, with it, the destruction of Old Eden.

"Which brings me back to these Adamites. Who I now recall Jordy telling me called themselves the Brethren of the Free Spirit. Who in turn, funnily enough, is often called the Holy Ghost, as if he was actually once alive. Like I said, they're dead ignorant of anything that isn't explicitly stated in what's left of their Bilge of Byblos, a word that refers to paper or papyrus as well the Levantine city not all that far from Sedon's Sidon.

"It seems that, in this ignorance of theirs, they fabricated some nonsensical notion of a perfect world that existed in the non-Edenite Garden of Eden before the fall of the first and, to them, not-at-all-hypothetical Adam and Eve. They fancy it an Age of Innocence and, in seeking to imitate it, they indulge in all sorts of sexually promiscuous activities.

"I'm more than surprised to see them still at it, though. I can say that because, again according to Jordy, they reckoned they could rut merrily away, without the risk of disease or pregnancy. They additionally reckoned, almost as an article of faith, that they could do so endlessly, till-death-do-us-stop sort of thing."

"Kind of like you constantly having it on with my Janna, Abe," smirked the fifth one there, Datong Harmonia, the Unity of both Balance and Panharmonium. "Only where you two started getting it on before anyone noticed was a Rose Garden, not an Apple Orchard."

"Hey, if it'd been an Apple Orchard, you'd have got suspicious, Harm."

"I still am; more so than ever thanks to that, sooth said."

========

Harmony was hardly the only one who blamed her deviant half-daughter falling for the Unity of Chaos on Hell's Belle, Sinistral Lust of Satanwyck. Abe's known paramour since the night of the twins' 18th birthdays, Bouncing Belialma was one of Thrygragos Varuna Mithras's two surviving, second-born Apple Goddesses. Her power focus was the Ruby Red Apple of Concupiscence – its colouration being one of the reasons Harmony suspected Lady Lust had now turned her attention to corrupting her half-son.

For her part Janna denied the pulchritudinous dazzler had anything to do with her opting for Chaos. She'd know if she was possessed, wouldn't she? (Actually she wouldn't; make that shouldn't. No one should be able to tell if they were or if they weren't occupied.) What was even more exceptional than her assertion that she could tell if she was, however, was the unexpected and thus doubly bizarre fact that she wasn't.

Even though Chance had failed to preserve what passed for Janna's chastity the night of her 18th birthday, her birthparents insisted she thenceforth be kept in line by an internal devil, preferably one not known for randiness. Accordingly, Harmony delegated Rastha Aragon to possess their impulsive and consequently too often delinquent, mutual daughter.

The Skinless Rasp couldn't disobey Harm, her eldest sister in Thrygragos Lazareme, so she had to no choice except to take over Janna howsoever prematurely now that her announced marriage to Squiggly had been cancelled due to her banns-boy being banished. Once her affair with Abe Chaos came to her attention, though, the lone female Unity demanded the no longer mysteriously missing flagellant come out and report. When she didn't, Harmony went into Janna the same as she did Mama Mel when she was both conceived and being born.

Disturbed as she was to discover her void of a devil, Balance was even more unbalanced to discover the truth behind her apparent infatuation with her immediate brother. It was nothing of the sort. Janna had seduced Chaos, not the other way around. What was as or more shocking, it turned out she'd done so deliberately.

An approaching diabolical, as well as initially loveless method of revenge, she'd done it to get back at her parents, for exiling Squiggly, and at Lord Order, both for killing the Quidnunc Legendarian and, no matter how accidentally, for non-lethally blasting her when he cathonitized Jordy's luscious Lady Luck, Fata Fortuna.

As for why the White Godling was no longer mysteriously missing, Janna had always been headstrong. Until Harmony came out of her (thus proving her half-daughter's better), no one realized Janna was so headstrong she could out-mind-wrestle a supposedly psychically superior Master Deva. The devil couldn't control her. She controlled the devil.

The ring Abe gave her as a token of his affection? It was a ringot, a made-for-devils prison pod, she reminded Harmony haughtily, as she nevertheless obligingly handed it over to her. Although forged by the Unities' not so much younger brother – the Anvil Artificer as devils had him, Tvasitar Smithmonger as antique Illuminaries had him – at his good-as-protectorate, the Brainrock-volcanic Sedon's Peak, the devic Prometheus didn't devil-devise them.

Ringots were the brainwave of their inventive cousin, firstborn Heat, Methandra Thanatos. Hot Stuff was the Mithradite also oft-times referred to as the Scarlet Seeress because she was something of a sorceress. She'd conceived the idea during the expansion of their comparatively short-lived but, fortunately for the Thanatoids, not altogether ill-starred Lathakran Empire in the 48th Century of the Dome.

Master Devas, the High Illuminary's thoroughly well-schooled daughter noted, used them to capture devic spirit beings much as even hybrid Utopians, like her birthparents, once could use Trinondev eyeorbs to do dot-ditto. The major difference was that ringots couldn't capture devic power foci. Rastha the Rasp, aka Skinless Aragon, had a Brainrock flail. Where was it?

Tvasitar-trinkets, the talismans empowering as well as helping to solidify third generational devils, are transmutable. Anyone can use them and they can look like anything. The ring Janna tit-for-tat gave Abe to cement their relationship? Oh, Chaos muttered, grinning sheepishly as he took it off his right ring finger and gave it to his immediate sister.

The ring, back to being a flail again, Harmony hid somewhere in her so-called High Seat, her primary domicile within the Gypsium Wall, aka Sedon's Hairband (as opposed to the Mystic Mountains, his geographical crown or headband). As for the Rasp, approaching irrationally angry at her for so thoroughly buggering up her assigned duties, namely her internal coverage of Janna Somata, she could easily have done a Lord Order to Wintry Moira and catasterized her potentially for all of eternity.

Instead, Harmony just fed her to All of Incain for a few token centuries of enforced rest. It was a relatively merciful, mutually agreed-upon, short term punishment; a fitting one for her being so weak-willed. It beat being ill-starred, that was for sure.

========

"Be that as it may," said the Librarian, concluding his presentation, "Should Squiggly's squiggles prove spot-on, or even if they just prove speckle-on, they apparently can rut merrily away without fear of venereal curses or other commonplace consequences. Then again it could be they just left their children at home."

There were no visible signs of illness or infection on any of the orgiastic revellers depicted. Nor were there any children observable in Squiggly's drawings. The fruit may have been disproportionately huge but the figures looked adult by any measurement. In spite of this, that wasn't what the Master finally picked up on.

"Wait a minute! You're saying these Adamites are actual Adamites, aren't you?"

"What would you make of these maybe manmade Tholoi if they aren't?"

Drek indicated a number of queer looking, usually domed, ornately designed and lavishly decorated, circular structures in a half dozen of the sketches. More pinkish than reddish, some of them perched precariously on even bigger balls or globes possibly meant to indicate teleportive gaps or holes through Cathonia; ones akin to aureoles the Death Head's Hellion opened for her deadly destructive, so-called empyrean vessels all those centuries ago.

"Tholos just means beehive," Melina appreciated, almost – given the seriousness of Drek's allegations – avoiding referential ironies. "Except, if those things were built by bees then the humans screwing those raspberries there weren't the only ones on this honeydew-ergot of yours." Almost, but not quite!

"Why wouldn't they be manmade?" queried Zal. A trained Illuminary, he knew what they were and what they did before they shut down. "Who else could make them?"

"Yazata Angelycs aren't confined to the Mystic Mountains," the Librarian pointed out, referring to the traditional builders of Tholoi Ghost or Guest Houses for the Gods, on both sides of the Dome, albeit for the most part thousands of years ago now. "The fact is, if they were, they'd more likely be radioactive than angelic these days. Plus, if you look carefully you'll spot a whole bunch of botched biota in these scenes. If I didn't know better I'd say we're looking at hellscapes."

"Demons aren't exactly noted for building anything, Specks," Harmony objected. "Tearing things down, especially if they can't eat it, that's what they're best at."

"That may be so," agreed her immediate sibling, "But Pandemonium is no more the abode of all demons than Evenstar is Dawnstar, other than she is of course."

"Fucking faeries!" grasped Harmony. "You're right. It has to be them. How did you figure it out, Abe?"

"Do give me credit for some intelligence, Harm. Who else could shrink non-fay-folk?"

========

Mariamne Dawnstar and Krepusyl Evenstar were one and the same Lazaremist Master Deva. There was nothing normal about many of her nominal subjects. In truth, there was nothing necessarily the same, even in terms of what might be considered intra-species commonalities such as heads, hands or feet about them either.

Roughly divided into two groupings – the summery Seelie Court, who were strongest between Beltane and Samhain, and the wintry Unseelie Court, who were strongest oppositely so – families of soulless faeries meandered, or trouped, throughout the Whole Earth. More often than not they did so invisibly, though many mortals nonetheless saw them as if as a shimmering when they paraded by, or else thought they'd spotted them, as if out of the corners of their eyes, then blinked and realized they'd just imagined it.

Worse than familial fays of either court were the tormented loners. Decidedly nasty when encountered against their will, they generally had enough residual decency to avoid contact even with each other. By their own estimation, by far the worst wights were the misanthropic redcaps. So-called because they wore headgear the colour of Squiggly's sketches of ripened fruit – as if to warn others to stay well away from them – they travelled in packs like predatory wolves or wild dogs. Fortunately, they were cowards and routed easily. It was further said that if you grab even one of their caps, the entire gang they belonged to would leave you alone if you gave it back.

What was the same about the otherwise ungodly, bordering on wholly un-wholesome host, besides the fact they worshipped Mother Earth, and her only when the whimsy hit them to worship anyone, was they were unprincipled pranksters to a man-woman-wight of them. They like nothing better than having fun. However, fun for one rarely means fun for many. Their kind of therefore fay-fairly-unfriendly amusement almost inevitably backfires unkindly on everyone except, more mostly than only once in a while, them.

For whatever reason – perhaps because she wanted to spare the Outer Earth more of their malicious mischievousness; perhaps because she grew fed-up pursu-ing her tactless '*truelove*' of the time, Tomcat Tattletail, who could never stay in one place for very long, not even in his grave; perhaps because he'd jilted her once too often; or perhaps because her real old man, her father rather than her half-fairy old man, insisted on it – Harmony finally decided to reseal the fay-ways she'd been using for so many decades to get to the Outer Earth with Brainrock-Gypsium's counteragent, Stopstone-Solidium.

Still, she was well aware that another thing fucking faeries had in common with each other was no one was more talented than they were when it came to detecting pathways through the Dome. So, had they unsealed her ways of half a century ago? Had they found new ones through the Sedon Sphere?

There was only one way to find out.

========

"You're with Abe on this, aren't you?" the Unity of Panharmonium demanded of the Librarian. "You think a portal's opened up on the edge of Marutia, don't you?"

"I think much more than that, Harmony. For one thing, to judge by Squiggly's drawings, I think a plentitude of portals have opened up. But mostly I think faerie farts are responsible for the botched biota who've been blotching the Cheek Lands for decades now."

"Best go check it out then, Specks," she put to him.

"That I shall. Care to accompany me, Abe?"

Chaos had been on his best behaviour since taking up with Janna. His looks reflected his happy mood. He was healthily tanned, washed regularly, kept his hair short and beard trimmed. His clothes were clean. He wore bright colours, not just black or blue. He only drank at meal times, never got drunk and, much more often than not, secreted his fearsome trident between-space. Nonetheless, even in his most handsome, least threatening state, he was always on the verge of unruliness.

Ordinarily he'd have jumped at the challenge. Today, though, after barely a moment's hesitation, he shook his head. "It'd be better if Harm went with you. Got a gal now don't I. Anyone wants a shot at me finds out I'm not around to protect her, well, that's why every man and his sister, save a certain sister of a certain Shreds – not to mention Thrygragos Everyman and his incomparably gorgeous, firstborn daughter – say devils should stick with devils."

"Or to mention Everyman's favourite bibliophile, put more inclusively. Which of course is why you didn't listen to any of us, isn't it?"

"You might have something there, Specks. Where's Don Delinquent Deodorant?"

"South," Harmony answered, not bothering to challenge Chaos's characterization of Order as Odour in topically apt, but for her embarrassingly echoing, fay-terms.

The only way their ageless, yet so very childish form of sibling rivalry would ever die would be if one or the other of her immediate brothers did just that, die, which was a near impossibility for immortals. Even ringots would be useless against them. She knew that because once, centuries ago now, before she knew the eyeorb-like devices existed, she learned the hard, and very hurtful, way how they worked.

Early on in the Mithradic third of the Year 4824, their maker – the Unities' younger brother in Lazareme, whom Illuminaries named Tvasitar Smithmonger, but devils addressed as Anvil the Artificer – pointed one at her. It didn't take, in all probability because the third-born Lazaremist, who was best thought of as the devic Prometheus, hadn't beaten her to an altogether unconscious pulp first.

It took him, though, shortly thereafter. Mind you, it did so only after she accessed her Nemesis persona, which she usually kept thoroughly subsumed. Still, there were instantaneously decisive, reaction-requiring occasions when recalling her, and thereafter resorting to howsoever-mindful violence, offered a become-mainly-mindlessly easier option than seeking to engage madmen, even if they were mad (as in justifiably angry) but brotherly devils, in rational arguments.

In normal times she both delighted in, and excelled at, the latter. That she proceeded to demonstrate just how excellently her Brainrock chains (what Tavy had in effect fashioned circa 2000 YD) transformed into barbwire-strung whips, well, the Era of Empires weren't normal times were they. Besides, albeit not by her, Tvasitar was hardly the first to be taken out that way, and too many of these last were their fellow Lazaremists. Pulping him unconscious only partially paid him back for making, if not devising, the damn things in the first place.

Despite her predilection for finding harmonious solutions, Harmony sometimes – like that time – acted as unbalanced as Chaos and Order did, especially around each other. That didn't mean she was their equal. It didn't mean she wasn't of course. But her self-confidence in that regard was sufficiently lacking she never wanted to try and prove it one way or another.

Plus, she was absolutely certain that if they ever really went at each other, or if she went at either one of them, the planet would be the only thing beaten to a pulp.

"About as far south as you can go in the Cheeks without it becoming the Jaw, if you have to know. I had a thought."

"Do share it then."

"Grandfather's missing. If only because of everything else that's going on, and not just in the Cheeks, that's a mystery in urgent need of demystification. The same thing happened, what, seven hundred odd years ago, who found him? Order doesn't drink but Jordy does and what's his favourite place to get pickled?"

"Not just place, brew," Chaos appreciated, having popped more than a few pilsners there himself over the centuries. "And the Dinq, Doinq, Danq doesn't do deliveries."

"Actually, it does – but only in a manner of speaking. First, you need a Brain-rock quill to draw deliveries to destinations."

"And that's been happening?"

"In a manner of speaking."

"So why aren't you there?"

"I was, until Specks far-spoke to me about Squiggly's squiggles. Besides, I was coming up here anyways. Order also isn't the sentimental sort. So I asked him to take up the vigil until I got back."

"Sentimental?" had to ask the Master of Marutia.

"The sort that comes up here to wish you a happy hundredth, put precisely."

"You remembered," clapped Zal's Mel, his wife of a quarter of that time. "How sweet!"

Melina's Zal of a husband wasn't so much so delighted. "You sure Drek didn't far-speak you about the announcement I'm making today?"

"That piddling blither of pomposity? My dear boy, I don't care how many agatine eyes Mel makes you wear, you Utopians have always been transparent to he and me."

"To Dad and the Bad, too," Chaos confirmed. "Bad Smell as well, dick-dildo!"

========

Something else needs be said about a certain not-quite-pureblood Hellion hag (one who couldn't resist changing her Q-name from 'Queer' to 'Quoits') besides the fact that she could keep secrets. While she was good at transmitting illnesses, she wasn't much good at curing them. Neither was the Master she served the longest.

Quoits was also lucky. That might have something to do with her devic half-mother, one she'd acquired when she was conceived on her parents' passage from Devic Eye-Land to Human Apple Eye-Isle just prior to the nominal beginning of the Age of Panharmonium circa 5000 YD. Then again it might not.

The Master she served the longest, though, was no more lucky than he was immune to at least one of the next-to-innumerable infections he and his predecessors had been having her bring through Tholoi from the Outer Earth for a couple of hundred years by now. Pure U-bloods, even if the vast majority were basically inbred morons by then, couldn't be possessed but, once in awhile, particularly virulent Whole Earth bugs bit them both ways.

Some might call that ironic. Others would call it karmic. One in particular, as per usual with him, would simply characterize it as the natural order of things.

****

6: Danq Discourtesies

End-Antheal 5476 – The Southern Cheek Lands

John Barleycorn wasn't dead.

It being Antheal – April in the European area of the then thought-flat planet by scabrous scads of its reprehensibly kept-ignorant natives – he wouldn't be. The harvest, his scything, was months away. Then again that John Barleycorn was a folkloric figment of bards, poets and/or roving troubadours on both sides of the Dome.

Even though he had nut-brown skin and wheat blond hair, this John Barleycorn – JB to his friends and clientele alike – was a barkeep at the Dinq, Doinq, Danq Cavern Tavern.

========

Sparky sauntered into the Danq purposely more casually than cockily.

Because everything came so effortlessly to him, it mustn't have registered that rainfall had been inundating the impassable – due to a complete absence of passes – Diluvian Mountain Range nigh on never-endingly since the 40 days and 40 nights of the Great Flood of Genesis itself. As a result of his sloppy, self-centred conceptualizing, he thoroughly blew any chance he had of entering anonymously by virtue of the fact he came in completely dry.

Reckoning himself ever so clever, he did recall to quell his hair's inclination to snap, crackle and pop, both visually and audibly. He further remembered to conceal his lightning blade between-space. It was still in its Stopstone scabbard of course, which was still strapped to his back, a thought away from manifesting in his hand. He greeted Barleycorn by nickname and ordered his usual pot of steaming hot Cathy, thus demonstrating anew how hopeless he was when it came to pretending he was anyone except himself.

A foul-tasting, but remarkably energizing, altogether non-alcoholic concoction of finely ground, thence dissolved and distilled Brainrock-Gypsium, Cathy was called such because it was little more than a hopped-up, terrestrial variant of life-preserving, though animation-suspending, Cathonic Fluid. Its multiple tens of thousands light years' pre-Earth originated, yet similarly prepared, and liquefied, constituent-cousin was what kept Cabalarkon, Sedon's Cabby the Daddy, he of the north-westernmost Weirdom of the same name, the Undying Utopian.

Even if its recipe included rotting fungi, the Danq was one of the few taverns on the Whole Earth to do a decent Cathy. That it could do so at all had everything to do with its relative proximity, across the devil-dredged and thereafter Diluvia-drenched Auditory Canal, to the westernmost extreme of the Gypsium Wall.

A geologically unstable, ultra hilly strip of terrain upwards to two hundred miles in width and spanning nearly eight hundred miles in length, it was another natural-looking, but Sedon-shaped landscape. Cresting most of it was an actual wall. Thick, though partially collapsing and no longer impenetrable, Cathy's concocters had no problem locating, then mining, blocks of the transitory Godstuff for preparatory purposes of stimulation more so than refreshment.

Head-worldly-wise, the Cattail Peninsula formed Sedon's Ponytail, hence why the Wall was also called Sedon's Hairband. Broken as it was, it nevertheless continued its exemplary service as an unmistakeable, devil-reinforced, geographical barrier between the eastern Head's Yajur-dominated occipital regions and Unholy Abaddon's de facto domain.

Although it had definitely seen better days, very few, if any, of those who passed over, under or around it were better looking than its Deva Dand, also an Over-Lady. When she wasn't elsewhere, the Danq's official owner, the Unity of Balance as well as Panharmonium, could usually be found dwelling at her mobile, now-you-see-it and now-you-don't, High Seat somewhere atop the Wall proper.

Today though, Sparky knew because she'd far-spoken as much to him earlier, she was a thousand miles to the northwest, visiting the Weirdom of Kanin City. Which, her being there, was most of the reason he'd deigned to come here. He would much rather run her through than run into her at the Danq – or anywhere else, for that matter.

Harmony was all that kept Order from crushing Chaos.

========

"Sorry, sir," JB apologized. "Run out, sir." Despite the newcomer manifestly feeling 2-eyed-courteous, the barkeep recognized him immediately. That he wasn't soaked thoroughly through undoubtedly helped with his ease of identification.

Here, on the far north-eastern slopes of Diluvia – what separated the Cheek Lands from Iraxas-Krachla, the Penile Peninsula or Sedon's Mutton Chop – and with the Auditory Canal as good as lapping at their feet, only devils and other self-psychopomps could enter the tavern's main cavern as if coming from the outside so seemingly weatherproof. That they could was due to the simple fact it didn't rain in the Weird of between-space.

"Who's the sponge?"

"Him, sir, the Mushroom Man. Although I can't rightly say which one's your dad, he and the Green Man he's with have been around a lot lately."

JB gestured across the huge, high-ceilinged enclosure. With its open and closed grills and fireplaces burning peat or charcoal, the cavern was exceptionally smoky. The horribly unhealthy haze rendered them difficult to make out but he was pointing in the direction of a pair of noticeable devils sitting at a run-of-the-mildew table. By far the more grotesque of the two seemed composed entirely of soil and biomass but, to both of the vainglorious Sparky's visible eyeballs, the other one looked much like he always did, as an elderly him.

"You're an atheist?" he inquired of the barkeep.

"How can anyone except devil-gods afford to be atheists on the Head, sir?" JB answered cheerily enough. Realizing whom he was dealing with he spoke rhetoric-ally, neither sarcastically nor, heaven as well commonsense forefend, disrespectfully. "I'm just a drunkard, sir; one that's partial to our own mushroom wine, the same as they both are ordinarily."

"Your fondness for your homemade home-wrecker must account for your per-ception of Thrygragos Everyman as a mushroom man. I see him differently, more like an old me with no electric hair. But the Green Man's definitely Byron's Bow-man, Djerrid Ruin. He almost always looks like a burl-headed, ambulatory tree stump with mossy branches for arms and torn-out roots for tramples."

"Which," JB replied, chancing a pun, "Going out on a limb, would account for the bow as well as the boughs. We don't get a lot of Byronics up here, sir. At least we don't get a lot of them up here with their third eye sticking out so brazenly."

"Better their third eye than their lightning blade."

"Very good, sir."

========

Thrygragos Lazareme and Djerrid Ruin were chatting with two poor, but human-looking white men and a boy standing in the aisle beside their table. The grey-haired, evidently once tonsured eldest of the three, who was dressed in a brown woollen robe, appeared to be well into his fifties. The blondish other man seemed somewhere in his twenties or very early thirties, so he might have been his son.

As for the youngster, he was maybe five or six at the absolute maximum. That meant either of the other men could have been his father. Then again the noxious miasma that passed for air in here was so dense it was impossible for him to tell if they looked at all alike. Maybe the boy was a waif or a foundling.

It being indoors, the strangers had doffed and were now carrying their oiled, woollen cloaks or blankets. Despite their distance across the cavern, these seemed of decent quality. Similarly, muddy and heavily scuffed as they were, so did the leather boots they wore. While that might mean they'd been well off once, it would have to have been 'once upon a time, long ago and faraway', to quote the taleteller he'd come here looking for.

Like himself, JB and, indeed, virtually everyone in the Cheeks who didn't wear a robe, gown or dress, the man and the lad dressed in trousers and shirts that might be made out of wool or else coarse linen. Yet their clothing looked patched or threadbare, as if it had been many, many months since they'd had a chance to change into something clean, let alone new.

Gazing at them, eyes already watering even though he'd only just arrived, he felt oddly unsettled. Since, other than his triplet brother, not much could disturb an arguably matchless Master Deva like himself, he reckoned he knew its cause. "The three scruffy looking fellows they're drinking with, they're demons?"

"They're not really drinking with them, sir. They're just waiting for takeout, as it were. They're not really demons either. They're Outer Earthlings. So the Green Man gave me to understand anyhow. Folks don't wash or shave much out there, I take it."

JB was certainly right about that. Although the boy was years too young to have a beard, the other two were rumpled, shaggy-doglike specimens of dubious humanity. "Outer Earthlings, eh?" said Sparky. "No wonder I mistook them for demons. They probably figure a scrub brush's some sort of bramble bush."

"If I hadn't been told differently, I'd have done the same. Truth told, I initially did. You should have been here when they walked in, sir. The smell they gave off, well, they reeked so foully they almost emptied the place."

"And the Danq doesn't serve pansies, does it?"

"Actually it does, sir. We here in the Danq are only prejudiced against not being paid properly. So long as they've the coin, we'll serve anybody, earthborn crud like cannibalistic cacodemons and red-capped faeries included. Mind you, we do draw the line on them bringing their dinner inside, especially if they want us to serve them, too, before they ... you know."

"Ask you to pass the salt and pepper?"

"Precisely. Myself, I've personally plied Plantagenet pansies plenty of their preferred brands of liquid fertilizer. I'd offer you some of our chlorophyll Cathy except the Byronic drained our stash before he went back to wine. You might have enjoyed it, sir. It's chock full of pressed wheat grass. Very good for you too, I hear from those who don't object to being poisoned."

"Just as well you're out of it," Sparky allowed. "I'm the Sky God type."

"And a mightily impressive one too, I dare say, sir. Those three there, though, walking in they had the odour of ordure and one thing even I know about demons is they're earthborn. Plus, they seem prone to facial pock-marking, like they've survived one pox or another. And that's the other thing I know about demons. They never get their semblances quite right, do they?"

"You'd better ask Chaos about that next time he pops by to pop a pill. I incinerate the blighters. He sleeps with them."

"The DDD is a civilized drinking establishment, sir. So I guess that makes it a good thing they aren't demons, particularly for them. Of course, should specialized incineration, or virtually any variety of, um, recreational arrangements and/or pre or post sleeping companions be desired, we have many different kinds of catered caves carved into the granite out back. You've the cash or the jewellery, give us a few days advance notice and we should be able to accommodate most any of your whims."

"I'll keep that in mind for next time. You hear anything more about them?"

"Only that the men are seekers after secrets, sir; ones who got lucky or unlucky, according to your point of view. As for the boy, I'm to gather he just did what boys tend to do and stuck his nose, feet and little lightning blade in somewhere they didn't belong. Youngest to oldest, the Green Man told me their names are Dire, Bosco and Twisted Tommy."

"Twisted Tommy?"

"That'd be the brown-robed fellow, sir. So your Mr Ruin told me, sir. I gather it's a play on his surname as well as his wretched personality. You probably can't see it with his back to us but he has a cross-like ornament strung round his neck with a disgusting depiction of a naked man crucified to it. Beastly beat-up and bloody he is too, sir – a first rate etching of a seriously sick subject. Ask me it's no wonder they call him Twisted Tommy."

"A Xuthrodites-duped monotheist, how very interesting. Even more interesting, he must be one of their misbegotten, holier-than-thou priests. I should have realized it straightaway. He obviously shaves the crown of his head when he has access to a razor. Harmony told me about suchlike slime. Misogynist pigs and horrendous hypocrites, she called them. Then she claimed she was being polite. She says they infest this Europe of theirs like humanoid leaches."

"The boss has said a lot worse than that to me, sir. *'Religion is the root of all evil out there.'* Verbatim, that is, and I can guarantee you she wasn't only talking about this Europe of theirs. She's been all over the Outer Earth. When she claims that wherever you go beyond the Dome, and in whatever language you hear it, the collective noun for their stomach-churning sort is a plague of priests, I believe her."

"And so you should. Devils can't lie."

"Even the bit about Outer Earthlings having different languages?"

"Even about that, although it's been any number of your human generations since I last traversed the Dome. Mind you, if you went out there yourself, you could both understand and speak to anyone you met in any language. The same goes for anyone who comes in here. The Legendarian claims it's got to do with the quality of our air, not the quality of our intelligence. You seen him lately, by the way? Harm thought he might be around."

"Myself, I'd say nay, sir. That is, to say aye, I haven't seen him lately, as in the last couple of years, since just before that day I long-distance filled order after order – no offense, sir – of premium spirits for him and what he called the Baby Byronics. Took some doing to get paid for it all too, sir, as I recall. Fortunately, the Green Man's eye-catching eyeful of a sister took care of the bar bill."

"But not the JB?"

"Not getting you, sir."

"Bar bill, but not the barkeep – APM All-Eyes is Uncle Moon-Face's Love Goddess."

"Ah well, as to that, circumspection is an occupational requirement around here so I couldn't possibly say."

"I suppose circumspection is preferable to circumcision. Or couldn't you say yay or nay to that either?"

"It is of course as you say, sir. I could perhaps answer you a mite more all-inclusively, though," JB quickly added, warily. "Since I hear he sometimes comes back female, I haven't seen anyone who might have been him or her. You'd best speak to management about that directly. He-or-she-Jordy is, um, reckoned something of a suppurating pustule around here. Talking about him fills spittoons, if you get my meaning, sir."

"Oh, really? Here's one for you then. I trust Twisted Tommy or, more likely, to judge by their ages, this Bosco fellow, is Dire's papa. Either/or the boy's way too young to be drinking."

"Too true, sir," Barleycorn allowed, knowing Lazaremists didn't believe in laws or their enforcement. Moral, as opposed to immoral or amoral anarchists, they relied on the guiding principle of the Golden Rule – namely tolerance, if not necessarily respect for their fellow man, woman, wight nor devil – to moderate individual as well as collective behaviour.

According to their tribal dogma, unqualified awareness of what's right and what's wrong attaches to every man and every woman, of any sentient species, at the moment of birth. Furthermore, anyone who seeks to impose unnatural standards amounts to the real criminal. Self-preservation starts and stops with everyone looking out for one another. Let it be and chances are it'll be benign.

That attitude, in their realms anyhow, seemed to work. Then again, if you displeased a devil-god, he or she could turn your life into a hell on earth next-to-instantly. To this day the torments the Lazaremists – and, admittedly, not just them – foisted upon the Utopian inhabitants of the Weirdom of Cabalarkon, where they still dare not go, during the reign of the fabled Death's Head Hellion all those centuries ago continued to be cited as pudding proof of that.

Sure, from an immortal's perspective, it'd be a non-lethal, living hell. But those close to you – provided they were experiencing the same, devil-wrought misery due to your nearness – might decide to avail you of the opportunity to experience hell post-mortem. And that most pristine expression of peer pressure seemed to work even better.

"Shall I cancel their order, sir?"

"A bit late for that, I'm afraid. They just took two buckets of beer each off that ice table your wench wheels around."

"That they did, sir. I wouldn't call her a wench, though; not if you don't want your voice to radically change pitch."

The waitress doing the wheeling suddenly shrieked in amazement more so than alarm. The three outsiders had just vanished between-space.

"Oh dear," gasped the barkeep. "I hope they paid first."

They had. Spotting Sparky as if for the first time, the woman nodded deferentially at the Green Man and the Mushroom Man, though to her the latter probably looked more satiric than fungous. Strolling borderline-nonchalantly over to the bar, she showed them the coins they'd handed her. If anything it looked as if they'd overpaid.

"Maybe there is a pot of gold at the end of the rainbow after all," she said meaningfully.

"One guarded by a leprechaun, I'm to appreciate," Sparky answered friendlily. Minus the startle-factor, he had no difficulty identifying her voice. It belonged to that of a millennia-long acquaintance and occasional lover, when he was the one shifting shapes.

Unbidden, yet responsively, he let shine his devic eye. Taking care not to burn her hands, he gave them the eyefire-once-over. This time she only yelped reflexively. The coins were under a glamour. In actuality they were a variety of sea urchin informally known as sand dollars, after the commonest coinage struck in the Byronics-dominated subcontinent of Aka Godbad, what were even more commonly known as Godbucks.

"I knew the weight was wrong," the waitress said. Nullifying her own splendour, she stood before them revealed as the famous fauna, Pusan Wanderlust.

"So, are you coming with us or what, Sparky?"

========

Next to the legendary 30-Year Man, Pusan was the most renowned and, in reality, only other, still extant deviant known to recur with any regularity. So long as one didn't count certain faerie allsorts as deviants, that is to say. Like Jordy, she came back in her own offspring, or their offspring, just as they were expiring or just after they'd expired. Also like 30-Beers, she always came back with a devic power focus. Hers wasn't a quill, though; it was a shepherd's pedum, crook or crosier.

Very much unlike him, however, she invariably came back as a woman as well as a fauna, a female faun. Since she couldn't shift shapes – besides visually, like most witches and almost any moderately gifted illusionist could – it was in that form, he as a male faun or satyr, that Sparky and her came together as lovers physically.

As the saying went, particularly with respect to her, Pusan was more bare than barely dressed. All she had on was a thin, delicately woven slip of lamb's wool that, while it did cover everything modesty generally recommended covering, including her protrusive breasts, goat's tail and cloven hind legs, from the looks of it the garment didn't cover anything very warmly.

For a woman – and she was every bit a woman – she was awfully hairy. However, other than on her head, from whence it flowed long and fiery freely, it was more akin to pinkish silk or ginger gossamer than even faintly furry. Her slender goatee was only perceptible up close and her horns were stunted, even dainty.

There was nothing of the barnyard about her scent. There was a great deal of the bordello about it, though. She positively oozed pheromones. Only Sinistral Lust's lesser-born lackeys, whom he'd also shared sacks and sometimes, yes, stacks of hay in barnyards, smelled like her. Enticing, thy name be Pusan.

In terms iconographic her pedum of a power focus suggested guardianship, à la the fairy godmother of not just rustic superstitions the world over. Evidently she was a big fan of iconography since she often took protective or preservative tasks upon herself as a form of perceived obligation. At times she did it so zealously she contributed to her own endgame for that recurrence.

Fauns were no more daemonic or fairy types than garudas, pterippi, related centaurs or elves. None of them could shift shapes naturally but, like the Legendarian, who could draw himself into different sexes, sizes, shapes and even species, most had learned an assortment of sometimes wildly diverse techniques that made it seem as if they were capable of metamorphism. They probably were products of Old Eden's cruel, millennium and a half pre-Flood-discredited, scientific experiments into the bits and bricks of life, though.

When they weren't calling her '*Goat*' – because she was decidedly capric or goatish – most of those who knew her called her '*Trailblazer*'. They did so because one of her more useful, non-knackering talents was trailing, tracking or just plain following folks through the Weird, the dark grey, universal substance of Samsara.

That made her a self-psychopomp, the same as many another exotic species (skyborn or Cathonic devils being only one of them). While that no more made her an earthborn or chthonic creature than it did a devic suicide – one who nevertheless retained their subtle matter, daemonic bodies until they were destroyed – her crook originally must have belonged to a devic deity.

Power foci were notoriously transmutable. As a result, an approaching endless debate had been ongoing for almost as long as she'd been around as to which devil the Anvil Artificer, Tvasitar Smithmonger, forged it for initially.

One candidate was the eponymous Roman goddess Fauna, the mythic wife of Faunus or Pan. Except, regardless of whether there was or there wasn't a devil-goddess worshipped under that name, it couldn't have been her because Pusan wasn't the marrying type. Besides, she started recurring a millennium or more before the city of Rome was even founded.

Whoever it was, most agreed Pusan's birthfather – the 1000-plus-years exterminated, but once self-succeeding deviant born Chrysaor Attis – disposed of her during the Outer Earth's man-hating mad goddesses' Middle Sea matriarchate of between roughly 2000 and 2500 YD. That might make her Byron's Capricorn. Except again, the millennia-vanished, watery Zodiacal was a goatfish rather than a terrestrial goat.

Byron's Capricorn did vanish during that selfsame era, though. Plus, devils were as changeable as their talismans. So, yes, it could have been her. Then again Byron's Capricorn was hardly the only matriarchally inclined, female supremacist the Attis disposed of way back when. He wasn't the only one seemingly on disposition duty during the era of the Goddess Culture either. The difference was most of the rest of those disposed of were male.

They weren't called *'man-hating mad goddesses'* because of docility or submissiveness, on their part, to patriarchal authority figures. They took to their task of fertilizing the ground, then keeping it irrigated, with enthusiasm – as well as, usually, with patriarchal authority figures they or their surrogates had married the year before they bled or had them bled dry.

For her part, Pusan ascribed her deviancy to an inheritance from her myrionymous, deviant dad, whose successions, particularly beyond the Dome, were often more celebrated than he was under his own name. That Attis was always humanoid, whereas she was always capric, she couldn't rationalize that away. As for why whomever's crosier transferred to her lifetime after lifetime, she put that down to its composition. Brainrock-Gypsium must just like her.

She'd been the Danq's manager for many generations – regenerations, put better. As JB warned him, without him picking up on its retrospectively unveiled significance, in her typically irrepressible manner she counted knackering those who offended her amongst her bric-a-brac multitude of knickknacks. Still and all, in fay-fairy-fairness to her Pusan did much prefer bed-balling to ball-busting.

So did he. The only balls he wanted to bust were those belonging to his immediate brother. The Unity of Disunity, Chaos as castrati, had a nice ring to it.

========

"Coming where?" he demanded of her.

"Gallivanting-get with it, Sparky. Where do you think? You can find sand dollars on any of the Head's four coasts, but these could only come from one area. Name me somewhere else you can conjure something coated in fantasy gold and forked over by non-fay-folks from the Outer Earth who promptly disappear? Into a fairy knoll of course!"

"I am with it. I meant specifically, not generally. Twilight's coastline must be thousands of miles long if you count the inter-nasal canals. And how can you be so sure they're pixilated? You're no devil. You can't read minds. What are you going to do, ask Evenstar not only for an okay to invade her realm, but where you should invade it?"

"We've already sussed out all that Jack and Jill shit. There's no need for either. Fucking faeries don't worship anyone, so that makes them fair game, no pun intended. Besides, those three didn't come from Twilight. They came from just beyond its borders. That takes them safely beyond Evenstar's at best token influence on the feeorin she lets run amok over there in Sedon's Outer Nose.

"That said, even if it didn't, the reality of where they did come from has the potential of being doubly dementia dodgy."

"A knoll, I got straightaway. The rest I'm not."

"You're definitely not getting anything from her in that condition," JB remarked, referring to the fact the Unity appeared humanoid.

He was smiling. The glares both Sparky and Pusan shot Barleycorn rendered him asking her for permission to take a bathroom break suddenly redundant. Fortunately, like many of the Danq's employees he kept a cave-cubicle, complete with wardrobe and dresser drawers, within the Cavern Tavern's innards.

"I'll look after the bar," she promised him, sniffing more than just the air.

"Thanks," said JB, as he scuttled off to attend to matters hygienic as well as sartorial.

"Mind you," Pusan carried on once he'd gone, "We're not sure where they came from actually qualifies as a devic protectorate. Going back to Thrygragon it wouldn't, that's pretty clear. The terms of your sister's Panharmonium Accord were reached by consensus and none of you anticipated non-Mithradites claiming territorial inviolability. However, from a neutral point of view, why shouldn't every Master Deva have the same rights as Mithradites?

"Think about it: It's the worshippers, not the worshipped, who make or break a protectorate anyways – at least it should be. Yet, even if you can agree on that, which Great Byron probably never would for his tribe, but which your father seemingly already has for your tribe, it might not be relevant. And if that sounds like I'm beating around the bush, well, I guess I am."

"Nothing new about that," Sparky cracked earthly.

"Be that as it may," she said, preferring to stick to elucidation mode rather than engage in a quip-wittedness contest, "It seems to me we're dealing with an entirely singular phenomenon; one that, hopefully, will never repeat itself. It's the equivalent of a piddled riddle wrapped in an enigmatic enema – a fairy knoll full of devil-eating wights situated in a portable protectorate primarily bolstered by Outer Earthlings brought through the Dome by ensnarers of seekers after secrets."

"You want us to blast their blessed but bedevilled butts back home, don't you?" he capsulated, cutting to the chase.

Fay-saying was contagious but even he couldn't deny that much more lethal contagions were permeating the Head like ringworm, and had been for a few centuries. Notwithstanding his own lack of concern, everybody seemed obsessed with various doomsday scenarios purporting to explain these admittedly disturbing developments. He was more interested in ordering a Cathy than conspiracy theories. Whatever will be will be, that's the natural order of things. Put better, that's the devic order of things, him being its peerless personification.

"If possible, yes," Pusan confirmed, thus reinforcing how seriously she took to her self-appointed responsibility as an all-around Good Shepherd. "Somebody has to plug their pipeline to Sed's Shed. I can only hope it's with them on the other side of it first. Sooth said, they better hope a dot-ditto because I don't know if Sangs can function beyond the Dome."

(Sangazurs were symbionts. They animated the Dead while, at the same time, allowing deceased individuals to retain their unique personas. That made them about the most useful form of azura to be found anywhere. It also made them the most prized. Their Valhalla-homeland having gone radioactive courtesy of the Idiot Twins – Tammuz and Osiraq as Illuminaries had them – going atomic in 4825, these days they were mostly found in the Bloodlands, Sedon's Inner Nose; hence its other name: New Valhalla.)

"Unfortunately, if it proves impossible to drive them out first then, needs be, we leave them far worse off than just tediously dead. We leave them both harmlessly immobile and thoroughly disinfected. In other words, we'll have to leave them burnt unto ash, the same as if they were cacodemons and not gaga-cliques of kaka-cretins."

"Which they're not – demons, not cretins. At least they aren't according to JB."

"It's not just according to JB. The Green Man isn't the only Byronic hereabouts or just gone walkabout, them inside them. APM All-Eyes has been coming around fairly regularly for a couple of years now, pretty much ever since you creamed Jordy. She was among the last devils to see him alive, save you."

"So I just gleaned, not creamed, from JB."

"From the way she acts – kind of haunted is my sense – both the boss and I are among the many who think she saw something weird before Jordy wandered off to reacquaint himself with Lady Luck, in her latest shell, but no one can get anything out of her. Like you, she seems to have forgotten whatever it was, always assuming there was anything weird."

"Believe me, there was. I don't usually go around blasting Jordies. In fact I never go around blasting Jordies. Ask me the Mithradites got away with one, just don't ask me how."

"Because you don't know, and what you don't know you can't answer. Myself, I do know that Byronics are like any other Master Deva. Sedon or no Sedon upstairs in the Sedon Sphere, they dare not kill. Neither do deviants like Jordy and me, but that's from personal choice. Yet killing could be on the horizon for the Lazareme-load of you. It's a price you might have to pay if you want to maintain your tribe's age and enough worshippers to keep it that way."

She knew more than she was saying. Sparky had no doubt of that. He also had no doubt she wasn't even close to being done quite yet. She immediately verified this sense of her. "Of course you might be able to hire an army or two to do it for you," she provided, predictably non-stop-yapping. (That, her constant conversing, was why he never stayed a faun for long.)

"Rearmed Mithrant legionnaires from nearby Apple Isle would probably do it. So might fighting forces from the even closer-by Bloods. Those loyal to Ruin, APM and their brothers and sisters in Great Byron from faraway Godbad, your own Rajputs, from almost as faraway Ophir-Moorset, or any army from any of the Cheeks' any other protectorates: I suppose they're all options. Therein lies the challenge your father faces, and therein lies your opportunity to help us repair the damage their incursion's caused."

"Do stop trying to try my patience, Goat. You come back but Rumour never did, not after the feeorin ate him anyhow. We kill; we cathonitize. Ask yourself this: How can we help repair anything dad can't anyways? Great Gods have to be worthy of exaltation. Lazareme isn't called Lord Lazy, the Lackland Libertine, because it's alliterative. He doesn't do anything because he can usually get us to do damn near everything he wants done for him. The *'damn near'* exclusion to that rule is doing everything except committing suicide."

"Well, you better come up with something, Sparky. Because, in keeping with precepts set out in your precious-to-me sister's Accord – as well as in the interests of maintaining the spirit of his freewheeling, freedom-first age – Thrygragos Lazareme finds himself on the horns of the proverbial dilemma."

"Better than the horns of a goat," he jeered. "Present company not always excepted unfortunately." As topical as it perhaps unintentionally was, she strove to ignore his gibe; succeeded as well.

"I've big ears," she nattered on. "I've caught the gist of what they're on about. Your father's mindful of what happened during the Era of Empires, which began not long after Thrygragon. He doesn't want to countenance myriad, albeit mostly Mithradite, militaries being unleashed in the Cheek Lands again.

"Neither does he want to authorize any of his devils invading a protectorate without the Dand's permission. That's due to the fact they could then be catasterized purely at his or her whim. It's a dick-dildo for putting them at risk of killing outsiders. They do, you do, you kill any lesser being, in my view that's quite correctly cause for instant cathonitization."

"Regardless of whether Grandfather's around or not?"

"Regardless of anything! As far I'm concerned killer devils should self-atomize."

"Yet we don't."

"How can you be so cocksure confident of that? You ever heard of, or come across, a killer devil that didn't end up ill-starred?"

"As a matter of fact I have, dozens of them. And so should you. Can't you recall the Infernal Equinox of whatever year it was?"

"4824/25 – and you should know bloody well I can't. I was still dancing the legless limbo when all that crap came down, as well as went up."

(At the beginning of Belialmam, on the Imbolc Day before the Empire of Lathakra ceased expanding on Samhain 4825 YD, hence the Ghostlands, Yajur actually killed her while they were making love in his Thunder and Lightning Dome. That, unbeknownst to her, she was booby-trapped, as in carrying a devil-eating or at least devil-hardening demon or two, explained his actions. It also explained his crack about her horns. Still, electrocution hurt as much or more as any other method of getting killed.)

"Besides, the Inferno you devils started in Grand Elysium doesn't prove anything. You were defending yourselves against the Deadhead Hellion and her cacodemons …"

"Death's Head."

"That too. And because you were acting self-defensively you set off a whatever Harmony called it …"

"Chain reaction."

"She would, wouldn't she. Anyhow, you lot were absolved of culpability back then for an appreciable reason. What makes you so hell-bent whatever I said won't happen automatically once you deliberately set out to slaughter a bunch of defenceless Outer Earthlings?"

She was clearly upsetting herself but, by his silence just as clearly, Sparky couldn't decide if it was needlessly or not. For a few moments he mulled over the intent of her words noncommittally. Evidently Everyman and Bodiless Byron, as represented by his bowman and, earlier on, by his all-eyed Venus, were trying to decide what to do with the outsiders. More personally pertinently, they were trying to decide if, in Grandfather's absence, they could get away with killing outsiders.

However, from what she'd just said, might there be another issue? Not all that long ago, in devic terms, Harmony spent years traversing the Dome with or in pursuit of her metamorphic as well, to her, irresistible faerie lover, Tomcat Tattletail. She could have brought back a veritable cesspit of foreign pestilences herself. That would make her as guilty of second-hand mass murder as the faeries or whosoever's been acting as ensnarers of seekers.

Obviously Grandfather Sedon didn't think that way. But, her being so harmoniously inclined, she might. Once she grasped the fullness of her culpability with respect to increasing, if not originating, the Head's potentially catastrophic contamination by germs she carried beneath the Dome, it might drive her to self-cathonitize.

As Harmony smarmily remarked, more than a few times over the centuries since the Infernal Equinox, she did not participate in lighting up Grand Elysium because she realized instinctively that thousands of mortals would die. Just because the Death's Head Hellion and her inflammatory demons could care less about human and humanoid casualties, that didn't make what the devils did right. They should have just buggered off, the same as she did, rather than adding to the carnage.

So, if unencumbered truth be told, was that why Father was here, tossing back sobering goblets of Cathy rather than beer, wine or spirits, as was his wont? Was he making deals to cover his precious daughter's beautiful behind? He'd had a soft spot for her almost as often as he'd had a hard-on for her. Sparky could only hope the Byronics weren't getting gulled.

"Aren't you forgetting the Mastery's Marutians?" he finally ventured.

"Ah, as to that, that's what makes it a conundrum sautéed in the mystery of misery then skewered with a quandary and baked in a poser."

"Fuck the fay-saying, Goat! Whose portable protectorate is it?"

"Your daddy's son, whose else?"

"So what's the problem? Devils can't disobey their fathers."

"Allow me to rephrase that. It's his deviant half-son's protectorate. Unlike you lot, we lot suffer no genetic compulsion to obey any bloody body. Our devic half-father might as well be our non-devic birthfather for all the difference that'd make. Just as importantly, it applies even when one's a Great God and the other's a Master of Marutia."

"Huh?"

"Hadn't you better make that *'duh'*?"

========

Sangazurs had many weaknesses. Like any azura – or any Master Deva, for that matter – they could be captured and held in a Trinondev's prison pod or a devil's ringot. Equally so, albeit unlike devils, they could be captured and held in soul sinks, a dryad or Acorn Ant's nut-ball, a wizard's eye-catcher or a Valkyrie's crystal skull.

These last, Valkyries, were always women. By Sisterhood affiliation they were also always Hecate-Hellions. You didn't have to be a Hellion in order to hold or even get hold of a crystal skull. Anyone could do that. Just as much so, what can be captured and held can also be released. You just had to smash it against whoever's deadhead.

The key was you had to know to do that. And to learn much about anything it generally helped to have someone decent to teach you.

****

7: Making a Mess of Melina's Mastery

End-Antheal 5476 – The Weirdom of Kanin City

Zalman Somata shared with the devils that had possessed his wife and father – as well as the one who was bagging his precious daughter on a near-daily basis – their distaste for Mithras Spawn. Nonetheless, like Thrygragos Lazareme and his firstborn, he was prepared to accept tradition and allow them to take over the Weirdom of Kanin City on New Year's Day 5500. What he wasn't prepared to do was serve under them.

So he deserted it.

========

Unless the monotheistic Church of Rome preserved it, well masked, within its recondite, all-male hierarchy, Cave Mithraism was a virtually extinct belief system beyond Cathonia. It still thrived beneath it, particularly on Apple Isle, Sedon's Human Eye-Isle. And so it should. None other than the Great God of Truth, Light, Justice and so much more, of civilization itself according to many, the island's egocentrically self-serving, original devic Dand or Overlord, none other than Thrygragos Varuna Mithras himself, promulgated it there not long after the Dome's Year Zero.

The sixth and next-to-last step up the ladder to its *'seventh heaven'* was the Heliodromus or sun-runner (which was what the word meant in the Roman version of Mithraism's ritualistic Latin). Mithradites did not have exclusive use of its parlance. In truth, although Mithraism was an all-male brotherhood – the same as allegedly pan-humanistic Xuthrodism and the Church's top-down chain of command remained to this day on the Outer Earth – each of the three devic tribes had, at the minimum, both a male and a female Heliodromus of their own.

Just as often called angels or jinn, these sun-runners ran messages between the Hidden Headworld's devil-gods. Most commonly they acted as envoys for second generational Great Gods, who rarely deigned to speak with any of their third generational triplets face-to-face, especially not to those born below, say, their first ten to twelve broods of three.

Thrygragos Lazareme only had his female Heliodromus left. His male dick-dildo – as devils indelicately differentiated when referring strictly to men and, well, feeling devilish – was one of the casualties his enormous family of still more than a hundred-strong Master Devas incurred during the expansion of the Empire of

Lathakra in the 48th Century of the Dome. Antique Illuminaries had her as Irisiel Mercherm; devils tended to call her Speedy.

As the Great God Everyman and Byron's Bowman drained their drinks in the Dinq, Doinq, Danq Cavern Tavern; as JB, John Barleycorn, replaced his smeared, sartorial non-splendours in one of its backend honeycomb of caves; as Sparky and Pusan Wanderlust concluded their conversation by its main bar; and, as it turned out, APM All-Eyes and two of her broods-younger sibs were up north about to be devil-devoured, mouse-like, by an oversexed crazy cat who generally stuck to canaries; she raced into Kanin City on her talarial winged sandals.

Quickly locating her querulous quarries – Irisiel did everything quickly, hence why devils called her Speedy – she pounded to a stop before them the merest of moments after the megalithic metropolis's popular Master, Zalman Somata, pronounced howsoever-temporary abandonment of the Weirdom on himself and those who would follow him. At their unspoken signal, she was forced to tramp turf while he drearily finished reciting his statement of resignation.

She thus heard him appoint his wife, Kanin's High Illuminary, to take his place until such time as he returned. Being for the most part unfamiliar with the behaviour of non-devils, it was difficult for her to gauge what provoked the loudest eruption of approbation from the multitude assembled in the Masters Palace's huge courtyard: he assigning Mistress Melina to take his place or his promise to come back to Kanin City and replace her someday. She reckoned the latter.

Zal's droning done, she mentally imparted an unusually long and detailed message from their father to the two firstborns and the Librarian. Although sending a Heliodromus in his stead amounted to a Thrygragos requesting rather than commanding compliance, they were heading in that direction anyhow. So, after exchanging no doubt meaningful but wordless glances, Drek and Harmony agreed to accompany her to the far west coast of Marutia, where Father Lazareme would by then be waiting for them.

Notwithstanding the additional information that Sraddha had become so much more than Squiggly's personal god – that he had become an actual divinity, one with his very own port of a protectorate, and that it encompassed a fairy knoll packed with a host of seekers after secrets from the Outer Earth carrying deadly diseases – Unholy Abaddon, the Unity of Chaos, declined to do a ditto. Once again he cited his fear for dear-heart Janna's good health and better beauty should he not be around to guarantee their continuance.

That was hardly all of it. Like Harmony he'd had a thought, an assortment of them in his disordered braincase.

========

Some began percolating the moment Harmony mentioned the Somatas were wearing agatine eyes, gemstones ensorcelled by tiptop Antheans like Melina and her fellow superiors. There was nothing special about that of course. Seemingly the moment after his immediate sister dispossessed her, less than a month ago, Janna herself took to wearing two or three of the dubious blings. He didn't care one way or the other. It wasn't like he was ever going to possess her, not on the inside anyhow.

As per usual Zalman had his inlaid in a ring. Melina had hers as one of many ruby-like jewels strung round her neck. Neither his nor hers glowed but Abe knew that unlike more conventional Tvasitar-trinkets – devic power foci, predominantly – non-glowing was part-and-parcel of their functionality. You didn't know they'd activated that way, let alone that they did anything once they were activated.

What agatine eyes did do was ensure those wearing them couldn't be possessed by devils any more than they could be read or compelled by them. That didn't make the gems the Ants' exclusory equivalent of ringots. For ringots to confine their target you first had to beat the devil into submission then confiscate his or her talisman. By contrast, agatine eyes were purely prophylactic. They only worked if a devil was trying to exert his or her unwanted influence on you and then they only negated his or her efforts to do so.

Over the course of the Dome's thousands of years, thousands of Ant Nightingales proved their efficacy in both regards over and over again. Nonetheless, devils being devils, any one of them could have coerced either of the Somatas to toss away his or hers anytime they desired. He being whom he was, Chaos Incarnate, Abe might be tempted to eyefire-burn them off. Although he could, by conviction he probably wouldn't thereupon possess them. But he would read them, as if by convection (to nearly rhyme and nearly alliterate at the same time).

Eyefire-burning them off would hurt. Janna wouldn't appreciate him discomforting her parents and he wouldn't appreciate her withholding her charms, assuming that's how she chose to get back at him. The girl had a mean streak. She was nothing if not vindictive. Besides, he was on his best behaviour.

Plus, Harmony was correct when she said they'd known of Zal's desire to leave here, long a Weirdom in name only, and where he intended to go as soon as he had a reasonable hope of reaching it in one piece: namely a Weirdom in every sense of its, to Abe and his fellow devils, anti-devic weirdness.

The Librarian speaking of the Outer Earth's Book of Byblos was something of a thought-trigger as well. *'For dust thou are, and unto dust thou shall return'* reminded him of how faeries shrunk folks. They sprinkled them with faeriedust, their all-purpose medium for enchantment. Additional thought-triggers were Drek's term for earthborn creepers (botched biota) and the fact that Squiggles could scribble in colour.

In a land beset by Time Quakes, ordinary transportation for ordinary folks was always an iffy endeavour. Given their unpredictable, seemingly random nature, such had been the case since they began in the aftershocks of Thrygragon, more than a thousand years earlier. Invariably frustratingly, depending on how they were made, or what they were made of, wheels et al could and oft-times would drop off and/or disintegrate mid-journey.

So how, other than with Godbucks and their northern, eastern or north-eastern, monetary equivalencies, did Squiggly manage to acquire the pressed flora or crushed minerals he'd require such that he could prepare tints to embellish his artwork? Colour's constituent elements often came from parts faraway and wildly separated. That made them hard to get, harder to preserve, as you tried to get them anywhere else, and extremely pricey.

While that last unquestionably had its attractions, there wasn't much of a demand for them either. That meant merchants still using the Hidden Headworld's far more ancient version of the Outer Earth's Silk Road, which had crisscrossed the

Marutian Cheeks since the Headlands filled in (including its canals, which for the most part were formerly oceanic troughs far too deep to fill in properly), seldom traded in the pernickety products.

Why would they? The near-certainty of being struck by a Time Quake made traversing the Cheek Lands a very long and very tedious plod at the best of times. They'd only risk it for big paydays or lucrative tradeoffs, such as authentic goods made by famous talents, and that almost never happened. Painters worked for patrons, not paint.

Irisiel provided some of the answer. Someone had Jordy's quill. So, for whoever had it, travelling between-space was an option. Of course Brainrock ink came in every shade of the rainbow anyhow. That meant that same somebody would never need to collect the components of colour anyways.

Derail that train of thought as if a tender on tracks in a coalmine, he advised himself. So he did. Whereupon he promptly had another one. That somebody had developed Jordy's love for the Danq's pilsners. But they were hardly an acquired taste. Abe preferred popping pills to lagers, ale or dark beers himself.

That somebody couldn't be the latest Legendarian, though. The Legendarian could be trusted to send IOUs rather than outright steal anything. And, no matter how seriously ill or otherwise close to death's door he may be, Squiggly couldn't be or become the latest Legendarian simply because he wasn't yet twenty. Said conclusions deliberated, yet still not vocalized, flattened a few more erratic brainwaves.

Upon further, albeit occasionally lips-moving-reflection, he determined the majority of his thoughts had practically nothing to do with fucking faeries or shrunken Adamites boning ripened fruit, Sraddha Somata's apparent apotheosis, Jordy's whereabouts or who had his quill. Neither was he overly concerned Janna's mama had become an Ant Nightingale a couple of months ago. She'd always been resourceful.

Yes, agatine eyes did make him wonder what else Zal and Mel or, as far as that went, what their other, much more delightful child might be attempting to conceal from them. But, no, most of his thoughts centred on the commonly accepted perception that Melina born Tethys was some sort of freakish mutation, a non-imbecilic yet nonetheless nearly pureblood Utopian.

He held no illusions about the Family Somata. Father, son and daughter were deviated hybrids, but they remained Hate-Sedon extraterrestrials at heart. While the hatred they held for devils was inbred and, as such, principally philosophical, mother might prove capable of pulling a Death's Head Hellion and getting away with it.

Worse than that, with their mighty Moloch of a grandfather no longer gracing the night's sky, Mistress Melina might be well along the road to success. Then again Master Morgan Abyss got that far herself, only to fall, at the end of her last day, both a radioactive and appropriately abysmal failure.

Unlike his father and some of his more selectively forgetful siblings, he never subscribed to the cant propagated by the Antediluvian Sisterhood of Flowery Anthea: namely, that it was named in honour of the long lost devic Anthea, Lazareme's highborn embodiment of the Spring Season. It was the other way around. Antique Illuminaries named their Anthea after the wife of Xuthros Hor, the Golden Age

Patriarch who caused the genocidal Genesea, thereby drowning, at the minimum, hundreds of thousands of normal men and women, of any and every species.

He wouldn't echo Harmony or the Librarian and rule preposterous the proposal Irisiel put to them, quoting their father, that her predecessors as Nightingales, Illuminaries and, now, as Masters of Weir had hatched *'a genuinely evil stratagem to rid the cosmos of devazurkind'*. As far as he was concerned, Mel might well be a willing participant in the, to them, *'ends justify the means corruption'* of a million or more of their reverential sustainers with cumulatively incurable illnesses. Of course, to be non-faerie fair to her, she might not be.

Paranoia couldn't be considered one of his characteristics. Neither was contemplating intentionally calamitous consequences, for what might be nothing more than a few coincidental inconveniences, one of his pastimes. He was Abe Chaos, though. He didn't need to sprout wings and flap them in order to generate a hurricane thousands of miles away in one of the Head's four oceans.

Sometimes all he had to do was sneeze.

========

Once, in a very long while, Ants and Illuminaries were one and the same. Then it became a question of degree. Which was more important – hating the Moloch and doing something about it, which might involve killing off his worshippers, or loving life and striving to enhance it, which shouldn't involve killing anyone, including Dark Sedon?

There were those who claimed that nothing mattered, that everything was predestined: fate, kismet or whatever. But where would the fun be if that were the case?

Might the answer to that, too, be in the stars?

========

Irisiel, Harmony and Drek took off between-space after witnessing Mel's inauguration as Kanin City's nominal Master of Weir. Abe swore not to go anywhere without Janna and wasn't about to renounce his vow now. He especially wasn't about to leave her alone after she informed him she didn't want to go anywhere potentially dangerous, not even in order to try and talk some seriously absent sense back into her beloved twin brother. She would, however, happily meet him in the rose garden later on.

He therefore dutifully, as much as dotingly, stood beside her as Zal and an unexpectedly numerous cortege of wannabe-Trinondevs set off on foot, horseback, donkeys and mule-drawn wagons for their weeks-long march west, to the Gulf of Corona, Sedon's Human Eye. There they intended to connect with Shreds' *'mission accomplished, dad'* crew of, ho-hum, co-conspirators and sail freshly constructed brigs a good perhaps thousand miles north.

What with dodging Time Quakes and tsunamis, they may or may not make it as far as the last remaining real Weirdom: that of the Undying Utopian, Sedon's thought-father. But, if they did and if they managed to make it back, they'd do so fancying themselves equipped as proper devil-slayers.

Ah well, Abe resigned himself as he watched them trek beyond the horizon, Grandfather Sedon only forbade guys like him killing prospective devotees, not prospective god-killers.

It was a shame in a way. He sort of liked his don't-wannabe in-laws.

========

Zal's announcement and departure immediately thereafter crammed merely a minor damper on the city's months pre-planned celebrations for commemorating his hundredth birthday. Starting with fireworks shortly huge after dark, it was simply too late to cancel the scheduled festivities. As a result, the mid-afternoon line-up to the Tethys Tomb wasn't what it usually was, but it was still lengthy. Manfully feigning good-natured tolerance, dumpy and 2-eyed anonymously docile-ditto, he entered it, for the first time ever, after a paltry half-hour wait.

He'd heard of how lavishly decorated its walls and ceiling were but, not surprisingly, the standalone statuary was just as spectacular. Quibble and Quidnunc had been fabulously talented muralists and rococo artists, albeit only after they became Quills. And Quill, singular, had been dazzling his patrons for coming on 1500 years. There must be close to a thousand years worth of the Legendarian Jordy's masterpieces in the ever-expanding edifice of the Masters Palace.

First as Squab then as Squib, once-Quibble and his students carried on the Legendarian's tradition of superb stonework while adding to the complex under Quid-Quill-Jordy's supervision. As fine as their sculpting skills were, though, he found the half dozen huge, painted and fancily framed landscapes hanging on the left and right sidewalls truly breathtaking. He recognized only one of the places depicted, but they were so splendidly rendered they had to be Jordy's work. It looked like you could walk into them and literally be wherever he'd done them initially.

What weren't anywhere near so striking were the mausoleum's two closed and peculiarly unadorned sepulchres. He reckoned that for someplace shrine-like, where not just rumour had it the Somatas intended to lay themselves to rest eventually, they shouldn't be so plain. They weren't made of lead or Stopstone-Solidium so he surreptitiously opened his 3rd eye and, borderline-dreading what he'd see, focused on their insides. He was right to dread what he saw of the dead. That is to say he was right to dread what he wouldn't see of them.

Squib's flesh had mostly decomposed in the intervening nearly two years; not so that of Quidnunc. Rather, if it had, Abe had no way of telling because there was nothing left of it to see. Quite conceivably his burial box had always been empty. But, short of grave robbers, how could that be? His brood brother admitted killing him what amounted to his second time bodily – the first time being when Quid was barely into his twenties and Harmony poked him in the chest with the (arguably) tainted tip of the Five Blades' medallion he'd just won.

Harm claimed she hadn't poked him hard enough to break the skin. Furthermore, even if she had, like Odour with respect to killing the Quid-Quill and cathonitizing Dame Chance 18 years later, she'd only done so inadvertently. She had no idea the tip was tainted, if it was, let alone that its nib had ejected, if it had. Indeed, reckoning it self-evident he'd died of a heart attack, apparently nobody checked it.

(That being the case, as Tethys himself would frequently remark when the subject did come up, no one asked Nobody what he, or she, discovered.)

Since devils were as incapable of lying as they were of disobeying their fathers, no one questioned Harmony's assertions either. Although the Legendarian insisted he always told the truth, insofar as he knew it, being a deviant Jordy was not so genetically constrained. He never confessed to it, though – and Abe, for one, never pressed him on the issue. But, if there was a guilty party everybody knew it had to be Squab-Quibble.

Although not unheard of, Quit-Quills were, historically speaking, as scarce as scared ghosts looking in a mirror and saying boo. Mostly that was because few Quills lasted until the termination of their 30-year life-extensions. Also on occasion, a Quill who was about to make it that far dropped dead the very second he or she reached it. That suggested Quill had an internal alarm clock that, howsoever irregularly, went off when their time was up.

So, yes, had a crime been committed then everyone knew Squab-Quibble, desirous of achieving the comparatively uncommon eminence of a Quit-Quill, had to be responsible for masterminding it. After all, dosing darts or needles were as old as the hills or jungles on both sides of the Dome, whereas rigging an ejectable nib had to be within bailiwick of a resourceful fellow like the Legendarian.

But, unless there was another, otherwise perfectly innocent explanation for all this, what if everyone except the real guilty party was wrong? What if … Sedon's Sharpest Teeth! Put a confirmatory checkmark in the square beside *'Blame Melina'*. First Harmony then Order, she was setting them up for a Luciferian-calibre fall. Killer devils got cathonitized.

Was he next? He had to be. Wait – who was she was setting him up to kill? Was she that suicidal? More to the point, was Grandfather Sedon that negligent?

Better make that a tentative checkmark.

========

Janna said she'd be waiting for him in the rose garden where they'd made love for the first time. (The first time for real, that is. Lady Lust turning herself into her lookalike on the night of Janna's 18th birthday didn't count.) She could do that. She could wait. Doing away with his maybe groundless suspicions re her mother's maliciousness came first on his to-do list.

Indeed, should looming revelations dictate it, he listed doing her third, after doing away with her murderous mom.

========

A sucker if ever there was one, at least when it came to her only daughter, Mel was nevertheless nobody's fool. Two incarnations of Jordan *'Quill'* Tethys were, however, her foil.

As dawn approached the morning after that tragic midsummer's night of 5474, her twins' 18th birthdays, she supervised the removal of the Quidnunc-Jordy's corpse from the palace. Seemingly lacking inspiration, let alone a proper morgue, she had it taken to the same outsized and intricately ornamented mausoleum-cum-monument – ultimately to themselves and their intended dynasty – wherein they'd laid the Squib-Squab-Quibble-Jordy's body less than 24-hours earlier.

There she had her retainers stretch him out on the bier upon which she herself might one day lay. Ostensibly so she could bid a teary farewell to the latest Legendarian in private, she insisted they all go and fetch a howsoever-temporary wooden coffin for his remains. Once they left her alone, she materialized a crystal skull out of the Weird and smashed it against the dead deviant's head. As she anticipated, he instantly sat up and began gulping great gushes of welcome air into his lungs.

What she didn't anticipate was that, before he could say boo, he broke into a big, broad grin. As ghastly as it was, it wasn't as cadaver-like as it was familiar – and not in the way the black, or Utopian, skinned Quidnunc Jordy was (make that should have been) familiar either. The prancing panpipe player at last night's pre-birthday bash, maybe? What was his name – Rhadamanthys? Could be; something weird like that anyway.

Harm seemed to know him, she recalled. Then he spotted her and his visage went from glee to glare. "You, you filthy throwback, you murdered me! Why?"

She hadn't really expected him to say boo but his attitude, once he realized where he was, and what she'd done to him, nonetheless took her aback. "Smarten up, Jordy," she retorted, after the briefest of pauses. "I didn't kill you. Your son Squiggly did, in a fit of justifiable jealousy if you ask me. I revivified you. Where's your gratitude?"

"Jordy, my beery butt, Illuminary," he very nearly spat at her. "Do you take me for a total toadstool? Harmony jabbed me but you poisoned the prick! That's why Sedon didn't cathonitize her. He knew you set her up."

Although she was still most of two years shy of her fiftieth birthday, the earliest age she could become eligible to be addressed as a Sister Superior of the Superior Sisterhood – as well as the earliest age she could become one in actuality – Mel had already absorbed the broadest scope of Ant Nightingale lore. She realized what must have occurred straightaway.

"Have it your own way, Quid. I didn't want to kill you but we couldn't afford to lose our Jordy then and we still can't. Truth told, we need you more than ever now. Something's happened to the miserable Moloch. His star's gone from the night's sky. That means Cabalarkon's free of his abhorrent lordship at long last."

Grand Elysium – Dark Sedon's cult centre since pre-Genesea times – became radioactive, and thus part of the consequently still uninhabitable Ghostlands, in 4825. Counter-intuitively, the Weirdom of Cabalarkon being populated almost exclusively by mainly pureblood Utopians, the mighty Eye-Mouth, when in the heavens, adopted what geographically replicated his Devic Eye-Land in order to take its place when he walked the Inner Earth.

"Tell you what, materialize your quill, draw Zal, me and our children up there, and we'll let you go off to do whatever you want after that."

"Including slicing and dicing you into so much pig slop?"

"Look, Harmony didn't really hurt you. She just set you adrift for a while. Now I've brought you back, so you owe me."

"Liar!"

He – Quidnunc's Sangazur-reanimated corpse – leapt off his bier intent upon grappling her to the ground. Then he was going to strangle the life out of her as comprehensively as his had been taken twice now. The futility of his exertions belatedly registered in the form of him grabbing thin air instead of her. Even more emphatically it registered in his consequential – not to mention bruising, badly bloodying and undignified – face-first collision with the stone floor.

Only when he attempted to haul himself into a kneeling position – and failed – did it dawn on him that he was the better part of two beer-guzzling decades away from his teenage peak of swordsmanship-robustness. By contrast, as he and almost everyone who knew her postulated, she was something of a pre-Earth, maybe even First Weirworld, U-blood made flesh.

Fifty for even earthborn purebloods was more like twenty-five for normal human beings. It didn't matter that they'd spent the last 18 years as deviants. Sooth said, the degree of abuse he'd put his howsoever-deviated body through might have made matters worse. And, oh right, she exercised on a daily basis. He did too, but just because he was adept at lifting buckets of beer with either hand, that didn't mean he was fit for much except being tied down and out.

She evaded him adroitly. Then she vanished, or seemed to vanish. Top drawer Antheans – not just fully fledged and pledged Ant Nightingales, let alone ones two years shy of becoming an official superior – were skilled illusionists. But he had bevies of bents of his own. He knew what she looked like. He could draw her back.

First he had get onto his feet. No go! His knees? How about over onto his bum? He could roll, couldn't he? Yes! And sit? Yes, again. Triumph trumped trauma. Pain passed. Breaks healed. He wiggled his fingers in front of his face bizarrely, whereupon he swore foully, if sort of funnily. "Fucking five; fucking ten; fucking witchcraft!"

Desperately, as if for the first time, he glowered at his surroundings. "Fucking Jordy! Let's hope you're still in me enough."

He did it this time, rolled the other way, knelt, then staggered to his feet with the help of a hand up, one outstretched as if out of nowhere. Or maybe it was that statue over there's hand elongated and made miraculously mobile. They were all so lifelike, weren't they? Jordy often described pure or near pureblood Utopian women as ambulatory alabaster, didn't he?

Clearly confused, no doubt deadhead-demented after enduring the ordeal of resurrection, he pushed her away just as she rematerialized, visually as well as physically, out of her *'Shelter'* between-space. She'd reflexively conjured it off an Anthean Agate she dropped at her feet the instant he came at her. That was something else not just top drawer Ants learned to do during their second 7-years of training. Education had its benefits.

Like the madman he'd presumably become thanks to her, still dead Quid raced toward a sidewall and leapt. He thereby hurled himself up at one of the paintings, whereupon he promptly disappeared into it. She tried to duplicate his phantasmal feat. Despite her heritage, there wasn't enough of a Jordy left in her. Either that or there was a devil as well as a Sang in him.

A 2-eyed one who pranced about smiling near ear-to-ear as he played a pan-pipe, perhaps?

========

It was less an impression than a notion.

Abe Chaos put it down to a suddenly, albeit only momentarily unsuppressed rush of fancifulness. He forgot it the instant he released her from his eye-lock. That'd be the one he'd been holding her in since bursting into her dayroom, tearing off her necklace and eyefire-melting it unto slag just as she became conscious he was there.

Even though he was on his best behaviour, he was no more in the mood to mess around with her than he was to prance, play or even smile.

========

"Which one?"

"The one of Theopolis Hill, if you have to know."

He did and, in a way, her answer made sense. Howsoever ironically, with its hundreds of often Tholos-shaped, mostly Yazata-built, temples or sanctuaries, Theopolis Hill was the only place he'd recognized when he'd been in the Tethys Tomb admiring Jordy's landscapes under an hour earlier. Dead again, but Sangazur-re-animated, Quidnunc must have felt it would provide a refuge, so long as he could get through to it.

Since he did, he clearly could. And he was right. It would have, if Mistress Melina were a devil, which she wasn't, just as perceptibly.

Chaos had always known she was anti-devic. Nonetheless, after gleaning her unto the edge of her soul, he was convinced she wasn't mass murderously so. Not in the sense that she was in any way culpable when it came to ensnaring seekers of secrets from beyond the Dome, and bringing them inside, she wasn't. That had probably been going on for hundreds of years before she was even born.

She, not the Legendarian, was the real driver behind Quidnunc's appointment with a hearse, as in Quid's death by pre-planned heart attack. That he'd confirmed. Furthermore, since her Masterly husband had initially agreed to pin the medal on the sacrificial donkey of a champion dummy, one who was too good at sword-fighting for his own good, Harmony had only been an accidental perpetrator. Knowing the needle was rigged to go off anyway, how could Zalman have refused the opportunity Harm presented to kill off the proverbial two birdbrains with one perforation?

So, did Zal or a Hellion or an Ant Superior, a Master of the usual somewhere else or, just perhaps, a malignant spirit like Strife or – and here was a strange thought – a Trigregos Sister put Mel up to snuffing out Quid's life the first time, in order to keep a Quill in Kanin City? She might hold the answer to that deep within her subconscious but, when it came right down to it, there was only one way to be absolutely sure of it.

Notwithstanding how unruly – as in rigorously ungovernable – and prone to recklessness he generally was, he felt unready to take it to that extreme quite yet. He had his principles. He didn't, he'd be as conniving, as manipulative, as Harmony, his father, his other siblings and most every other devil were when it came to possessing people.

No one was worse than Ordure in that regard. No one was worse than him, period. He used to take over Quidnunc constantly, when the lad was a teenager, solely for the sake of sport. And look where it got Quid twenty years ago, almost got Harm back then, did get Quid-Quill and Fata Fortuna two years ago, and should have got him as well, when he foolishly finished what Squiggly started in Janna's bedroom the night of her birthday/bequeathal/betrothal bash.

Still, as awful they were, they were devil-gods. Other than Odour, just for being Odour, they could be forgiven. So could any and every one else, even Hecate-Hellions. It was just that, when it came to Hellions, as a general rule of pricking thumbs and something wicked this way comes, you came across one it'd be best you fed her to cacodemon-crocodiles.

They had to eat too.

========

"What does it matter?" Melina challenged him. "It's almost two years ago."

"And he tried but couldn't conjure Rumour's quill?"

"That's how it looked to me, sounded like it too, unless he's ordinarily poly-dactyl, which he isn't. I thought he could manifest it over any distance. Jordy can; at least I think he can. That's one of his stacks of knacks, isn't it? I wasn't thinking, though. Quidnunc wasn't Quid-Quill anymore was he. He was Quid-Sang. Strictly speaking he wasn't even alive."

"So how did he end up with it?"

"Couldn't say, could I? Or didn't you probe me that deeply?"

"I can do a lot more, or a lot worse, than probe you, Hellion."

Hecate (or Herta) was a pre-devic, reputedly Edenite deity. The Mother-Earth-worshipping, demon-welcoming – and oft-times demon-complicit – Hellion Sisterhood was so old it predated the Golden Age of Humanity. Morgan Abyss, the Death's Head Master of Cabalarkon's Weirdom hundreds of years ago, was a Hellion. And so, from the depths he had read of her, was Melina nee Tethys.

"Sure, you can kill me. You going to kill me, Uncle Abe?"

"You'd never worship any of us, would you?"

"What an appalling conceit! How dare you ask me that?"

"And you'd love it if I killed you because then you wouldn't have to tell me what else you know."

"Actually, I haven't anything approximating a death's wish. So, if you don't mind, how about I tell you whatever you want to know right now?"

"Fine, you do that. I can always kill you later."

"You kill me, Janna will be miffed."

"True enough. Speak freely and fear zilch multiplied by zip."

"That's more like it; more like you, and your father, and your immediate siblings, too. I can't say, but I sure can speculate."

"How many ears would you like me to have?"

After the manner he'd been toying with her – if threatening to kill someone could be called toying and not, say, out-and-out cruelty – she felt no urge to reward his arrogant attempt at wit with the slightest flicker of amusement. Devils could be all ears if they wanted to be. She'd met one who regularly appeared to be all eyes. What they weren't, ever, was humorous.

"Janna found his cap wedged between the cushions of the couch they'd been screwing on," she provided, "His quill was still stuck in it." She fixed him in her gaze unflinchingly. She trusted she'd also fixed him in it unnervingly, for him. Eye-locks were a devic specialty but she was pretty good at them too. Zal hated it when she did it to him.

"Rather, she found it in the couch Jordy and your bitch sister, Wintry Moira, so unforgivably occupying her, had been screwing on. Janna tried to keep it to herself but proper mothers – not half-mothers like Harmony, another of your bitch sisters – always know when their daughters are trying to keep something from them.

"Anyhow, she snuck his cap, his quill still in it, to Squiggly just before Zal banished him. He's had it for going on two years now and counting."

"Counting?"

Abe Chaos was her uncle, albeit 1500 years removed. The first Legendarian was the half-son of a pair of his slightly lower-born siblings. Antique Illuminaries of Weir interchangeably called Jordy's half-mother Metisophia and/or Titanic Metis, after an Outer Earth, Middle Sea, pre-Olympian goddess of female sovereignty. A second-born, her fellow devils addressed her, respectfully, as either Wisdom or Sophia of Lazareme.

They didn't do so because her triplet sisters were Mariamne Dawnstar, once of the Land of faeries-friendly Daybreak (nowadays Krepusyl Evenstar, the Grey Lady of the faeries-fraught Grey Land of Twilight), and the devic Flowery Anthea, whom Mel's predecessors of long, long ago had admired and thus named appropriately. They addressed her respectfully because her abilities could affect devils.

"They're sharing it, Sang-Quid and the squiggle-kid. At least that's what I'm speculating they are. Hence, among other things," she added, without prompting, "The coloured artwork; hence, just as much so, the pointlessness of your Beaming Balance sending your bleeding Body Odour to the Danq in search of a legit Legendarian."

She apprehended wish-fulfillment wasn't on today's agenda. All the same, she prayed that, by playing on his intense dislike, more, his oft-expressed contempt for Lord Order, she'd ingratiate herself to him. She was also gambling that he, every bit as diabolical a dastard as any other devil, nevertheless felt some degree of genuine affection for her Janna.

It wasn't that she was worried the amoral, daughter-diddling slime-bucket would strike her. Janna or no Janna, he probably would, very hard too. But, with him being a Master Deva, he undoubtedly wouldn't strike her fatally. Neither did the fact she'd already put on her makeup for tonight's coming festivities, and would hate to have to redo it, agitate her.

When it all came down to dust – not faeriedust, her being not dead-and-dusted – all she really wanted was for him to leave her alone. Just because the proverbial cat was out of the bag, that didn't mean there weren't more cats in it; this fifty year old bag in particular. Nor did it mean there weren't more bags secreted deeper within her psyche.

Unlike devils and Great Gods above them, Nightingales weren't born to their exalted status. They earned it.

"Zal and I enjoy the Legendarian being around as much or more than any of you devils do. That said, and unless something deathly has happened to a Jordan Q Tethys of any name – so long as he or she's over twenty years old – since Squiggly scribbled his own squiggles, I reckon our pal's still dancing the limbless limbo in some otherworldly Limbo."

Thrygragos Everyman coined phrases. *'By the pricking of my thumbs, something wicked this way comes'*: he'd made that up millennia ago as a reference to anyone he could foretell was approaching him for a favour rather than the pleasure of his company. *'If wishes were horses there'd be a stampede'*: that one he coined with Titanic Metis in mind.

As well as shifting shapes, so long as they had power foci more so than de-brained daemonic bodies, devils could transport themselves through the Weird. With little more than a flash they were there, wherever there was at the moment.

Mel's wished-for-flashes were nowhere near a stampede. Regardless of how much she devoutly desired him to be elsewhere right this minute, he wasn't responding.

She could tell him to fuck off. More politely, she could ask him to please fuck off. But, regardless also of their remote relationship, he didn't strike her as feeling cooperative. She didn't either. She just didn't have much choice in the matter. Minus her agatine eyes, he could compel her as readily as he could glean her or any other devil would possess her.

"Very alliterative, Master," Chaos conceded, using her title as of today, if not for much longer, condescendingly. "Very extraordinary as well. Not everyone can keep stuff from us; especially not ones we've occupied, like Harm has you and your delectable daughter."

This time Melina did smile, and not just in relief. She'd mistaken the menace in his tone for a begrudging approval of her skills. "Not everyone is an Ant Nightingale, Abe. Or has a wife who's one, in Zal's case." She reckoned her sucking-up had done the trick. What she should have done was shut up.

"Now, if you'll excuse me, I've a number of public engagements to attend."

"And one very public announcement to make. Since you'll be making it, and you're not deaf, you might expect to hear yourself make it, too. For my part, well, I expect you already realize that whatever a Sangazur can do, a devil can do better."

"You bastard!"

"Wrong about that too, witch. It's my mother I'm not too sure about."

========

Janna Somata stood beside her Mama Melina on the viewing balcony overlooking the massive courtyard external to the Masters Palace. A few hours earlier, and from exactly the same vantage, her father had made an almost identical announcement. Understandably, the cheering was more subdued this time.

Kanin City had never had a teenage Master of Weir before.

The early evening fireworks were spectacular, though. And so they should be. Like his Great God of a father, there was nothing Abe Chaos enjoyed more that to make a spectacle out of his own self.

****

8: Getting Sparky's Goat

End-Antheal 5476 – The Southern Cheek Lands

Third generational Master Devas were and are triplets.

========

As in the normal course of events for most species, one father, a Great God in their case, impregnates one mother, a similarly second generational Great Goddess, one of three. These were – and may yet be, somewhere in the cosmos – the Trigregos Sisters. Like their Father Sedon and the Thrygragos Brothers they always had names: Demeter the Body, Sapiendev the Mind, and Devaura the Spirit.

In terms of personal mythologies, Chaos and Order both claimed their womb-mother was Demeter because they felt themselves, self-evidently, faultlessly perfect physical specimens. Most everyone else believed Yajur's mother was Sapiendev due to the fact that, as his father put it, coining a phrase, he had a mind like a steel claptrap.

Judging by how swiftly his *'huh'* became her *'duh'*, Pusan Wanderlust had to agree with Lazareme's assessment. Outwardly, Sparky positively gleamed with brilliance. Internally, his synapses snapped akin to someone just after having had a mud bath, yet prior to completing the cleansing process with a rinsing shower. They kind of stuck as well as stunk. In other words, as Pusan would put it, if he weren't such a mind reader, they also kind of sucked.

"Sraddha?" he wondered demonstrably. "How can Shreds have a devic protectorate? He's no devil." He might not be dumb as they come, but he wasn't smart as a spark smarts against skin either. It had clearly slipped through the sieve that passed for his cerebral cortex what twin sister Janna did to Rastha Aragon not all that long ago in Kanin City.

"I suppose that would depend on your definition of devil, wouldn't it?" Pusan verbally counterpunched, daringly sarcastically. "Under the Dome, weirdness and deviancy do tend to go hand-in-hand. From what APM told me before she went off inside him, Twisted Tommy thinks the word *'deviant'* is a synonym for sinner.

"It further follows that he reckons sinners are creatures of evil, as in the Devil. We deviants have devils – little gods, as certain still paganistically-inclined Outer Earthlings have the licentious lot of you – as our half-mother or half-father or both.

That means our half-great-grandfather, on at least one side of the bed, is indeed the Devil Himself. So I can agree with him on that much. You made up your mind yet?"

"Why do you care?"

"Like I said, somebody has to care. Fauns aren't fighters, we're lovers, so I'm happy to leave the big picture for you bickering blighters to resolve. Me, I'll concentrate on the small picture; especially on a guy or gal who's really good at drawing small pictures."

"Now you're talking about the Legendarian, not Sraddha Somata."

"That I am, though I'm only sort of talking about the Legendarian. Saying that, the way I have it figured one leads to the other."

"I'll chomp. How so?"

"Just don't chomp on my head, okay?"

"I ate before I came here."

"Good." She gave him a twinkle. He didn't return it. That was good as well. She wasn't in the mood anyways. Which for her was similar to saying a hawk wasn't in the mood for flying or a shark for swimming. She was almost always in the mood. "Look, Jordy's nuts about beer, right. Everyone who knows him knows that. So it follows that every Jordy is nuts about beer – double duh that."

"Come to think of it, I am feeling a mite peckish."

"The beer nuts are behind the bar." Mouth shut, he jutted his jaw out attentively. Encouraged by his sudden, more so than sullen, silence she carried on dutifully. "This may be the first time he's sent three outsiders to do his dirty deeds; emphasis on dirty, not to mention stinky. More likely it may only be the first time we've caught them.

"It's certainly the first time we've caught him, because heretofore we only suspected what's been going on – and that not for long. But this kind of crap has been going on for the better part of a year now. It's so queer it begs bags of queries, to fay-say some more."

"Maybe I will have a chew – but not on beer nuts. You only need the one ear. Of course that's true for kidneys, too, and they're nowhere near as chewy as ears, more flavourful too."

"All right, all right. I got you." Did something flicker in her forehead, like a warning light in Kanin City back when everything worked properly? Was she possessed? Had he just imagined it? She was an illusionist.

"It started small enough. So small no one noticed a few corked bottles of pilsners, or the occasional stein of the stuff, disappearing on a near nightly basis. Then one day JB spotted a bucket of the benighted brew do just that, right off the shelf, as he entered one of our cold-caves for more of the same. He did a reverse inventory and realized that much more than a trifling trough or two of typical Tethys-tipple had gone missing over the last quite a while." She paused. He was listening. She continued, forehead glistening.

"You're us, what's your first thought? The Danq's got fucking faeries, right? And not the ones we usually have, the almost always female, mushroom-munching leles who take such a delight mocking Harmony by donning chain mail, the better to rattle about noisily when they get ripped and start dancing dementedly."

(There were those who said that leles were Harmony's azura daughters animating mischievous wights. However, those who said it were more likely the mischievous ones since, generally speaking, azuras couldn't animate anything except dead things.)

"Well, I can track faeries through the Weird as readily as I can dorky devils or any other self-psychopomp. Except, there weren't any devils, faeries, or psychos around that I could detect. The bottles and buckets of bonny booze were just plain vanishing.

"Odoriferous oodles of poodles like pilsner. So I'm not thinking Jordy at this point, mark. Sooth said, I'm still not thinking Jordy. He's always been trustworthy. Rather, put better, he's always been trustworthy monetarily. He'd never, ever, last a full 30-year allotment of lifetime if he wasn't, and he's lasted lascivious loads of them." She paused. Still two-eyed Yajur was giving her another of those hungry looks.

"Well," she quickly qualified, on second thought, "Maybe not lascivious loads, but he's lasted a fecund few of them." If Tethys knew how many lifetimes he'd had since his first one began circa 4000 YD he'd always kept it to himself.

"At any rate, if it was him, and he couldn't afford to pay right away, he'd just draw his pills to wherever he is, or was, and leave an IOU behind. He didn't. Ergo, it's not him, ergo the thought never crossing my mind. It has to be faerie tricksters who've learned a nasty new wrinkle on an old wart. Needles to slay, while it's not like me and the Danq are about to go broke subsidizing a gang of red-capped bandits, I contact the boss anyhow."

"Needles to slay?" Sparky demanded.

(That was how some said Harmony slew Quidnunc Tethys the first time: by puncturing his chest with a needle, even if it was actually more like a pre-poisoned pin. Slew Quid before he in effect slew him a second time, he reminded himself. Was Pusan Wanderlust involved in that? She was there, in the Masters Palace, back in 5474, he couldn't help recalling.)

"I'm fay-saying. It's a joke."

"Jokes can choke," he put to her. Appreciating that the Moloch Sedon didn't consider devils killing her a cathonitizing crime, she chose to complete her runaway train of thought as if she'd never made it.

"We change labels. We change what the bottles and jars look like. We change cold rooms. We post guards. We post me! APM even lends us some of her fancy *'flutter-eyes'*, azuras that can far-see as well as far-fly; via between-space as well, ditto that dot. Stuff still disappears, without any trail any of us can spot let alone follow.

"By now we're only filling anything dinky on a per order, cash on the notorious barrelhead basis. Containers we used to store pills in for takeout or local delivery, we fill with water. Finally, whoever's responsible for all this tom-thievery must get pissed off about not being able to get pissed up on what he or she's been vanishing, because one night an entire barrel-room of kegs full of pilsners goes poof."

"The room or just the kegs in the room?"

"Pardon my imprecision, Milord Specificity Electricity. The kegs – the room doesn't and neither do the guards we've posted inside it, some of whom are preoccupied in the spiritual sense of being prepossessed. That's when we start thinking Jordy."

"Because his quill can't affect sentient beings."

"Because, unless they're unconsciou, it can't without him first getting their expressed permission, that's true as beer isn't glue. Also, he's neither a creationist nor an Etherealist. He can't draw doodle then make it drool, if you know what I mean. It has to come from somewhere it exists, in reality, before he can draw it drinkable into whatever bolthole he's hiding out in for whatever reason."

"And it came from here, I got you now. Got today's vanishing act, too. The Outworlders gave him permission to draw them thither, here, and thence hither, back there to wherever."

"But not before your devious daddy read them thoroughly, through and through, then imparted what he learned to the renal rest of us. That's how we know how, who, where they've gone and what to expect when we get there."

"We?"

"His Angela of an angel's earning her wings. She's been in and out of here a half dozen times today alone that I've noticed. Plus, APM and a couple of her Baby Byronics are there already."

"They hitched a ride?"

"More like snatched one – the outsiders won't realize they're occupied."

"Why'd dad bring them into the act anyhow? He's the three of us; you just said Speedy's been about; and we've dozens of brothers and sisters besides Speedy who'll gladly do anything we require of them. Well, maybe not gladly, but you get what I'm getting at."

"They've got it too; the Byronics, I mean. The plagues and poxes – not one disease but many diseases – have swept south, through Sedon's Outer Nose, as well as north and east, across the Cheeks to at least Androgynia, if not as far as your realms in the Back Head. They've reached Godbad big time, bad time, bingo-bongo, and they can't handle it."

"So Bodiless Byron sent them here looking for dad?"

"While he and his bigger wigs stayed in the subcontinent pretending they can handle it, yeah. And that includes his two biggest wigs, the Silverclouds crowding more so than crowning his Byronhead – though, to be accurate, he sent APM and her Baby Byronics here looking for Harmony, not Everyman."

"Why does that surprise me not?"

"Because you're such a jolt of genius in the cranial cavity, it goes without saying. Your dad was here already. Boss brought him over from Tympani because, hey, when everything else fails whom would you call? It is his Age and you banged the button spot-on when you said Great Gods have to be good for something besides jerking you around like chumps on chains."

"The Libertine and the Legendarian are drinking buds from way back. He used to think Jordy's what became of Rumour – arguably his favourite son after me – once he committed devic suicide. Dad wasn't the only one who reckoned Rumour topped himself in order escape the Dream Thanatoid settling their score after his big mouth helped scuttle the Crimson Conspiracy, helped turn it into a Crimson Debacle, but he was one of the last holdouts in that respect.

"That said, no matter how belatedly he, unlike the rest of us, came to accept Rumour was eaten by faeries, and that Jordy's just a recurring deviant, like you and your first father the Attis before you, there's no denying they've forged some pretty strong bonds over the centuries. He usually knows exactly where Jordy is."

"That's what Harmony said," agreed Pusan. "Except he doesn't this time does he."

"Because he hasn't recurred," Yajur extrapolated. "Someone has his quill."

"Not just someone; someone who loves his pills."

"That's quite the coincidence."

"So it is, which of course means it isn't; a coincidence, I mean. But she also said the Lord Laziest Lazareme does his best work when it's in his best interest to do his best work. Needless to say – please note the non-fay-saying – the Danq will go broke if we don't have any clients left. We're dead, though, what do we care?

"But, that happens, what happens to he and she, ye and every other itty-bitty devil-god on the whole of the Hidden Headworld? Without any adherents to call your own, you'll go as far down the sinkhole to oblivion as you can and probably do deserve to go."

"Now you're overreacting. As much as the earthborn despise the skyborn – always assuming they're the ones responsible – even if your theory's right, and I'm not saying it is, fucking faeries can't possibly expect that to be the end-result of all these diseases they've been importing over the decades.

"Nothing's untreatable. Immunities do develop. From what Jordy himself tells us, there's been bubonic plague on the Outer Earth for hundreds, maybe even thousands, of years. Outer Earthlings still thrive, if what they call living can also be called thriving."

"There's that orderly crap-trap of yours at work again, Sparky. Sure they do, and some folks have a natural resistance to blings of things. Moreover, diseases don't affect devils so they don't affect their deviant offspring, so far anyhow. On top of that, fickle-as-pickles Pucks and their daemonic cousins aren't exactly known for planning ahead; never have been. I may be capric, but chthonic critters are so capricious they have as much trouble bothering with a bathroom as they do grasping why anyone would want to bother with one.

"And, just by the bye, it's no theory. I've heard everything that needs hearing and thought through magnums more. So many diseases, one after the other, spread wherever one or another goes, often only incipient, an outbreak of a new or mutated strain of some such horseshit seemingly every other year or so? And for so long, maybe as long your Masterly half-son's been alive, maybe longer, a ton of shit-bricks longer?

"You really do start to wonder. You better or you're already as brain-dead as you're going to be bodily sooner than later. This keeps up, eventually everyone except devils – and presumably the Mother Earthlings themselves – are going to be affected. That happens and it will be all over. It's as if the ensnarers of seekers are intentionally snaring non-fay folks with exotic contagions instead of healthy curiosities."

"You can't seriously be trying to tell me fucking faeries are the masterminds behind the plagues and poxes afflicting the Head."

"Not behind necessarily. But complicit, I'd say almost certainly, and not just because they don't get sick either. Someone has to locate the cracks in the Dome and there's no denying fays are the best at that. The only thing I can't be sure of is whether Utopians are just more hygienic than immune. I'm hypothesizing the latter, especially if the latter's from Cabalarkon, where Sedon won't let me go, let alone any of you, in order to prove it one way or the other."

It made some degree of sense, Sparky almost had to admit. Except, another thing faeries weren't known for was patience. Something as time-consuming as planning would be as beyond most of them as searching out a privy, to use her example. But, even if most Utopians were complete conservatives – in the sense of never wanting to change anything, especially when it came to surviving long enough to dispose of the Devil and his devil-spawn – faeries were famous for being as much Hate-Sedon hedonists as, say, any Utopian, pureblood, hybrid or otherwise.

It therefore should not have come as a surprise that they might be in cahoots. The real wonderment was why it took them this long to form an alliance. After all, hundreds of years ago Morgan Abyss allied her Utopians with Satanwyck's demons. Indeed, speculative hindsight going back howsoever-many and more centuries had her as being part demon herself; possibly even an avatar of Primeval Lilith, the Demon Queen of the Night.

Mass murder did not qualify as mischief in most people's books, but when you can come back just by being dusted with your own ashes, mortality amongst fays was almost as rare as morality. Much the same could be said about believers in cognitive reincarnation. Or would, if it existed for anyone other than, say, Jordan Tethys or Pusan Wanderlust, which it didn't. At least it didn't any longer and never did very commonly.

"Impossible!" Yajur forced himself to disbelieve, albeit more petulantly than genuinely. "What you're suggesting is so unimaginable it'd require a global suicide pact: an anti-devil conspiracy so colossal, so ultimately uncontrollable, you might as well blow up the planet as yourself. How could you contain something that deadly?"

"Bravo, Sparky! You couldn't. I couldn't. Anyone else shouldn't. But Cabby's Utopians may not care about anything else; let alone anyone else. Even if idiocy rates in their Weirdom are not accelerating, which I suspect they are, and are merely as unabated as imbecility was long before even the Death's Head Hellion's day, they have to realize time has got to be running out on them to get rid of the loathsome lunch-pail of you lot.

"Have to say I'm more inclined to call it a burial plot, though. It's funnier that way. Or, come to think of it, maybe plop's a better way of describing suchlike shit. Yeah, that's it: A burial plot with the whole of the Head being the plop to bury!"

========

Normality for Master Devas deviates not at the moment of conception, but milliseconds prior to parturition, when his or her diabolical mother splits – or split, many, many, multiple multi-millennia ago pre-Earth – into one of the Trigregos Sisters. Each of those selfsame three, perhaps not altogether distinct individuals thereafter proceeds to simultaneously give birth to a set of immediate siblings subsequently known as a 'brood' or, more pejoratively, as a 'litter'.

However, according to semi-knowledgeable pseudo-savants such as the devic Librarian, Biblio Drek, they didn't so much split as always were three-in-one. In other words, they were a triad or trinity along the lines of – though hardly identical to – the three Great Gods, who'd been down to two since Thrygragon.

========

As for where they were now, who could say? Maybe they were dead. If so, that was fine with most devils. At the end the Sisters hated their offspring almost as much as they hated their brothers and solitary engenderer, the Moloch Sedon, whom they regarded as rapists. Along with apparent sterility, at least in terms of having any more Master Devas, that was why the devils' grandfather abandoned them on the second Weirworld. And that was something like 200,000 light years earlier in terms of space, if not necessarily the chronological passage of linear time that it took the Sedonshem to cross all that distance to the Whole Earth.

Of course, assuming they still existed somewhere, no matter how much they hated their impregnators and solitary engenderer it probably only rivalled the hatred the earthborn had for the skyborn, on this planet, or pureblood Utopians had for devils anywhere. It had to non-lunch pale compared to the hatred the Unity of Chaos held for the Unity of Order and vice versa. Which, largely at their daughters' diddling, Lazareme-lazy of a father's insistence, left the Unity of Harmony in a loveless position seemingly, if mostly figuratively, forever stuck betwixt and between the two of them.

When your name as well as your attribute is just that, Harmony (or Datong Harmonia – two words that meant the same thing – as antique Illuminaries had her), loveless relations do not appeal. Truth told, they amount to more of a vexation than anything else. As a result she had a history – or a her-story, as she preferred – of searching out loving relationships. One of her most fulfilling, as well as relatively recent, affairs of the heart involved an underneath-human, overtop-faerie most commonly called Tomcat Tattletail (with a *'tail'* rather than a *'tale'*).

Daughters' diddling daddy accounted for much of its long-lastingness. Rather, the fellow's many-thought-deliberate resemblance to daughters' diddling daddy did. There was always more to it than just that, though. For one thing, Tomcat could sing like he'd swallowed the golden canary for breakfast and ate it again for lunch and dinner.

For another, he could just as easily look at any instrument there was and instantly be able to play it, as she put it, highly harmoniously, the same as he did her. While there was nothing he loved better than loving, he loved nothing next than composing and performing dance music live. Everything he did Harmony found irresistible. However, like fucking faeries everywhere, he never did anything for free.

More an underappreciated loner than a pernicious, red-capped renegade from either of the two faerie courts, Tomcat had always professed to disdain reprehensible behaviour of any description. Still, the wrong people in the wrong bedrooms kept catching him. Consequently, no matter how good his intentions had been, to his mind at any rate, she all too often had to bring his corpse back in here, where what amounted to the fays' magic was strongest, in order to incinerate it, then dust a successor.

Thus revitalized, he predictably proved as ever restless as he was essentially rootless and promptly wandered off again. Nonetheless, so love-struck was she, Harmony would go after him again and again and again. Until one day she'd returned to the Head empty-handed. Jordan Tethys, for one, reckoned Tomcat had just up and vanished out there. It was definitely something he'd do.

Thus, equally so, it was precisely the sort of thing he might reckon correctly, if indeed it was a matter of like father, like son.

========

"Try this on for transitory size, Sparky," said Pusan, as she continued to bleat at Lightning Lord Yajur, the no matter how poorly disguised Unity of Order, in the Dinq Doing Danq Cavern Tavern. Very much happily, for her, she also continued to do so non-electrically, as in without having been electrified let alone electrocuted.

Again!

========

"Why would Jordy send someone for his pills? Why wouldn't he come himself? We're bosom buddies; though I doubt Harmony's ever privileged him with more than a fleeting glimpse of her bosom. Nips-tips-point being, we've known him or her forever, for him or her. It could be she couldn't. It could be he's a prisoner. It could be they're sick, one or the other. It could be a bunch of beeswax-bumblebees buzzing in the beehive that passes for his brain box. Yet, like I said, whatever else it could be, it looks like a trap to me."

"Jordy laying a trap? Come on, Goat, get real."

"I am real. Touch me don't I ruminate? And it's mostly your fault, Sparks."

"My fault! Now you're really annoying me. Who are you on about this time?"

"If you can't open your mind, at least try to open your ears. The Jordy I know and love always pays his bills. You not only killed our Jordy; you got away with it. Like you said, though, killing Jordy doesn't count any more than killing me does. So here's my answer: Whoever has his quill. He's the one laying the trap."

"And who might he be?"

"You call me *'Goat'*. Goats are ruminants, on that we can regurgitate confluence if not flatulence. That said, after you bake the poser, but before you start to chew the confounded, you'll probably want to salt and pepper the perplexity. I did. Then I spewed and chewed on it some more. That's what makes us ruminants. We ruminate; we re-chew anew our spew.

"Finally I swallowed it, whereupon I burped and farted both. Methane thus dispensed, what also came out so resembled palpable I'm disgusted it hadn't occurred to me already."

"It being – besides revolting – what?"

"Regardless of his or her name, every Legendarian eventually has to die twice. The first time he or she dies, he or she acquires our Jordy, who's almost always one of their progenitors from within a generation or two. Their second death, if he or she hasn't outlived his or her thirty years of having him, like Squab did, he or she loses our Jordy forevermore on account of he or she's dead forevermore.

"The purest puzzlement is how someone can kill a Jordy psychically, yet not physically? Readily resolved, eh?"

"He or she's not dead in the sense of not moving about anymore. I was wondering why you brought up Sangs."

"Wonder no longer. When Sangazurs reanimate the drearily departed they preserve an individual's persona. Evidently when a Sang reanimates a Jordy, after the body's second death, they in effect reactivate the body's original personality."

"So the trap being laid is for his killer."

"Thus my burp."

"And your fart."

"That too, equally stinky – but thus only results in the how, not the why. To me, the whole thing smells of something gone sadly awry. But you killing Jordy and cathonitizing Fata Fortuna on the same night Star Sedon disappears, well, might there not be a counter-plop? Or a side plop – her wanting revenge on you so bad she's accidentally or intentionally twigged us to what's really been going on all these years?"

"Her misfortune's our good fortune."

"Or not. The chance is there for the taking is all I'm really saying. It all depends on how you take it."

========

According to some demonologists ieles (as opposed to the Danq's dancing leles) are forever scrawny, cat-like horrors nevertheless cursed with an insatiable thirst for blood. As a fairy changeling, Tomcat Tattletail probably wasn't an iele. He might have been a 'mora', however. They had somewhat similar traits and he did sometimes claim that his devic half-mother was Wintry Moira, Dame Chance.

What definitely was true was that moras were living nightmares. Nonetheless, regardless of whatever sort of faerie fart he might be, his name probably should have been Tommy Trouble.

Just as unluckily, what it likely was originally was Rumour of Lazareme.

========

Theoretically, no normal Outer Earthling knew that a Hidden Continent of Sedon's Head actually existed. Neither did any fully indoctrinated adepts of the still extant, but anciently rendered ignorant, Xuthrodite Brotherhood. Nor, as far as that went, did members of any of the Outer Earth's similarly nowhere-near-enlightened-anymore witch-sisterhoods.

Even though the notion of an Inner Earth, a Shadowland or an Eternal Elsewhere was fabled virtually everywhere you went out there, it was not under any suchlike site-specific name – or, for that matter, under any dome, site-specific or otherwise. That was for sure. Even *'Yenne Velt'*, the Cabbalistic term for, only possibly, the Headworld, just meant *'otherworld'* in Yiddish.

While that should mean no outsider could get within Cathonia unless it was inadvertently, the keyword was normal; which, his or her pretensions aside, Xuthrodites and members of witch-sisterhood essentially were beyond the Dome. Equally in theory, with the well-known exceptions of Pyrame Silverstar and Sedon himself (due to the fact they were who they were), no other devil – not firstborns, nor even Great Gods – could get through it, in either direction.

However, over the multiple multi-millennia of her existence Harmony had earned an impressive reputation of proving preposterous the theoretical. 50 up to

100 or more years' latterly, she'd been there and back many times in pursuit of her ostensible then-truelove: the selfsame enchanting, yet otherwise worthless gleeman whom many believed looked, when he was in here, like her notion of what her father should look like on purpose.

Because he was far more familiar than she was with not just the air out there, a pre-Quibble Legendarian accompanied her on many of those excursions. Their egress and re-entry points were an interlinked set of Tholos temples. Once hundreds, perhaps thousands of these beehive-shaped Guest Houses for – depending on one's perspective – gods or ghosts, dotted both sides of the Sedon Sphere. In Tethys-terms, every one of them had a heartthrob-hearthstone powering it.

Again depending on one's preferred phraseology, every one of these heartthrob-hearthstones was composed of the Godstuff alternately known as Brainrock or Gypsium. After many centuries of inactivity, call it morbidity, one in particular had begun beating again. One typically led to another.

Inexplicably, a dozen or more, trans-Dome departure or arrival dots must have done dotty ditto, as not just the Legendarian would have alliterated it. The howsoever-delayed, and undeniably deadly dreadful, ramifications of these multiple breaches in the Cathonic Zone were only now becoming apparent to the top dog top gods of those normally in here.

"Actually," Sparky put to Pusan, grasping a few more strands of what she was ultimately leading up to and not liking it, "What you're really talking about is Grandfather embarking on another Sedonplay isn't it. Did it never occur to you Lady Luck might be as yappy as you are? Surely you've heard what superstitious nits say about the stars influencing your future."

Being a goatish nymph with an admiration for all manner of satiric beasts – not that Lord Yajur suffered from satyriasis as such – Pusan allowed herself a giggle of glee.

"Unhappy happenstance forcing Sedon to match it with deleterious deliberateness, that's how I had it figured. But Lady Luck's predilection for endless babbling driving your granddaddy out of Cathonia, just so he could avoid listening to it everlastingly, is certainly a novel notion. I can't see it myself but you never know do you."

"And we can't ask him, can we?"

"Sure we could, if we knew where he was hiding. Your father sent his Angela of an angel to the Sed-Sphere, too, and either she couldn't find him, which is pretty hard to feature, him being the biggest and brightest star in the night's sky, or he wasn't there. Did you whack the Moloch Sedon when you thought you were whacking Gravedigger?"

"And why would Grandfather have been pretending to be the Nergalid?"

"So he could pleasure himself of Janna Somata is the obvious answer to that. She does have silver hair and he's always had a thing for women with silvery hair. Recollect that trainee Valkyrie after Thrygragon, one of the Jordy of that era's multitude, whatever her name was? Ute, that was it. Hell's teeth, witness Pyrame Silverstar. She doesn't have to have silver hair when she's pretending to be wholly human. But she does, because that's the way he likes her."

"Which doesn't in any way answer what I asked."

"No, it doesn't, does it. To be honest, I have no idea why he'd want to look like the Nergalid. I suppose that's something else we'll have to ask him once he's either back or we find out where he's hiding. Guess I better start making a list. So?"

"I'm coming. I can't wait to see how Harm's going to wiggle out of this one."

"Me, I'm more interested in seeing how Quidnunc's going to wangle her into it."

========

As the Great God Everyman and Byron's Bowman drained their drinks; as JB, John Barleycorn, replaced his smeared, sartorial non-splendours in one of its backend honeycomb of caves; as Sparky and Pusan Wanderlust concluded their conversation in front of the Dinq Doinq Danq Cavern Tavern's main bar; and, as it turned out, APM All-Eyes and two of her broods-younger sibs were up north being faerie-fed-backwards, mouse-like, by an oversexed crazy cat who generally stuck to canaries; Lazareme's angel, Irisiel Mercherm as ancient Utopians had her, raced into the Weirdom of Kanin City on talarial winged sandals.

About the same time an ancient, in terms of longevity, but still noticeably breathing, albeit unhealthily heavily so, white-as-light Utopian stepped out of a teleport-hole of her own conjuring. It wasn't into the master bedroom of the Masters Palace in Kanin City; it was, however, into a master bedroom in a Masters Palace.

The once millennium-child, long-nowadays-decrepit skin-bag of osteoporotic bones, was no Quill Tethys either, though she was a Jordan Tethys. Her 'Q' name of personal choice was 'Quoits'. As for the Master in the master bedroom of said Masters Palace, the longevity bit applied to him as well, albeit not quite as much as it did to her.

Ditto the breathing bit – for a few more minutes anyhow.

========

"Quid's after her too?"

"Quid's who's setting the trap, bright light. But he isn't the only one – more like the third or fourth one, I'm figuring. You see, I didn't burp and fart just once, Sparky."

"No," a male faun said to her, an older Yajur said to him. "Someone like you almost certainly does both a dozen times a day," their father or grandfather, as the case may be if Pusan wasn't as many speculated a devic suicide, added conspiratorially. "I know I do."

Guffawing out loud, more to himself than to anyone else, an actually clean-shaven, blue-skinned, golden-haired Thrygragos Lazareme slapped him, then her, between his then hers shoulder blades. He did it so hard that they each spat out the last of the beer nuts they'd been popping into their mouths as they spoke.

"But, just so we're clear, you're coming because I'm telling you to come."

"I knew it," Sparky smirked. "You need our protection."

"Don't be daft, boy. While it's true that having to listen to Miss Fortune never-endingly nattering into your stellar ear-hole would be a fate presumably worse than even death for an immortal, you're coming because the Goat's right. Father Sedon did bugger off on purpose. He didn't bugger off because he doesn't want to have to ill-star you or Harmony, though. Rather, he doesn't want to have to do that yet. It's me he doesn't want to have to cathonitize."

"You're going to authorize us killing the outsiders?"

"Authorizing you to commit devic suicide is not within my prerogative. All I'm going to tell any of you to do is give the outsiders royal hell. Isn't that true, Mithradite?"

On cue Zuvem Nergalis (the 2-years-earlier, falsely accused, black-as-midnight *'Planter'* of the three Nergalids, hence not just Pusan also referring to him as *'Grave-digger'*), talismanic spade Brainrock-glowing in hand, manifested himself beside the Great God and Byron's Bowman: "It'll be my pleasure, uncle dirt-bag."

Sparky despised Gravedigger for any number of reasons besides a disrespectful attitude towards his father, whose age it was despite Harmony claiming it was that of this semi-mythical Panharmonium of hers. The Nergalid somehow or other not being inside the Legendarian most of two years ago, when he distinctly saw him shining therein, was only the latest of them.

If he hadn't judged he was cathonitizing Zuvem, he would never have finished what Squiggly started, thereby killing that Jordy for the second time and ill-starring his own wintry sister. He nevertheless instantly appreciated there was nothing of the *'as if'* about his sudden appearance. His father loved theatrics.

"I'm shocked you didn't say *'I can dig it'*," did say Pusan Wanderlust.

"Why would he?" proffered the Green Man, Djerrid Ruin, Byron's Bowman. "As I understand it, we're all going to dig it."

"Then shovel it into the bitch's ditch," concurred the Nergalid.

The ditch-reference was to the Gulf of Corona, Sedon's Human Eye. The bitch, a myrionymous Mithradite, was one of his eldest sisters, a second-born Apple God-dess like the Nergalid's current flame, Sinistral Lust of Satanwyck: the one who hadn't been seen – not for sure – for over 1,400 years. A sample of her names included Kore-Eris, Kore-Discord, Marut Kanin, Fitna Marutia, or just plain Ma-rutia, the same as the Cheek Lands themselves.

That last was the specific name Nergalis was thinking of right that minute. But it might well have been Strife, the first and probably the most common of her many names.

If he had, except for capitalizing the letter *'S'*, he wouldn't have been far wrong.

========

Far to the north, in the Weirdom of Cabalarkon, its Master finally died after a de-cades long illness. His, by pre-agreement, consensus successor, who was even older than he was in terms of centuries, not decades, dutifully took possession of his regalia: the so-called six Great Godly Glories. They were the Mask of Byron, the Cross of Mithras, Lazareme's Cloak of Many Colours, the Amateramirror, the Susasword and the Crimson Corona.

Utopians of Weir called these last the three Sacred Objects because they were dedi-cated to the Trigregos Sisters: Devaura, Demeter and Sapiendev. Reputedly the approach-ing impossibly long ago abandoned, second generational Great Goddesses hated their solitary father, their by now only two remaining brothers, and their hundreds of offspring as much or more than every pureblood and most hybrid Utopians did.

Even though many generations separated them, the terrible twins' Mama Melina nee Tethys nowadays Somata sometimes called the new Master of Weir Granny Jordy.

****

9: Herta Heartthrob

Circa 4828 Year of the Dome – Beneath the Weirdom of Cabalarkon

The hugely oversized, though self-evidently not impossibly mobile, 3-eyed she-sphinx called herself All the Invincible.

========

Although she had back-wings, a lioness's body, a serpentine tail, and an extremely attractive face, she was no more all of the sphinxes on the Whole Earth than, as she discovered to her abiding horror on Thrygragon, she was invincible. She was, however, familiar with where she'd materialized out of between-space, for it was from here that All, in her role as Mandroid Monster Maker, mined the chthonic crud she used to manufacture the golem-like automatons.

That wasn't what she was here to do today, though. Neither was her presence altogether voluntary. A devil controlled her, the only devil who could control her: Pyrame Silverstar, the devic mother of the sedons, small case, on both sides of the Dome. It was Pyrame's face staring out of All; that made it Pyrame's third eye as well.

Having previously far-seen it, the Pauper Priestess easily found the corpse she was looking for; she also found six talismans no devil ever wanted to touch, but she nevertheless expected to find in the Hell-Well beneath Cabalarkon, hence her bringing All. As for whether she also found, and reclaimed, her demon, stuck inside an immobilized, but very familiar-looking body, she convinced herself that wasn't at all possible, pun not intended.

Once she retrieved it on Midsummer Day 4825, she never lost it again.

All in all then, pun intended this time (for, despite having to endure travails wholly inappropriate for a goddess of both her exalted and effectively unique stature, she prided herself on maintaining an upbeat, positive attitude), Pyrame was highly pleased with her day's venture into Subterranean Absudyl. She was curious as to what Harmony's daemonic body, minus a face, was doing down here, though. Most devils didn't keep spares.

Then again, a few devils believed that the Unity of Balance (in addition to, as she personally preferred, Panharmonium) didn't need a debrained daemonic body in order to maintain solidity; that she was almost all Brainrock the same as All was almost all Stopstone, its counterforce. That probably wasn't true, but it made for a decent rumour.

She made a mental note to ask Harm for confirmation one of these centuries.

========

Antheal 30, 5476 YD – The Garden of Earthy Delights, Coast of Corona

In Kanin City, Lazareme's Angela (whom long gone Illuminaries of Weir named Irisiel Mercherm after a typically eccentric selection of Middle Sea messenger-deities) finished conveying their mutual father's request that they – Harmony, Chaos and the Librarian – join him on the Corona Coast. Simultaneously, on that selfsame, faraway coastline, a Head-worldly heterochthonous threesome materialized out of the Weird beer-buckets in hands.

Carrying stuff, and not just beer, that was their specialty.

========

When incarnations of the legendary 30-Year Man came back from the Outer Earth, he or she often entertained his or her delighted listeners by mocking the idiosyncratic or, more accurately to most of them, idiotic belief systems prevalent beyond the Dome. Dire, Bosco and Twisted Tommy didn't look sick so maybe there was something to be said about not washing. Their being in here at all, though, suggested a far likelier scenario.

They might well be immune to them, but they and their predecessors nevertheless must have brought the bugs blighting the Cheeks with them when they first began coming through the Dome via reactivated Tholoi or some other sort of as yet unidentified teleportive ring-holes. Moreover, the plagues and poxes – not one disease but many diseases – had been ravaging the land for much longer than Zalman Somata's 100-year lifetime.

That indicated their precursors had started the whole pernicious process, the very harvest that the Head was reaping today, decades before Harmony commenced to traversing Cathonia regularly not all that long before the turn of this, the 55th Century of the Dome. Her excuse throughout so much of that time was she'd once again become incurably enamoured by the sensually seductive fairy-type, Tomcat Tattletail, whom she speculated was an incarnation of her father, Thrygragos Lazareme.

None of what subsequently transpired could be considered her fault, could it? That would certainly be her father's argument to his father, should it come to that. The Moloch Sedon's absence from Cathonia – or at least his visible absence – naturally negated the necessity of any such an argument. It therefore wouldn't come to that until he, the mighty Eye-Mouth in the sky, did come back.

If anything, he'd say to Sedon when he finally did, blame it on love.

========

The threesome stepped out of between-space into a windowless dining hall lit by fairy carbuncles – fabulous garnets that generated their own luminescence as if by, yes, magic. It was situated well within a ball-like, partially underground, cobalt-coloured and hence metallic-looking bunker; one topped with a sculpted, very much flamboyantly overwrought hoodoo that, with its ornamental curlicues, architecturally approached the filigree-flowery.

Many of those there couldn't have been happier. One wasn't. That one, a *'dobury'* by the name of Nanapollo, stuck a finger times two into each of the beer-bearers nostrils.

'Doburies', sometimes also, mistakenly, known as *'snot-snakes'*, were a lumpy, very much dough-like faerie genus – an anthropomorphic tub of lard bleached white, to supply their most widespread depiction. Polydactyl, they always had too many fingers on, only usually, two hands. Today was one of those unusual days.

There were three of them and only one of him. Consequently, Nanapollo extended three hands on three arms. The third's elbow, wrist and finger joints hinged appropriately. However, growing out of the top of his chest as the arm did, it was akin to a skinny, grotesque goitre. As monstrous as it appeared, the generative effort didn't particularly pain him. He nevertheless grimaced as he did so.

The Outer Earthlings who'd been at the Danq did too, bracing themselves psychologically as he latched six fingers securely within their six nostrils. They'd endured this predictability-to-the-point-of-routine ritual more than a few times before, after much the same missions as well, albeit to different canteens elsewhere on the Hidden Continent of Sedon's Head. (The Danq was hardly the only beer hall that brewed fine pilsners. Pure pill-lovers merely judged it the best.)

Insertion accomplished unquestionably unenthusiastically, yet both professionally and therefore satisfactorily – Utopian biomages deliberately bred doburies largely for just this function – Nanapollo took a deep breath. It was the start of a preparatory sigh of resignation at the anticipated futility of the non-results. Which was why he was not, and would not be, happy.

With previously practised-to-precision ease, he promptly jettisoned all six fingers up the trio's nostrils. And that, jettisoning his fingers, did hurt. Then, joy of toys, for the first time in what amounted to a near-lifetime of doing dick-ditto, he was rewarded for his pains. First, Dire – whose given name was Albrecht and whose surname, Durer or Thurer, did mean doormaker – clutched his throat and started to gag. Next, Bosco convulsed as if he was about to vomit. Twisted Tommy beat them to it by milliseconds.

Except, the matter they expelled did not meet the traditional definition of vomit as the contents of one's stomach. In truth, what they ejected had never reached anyone's stomach. The devils thereby purged hadn't been swallowed so much as they'd swallowed, in unseen stealth mode, the Outer Earthlings. As for Utopian biomages, with comparatively squeamish Quoits' concurrence, they and their eyeorb-armed brethren, the Trinondev Warriors of Weir, had been banned from the protectorate.

You want to wipe out devils? Sometimes you have to deal with the mothers-hating brothers- and sisters-humpers.

========

Dire's birth year was 5471, Year of the Dome. Bosco's was 5450, also YD, not that any of them were born within the Cathonic Zone, as the Dome was more correctly known. Twisted Tommy was born in 5420, the equivalent of 1420 AD in the flat-earth Europe beyond many tholoi-linked parts of it.

The flat earth was hardly everything he believed in either.

========

Tomas de Torquemada, easily the eldest of the three non-native-born out-siders, ended up with *'Twisted'* when *'Torqued'* didn't take as a nickname. As those in the Danq, those who knew of the Outer Earth's much more than millennium-plus descent into its current sorry state of superstitious ignorance, correctly suspected, he was indeed a once-tonsured preaching friar.

A mean-spirited, judgemental man by almost anyone's estimation, in his fifty-plus years of breath he had thus far acquired only one howsoever-prestigious claim to fame. That was as the confessor of the recently proclaimed queen of the kingdom of Castile, a position he'd held since Isabella was an Infanta. Of course that was be-fore he went for a walk in the monastery's grounds one pleasant afternoon a while back now.

In what could not by any measure have been a coincidence, that fateful after-noon he befriended a complete stranger; one who subsequently took him inside, in his case, a long abandoned, tumbledown chapel. Built in the round supposedly such that the Devil, singular, could not hide in its shadows, very much ironically the chapel turned out to contain a between-space gateway leading to a reputedly Africa-sized landmass enclosed by this acknowledged Satan Sphere of his hosts; devils, demons and deviants that so many of them apparently were.

Until then it was a day not unlike many other days: a day, as it also turned out, not unlike many another when it came to a great many others, expressed more in-clusively. His similarly invasive companions-in-contamination, he now knew, num-bered in the hundreds, if not the thousands. Persuasive, presumably autochthonous strangers of either sex had been escorting men and women like him hither for at least a century and, most likely, much more.

The main difference between him and most of them was that he had no in-tention of staying on the Head until the day he died, of whatever cause. That was because he had faith, what some of his hosts decried as an affliction that relieved the afflicted of the need to think. Be that as it may, Twisted Tommy did not consider himself afflicted; he considered himself blessed.

The Lord, in His ineffable wisdom, may have delivered him to this ghastly, though hardly ungodly, realm. But He, capitalized, never did anything without reason. Therefore he, small case, being in here was nowhere near as unaccountable to him as it was to the vast majority of those who shared not so much his despairing doom as, potentially anyhow, his glorious destiny.

As far as he was concerned, said-despair would automatically change to said-glory once he returned home. Returning home, though, that was the non-what-soever-proverbial, thorny bush surrounding his ramshackle hovel on the edge of the oddly often sunny, coastal mudflats. Which was why he'd volunteered to fetch hither the chief beer-guzzler's pills.

Here, a comparative aureole of brightness in a misty, grey land of seemingly unending bleakness, was a garden of earthy even more so than earthly delights. Here the Devil's spawn ruled so unchallenged that wanton Jezebels cavorted shamelessly with execrable, sexually seemingly inexhaustible imps. Here lost men, such as the bulk of his fellow, initially off-Headworld travellers, spent their sacred seed, literally, on overripe fruit. Yet even in this pagan paradise of theirs, favours rendered gener-ally begot favours repaid.

Surely anyone who could draw him from one place to another in here could draw him back to where he came from out there. And, once he was safely home in Iberia, infidels beware. Because, with Queen Isabella's well-cultivated patronage, here was precisely where he'd be consigning Jews, Saracens, heretics, apostates and the irreligious sum of their thus already damned cohort – here, to this Living Hell less within than on the Whole Earth.

What's more, he'd send them through as alive as He had he himself. That way they could help finish what he'd been privileged to prolong: namely, its utter annihilation as anything except a become-barren wasteland for the ambulatory dead and the irreversibly irredeemable; one that may then finally sink to the lightless gloom of the ocean's floor the way it should have during the apogee of the Great Flood of Genesis.

That the chief beer-guzzler, an undeniably staggeringly talented artist who could draw anything, as well anyone anywhere, stunk abominably, like a decaying corpse, didn't surprise Twisted Tommy. It especially didn't once he found out that that was exactly what he was – a somehow still mobile dead man his living son, also present, sometimes called *'Deadnunk'*. Neither did the fact the stranger he'd befriended in his monastery's green quickly proved himself a shape-shifter.

Then again, why anyone would want to spend most of his time in here looking like an anthropomorphic tomcat, in a leopard-skin jacket and matching leotards, complete with codpiece no less, did strike him as cat-curious. What didn't strike him anywhere near as curious was that cats were the only domesticated animals never mentioned in the Holy Bible. He knew why that was now. They weren't just demon familiars; they were also demons.

What did surprise him, however, was that the darkish-skinned, 3-eyed divinity they all seemed to worship – or at least defer to – wanted to wipe out his own kind, devils the lot of them, as much or more than he did. And it wasn't so he could thereafter rule the roost all by his lonesome self either. It was because that was his duty as a true, so-called Utopian.

Would the Almighty really reward a recidivist Lucifer, let alone a godless atheist, with a paradisiacal afterlife everlasting? Mysterious ways indeed!

========

An oddly orange-and-brown-striped, more furry- than hairy-headed and hence terribly tigerish roving minstrel smiled rather too broadly for an actual man. (Which of course he wasn't, nowhere near.) The panpipe-playing troubadour's work-in-progress lover, the winged, otherwise apparently permanently perplexed beauty standing beside him, dotted his ditto.

That would be she whom, despite her worn, sackcloth gown, almost everybody who saw her, young and old, male and female, there-then and then-and-there not there, considered altogether too knockdown-gorgeous for her own good. That, therefore, would also be the lone scum demon present.

What they ejected had never reached anyone's stomach yet – also best to make that – because, for the two categorical demons, it was feeding time. Or should have been.

========

His faerie parents named the dobury presciently. The three Outer Earthlings did not puke out, as if venting themselves, snakes made of nasal mucus, though due to a superficial resemblance that's how the term *'snot-snakes'* derived. Nor did it, whatever they puked out was constituently, turn into snakes. Olympian Apollo had initially been worshipped as a Mouse God and that's what whatever it was speedily became, ever so appropriately: three demonic approximations of long-tailed mice.

Despite, as not just the dobury's presence indicated, they were in a fairyland of sorts, they were not as per the nursery rhyme. On the contrary, far from being blind, two of what amounted to Nanapollo's trademark vermin had three eyes whereas the other one seemed sprinkled with so many multifarious-same she was verging on all eyes. Besides where they came from, that kind of gave away the fact they weren't real mice.

They weren't demons hardening into the shape of mice either. But, while it might not be accurate, or even intuitive, to call them demonic, what else would you call them: phlegmatic, as in faerie phlegm? That would be even less right. Then again it probably wouldn't hurt their feelings. Always assuming suchlike curiosities had the brainpower to have feelings, which they did and they didn't.

Doburies kept virtually everything they could conceivably, in exceedingly fanciful theory, impart to their snot-snakes with respect to intelligence where it belonged: namely, in their own nodular noggins. That meant the resultant expectorations weren't just seriously deficient in terms of their own brain matter; they were absolutely devoid of it.

So, being basically brainless, how was it they could reflexively try to get away? Snot no more ambulates than amber does. The answer to that was obvious to all except the three outsiders there. The grinning gleeman currently doing his best to impersonate a fiendishly feline humanoid was merely the quickest to react.

When it came to devils he was far more indiscriminate than her.

========

Bosco's birth name was Jeroen (Jerome) Anthonissen van Aken.

========

Like the precocious, sometimes tryingly enthusiastic boy with the superlative natural talents, he had artistic pretensions. Indeed, prior to being lured inside by the not-then-winged temptress so much slower to react than the smiling shape-shifter, he felt himself well advanced along the road to the leisurely life of a professional painter. Specializing in unflinchingly harsh, yet highly lucrative, religious subjects, he signed those few, to-him-acceptable paintings he did sign as Hieronymous Bosch.

Like Twisted Tommy, Bosco desired little more than to be drawn back to from whence he came. The preposterous paradise they lived in, thanks to Sraddha Somata; the sights he'd seen hereabouts; the activities he'd not just witnessed but participated in firsthand, and not just with his hands either; as horrendously improbable as all of this was, he'd promised himself that if ever did get back home, he would never leave it again.

He couldn't. There'd be too much work to do.

Sculpted sandstone hoodoos, many on rounded bases, garishly glazed and brightly shined; all manner of mutated plants and bizarre animals, some of whom could speak; freakish demons disporting not so much nightmarishly as feverishly; 3-eyed devils, albeit – so far – none with horns, cloven hoofs or barbed tails; fucking faeries shrinking men and engorging fruit as if at whim! Lasciviousness unmitigated!

Lady Lust personified – as a melancholy angel no less: a winged, even for this particular Head, presumably supernatural being so nevertheless irresistible you didn't
need a filthy imagination to become aroused.

God above this worldly welkin, the Devil up there too, though nowhere near
as beyond stratospheric, the high art they'd inspire. The brain positively boggled
with possibilities.

He may not be as latently gifted as Dire, the boy amongst the returning men.
Nor was he as patently talented as the dead man obviously was, with or without that
ever-glowing quill of his, the one that made its own colours. But, being abstemious,
yet relatively open-minded – especially when compared to the intolerant and, as a
result, largely intolerable Tommy Torquemada – he had a far more reliable as well
as vivid memory.

The same as perhaps thousands before them, Twisted Tommy and Bosco
thought themselves privileged seekers after secrets more so than as the largely unaffected carriers of contagion for which they'd been recruited. There was no bigger secret beyond the Cathonic Dome than that there was a Cathonic Dome. The
second biggest secret was that there was an entire continent hidden underneath it.

They'd heard from their hosts, but couldn't yet know from direct experience,
that ordinary folks who made it both in here, then back there, seldom retained re-
collections of their experience for long. To them it often seemed like a pipedream or,
if they'd been gone for very long, an egregious case of waking amnesia.

Overall though, while it might be too bad for them in that they'd never get to
profit from revealing the secrets they thus learned from coming in here, that wasn't
much of a price to pay. Those they came in contact with because, wittingly or un-
wittingly, the viruses, ill humours, transmissive malignancies or whatever else they
brought with them slowly killed off those on the inside, they were the ones who paid
the really serious price.

All things considered then, it might not be much of a tragedy if what they were
informed the Dome did to returnees once they got back outside proved correct.
Especially given the evil times out there, Bosco certainly wouldn't mind if the whole
thing left him speechless. He was, however, convinced there was no way it would
leave him sightless.

Rather, there was no way it would leave him incapable of portraying viscerally
affective sights in a visually effective manner. Plus, considering how he used to make
his living, he would never have any reservations when it came to painting pastiches
no matter how perverse they might look at first glance – though first blush might be
a better way of qualifying it.

So, yes, he prayed the dead man would shortly draw him back to his home in
's-Hertogenbosch, which he tended to refer to as Den Bosch, hence his signatory
surname. Failing that, he prayed that as a supplemental, fallback plan he'd at least
draw him to the other side of the circular bandstand in his hometown. After all, it
was from there that he and the otherworldly stunner somehow or other departed
the Outer Earth originally.

He had no qualms about Dire. The evil times out there had nothing to do with
five year olds. They did have a lot to do with the other one, though. That made the
Dominican from the Iberian Peninsula an entirely different issue. So, if possible, he

prayed even more fervently that, should they get back to the other side safely, the uncompromising, holier-than-Jesus bastard didn't sic the goddamned Inquisition on him.

Twisted Tommy was a Black Friar. And even if, thanks largely to everything he'd experienced beneath this overarching Dome of theirs, Bosco wasn't any longer, the dangerously devout Burgundian-cum-Hapsburg Netherlands where he came from, and felt he would soon return to, still was a nominally Papist realm.

Vengeance may belong to the Lord but, both out there again, Tommy might not prove beyond attempting to silence witnesses to the Lord's manifest folly of countenancing the existence of this Hidden Continent of Sedon's Head. Quietly hunkering down in Den Bosch for the remainder of his life might be the only sensible way to prolong just that, his life.

That sworn never aloud, accurately capturing in pulsations-provoking lines and hues just a few of the mortal delights, the fantastical figures, and the approaching surreal shapes this seemingly forever-fluctuating garden protectorate provided on a nearly daily basis (paradise, Tatty Tom told him, originally meant a walled garden, nothing more), that would be his masterpiece, his assurance of an immortality regardless of his soul's immanent persistence.

And all he had to do was physically survive long enough to paint it.

========

For his part, being so young Dire retained vague memories of his mother breast-feeding him. Thus, when his latest hero – funnily, Squiggly was his name – used words like 'scrumptious' and 'succulent' when referring to the melancholy angel, the child knew exactly what he meant. And it had nothing to do with her wings.

What he didn't understand was what the black-skinned, smelly old dead man – Drang hated him – in an evidently non-Sedon-Speak observation, meant by a 'puta with a putto'.

He did know what 'jealousy' meant, though. The puta's putto epitomized it.

========

Startled as they had to be by such revolting developments, the Byronic Master Devas already effectively trapped within the resinous, rapidly solidifying, snot-snake effluvia retained a modicum of their vastly superior wits. Activating legs where mice usually had legs, they sought to scamper to safety.

Too late! Tomcat Tattletail pounced, smacking the three taxonomically whatever-they-were dazed thoroughly starry. Picking them each up by their snaky tails, that Tom, Tatty Tom as he was nicknamed this time around, proceeded to proffer the multi-eyed and, hence, prettiest critter to the impromptu gathering's 3-eyed acclaimed god – another mostly black-skinned mixed-blood, one who shaved his pate bald, though not his face, and was apparently altogether alive since, whenever he accidentally cut himself, he bled.

Sitting anticipatorily as he was at the head of the table, eating puke may or may not appeal to Sraddha Somata. However, even if he couldn't be sure of their tribal affiliations, he knew precisely what the murine crud they were about to eat was underneath the resultantly doughy exterior the outsiders expelled.

Having, at least for the time-being-distinct from every non-mouse there, three eyes, he had no desire to share their indulgence. It might, he could have been thinking, set a lousy example in both senses of the word: poor and lice-ridden, which most rodents were. After all, while it was always better to eat than be eaten, he could be next in line. Or, put better, his internal godhood, what made him their acclaimed god, could be next in line.

"I'll just have a chilled glass of that excellent pill, thanks all the same, Tatty Tom."

Seemingly unperturbed by his lord's polite yet nonetheless mild rebuke, Tomcat popped the liveliest one like an after-dinner mint. "Hmm," he savoured as if a connoisseur in such matters. "Tastes kind of fishy, for a mouse. Wonder if it's Pyçonja?" Crunching it taste-buds-contemplatively, he made his decision. "Has to be," he declared.

The same as their mother and father before them, Sraddha and twin sister Janna received extensive Illuminary-training whilst growing up in and around Kanin City. Shreds, to give him his nickname, was therefore well aware from his school days that old-time Illuminaries often intermingled humour with a sometimes-deplorable lack of imagination once they began coming back from the Outer Earth (circa the early to middle of the 4th Century of the Dome) and started giving Master Devas their subsequently commonest appellations.

The vast majority came from names ascribed to the then-almost-exclusively pagan, and consequently polytheistic outsiders' top dog top gods. In arguable truth, many of these so-called divinities may well have been the Inner Earth's devil-gods transplanted (often for hundreds of years, some for well over a millennium). Watery Pyçonja, whose supplementary surname was Volant because she had wings and could fly, had a somewhat different pedigree. She was one of Unmoving Byron's dozen Zodiacals, the one representative of, as might be expected, the astrological sign of Pisces.

Pleased with his pick Tomcat offered the most multiply multi-eyed beastie to his acknowledged-untouchable gal-pal: "Want an APM, Herta?" he ventured indulgently, intuiting the correct identity of the fossilizing devil by the sheer amount of eyeballs the mucous-mouse sported. "Or would you prefer a hot dog?"

Almost anthropomorphically, Dire's Drang looked askance at that. He settled his head back between his paws again before anyone except the speaker himself noticed. Cats and dogs got along like, well, cats and dogs. Tatty Tom was no different in that respect. He'd been wary of Drang ever since Herta and the putto brought him through with the sickly boy. (Interestingly, as the cupid had foreseen, Dire started feeling much better virtually the moment he arrived on the Head. Not just the air in here really was conducive to good health.)

For his part, Shreds didn't need any of the eerie insight so often attributed to felines in order to figure out who the distinctly tubular third mousy had to be: yet another female Byronic, Camorva Freeflight, after whom the month of Kamor was named. Her Dachshund-like shape, albeit as a rodent not a dog, left little doubt of that. Hot rat wouldn't have been as humorous and the tigerish metamorph with the silken singing voice did pride himself on his sense of same. Just about everything amused him, hence perhaps why he was as often as not smiling.

As Shreds had also heard tell, albeit mostly from Tattletail – but definitely not from his teachers back home, who wouldn't have known the so-called *'scum'* demon even existed – she deemed herself Herta Heartthrob. (Herta was a word-jumble of Earth, as in the planet from whence she gained chthonic corporeality. The truly ancient Edenites' triple goddess Hecate was occasionally recalled as, dependent on one's pronunciation, Herta, Erda or Hertha. Titanic Rhea, mother of Olympian Zeus, and his sister-spouse Hera, were analogous anagrams for the same mythological, even fictitious, entity.)

The self-evidently melancholy angel did so years ago now; not long after he, Tatty Tom, found her somewhat deteriorated, yet still unmistakeably shapely, form deep beneath that other Weirdom, Cabalarkon. That was hardly all he found there either, for laying near her attractive clumpishness was some sort of almond-egg with her – and not just her – face etched upon it. This he picked up and, pineal gland-like, stuck into her putty of a brainpan, thereby reactivating her howsoever-borderline brainlessly.

"Devils generally don't agree with me," she apologized, somewhat surprisingly to young Somata's mind. Most demons liked nothing better than to munch on devils. "Besides, I'm saving my appetite for someone far more substantial than any lowly third-born, one from the wrong tribe to boot. You did promise me, Tom."

"That I did, my love," Tomcat acknowledged, having – Shreds correctly reckoned – anticipated she would decline to partake. "And that I shall deliver; momentarily, I believe."

"They do me," deadpanned Deadnunk (as in Quidnunc) Tethys, who had plans of his own for that selfsame substantial personage – his last-touch murderer.

"I'll try one," enthused Squiggly Tethys, experimental as always.

"You would," grinned Shreds. Despite his comparatively recent ascendancy to localized godhood, dead-dad Quid's increasingly insouciant live-son was about the only person in this perverse port of a protectorate (what the Lazaremist Fop, Faustus Vladuca, allowed him to set up then make his own) who continued to refer to him by his childhood nickname.

"You'll pop anything. Give him the one with all the eyeballs, Tom. It's still squirming. Which is to say it's still squiggling."

Many of the ocular orbs blinked, not so much on cue as in absolute panic. What happened next couldn't have been unexpected. In fact, given whom they were dealing with, it should have been predictable. Before Squiggly could make like a tomcat himself and swallow the mishmash thingy, a number of them did a different kind of swallow, a birdie kind of swallow. They exploded out of the mucous-mouse, took wing and attempted to flutter-eye away.

Herta might have been waiting for her opportunity to demonstrate to her heartthrob – the Tomcat of the Tattletail strain, not the torqued Tom of the twisted Torquemada extreme – that she was getting better and better week by week, if not quite yet day by day or hour by hour. As if she'd been practising it for months, she quickly rendered her forearms and hands into her version of a flyswatter. Rather, she rendered them into her version of flypaper; whereupon she promptly swatted the swallowing-eyes stuck to it.

Being daemonic her figure was mutable. Consequently, she wasn't averse to snacking before supper; no doubt figured, mindful of Tom's assurance of a Harm-full main course, that it wouldn't do her any lasting harm. Plus, even though devils as a whole disagreed with her, she also wasn't averse to nibbling on bits and bites of them; their eyeballs in particular.

Of them Byron's Venus, Aphropsyche Morningstar, had ample; hence APM All-Eyes.

========

Minus all but a couple of those eyes, the Dobury's effluvia dissolved into a non-murine mucilage that dribbled onto the table. Deadnunk, formerly Quidnunc then Quid-Quill, scooped the mess up and in the next motion swallowed it. Dead as he was his taste buds must have remained functional to some degree because his face screwed up in enough of a grimace that Squiggly reconsidered accepting the proffered hot dog.

"Give it to the beast," he said second-thoughtfully.

"A dog for a dog," agreed Tatty Tom, evidently liking the idea. He tossed the elongated mouse at Drang. "Don't choke. Or, if you do, do it quietly."

Drang gobbled the critter instantly. He no more choked on it than hound became dachshund. At least he didn't right away.

========

Regardless of whether today's Tatty Tom was all that what was left of his faerie-dusted half-father, Rumour of Lazareme, an incarnation of Jordan *'Quill'* Tethys was wrong when he reckoned the notoriously womanizing, panpipe-playing trickster had just up and vanished beyond the Dome all those decades ago now.

It was definitely something he, the Legendarian Quill, would do of course. Thus, equally so, it was precisely the sort of thing he might reckon rightly, if it was indeed a matter of like father, like son. Which it was, in a manner of speaking, as in when either/or had howsoever-irrationally fallen head-over-heels-backwards in love. He'd vanished because he didn't want to be found anymore: not by Harmony, who was always too cloying for a more than just freedom-lusting rambler like him; backwards because, ultimately, he didn't fall for Harm. He fell for her fleshy eidolon or idealized simulation given a renewed semblance of life.

Tomcat had been faerie-dusted over and over again. That made him a chthonic critter. Herta Heartthrob was at least as much so, albeit far more demonically so than fay-facric-fairly much so. Although initially little more than another of Magnus Minus's leftover mud-monsters, thanks notably to Tom and his very slow to age sponsor, Quoits Tethys, she was also substantially Harmony; as in increasingly large measure her substance.

(Harmony going through the Dome in hopes of relocating the ever-wayward Tattletail and bringing him back to the Dome didn't go unnoticed by the Utopian Hellion and her feeorin allies. Every time Harmony used a Brainrock hearthstone to traverse the Dome, her daemonic body left behind a minute but substantive residue. Quoits had her biomages scrape off this filmy scunge and save it just in case it might come in handy someday.

(It did indeed come in useful, whole bodily as well as just handily. Herta smeared it on as moisturizer whenever, like sugar cubes for a compliant donkey, Quoits deigned to reward her for a good – as in highly contagious – catch beyond the Dome. For her part, Herta reckoned it gave her skin lustre as well as even more of the Unity's memories.)

True, while she had all the animation she'd ever need, she lacked Harmony's essential animus. (No surprise there. Demons, unlike devils, were soulless whereas devils were basically spirit beings. Besides, Tom had promised her just that, the Unity's animus – or at least promised her the opportunity to assimilate it.) True also, her brain remained a work in progress, but demons were always more body than brain.

Her body worked just fine, thank you. And, unlike Harm's equivalent, it wasn't incapable of generating fully physical fruit of their loins' lovemaking. That very fruit, one of what were once, fleetingly, many, but nowadays were only him, chose that moment to flutter into Sraddha's localized protectorate. It wasn't Love per se. It was, however, their latest and thus far longest lasting lovechild.

And he was a be-winged, but hornless cupid – the puta's putto as Squiggly's Deadnunk dad characterized him.

"What is it?" 3-eyed Shreds demanded of the newcomer, Dire's recruiter.

"They're out there, maybe forty or fifty of them, and there's plenty more than just Lazaremists out there. My stomach ache recognized guys and gals, and gal-guys or guy-gals, from all three tribes, including the bloody stupid toad with a bloody stupider mitre on his head. It's like a convention of titans, only most of them are way bigger than titans. Some are way bigger than trees too."

"Is she one?" dead Quid wanted to know, no longer gagging on the Dobury's spume.

"Micro-Mass-Murderous Mistress Misery," the putto replied semi-sarcastically, as well as mostly disrespectfully, "Thy name be Mama Melina nee Tethys Somata? Not that I could see, deadhead. Your half-grandfather Sparky is, though, Shreds. So are the Goat and your other miserable mom, Comes-to-Harm-Harmony."

Reflexively Tatty Tom did his transmogrification trick. A plinth-worthy, godly handsome, golden-haired, green-eyed (albeit without them being as intensely ver-dant as those of the putto) and blue-skinned young man, one those there knew wasn't much of a man at all, replaced the manly moggy. He kept his leopard leotards and jacket, though. Plus, perhaps in deference to the magisterial form he'd taken on, he did make a point of enlarging the codpiece he wore over his tights flatteringly.

"Him too," said the putto, evidently unaware that Thrygragos Lazareme was also Sraddha's *'googly-woogly'* half-father (to quote the truly terrible twins directly). In that regard the Cupid-like self-psychopomp was hardly the only one, though the fact that Zal and Mel's only children could control devils foolish enough to possess them should have made that obvious.

"Harmony will be ever so pleased to see you again," smirked Herta self-pro-nounced Heartthrob, feigning admiration for Tatty Tom's well-practised re-embodi-ment of the Helios-like Great God, aka Thrygragos Everyman. "She'll probably cream her mail in anticipation of linking up with you come tonight."

"With me around she ordinarily wouldn't rust it off; she'd strip it off. But you're right. So long as you're around, my love, it's not me who's going to get into her. It's you."

"Best we get to it then," said Shreds, rising to his feet. Hardly for the first time his right hand glowed as if gloved with a devic power focus, which it was – the Fop's fang-fingered Tvasitar talisman. Pal Squiggly had never before produced a panpipe, however. Nor was he the usual one to sprout an extra eye.

"Better and bitter. Care for a lively marching tune, boys?"

Another thing about devils was that they were really very good at body-bouncing.

========

"That's it?" Sparky sounded surprised at the hoodoo hamlet's lack of size.

"The mist over here and the blue sky over there kind of gives that away for free, Order," Thrygragos Lazareme noted drolly. "Still, it does seem barely a sty on the eye."

"Technically speaking, dad," the Librarian, Biblio Drek as antique Illuminaries of Weir named him, corrected the Great God his father, "A sty's on the eyelid. Sraddha and the Fop's bitty bump of a pimply protectorate is beneath Sedon's Human's Eye. Which, as you may have heard, is the Gulf of Corona and thus watery, hence the spiffy new barques out there."

"So what?" the Great God said, dismissing his observation with a wave. "If the sty offends cut it out, I say."

****

10: Deva-Dand Depilated

5476 Retrospective Perspective

A peculiarity novel to Masters of the Weirdom of Cabalarkon on the once Whole Earth – as distinct from captains of Utopian millennial or generational ships pre-Earth – was that they ruled by unspoken yet implacable consensus. The only real way to tell if they had the support necessary to lord over everyone living within Sedon's Devic Eye-Land was if everything essentially extraterrestrial continued to work properly. It didn't, or stopped while they were ruling, then that was it for their reign. Exit stage exile, as the saying went.

Such was the self-centred mental might of Daddy Cabby's Idiots of Weir, as funnelled through their Masters of same.

It did nothing to ensure their longevity, or comparative lack thereof, though.

========

When he was both alive and a Quill, then a Quit-Quill, Jordan (born Quibble, become Squab then Squib) Tethys claimed no recent commonality of blood with his Missus Master at the time, that of Kanin City. Such a declaration seemed straightforwardly confirmable. Until they died not all that long ago, of one affliction or another, her parents claimed the same thing – on behalf of their parents, dot-ditto. And, one would hope, they should know.

Melina nee Tethys Somata was almost as white as that Quill's son Quidnunc, Mel's Zal of a husband, and most mixed-blood Utopians (admittedly the men more so than the women) in the Hidden Headworld's 55th Century were black or blackish. However, up until maybe a thousand years earlier, Utopian females living in the Weirdom of Kanin City were often almost as white as ambulatory alabaster.

Reputedly they still were in the Weirdom of Cabalarkon; reputedly because, for non-devils, it had been impossible to reach since nearly a year after Star Sedon failed to shine that first night in late Tantalar 4824. In truth, decades passed before anyone except said devils realized the Weirdom hadn't become part of the aptly dubbed Ghostlands any more than Sedon had become a ghost back on that year's Mithramas Day.

Hybrid- and the moderately few pureblood-Utopians dwelling in unaffected areas – such as the Head's Occipital Regions, the Lake and Floodlands (sometimes called Sedon's Brow or Sweat Glands), Apple Isle or Sedon's Cheek, Crown and

Cranium – quickly grew anxious for news of their sometimes quite literal forbearers. They couldn't confirm either their best or their worst scenarios, though, because they could no longer travel there.

First off, in some cases fatally, they discovered that the instinctual, if not necessarily semi-sentient, yet always alive exotics they used to use to fly there on, or with, refused to cross the Ghosts. As Quill Tethys often put it, these exotics might all be somewhat birdlike. However, that did not necessarily mean they were birdbrains.

Suchlike beasties included the great gasbags often called blimps, trained pterosaurs, wyverns or *'vouivres'*, vultyrie, Pegasus-psychopomps (*'pegasi'* being the proper plural {as opposed to the wholly incorrect, but commonly used, Pegasuses} – *'pterippus'*, meaning winged horse, plural *'pterippi'*, was an interchangeable term), the Valkyries' psycho-swans, winged agathodaemons (who, thankfully, were often vegetarian), yazata Angelycs (who were never anything except meat-eaters), and hollow-boned, avian-human garudas, to name a mere smattering of their specialized ilk.

For those who had access to the aforementioned, generally organic, if not (excepting garudas) overly intelligent psychos, ones who could also get there between-space, presume anew. When they went off, the deadly, radiant forces released by the newly christened Idiot or, as accurately, Atomic Twins did much more than rebound off the hastily erected Sedon Sphere around Cabalarkon Eye-Land proper and thereafter spread across the Ghosts' externally. Their thus-released, patently not-just-airborne, radioactive toxins permeated even the dark-grey matter making up the universal substance of Samsara in the Upper Head.

Interminable storms and atmospheric upheavals prevented Utopians reaching Cabalarkon via their Brainrock-powered, VTOL vehicles: the originally extra-terrestrial vimanas they called cosmicars, of which by then very few serviceable ones were left beyond that premier Weirdom. (Vimanas should never be confused with vahanas, the self-psychopomps of sub-continental Indian or, more precisely, Hindu legend.)

Regular mortals died trying to reach it by sea – Fearsome Fobbiat, the Hidden Headworld's western ocean, earned its unappealing modifier. Mortals also died after giving up the attempt and trying to return to from whence they came. Hold hands with a witch and seek to traverse the Weird to previously laid-down stepping-stones? Forget it. Either they didn't work there anymore or, to a one, they'd been gathered up and disposed of in Cabalarkon's astrophysical furnaces.

Immortal devazurs, even second generational Great Gods and their third generational firstborn, the three Unities included, avoided Cabalarkon like the proverbial plague, non-capitalized. (Plague, capitalized, was how devils tended to address an eighth-born Mithradite, the Apocalyptic of Disease – aka Carcinogen the Leper, as old-time Utopians returning from the Outer Earth in the Head's 4th Century named him howsoever luridly.)

Other than at a high-in-the-sky distance, or via far-sent castings of insubstantial facsimiles, they always had for the same simple reason Cabby's morons funnelled their mental might through their Masters in order to power that Weirdom's Mother Machine. That reason? Self-preservation.

Whatever else he, she or betwixt and between may be, even the dimmest devil wasn't that dumb. Unless at least one of their parents was a member of the otherwise disenfranchised Sarpedon underclass, a majority or near-majority of pure U-bloods might well be inbred imbecilic. However, assuming anyone was still alive up there, their Trinondev Warriors Elite would still have functional eye-staves and the eyeorbs that went with them.

Among their plethora of purposes, eyeorbs atop eye-staves did literally devastating duty as devazur prison pods. As Abe Chaos discovered when he scattered his brain into the doofus either he or Magnus Minus made in his likeness then deployed (on the Summer Solstice of 4825) they were just as effective against subtle matter demons. Even the fourth generational, non-devic portion of devazurkind, the lowly azuras themselves, weren't exempt – though, in their case, Utopian Trinondevs usually found the effort required to imprison them too much of a bother.

They didn't want to fill up their precious eyeorbs with the near-useless things, a fate that befell so many of Kanin City's Warriors Elite in the Medusa's Meadow on Thrygragon (emphasis on fell, mostly from great heights, as their cosmicars crashed and burned). They did then they'd have to switch to a fresh bulb before their eye-stave worked properly again.

In a way similarly, once the threat posed by the Death's Head Hellion passed in 4825, most devils didn't feel like sending their genetically loyal, spirit being offspring into Cabalarkon, where they might be sucked out of effective existence. Although not good for much else, azuras did help secure nourishing worshippers for their parents and that, in turn, rendered them too valuable to chance losing so gainlessly.

As devils already knew, found out firsthand from Pyrame Silverstar, some years after Morgan Abyss's misbegotten Mastery ended, or learned second-hand from taletellers, some of whom were neither human nor devazur, the Weirdom had a huge Stopstone-lined vault full of the detachable bulbs; ones that the Devil Sedon showed no inclination to empty until he apparently changed his mind on Mithramas Day 4824. That was precisely why Star Him failed to shine out of the Him Sphere for so many months in a row back then.

The main weapon of a basically homogenous society composed almost exclusively of Hate-Sedon Utopians, unless they were deliberately tuned otherwise via force of will (which they often were in Kanin City until Pyrame's Mithradite successors abolished them decades after Thrygragon), a prison pod triggered the moment it detected a devil within the environs of a Weirdom or, for that matter, anywhere close by (so long as it wasn't in a devic protectorate).

Cabalarkon's remarkably still at least semi-functional approximation of First Weir's Mother Machine also manufactured eyeorbs. That fact negated any opportunity devils might have to altogether eliminate the fabulous fabrications. You couldn't destroy what you couldn't reach; not without risking Cabby the Daddy, that was for sure. And Sedon would never again allow anyone or anything to endanger what was left of his thought-father, he in his tub of life-supporting, but animation-suspending, Cathonic Fluid.

Earth-made eyeorbs had no more effect on Sedon than siphoning seawater into pint bottles would have on an ocean. Be that as it may, the vast majority of prison pods in that Weirdom's Stopstone-lined vault contained Master Devas captured pre-planet. Composed therefore of far sturdier stuff, once vacated they shredded him, the approaching almightiest of mighty devils. Then they confined said shreds automatically, as if confetti gumballs swept simultaneously into dozens of dustbins.

The devils he freed? Them its Mother Machine-manufactured eyeorbs could handle.

========

"I thought you wanted us to dig it out," said Sparky, back to being altogether Lightning Lord Yajur, the Unity of Order.

"Dig, cut, what difference does it make?" snorted his Great God of a father.

========

Like almost all the other devils there, his sister Unity included, Yajur had made himself enormous in order to match (if, circumspectly, not to exceed) Lazareme's uncharacteristically extravagant self-indulgence. Lacking much in the way of imagination, devils were prone to supersize themselves vainly when out and about in public anyways. They loved to awe as much as their worshippers loved being awed. Being the occasional recipient of a wow-factor jolt was addictive. It legitimized the veneration they afforded their consequential devil-gods.

(Generally speaking, the Great God shunned ostentation. Nonetheless, if only to mark the for-him-unprecedented significance of today's anticipated events, he towered above the nearest treetops. Thrygragos Varuna Mithras yielded to just such a height of hubris on Thrygragon and look where it got him – stoned immobile, bodily pulverized, with his head pulped and stuffed in Lazareme's pillowcase on Tympani for well over a thousand years and counting.)

"You lot want to keep your godhood, you have to earn it like never before. Remember, the hopes and prayers of the entire Headworld are with you. Fail and it isn't just your adherents who'll succumb to the endless malignancies brought in here by those over there and their Sedon-cursed leadership, whoever they are. The future of the entire devazur race could be just as fatally fucked up, down, and every which other way you can imagine.

"So bulk up even more, fan out and get to welkin-work."

========

Credit for laying the trap to take Sedon out, as in into dozens of extraterrestrial eyeorbs, belonged to the selfsame, notoriously viperous Master Morgan Abyss.

========

Mythologized only later on as the Death's Head Hellion, she proved as much of a Hate-Sedon fanatic as any properly brought up Utopian of Weir. Nonetheless, with her adopted realm about to suffer the same doom then befalling the Laughing Lands of so many pantheistic paradises, Master Morg faced, for her, two equally detestable choices: release Sedon or die, painfully and slowly, along with most of your people, of incurable radiation poisoning.

While to this day arguments abounded as to why she did it, she chose the first. Whether or not he was aware Cabalarkon (his thought-father) was at that precise minute a *'guest'* of the Lazaremists between-space off Tympani, and therefore no longer in the Weirdom, he promptly saved Cabalarkon (the place) the same as he'd protected the archipelago of Pacifica 4,825 years earlier. He enclosed his forehead's cartographic Eye-Land with some of what part of his essence he wasn't already using to maintain Cathonia.

Then, in typical Sedonic fashion, he ensured she'd also chosen the second, albeit not of radiation poisoning.

As similar as their names sounded, Morgan Abyss probably had no more hint of a Jordan *'Quill'* Tethys within her then than Melina born Tethys did now. She certainly never became a Quill, not that anyone recorded at any rate. Yet, to the best that selfsame anybody knew – or the Legendarian ever acknowledged – a replacement Quill didn't incarnate until a few years after her demise either overtop the northern sector of the Slopes of the Sleepers or upon impacting against them from a long, long way up.

(Then again, from reports provided after the Legendarian confirmed, without ever going there, that Cabalarkon had not become part of the Ghostlands, her body disappeared for what in the end proved to be an easily explicable period of time. Of course, unlike devils Quills could lie. So maybe there was a very brief sort of interregnum during which time she did become the legendary 30-Year Woman. If so, though, Quill not acknowledging it was atypical of him/her.)

Morg also didn't die as readily as any Tethys had died or did die either before or after her. A deadly doctored pin pricked or expelled into his or her chest would (and not so comparatively long ago did) do for him or her straightaway. By contrast, only repeated jolts of lightning did for Master Morg so many centuries ago.

Sometimes what Sedon lacked in creativity he made up for in perseverance.

========

Ah, but did the mighty Moloch never again altogether back in the sky cause the lightning strikes that brought the Death's Head Hellion plunging earthwards, smoking all the way? Might it have been Harmony, her father, one of her brood brothers, or any number of other devils from any one of the three tribes? Did it matter? Not to that Master it didn't.

Not any more than what disease, unless it was just old age, finished off Quoits Tethys's longest serving Master it didn't. Dead may not necessarily be dead on the Hidden Continent of Sedon's Head, not always. But dead was nevertheless still dead in most cases (or coffins, as the case may be).

For the time being anyhow!

========

She might have been deceased already. Perhaps more likely, a spark of life yet lingered when the bolts finally blasted her out of her airborne jalopy – her Battle Beetle or lady buggy, as Morg had it, or her all-eyes contraption, as Quill-Quidnunc termed it much to APM's annoyance hours before Dark Sedon vanished the last time to date.

That she lasted so long, endured so much, came down not to Pyrame Silverstar and her demon; not according to Pyrame it didn't. It came down to six other reasons – namely, to-non-devils, the six Sacred Objects less controversially known as the Thrygragos and Trigregos Talismans: the Mask of Byron, the Cross of Mithras, Lazareme's Cloak of Many Colours, the Amateramirror or Soul of Devaura, the Susasword or Body of Demeter and the Crimson Corona or Mind of Sapiendev.

Wearing or wielding the Great Godly Glories accounted for the well over two-millennia success story of Taurus Chrysaor Attis, the Universal Soldier and, among many another accomplishment, Pusan Wanderlust's equally recurring, deviant father – equally recurring until Thrygragon, that is. The first three almost gave Mithras the victory he so desperately desired on his 4376 Feast Day, whereas the last three damn near did for him.

Wearing or wielding all six allowed Master Morg to make her *'gargoyle'* appear as Faceless Strife in Azky of 4825. (On that year's Hymeneal Day, taletellers would have added, regardless of whether most of their listeners had heard it before. That was when she massacred the non-devils attending Quack Tethys's wedding in what was effectively Djerrid Ruin's protectorate in Goatwood, Sedon's Beard, with a golden apple-bomb: a splatter-packed, anti-personnel grenade prepared in the Weirdom.)

That, instead of Strife's telltale geyser of red hair, she sported a hilt-downwards, crimson blade upwards, substitute for a topknot might have given away the source of her gargoyle. Then again sometimes Master Devas aren't as insightful as they think they are. Moreover, probably no devil save, perhaps, Sedon or Pyrame, both of whom could operate in Weirdoms replete with eyeorbs with impunity, had seen the Susasword since Thrygragon. Besides, even if anyone had, it likely never would have occurred to them that it could have been wielded let alone worn in such a manner.

Were she the taleteller, the Pauper Priestess, once she resurfaced inside of All, Incain's self-proclaimed invincible She-Sphinx, on the Prison Beach years afterwards, would conclude her dissertation, for the time being anyhow, with words to the effect that all six just as likely contributed to the disappearance of Morg's corpse (if not, as she herself eventually discovered, howsoever conveniently, its complete absence).

As a Master Deva, Pyrame could no more manufacture what she thereupon claimed was the truth than she could knowingly disseminate unqualified falsehoods. However, her evidently still at least partially be-brained demon could, especially if it was dominant when she finally returned to the Prison Beach from the Outer Earth. In many respects it was therefore fortunate for the Sed-sons' lone known mom that there was some support for her rendition of reality.

The Thanatoids of Lathakra may be forevermore moribund (after barely surviving the Atomic Twins exploding), but their friends weren't – and their friends (notably the extremely powerful firstborns, Abe Chaos and the Silverclouds of Thrygragos Byron) weren't always favourably inclined towards Pyrame.

Additionally, jealous of Sedon's affection for her, not them, neither of Strife's remaining, second-born brood sisters (the Apple Goddesses Divine Coueranna and Lady Lust) counted themselves fans of hers. Potentially even more humiliatingly, as a ninth-born she was vulnerable to dominance by every Mithradite senior to her: among them the likes of the male Nergalids, the male Apocalyptics, and the Reptilians of Sedon's Brow, all of whom lost vast numbers of their followers when the Atomic or Idiot Twins went off.

Quill Tethys, the legendary 30-Year Man, or Woman, was hardly the only person who could read tee-tee tails recounting the essential chain of events. He certainly wasn't the only one who could hear a tee-tee vocalize the tale whenever somebody pulled its tail and thereafter listened to it speak. Since tee-tees were, in all likelihood, daemonic, it further stood to reason that their oft-repeated, and notably consistent, versions of what happened once Morg was blasted out of her lady buggy by bolts released by whomever were largely factual.

If tee-tees or their tails could count as verification, the Pauper Priestess's corollary assertion that Morg, abetted by the Six Great Godly Glories, was, one hundred percent, the blameworthy party (for enraging the Thanatoids with her empyrean vessels) rang true. Furthermore, her attestations coupled with corroboratory explanations relayed by tee-tees, one way or another, not only absolved her and/or her demon of culpability for what the Idiot Twins did to the Upper Head, and so many of its inhabitants, it made sense.

Tantal and Methandra Thanatos should have called off their armies, plain and simple.

========

Sraddha Somata, possessed as he had been by Faustus Vladuca ever since his 18th birthday, along with those who'd come with him from Kanin City, came across the then typically fog-covered hoodoo hamlet (where they thereafter hunkered down to build their ships) during the Mithradic Quadrant of 5474 YD. Many of those his father and mother sent with him were carpenters, lumberjacks and shipwrights who'd learned their trade on the other side of Marutia, on the shores of the Aural Sea.

They didn't need to be any of that to be struck by one thing more than anything else. The coastal village, with its suspiciously out-of-place hoodoos, already had metalworkers.

Finally, after months of searching, they'd crossed the boundary of Time-Quakes.

========

If the lightning bolts that riveted Morg, over and over again, hadn't done for her already, then surely hitting the ground from such a height must have. On the other hand, if she somehow still breathed, then the Head's fabulously female Perpetual Presence (adult) was right. As beneficial as devic possession often was, even Pyrame and/or her demon (be it Primeval Lilith, who or whatever) couldn't have kept her alive after such a drop.

As for what happened next, power foci allowed anyone wielding them to slash through between-space. That much was irrefutable.

Soon after the Spring Equinox beginning of the extraordinary year of 4825, Pyrame petitioned Thrygragos Lazareme to resurrect the Daemonicus wannabe, Magnus Minus, a debauched demiurge if ever there was one. The Great God assigned Unholy Abaddon, the Unity of Chaos, the task. Admiral Abe, as Pyrame thereafter started referring to him, succeeded admirably as well. Together, he and the dipsomaniac monster-maker did much more than craft the simulacrum that so trashed Master Morg's long-planned marriage to Tomcat Tattletail came the Summer Solstice.

(That would be aka-Squirrelly, the chthonic creep whom she had faeriedust-resuscitated just that morning. The night before – a night not so much moonlit as Byron-lit – Q-Troupe's troublesome troubadour had been playing Dame Chance's Triskelion, morphed into a set of panpipes, for Quiff Tethys and members of the Sarpedon underclass in the Masters Glade. Very much intent upon spoiling their fun, Thrygragos Everyman far-sent his phantasmal self there for an equally electrifying encounter with Terribly Terrific Tom, he centuries pre-Tatty.)

As a latter day Daemonicus, the minutely mighty Minotaurus of Minius (after himself) felt obliged to fashion himself some suitably simpering subjects to oppress. After all, what was the point of being a bull-headed, not to mention bull-balled, demon king if you didn't have any lack-wit lickspittle to trod into the dirt beneath your feet – or paws, as the saddlebag may be. Just as much so, every demon king, taurine or otherwise, should have a demon queen, bovine or not. So he made himself a selection of concupiscent concubines to try out; made some for Abe Chaos to sample as well.

Abe quickly set his mind on a solitary offering thus obtainable from Minus's unnatural smorgasbord. She was, naturally, the spitting image of Harmony. Who else?

After, for Chaos, the borderline disaster of Midsummer's Day – absolute disaster for that fissile fusion of Tom-Squirrelly and an irrevocable one for his undercoating, Quiff Tethys – he left her behind. At that point, appearances deceiving, the mighty Minotaurus proved himself not entirely a twit-nit and took her over, as well as in every other manner imaginable, under, sideways and down included. The oversized genitalia he'd given himself ever-so-egocentrically had never been put to more enjoyable use.

Far more importantly for Magnus Minus in terms terminal, Abe Chaos never came back to Minius after that Solstice Day. Neither did he delegate anyone else to return there in order to replenish the supply of pilsners that he, on Pyrame's instructions, employed to resurrect him not so much in the first place as in the howsoever-many centuries it had been since the last time he'd been up and rutting. (Or running, put less entertainingly.)

So it was that, more than five months later, the by then far more mightily minute Minotaurus was subsisting mostly on fumes. As for his not-quite-as-malicious minions (compared to Morg's Satanwyck recruits of the previous winter, in particular the highly inflammatory ones in Grand Elysium on New Years Eve), nary a ungodly underling was more than an inanimate lump.

Add the Harmony husk to those he'd breathed life into in true, demiurgic fashion – the conflations that had survived the conflagration Hot Stuff (Miss Myth, Methandra Thanatos) set off in Satanwyck's extension of the Upper Head's Hell-Well on Lunasa Day, once it finally burnt itself out weeks later in Absudyl/Minius. His by then, again, self-made-official Demon Queen was, however, much more provocatively preserved than any of the others.

She was still shiny-smooth and scarcely smouldering, emphasis on scarcely. Minus, like Abe once his father insisted he break from the Thanatoids, wasn't much interested in tantalization. There was no need for disrobing if you hadn't bothered to fashion much in the way of clothing to start. All Minus really needed to get her going again, besides more beer for himself, was a spark of life.

As Lazareme aphorized decades before he heard Pyrame's version of events, let alone read or heard any tee-tee's pretty much dot-ditto: *'Fortune favours flukiness'*. Come that year's Samhain, just that, a spark of at least half-life, fell out of the sky. Rather, Absudyl/Minius being underground, it fell through its ceiling, underneath the Hills or Slopes of the Sleepers.

Magnus was as-yet-unaccountably drawn to it; whereupon he brought it back to his bullring (as Abe Chaos jokingly referred to the circular, beehive-like pavilion Minus constructed to become his palace). There he somehow or other transferred it to the Harmony husk. No doubt much merriment, not to mention happy hump-ing, ensued. Or had done prior to Pyrame venturing downstairs into Minius where she retrieved Morg's body, the six Godly Glories with it.

To hear her tell it, once she brought her corpse back to the surface, Utopians cremated it on a pyre (not a Pyrame), the ashes to sprinkle on some wannabe Master-in-waiting, albeit with no faerie-noticeable effect. The Thrygragos and Trigregos Talismans, again to hear her tell it, she re-deposited in the Weirdom's Stopstone vault, along with eyeorbs containing all the recaptured devils and the empty-again, extraterrestrial prison pods that used to hold the fabulously male (always adult) Perpetual Presence.

As for the devils' approaching-almighty All-Father, once they both returned to the Inner Earth he, Sedon, went visibly back into the night's sky, a dark star no longer.

========

Responsive – notwithstanding Harmony's pumping for Panharmonium – to the Great God whose age this was, the devils did just that. They fanned out.

So Old-Growth-massive had they made themselves, it must have looked to those in the surprisingly sunny coastal hamlet, particularly to those who were standing lookout atop the stumpy hill around which the town was built, as if a ribbon of forest had up and marched around them. And it had, up to and, in a few cases, root, branch and tree trunk deep in the peripheral tide line.

The instructions came from Thrygragos Everyman but their look had to have come from Djerrid Ruin, Byron's Bowman. The dig-it-out bit, that undoubtedly derived from Zuvem Nergalis, the devic Planter, aka also Gravedigger. The sincerest form of flattery and/or imitative words to that effect, Lazareme might have been thinking about coining.

Just before everything went not so much pear-shaped as out of sight, if not mind.

========

Pass forward hundreds of years.

Magnus Minus had long ago shrunk out of noteworthy prominence yet again. Before doing so he must have happily humped the spark that animated his Demon Queen right out of her skull. It must have come out complete with a face showing disappointment, not delight, because that's what Tomcat Tattletail came across all those centuries later when he ventured below Cabalarkon with his superior, the elderly but still remarkably spritely Quoits Tethys.

In terms classificatory, it had to be some sort of calcified soul sink similar, if not identical, to the crystal skulls Hellions, Valkyries and Rakshas demons used to carry around Sangazur spirit-selves, an adder- or hag-stone, a druid's Gnostic egg, or the acorns a jilted dryad tried to use against Quill Tethys on Thrygragon. This one was shaped like an almond (called a *'vesica piscis'* beyond the Dome) and had said sad face still etched upon it.

It must have landed right in front of the Harmony husk, suddenly both inanimate and faceless (ironically just like Strife), whereupon it was abandoned. Must have, because that's where he spotted it. Since, having a face, no matter how heartache-sad, it seemed to belong there, he experimentally slotted it right back into the otherwise featureless protuberance plopped atop the neck- and shoulders-like formations surmounting her barely deteriorated torso.

Tomcat Tattletail must be something of an until-then-unrealized demiurge himself. Like a binary weapon along the lines of a Utopian eye-stave and the eyeorb atop it, re-inserting it did the trick. She instantly filled out both bodily and facially, bounteously and beautifully dot-ditto. She did much more than just reactivate, too. She started right back doing what she must have been busy doing with Magnus Minus when he humped her face off.

She did him, swiftly tumescent Tom, right there on the cold, earthen floor of Subterranean Absudyl. Did him so unforgettably passionately, they'd been a couple ever since.

========

Antheal 30, 5476 YD – The Garden of Earthy Delights, Coast of Corona

The puta's putto had lasted as long as it had not because Herta and Tomcat were getting better and better at whelping them. It had lasted so long because it had a particularly tasty meal shortly after Heartthrob bore him. That meal was why he'd developed so many handy bents – particularly useful being the one that let him smell out contagion-carriers on the Outer Earth.

"Um, boss," the anything-but-stupid cupid put to 3-eyed Squiggly, "I wasn't kidding about the tree-topping titans. You march out of here, won't they recognize you right away?"

"Not envious are you?"

"Well, yes, but besides that ... "

"As you should appreciate more than most, I prefer my daemonic bodies debrained."

========

The Fop, Faustus Vladuca, had been in Grand Elysium on Lilith Eve, as some devils came to call the slaughterhouse of a furnace they ignited on New Years Eve in 4824/5. He'd heard Harmony's cry: "Don't blast them – bugger off!" But, it not coming from his father, he'd been among the many who paid her no immediate heed.

Sooth said, even though he almost instantly realized they were inadvertently immolating innocent, worship-filled sentient beings, he was among the few who kept blasting away. He was a Black Godling. He reckoned sacrificing animals to devil-gods like himself was just fine. Besides, they weren't self-cathonitizing for their dire deeds, so why stop?

(Devils being devils, they derisively derived the term Lilith Eve from an inspired meshing of Adam's first wife in Hebrew folklore, Primeval Lilith, and Adam's second wife, the one formed from his rib, whose name the Outer Earth's Book Byblos gave as Eve. They were motivated to do so because incendiary but non-individualized proto-daemons, like those the fabled Demon Queen of the Night must have ruled alongside King Daemonicus centuries prior to the Sedonshem landing atop Kanin City, in the year 669 pre-Dome, coated the conurbation as if with wight-whitewash.

(As far as the Legendarian was concerned, that devils set off these proto-demons with reflexive bursts of eyefire didn't cost them the right to be worshiped as gods or goddesses. Not stopping the moment they realized what they were doing to those mortals caught up in the baleful blaze resulting did.)

The Fop had also heard the Thanatoids' subsequent injunction to abandon Elysium and reconvene in the Medusa's Meadow, hundreds of miles to the southeast in Sedon's Mole. He heeded them, reluctantly, but he still didn't flee immediately. That meant he witnessed how the firstborns dealt with the drone-bombers, sent from wherever, that were adding to the inferno devils started with their eyefire.

Belatedly, if only to see if he could do it too, he'd even joined them in taking out, and taking into themselves, the Brainrock (or Gypsium) fuel the drones used for propulsion. That not only stopped said drones dropping their incendiary loads, it dropped them. It was also something he never forgot.

And if he never forgot it then his shell (who was actually controlling him, not the other way around, the way it should be) had no difficulty formulating a counter-stroke appropriate to the enemy. The mass of Master Devas Thrygragos Lazareme gathered at his side just beyond his hamlet-sized port-protectorate on the Gulf of Corona's generally misty shoreline had much the same weakness Utopian Trinon-devs did. They relied on one weapon to the exclusion of others.

And devic power foci were composed of the same miraculous Godstuff that fuelled the drone-bombers overtop of Grand Elysium all those centuries ago.

========

"What the fuck!"
The curse erupted out of Zuvem Nergalis, the Nergalids' fourth-born Planter, the first to dig his Brainrock spade into the turf within the environs of Shreds' protectorate. His spade's blade-end had just vanished. Too late other devils who'd ventured too close to the hoodoo-hamlet lost the bulk of their transformed power foci doing exactly the same thing.
"To me!" cried Thrygragos Lazareme.

========

To him dozens of the luckily faraway ones, many carrying their shell-shocked and therefore unluckily too close brothers and sisters, did just that.

(Devils didn't instantly revert to spirit beings when their power foci vanished. There would have been no need for ringots if they did – disarm or wipe out their Tvasitar talismans and, so long as you wore a witch-stone or something similarly ensorcelled against possession you'd never have to worry about the despicable extra-terrestrials. Likewise, just because most of their talismans disappeared that didn't mean all of them did.)

The Great God shrank back to his normal, human-size. So too did those flank-ing him, his two firstborn there, the Unities of Order and Balance. Biblio Drek and Pusan Wanderlust, who'd led Yajur-Sparky, Thrygragos Lazareme and Djerrid Ruin through the Weird from the DDD, were the first to reach his side.

Pusan hadn't bothered to increase her size; hadn't even bothered with an illu-sionary enlargement. While that didn't indicate she wasn't possessed, it didn't mean she was either. However, she'd been around long enough to be as aware as the others were as to what had just transpired.

"Perhaps you should have knocked," she suggested, completely uncowed by the company she was keeping. (Of course, faunas being more goat than much of anything else, except humanoid, she probably couldn't have been cowed anyhow.)

"Or sent a heliodromus in first," Lazareme's lily-livered Librarian, his 3-lens power focus still firmly perched on his nose, proposed, albeit for the first time out loud. As the other fifty or more devil-gods who'd come to the outskirts of what appeared to be a boat-builders' howsoever incongruously bright village returned to the Great God's side, Drek added: "Maybe we could have negotiated a way out of this mess."

"You can't negotiate with heartless fanatics," Lord Yajur snorted. "Not when they're intent upon wiping out all life in here. Father was right to seek to wipe them out first."

"That wasn't my intention," Lazareme begged to differ. "Forget how clear it is over there and how misty it is over here, Order. Look at the town; look at the buildings, not the beehive tholoi or fairy chimneys or whatever they're called."

"Differential erosion," said the know-it-all Librarian. "Sandstone hoodoos are caused by differential erosion. Except they're not usually found on the coast."

"Precisely what I'm getting at," said Lazareme, showing remarkable restraint. Almost no one besides firstborns would ordinarily dare to interrupt a Great God. "The Fop, through Shreds, accounts for the sunshine. Mithradites witch weather all the time in their protectorates. It's about the only trick they can get away with on a regular basis. So there's no real reason we Lazaremists can't either."

"If we had protectorates," said Yajur.

(While Lazaremists, particularly on Chaos's Cattail Peninsula and in Order's occipital region, had spheres of influence, they didn't have protectorates per se.)

"Just so. Likewise Shreds, the Fop, and those who came with them from Kanin City might have built the ships out there, but they didn't build this place. It's plainly been here too long for that. And if that oversexed tit on the shore doesn't tell you who did, it should at least tell you why they chose this spot. Fucking faeries are tremendously accommodating hosts when they put their minds to it. Outsiders give them folks to fuck with besides each other."

"The hill's a fairy mound," Yajur twigged.

"So are the hoodoos I'm thinking, at least they're shaped by faeries."

"That's what Abe was saying back in Kanin," Datong Harmonia, the Unity officially of just that, Harmony, recalled.

"Kudos for Chaos then," Lazareme half-heartedly applauded. "Fairies are fickle, prone to impulsiveness. They like to be entertained, though. And, if only because they're such wilfully credulous vapour-heads, Outer Earthlings have always had tremendous entertainment value. But faeries are also creatures of habit; they've lazy brains, tend to do the same things over and over again, as if by ridiculous rote. That was fun once, let's do it again. I call it spontaneous redundancy for dunce-cap dummies."

"You would," said Harmony.

"Indeed I would. These guys have been at it for so long, they're stuck in a rut. A good soaking's the best wakeup call there is. Toss the sods into the sea, sod and all, and they'd soon see the error of their ways. At least that's how I had it reckoned. Yet even the best laid plans of gods can sometimes go the way of men – into the dumpster, if not the drink; at least not immediately. I see that now. Faeries aren't the real problem; not anymore they aren't."

The Great God turned to address the first born of his eldest threesome directly. "You see the predicament we're in, Harm?" Everyman demanded of her. "By constraints made explicit by your Panharmonium Accord, devic protectorates are inviolable. Does the Fop's constitute a devic protectorate? Does it especially when it's Shreds controlling him rather than the other way round? Or does it just because we've obliged ourselves to leave them alone?

"Well, we've our answers now. They're inviolable because the dandy devils internally worshipped within them thereby gain the power to enforce their inviolability. Much the same thing happens in a proper Weirdom or on a Utopian millennial ship, assuming there still are such things travelling the stars. I've said it before and I'll say it again: Mental might makes minnows into mega-sharks when they concentrate collectively."

"Don't be such a wiener," Harmonia responded, howsoever rudely. "My own patently preposterous pretensions aside, it's still at least nominally your age, dad. For the sake of the Head, you say that isn't the fish boat, it isn't."

"Well, whatever else we've accomplished," Pusan observed, inclining her altogether-intact shepherd's crook towards the township. "It looks like we've got their attention."

Like ants from an anthill they were filing out of the main mound, the dozens of wooden shacks and the ages-old hoodoo habitations. Perhaps a third of them were grotesque freaks, though not all of these were chthonic critters. Some, like the big-footed monopods known as Skiapods and the headless, topless, but never faceless (since their faces were on their chests) Blemmyes weren't daemons or faeries. Indeed, both were reported as then still extant human species by Pliny the Elder in the 1st Century of the modern era on the Outer Earth.

Similarly, while many definitely were earthborn nasties, a stunning amount of those heading towards them might have stepped out of mediaeval bestiaries still popular beyond the Dome. It being just across the Gulf of Corona, Sedon's Human Eye, from Apple Isle, where all manner of the Hidden Headworld's exotics coexisted in remarkable concord, for a Mithradite protectorate, a strong minority of these oddities were fairly non-faerie familiar. There were even a few Saurs among them.

As for the centaurs formerly of the Iraxas Peninsula (Sedon's Mutton Chop), their Byronic devil-god, ever-changing Chimaera (Glimmenmare), was among those returning to Thrygragos Lazareme's side minus most of his power focus. (Ordinarily a multi-spiked club or mace on a rigid shaft, it wasn't precisely a *'Morgenstern'* or *'morning star'*, a flail weapon better known as a *'holy water sprinkler'* like that wielded by Krepusyl Evenstar, who didn't appear to be there, but it wasn't faraway.)

Regardless of their pedigree, hundreds of the thousand or so coming their direction looked altogether human. As if hearing the same, inner-ears-only command as the faerie farts and the likely outsiders, a few were naked, evidently having been roused while in the act of arousal, be it with fruit or otherwise. Many more wore clothes, though.

Some – like the boy Dire, who'd been in the Danq, albeit without the dog sidling along beside him – were children. Not to put the Judge Druj lie to observations Harmony and the Librarian made while considering Squiggly's squiggles back in Kanin City, however, a huge plurality looked to be adults. Many also had white skin, the same as the preponderance of those living in the Outer Earth continent of Europe. Of these, most of the men had beards and long, shaggy hair.

Be they male or female, all had two eyes. (Of course that didn't mean no one was possessed.) No matter how rumpled, shabby and worn out it appeared, Pusan approved of their woollen clothing. Plenty of presumably local Marutians had joined those advancing towards the devils gathered on the outskirts of the hamlet. Indeed, not surprisingly given they were virtually in the Grey Land of Twilight, with the Mastery's border not far to the east, suchlike made up the vast majority of the marchers.

Although collectively a much more heterogeneous-looking part of the approaching mob, a goodly proportion of the men amongst them were unusually tall, black-skinned, clean shaven, and lanky. By contrast many of the women on the face of it walking alongside the ebon stringbeans were shorter, starkly whiter and noticeably statuesque, in all senses of the word.

The greater fraction of these men and women wore bucolic brown robes, just like the locals and many of the outsiders, but some had blue, or bluish, linen tatters sticking out from underneath their rustic garments. A few had hoods pulled up and a few less even had telltale veils drawn. To a one they carried oddly metallic-looking staffs, albeit without anything orb-, eye- or egg-like topping them. Who they were, and where they might have come from, may have registered with some of the more with it devils, though not with very many of them.

Harmony was too busy double-taking to count among the perspicacious.

========

One day, or days, Bosco had already vowed, he'd paint perhaps only a portion of the sights he'd witnessed in this garden of earthy delights since he arrived here from Den Bosch. They'd include the fruit-fuckers, the oversized fruit they fucked, the hoodoo-tholoi, red, blue, yellow, whatever colour they woke up with that morning.

There'd be the huge musical instruments, some with bodies appended to them. There'd be dancing legs with the torsos of birds or more fruit. There'd be men without torsos, just legs and a head. There'd be two legged, furry and cynocephalic dog men, feline moras or ieles with fangs and/or claws that were more wolf-like than catlike, weasels that strutted around upright, birds he rode even though they were no bigger than the birds at home. There'd be the dobury, the multi-eyed mice and there'd be Tatty Tom, swallowing the fishy one.

This last, currently Harmony's idea of what her father should look like, a blue-skinned actual Apollo with sun-blond hair, strutted peacock-proudly at their head. That her father was standing beside her wasn't what tipped her off it wasn't the Great God. Neither was the fact that he only had two eyes. It was the beating of her howsoever-daemonic heart.

And it still went thump, thump, thump; not dump the dummy, dumbbell.

========

She knew him. She loved him. He was Tomcat Tattletail, he whom she kept going beyond the Dome to find, and be with, all those decades ago.

And striding, not flying, right beside Tomcat was, except for the wings, peahen-her.

****

11: Q for Key

·*"Uh, oh," someone said – someone stepping out of the Weird on the opposite side of Harmony from Thrygragos Lazareme and Lightning Lord Yajur.*

========

The lone female Unity instantly recognized the voice. Lazareme and Order did too. She whirled but their father spoke before she could. "About time you got here, Abe."

"Thought you weren't coming," said the Librarian.

Biblio Drek, as antique Illuminaries had him, was standing just behind the now front four with Pusan Wanderlust, as her parents had her. Beside her was an ever-changing Byronic, a second-born Nucleoid currently in the form of a centaur. Currently also a mare despite often being referred to as Byron's Stallion, he was using his human hands to swat at what wasn't precisely a horsefly; was in fact a flying eyeball, aka a flutter-eye or, sometimes, a little angel. It seemed to be shuddering. What it was actually doing was transmitting.

"I'm Chaos," Unholy Abaddon started to answer his much younger brother. "I changed my mind. What did you expect I'd do – remain resolute?" Before he could explain anything further (or not, as was the more likely scenario), his golden-gorgeous brood sister, at least outwardly not quite yet in Nemesis reds and blacks, demanded a different one.

"Uh, oh?"

"I kind of forgot about her," he admitted sheepishly.

(In doing so he thus established, once and for all time, not to mention against all odds, that a massive, near-naked, ten-foot tall, bloody-skinned barbarian berserker, one who had a big, seriously unkempt, black beard, tangles of hopelessly entwined hair stretching past his shoulder blades, with a half-circle of lit sparklers sticking out of it, and carrying a right royally wicked-looking trident that glowed positively volcanically, could look sheepish.)

"The wings are a nice touch, though; never thought to add wings. Bullring already had down cushions, or reasonable facsimiles."

"You made that?" Her expression darkened; her skin tone colouring towards the reddish aspect of the spectrum. Nemesis wasn't far away now. "In a bloody bullring?"

"A ring of bullshit if you prefer, of the mightily misanthropic Minotaurus variety ... What would you call it – a subterranean Stonehenge for doltish demiurges, a boneheads' bedlam beneath the bedrock, a barfing beer bucket for baloney brains, a chthonic Colosseum for cretinous cabbages, a Hell-Well honey house for severely soused simpletons?

"I did, all of the above and moronic more." Standing on the Twilight side of the divide between misty grey and clear blue sky, he couldn't help fay-saying. "Was days' drunk, wasn't I. And, before you start getting purple-puss-pissed, Harm, I had parental permission to boot; better make that to booze. Besides, it was five or six centuries ago."

"For fuck's sake," muttered Pusan Wanderlust.

"Predominantly," Chaos confirmed, borderline predictably, as Lazareme and Yajur, having finally figured out what both Harmony and Pusan already had, exchanged silent glances.

Neither dared speak. Personally painfully mindful of Harmony's tendency to thrash out with her broken-ended chains when she was applecart-upset, neither even smiled. Devils could, however, read minds. It required no small measure of concentration, though, and fortunately for the rest of them, right this minute she seemed to be concentrating very hard on maintaining what little was left of her cool.

"I see," said Harmony, apparently having succeeded – though she might have been assaying a weak joke from the letters I and C, meaning intercourse. "Then you deal with her."

"Gladly," Abaddon agreed, happy for the reprieve.

"No," countermanded their impossible-to-disobey father, who had himself weathered a wealth of welts wrought from the lash of the lass's wrath, to non-vocally fay-say some. Which was hard not to do when standing in Twilight (as twilight itself descended on the Head's not quite farthest west coast).

The Great God was as aware as Harmony must have been – but, having just come from making a display of himself in Kanin City, Chaos would not have been – as to what had just happened to so many of their fellow devils and their Brainrock power foci. His use of command mode was therefore perfectly in keeping with the situation. Harm, he must have reckoned, without having to read her mind, hadn't lost her cool; she'd gone completely cold.

She was so angry she'd willingly sacrifice her unholy brother for his, to her, inexcusable temerity. But what if Shreds-Vladuca could absorb his trident, its sheathe, but not his actual Tvasitar talisman, the Chaos Blade itself? Might thereby baring it be the same as if Abe had actually drawn it. Would it precipitate the end of everything as so many feared?

He hated ordering anyone to do anything but his unequivocal 'no' seemed to him in no way avoidable given the circumstances. So was something else – Plan B. "Evenstar," Lazareme put to Pusan, sounding nevertheless reluctant. "Twilight's as good as your protectorate. So you're forever telling me anyhow. Prove it, eject that sty beneath the eye into the gulf and you can have it unconditionally, with my blessing."

   (Lightning Lord Yajur, as Sparky, had wondered rightly when he suspected she was possessed. What he would have wondered wrongly was whether his father would ever grant any of his children leave to set up their own inviolable protectorate. Freedom of movement, as well as of worship, was the Lazaremist way. Until now it was, that is.)

Pusan nodded, sprouted a third eye but, as if having second thoughts, hesitated before Krepusyl Evenstar – Lazareme's Venus, who, back when Twilight was Daybreak and therefore on the other side of the Hidden Headworld, was once Mariamne Dawnstar – fully manifested herself. Goats could be as stubborn as donkeys.

"All that'll prove is faeries don't worship anyone, which we already know. Mind you, we might learn if they and their fellow fuckups are better at swimming than drowning."

"Don't be too sure of that," provoked Yajur, demonstrating a cunning intelligence akin to that of his libertine, more so than libertarian, father. He was three-eyeing Thrygragos Everyman – Every God? – ever so tellingly. In the usual scheme of things fathers challenged their sons, not the other around. Lazaremists, though, were natural-born contrarians.

"Time for Plan C I guess," said-dad mumbled louder than he probably wanted – taking hints, especially when they were more like risks, was something else he hated to do. "C as in could-be-calamitous."

"How about could-be-cavalry?" inquired the centaur, just as he (once again a he, rather) morphed into a wings-flapping seabra.

   (A form of seahorse native to Akadan, the Hidden Headworld's interior ocean, which lay south of Iraxas, between the Cattail Peninsula and the Godbadian subcontinent, seabras generally had fishy back-ends for front legs but horsy back ones. His, ex-hers, had sandy brown colouring with zebra-like stripes on the head and shoulders. The Nucleoid added flapping wings in order to keep from flopping about the ground like the proverbial Piscine out of water.)

"Horses scare the crap out of commoners, even centaur commoners, but seriously spooky psychopomps are even more terrifying. If you're equestrian-inclined thusly, you're in luck. I just happen to have a most nightmarish assortment of psychotic equines with me between-space. They're going begging, so speak now and they're yours for a scream."

Chimaera Glimmenmare, as Illuminaries had him, or her, had had enough time to read, if he had the nerve, his uncle's mind. Even if he hadn't, the cyclopean horsefly (in terms of eyeballs, one, not size) he'd reflexively attempted to squash had managed to impart enough details re what was really going on in the hoodoo hamlet for him to realize what Lazareme had to do.

"Thanks for the offer," the Great God responded, having heard much the same telepathic urging to take action unilaterally. "We'll have four of your finest. Make them pegasi instead of ankle-soars. If memory serves, they're cathonitizers."

"Pterippi," the Librarian corrected his father, to no noticeable effect.

"Not to mention extinct," Chimaera contributed, completely ignoring Drek.

"Not to mention," Lazareme repeated, regarding Chaos uncertainly.

(Omnivore ankle-soars – as opposed to herbivore ankylosaurs, who were quad-ruped dinosaurs most commonly found in the Floodlands, the protectorate of the Mithradite Reptilian Klizarod Rex, yet another who'd just lost most of his power focus – had bitty wings called talarias on their ankles, which were properly called fetlocks.

(Lazareme had likely been referring to ravendeer. Larger than most horses when fully grown, they did indeed have the wings of Hermes or Mercury on their upper hooves. They hadn't been wiped out, though; not altogether. Sooth said, interrelated families of the exotic leftovers from the pre-Dome Golden Age of Humankind still roamed the Whiplash Range just above the Prison Beach of Incain. Howsoever iron-ically, Chaos kept suchlike sustainable herds viable so he could hunt the big bucks more so than the docile does at his leisure.

(Nonetheless, Chimaera was half-right. The ones that could grow telescopic unicorn horns, which was what made them cathonitizers prior to circa 3500 YD, after which time devils did hunt them nigh unto extinction, could no longer be found on the Inner Earth of Sedon's Head. As for whether they were found any-where else, that he didn't want to know.)

"Prefer any particular colour?"

"I believe white, black, red and pale are stipulated for suchlike silliness."

"Read my mind, didn't you."

"Didn't need to, Nucleoid. Besides, reading always puts me to sleep and right now we need to more than just look lively."

========

Unlike many devils – though not unlike his scrumptious first of three first-born, she of the female persuasion, and, astonishing to some, not unlike a number of Byronics either (apparently they were still worshipped in the huge continental landmasses he, like the time-tumbling Dual Entities, called the Americas for some reason; hence Chimaera autonomously mimicking a quagga rather than a zebra when he made himself into a winged seabra) – Thrygragos Lazareme had read the Outer Earth Book of Byblos.

He consequently recalled Revelations (more correctly the Revelation of St John the Divine), from whence latter day Illuminaries (early in the 5th Millennium of the Dome) derived Chaos's name, Unholy Abaddon, after centuries of failing to agree on a more fitting moniker for him. (Because of the trident, they could have gone for Shiva or Shankar, or quirky variations thereof. But the notion of an extremely highborn devil whose alternative appellation would therefore be *'Destroyer of Worlds'* presumably tempted fate too much for their taste.)

Chimaera may or may not still be worshipped out there. Where he might be worshipped, in these Americas, may or may not have seen a copy of this Bible as yet. But he had heard of what it contained. Thanks to Pyrame Silverstar, the Legendarian and Harmony, among others, copies of it were printed in here, so he may well have read it himself. Obviously certain other devils had because Lazareme was hardly the first to request those particular colours.

In the monotheists' Bible, conquest rides a white horse; war a red horse; fam-ine a black horse; and plague a sickly pale green horse named Death. In devic terms, the male and female Apocalyptics were Mithradites. In that context, conquest was likely Catastrophe or Disaster whereas, while there was a Famine (Calcutta Famish to Illuminaries), these days the fourth equestrian harbinger of doomsday would be a different Death (the rider not the ridden, sickly or otherwise). That would be the gorgon Harmony disparagingly dubbed Mundane Murder, the Primary Apocalyptics' acknowledged favourite since Thrygragon.

As exemplified by Famine and the much later-born Medusa (who started calling herself Mater Matare, Mother Murder, upon her release from All of Incain earlier that Mithramas Day in 4376), the Apocalyptics actually numbered a few more than four. The head horrors, who were resolutely male, weren't overly pleased to be lumped in with their juniors, sisters the loathsome load of them. They liked to stand out from the rest of their properly branded-baleful brethren.

Anticipating Lazareme might call upon them to join in the inevitable mass mayhem everyone figured was coming, they huddled amongst themselves and decided to indulge their inbred flair for the dramatic. They therefore asked Chimaera to provide them mounts appropriate to the task. Appreciating that if wishes were horses, there'd be a stampede, but no fraught flying after frightful faeries, he brought them seriously spooky psychopomps instead.

Then, Lazareme's Plan A having less terminal consequences than most of Chimaera's siblings and cousins presupposed it would, War (Mars Bellona, whose head was skinless), Plague (Carcinogen the Leper, whose head was bandaged like a mummy, as was the rest of his body), Death (the Medusa, Mater Matare, whose stone-staring, putative head the female Unity confiscated in the aftermath of Thrygragon) and Catastrophe (Nakba Ramazar, who had no head whatsoever) went and got most of their nominal power foci absorbed by whomever.

As a result, they would not be charging into any upcoming slaughter, let alone on any chargers, spooky or otherwise; not if they were smart they wouldn't. On the contrary, depending on how much of their Tvasitar talismans were left they'd more likely be fleeing it – if they could. Still, psychos chomping at the bit to get going might mean he'd be the one to get bit first.

Waste not, eh wot, Chimaera aphorized internally, echoing Lazareme.

========

"Four," Lord Yajur all but groaned.

"You don't think I'm going in there alone, do you?" the Great God said to his first-born.

"Actually," he responded, "That's precisely what I thought."

"More fool you then," Harm contributed chillily. "When it comes to following orders, thinking isn't a option. I'd have thought you'd have appreciated that better than anyone, Order."

========

Having been informed some time ago by sister APM (a third-born) and brother Djerrid Ruin (an even lower born Zodiacal) of what was going on up here, in what was more the Lazaremist Krepusyl Evenstar's Land of Twilight than the Mithradites' Marutia, Chimaera Glimmenmare shared with not just them a sense of the inevitable. The only realistic remedy to what was ailing the Hidden Headworld was a merciless culling of contagion-carrying interlopers – and that, unavoidably, would result in the killing of uninfected, otherwise innocent and potentially worshipful bystanders.

Almost any and every devil with a modicum of intelligence reckoned identically. Which, since they learned centuries earlier that they didn't self-cathonitize when they slew lesser beings, probably explained why Grandfather Sedon had absented himself from the night's sky for so long. (You're not there, you can't ill-star anyone, can you?)

"Just make it snappy," the no longer mono-balled horsefly said seconds after she completed her transformation into a different Venus (Byron's instead of Lazareme's), albeit also a Cyclops, a very faint but very pretty Cyclops. "Before the hellacious Harmony gets a chance to swallow the rest of me. Watch it, though. She's a Sedon-cursed demoness but he's way worse. He's the embodiment of bad. He's the Smiling Fiend."

"What?" Lazareme demanded of APM One-Eyes. "Who? Where?"

"Him, you, there!"

========

That second-born Chimaera was a Byronic only partially accounted for his offer of scary psychopomps as mounts for the three Unities and their father. It almost entirely accounted for his mind-reading goad. If Biblical justice was required then it'd best be delivered Biblically, hence the handpicked psychos he whistled for that very second.

Just as they pranced into sight ...

========

"Up umbrellas," cried Pusan Wanderlust presciently (unless it was Krepusyl doing the yelling through her, land-sensitively). "It's going to blow."

All eyes – including APM's one eye – went to her. The remarkably recurring fauna was back to having only two of her own but her shepherd's crook wasn't that anymore. Neither was it Evenstar's holy water sprinkler. She'd turned it into an oversized beach umbrella, which she promptly used to shade both her and the Great God.

"So that's where all the Brainrock went," muttered Yajur, as he followed suit.

It glowed before it blew but blow it did, it being the hoodoo hamlet's main mound – what Lazareme had correctly identified as a fairy knoll, hill, Sithein or sidhe (though the last two words as often referred to the dwellers as they did where they dwelled). Then it was the resultant mushroom cloud that glowed, albeit not exactly the same as the mushroom cloud that formed after the Idiot Twins blew on Samhain 4825.

For one thing it was neither instantly fatal nor necessarily poisonous, let alone long-lastingly so. Certainly no one immediately dropped dead because of it, though virtually everyone below it, including most of the devils on the misty side of the otherwise unmarked divide, did drop to their knees or bellies. It didn't smile fiendishly either. It could have of course – had the god-devil who caused it been more creative or, as far as that went, aware enough to be intentionally indicative as to the true identity of the cupid's boss and APM's not entirely demonic bogey man.

As for that god-devil, he was surmounting it. Sraddha Somata sat in a somehow airborne throne surrounded by a luminescent corona (non-capitalized, as in not the Gulf thereof).

For Bosco it was something else to paint: a three-eyed, dark-skinned, bearded yet shaved-bald god or demigod sitting up there amidst a veritable nimbus of Gypsium glory. He wouldn't call it *'The Last Judgement'* but the slimy jerk who sold his best paintings to the Church, for a much bigger cut than he deserved, probably would – after insisting he change Sraddha to Christ of course.

(*Last Judgements* had nothing to do with Judge Druj, another name for the fiendish Smiler, but they were very popular in mainly, if not wholly, or holy, Roman Catholic Europe. Popinjay preachers would be unemployed without them. And, from what his fellow seekers told him, in this ever so practical Universal Tongue of theirs, so would not just Catholic clerics there or anywhere else. Priests, in their shared humble, were a blight on the landscape.)

Whereupon, at that precise moment, something even odder, yet almost as memorable, happened. Clearly someone had already made a last judgement on someone else.

Hopes of returning to Den Bosch may yet prove pipedreams.

========

Devils once devoured could bear grudges.

========

In 4824/5, members of Dame Chance's Q-Troupe made up Q-names for their era's *'Q for Squirrelly'*. Two they kept repeating were Qatty and Qaprine; the former because Tattletail told them, not jokingly, that his first name was Tomcat and the latter because they considered him something of a satyr, male faun, Faunus or modern day Pan.

Since he didn't have cloven hooves – at least he didn't visibly have them on a daily basis – they did so due to the fact he played a panpipe as proficiently as he did compellingly. Plus, if Master Morg was any indication, he really was very good at seducing water nymphs. She was, as the Legendarian could attest, had he or she been around, and in any position to tell tales, or read tee-tee tails, during the last few months of her reign as Master of Weir, a Melusine Piscine.

Among the outsiders the thus far endlessly recompiled – if not, as yet, convincingly classified – faerie fart subsequently (post Pied Piper of Hamelin) lured inside on behalf of Quoits Tethys, a decent number were French. As he remarked, this time jokingly, they in effect gave him a Q-name in their tongue, not Sedon Speak. That name was *'qui'*, meaning *'who'*, with plenty of expletives added once he brought them here, via whichever tholoi he was using at the time, and they realized they weren't in France anymore.

Qui was pronounced *key* and, though they knew it not, that's what he was; had been not just since Quidnunc the Deadnunk Dad came across the Gulf of Corona to join son Squiggly in the hoodoo hamlet. Had been long before that, truth told; had just been, courtesy of the Thunder and Lightning Lord, temporarily out of action for a couple of years.

He may not have been Quid's murderer the first time. Nor, technically speaking, was he his killer the second time, when Quid was the then latest Legendarian. (He was only in him, intentionally looking like Zuvem Nergalis, whom he disliked intensely due to the Nergalid's pretensions of ruling hell as if it belonged to him instead of Demon King Sedon.) He was, however, the devils' bipartite enemy within; had been since Year of the Dome circa 2000.

(That was when the Dual Entities, during the seventh occasion they'd tumbled through time, mistook his physicality more so than personality for his father, not his grandfather, the Moloch Sedon. They thereupon sought to assassinate him by asteroid. Very much unfortunately for the residents of a pair of Outer Earth conurbations known as Sodom and Gomorrah, they only succeeded in fusing his somehow surviving spirit-being-self with the remnants of Dissolved Daemonicus, Primeval Lilith's forever mate and thus the pre-Sedon King of Demons.)

He was the one the last of APM's flutter-eyes, the last of APM dot-ditto, identified as the Smiling Fiend. That she had managed to warn them about him, aka Smiler, was doubly or trebly remarkable due to the fact that by far and away his most forgettable attribute was that no one could remember he even existed unless he wanted them to do just that.

It could be she registered him when he appeared in front of her and her Baby Byronics (in Kanin City's extended Great Hall, on the midsummer's night of 5474) moments before he slipped into the Legendarian. That she hadn't forgotten him right away, like the others there did, could be because what she then registered with all those eyes of hers at least one retained until now. Then again it could have been some sort of rudimentary, borderline-racial memory.

Devils knew whom he was the moment he allowed them to see him. Every devil also had traits unique unto his or her self, hence their individual attributes. Perhaps her multitude of eyes allowed her to see him no matter whom he was possessing. Sinistral Envy knew whom he was in the context of the hoodoo hamlet and maybe the other devil there, the Fop, Faustus Vladuca, did too. Maybe one of the seekers of secrets, Twisted Tommy or Bosco, sublimated memory of his comings and goings up here and APM picked up on it once she took him over in the Danq.

Maybe he'd just screwed up. It would hardly be the first time. He'd been caught in an eyeorb for hundreds of years after Thrygragon. If the Death's Head Hellion, Cabalarkon's then Master Morgan Abyss, had not transferred him into a ringot, then stuck him into that era's Tomcat Tattletail, he might be in one still.

As it was, that Tattletail had not only eaten him he'd kept him down – until Abe's daemonic doppelganger diced him up right smartly, that is. Master Morg thereupon got him into another ringot for a time; one manufactured in the Weirdom, not by Tvasitar Smithmonger. So, sure, screwing up was a distinct possibility.

Whatever the truth of the matter was, the last of APM's flutter-eyes must have already skedaddled by the time he made his latest appearance.

========

She was right about something else, though. He was way worse than Herta Heartthrob. He might have been way worse than the Devil Sedon, if the two weren't one and the same.

He was the A in the VAM Entity – Varuna Ahriman Mithras, the Moloch's firstborn.

========

They were picking themselves off the turf on both sides of the imperceptible, save for atmospherically, demarcation differentiating Shreds-Vladuca's creepily creeping protectorate from eponymous Evenstar's dreary, de facto one, Crepuscule, the Land of Twilight. Some hadn't gone down; therefore didn't need to pick themselves up. The three Unities and their father were foremost amongst the devils but, on the still dimly sunny – and now noticeably encroaching – seaside of the delineation, Tomcat Tattletail (APM's *'him, you, there!'*) had barely buckled.

Someone suddenly appeared behind him. That someone, coming out of the nowhere that was the everywhere of the universal substance between-space, held a Brainrock blade. That someone thereupon struck off Tomcat's beautiful blue-skinned, green-eyed and blond-haired neck noodle with it.

That someone was not a devil. He wasn't even possessed by one. He was, however, possessed by a Hellion's Sangazur – said Hellion being the relatively recently minted Ant Nightingale, Superior Somata, Melina born Tethys, Granny Jordy's multiple-generations-removed niece. Wouldn't be ambulant otherwise.

As the rest of him crumbled, Tattletail's sun-godhead of a noble noggin tumbled through the air. It shouldn't be able to do that. It hit the ground and kept on rolling across the undrawn line toward its inspiration (the Helios-like Thrygragos), that Great God's cohort of devic offspring, their Byronic and Mithradite cousins, and the capric deviant, occupied as she was by the closest Harmony came to have a friend amongst her many, mainly envious, younger sisters.

It shouldn't be able to do that either. Neither was it as if it had sprouted wings and taken flight like one of APM's myriad little angels. It had, however, altered by the time Unholy Abaddon, the Unity of Chaos, stopped it as if settling an ordinary soccer ball – soccer, called soccer, being by far the most popular game on the entire Hidden Continent of Sedon's Head. (Something else the Headworld could thank the time-tumbling Dual Entities for besides the mighty Moloch and everyone, and everything, that followed him.)

Tatty Tom's head had become the head of, well, a vaguely humanoid tomcat. The likes of the Librarian might have pointed knowingly then claimed it as proof that Tattletail was a *'mora'* or, arguably less accurately, an *'iele'*. Pusan and Evenstar, collectively as one, or individually as two (which they weren't right now), would have been absolutely precise.

They'd have seen it as proof positive he was a *'lutin mora'*, a faerie type re-nowned as lovers of wine, women and song who, in their most unguarded moments, had catheads of the non-ship variety (especially when, as now, they were dead – or momentarily so at any rate). He was still a candidate for a fairy oven but perhaps not for much longer.

Harmony gaped in mounting fury at the severed cat's head at their feet. It was looking directly at them, its eyes seemingly still alive, which Tatty Tom being a fairy-type they likely still were – faeries were almost as preservative as devils. Reflexively Lazareme grabbed her left forearm with his right hand. At the same time, with his other one, he gripped Yajur-Sparky's sword arm. He thus restrained them both by his touch alone.

"Shall I dust him, my diddling dear?" Tomcat's killer shouted. As her father had already deduced, it was an invitation to disaster, albeit directed at Harmony and not her at brother Abe, the admitted demiurge behind Herta Heartthrob. "No, methinks you'll have to do that yourself. I did the crumbling, he did the tumbling, you come a-collecting and we'll all get to rumbling."

In life, Tomcat was renowned for never being able to make anything rhyme. In death it appeared he'd inspired poetic aspirations from his very familiar looking assailant.

"Guess I was wrong about you, Sparky," Pusan admitted.

"How so, Goat?"

"You aren't altogether to blame for everything that's gone wrong. Harm is too."

"Let's ride," shouted Chaos. Perhaps reckoning no one else would take it, he'd chosen the sickly-looking, pale green psychopomp.

"You serious about this, dad?" Yajur asked, on the verge of breaking loose and racing after his hated brother. There was no way Chaos was going to hoard the glory Order deserved.

"Never more so," swore Lazareme, releasing his iron grip on both Unities. "That's pre-Quill Quid, your pet swordsman from decades ago. He's at least dead. Finish the job. Your demonic double's yours to do with as you please, Harm. Abe, I want that cat-crap's body. He's a date at Sedon's Peak. Goat, you keep the misbegotten faerie-fucker's head. And since I'm going to have to play hero, the white psycho is mine."

Yajur wasted no time; leapt on the red horse, leaving the black one for Harmony. "Who's your target, dad?" he demanded as he drew his always sparking lightning blade.

"Who do you think?"

Balance trays ever so fittingly depending from her chain-ends, thereby mimicking scales should anyone imagine a pivotal bar spanning her from shoulder to shoulder, Harmony did a ditto. Following suit, Lazareme hopped onto his winged Pegasus. The creature reared archly but the Great God, chortling merrily, reined it down. Giving his own, godhood's-in-the-eye-of-the-beholder's head dozens of sun-rays, he rendered himself akin to portraits and statues of sun gods found throughout the Whole Earth.

By now clearly enjoying the moment, he wheeled the psycho expertly, as if he did it everyday, such that he could face the rest of the devils gathered in the cool immediacy of the Grey Land. To them Thrygragos Everyman may have looked like their father, themselves, the Moloch Sedon or even as the tabby trickster, Tomcat Tattletail, typically presented him.

"I'm a traditionalist, Ruin," he addressed Byron's Green Man, who probably saw him as Lazareme would have himself. After all, the sun was the source of life for superficial plants and John Barleycorn's mushroom man (not that mushrooms were necessarily superficial) had an affinity for botany. "So I'll take your bough-bow — some elves might require striking.

"The rest of you, back on your knees. Or get there, if you have them. Prayer power's most of everything we'll need to make the day ours. Oh, and the promise of beer afterwards. At the Danq of course. Your treat, Harmony." (Despite the fact that it was on the north-easternmost slope of the Diluvian Mountain Range, and therefore in what was traditionally Mithradite territory, the self-anointed Unity of Panharmonium had long claimed the Danq as her own.)

Although as a Byronic not genetically obliged to do so, Djerrid Ruin obedi-ently tossed the Great God his bow and quiver full of Brainrock arrows (elf-struck being a euphemism for having a stroke). He thereupon abased himself suitably ab-jectly. Even those who didn't have knees, notably Chimaera Glimmenmare, who'd just changed into some sort of spastic blob of wormy protoplasm, suddenly got as low as they could go, whereupon they began lowing or chanting or mumbling nei-ther nonsensically nor counterproductively.

To praise (if, being individualistic devils, not outright venerate) and/or impor-tune the Unities and their father, the devils intoned incantations that were old long before the Devil Sedon formed the Sedonshem and fled New Weirworld multiple tens of thousand years earlier. If only out of self-interest, they did so heart and soul, with a genuine passion. To do otherwise might negate the effectiveness of their ef-forts.

In this they were doing precisely what Lazareme knew they had to in order for them to have any opportunity for success. By genuinely channelling the hopes and desires of damn near an entire Headworld into the four horsemen, they were funnel-ling the consensual wherewithal for them to prevail at any cost. They were in effect empowering them as never before.

Unless, that is, the top god Lazaremists could have done it without them and their prayers all along. Which, if true, was a far, far scarier prospect than colour-coordinated psychos.

========

The damn near exceptions were pureblood Utopians, mixed U-bloods of an inveter-ate Hate-Sedon predisposition and those already damned or at least soulless.

========

Of those there, on the fog-free side of the atmospheric fence, smiles to match Tatty Tom's on much better days were cracking no matter how fractal faces ear-to-ear. They, (mostly) mortals, were about to triumph over their (practically) immortal oppressors. Oh, bards would sing of this day forevermore. So might a troubadour named Tomcat Tattletail, so long as he wasn't disintegrated too dreadfully.

(After the events of Midsummer Day 4825 Morgan Abyss hadn't been able to salvage enough of that era's Squirrely of a Tomcat to, as she put it, recompile him. Quoits Tethys, though, learned of him hundreds of years later, while she was receiv-ing Illuminary training. She liked what she discovered and so did her reigning Mas-ter at the time. Harmony was a hopeless idealist, a sap for the notion of romantic love. Utopian biomages made faeries to order.)

The four foremost devic divinities of this day and age, sufficiently incensed to be thus successfully lured into an altogether antagonistic devil's inviolable protector-ate, spurred their mounts towards the expanding and thus anything except imagin-ary boundary betwixt their drear and Shreds' clear.

They were about to receive incontrovertible pudding proof that the Biblical Book of Revelations was wrong. Sight of the Four Horsemen (even if one of them was, non-traditionally, a horsewoman) didn't mark endgame everyone. It marked endgame Thrygragos Everyman and his three just as foolhardy firstborn.

The Lazaremist extremists jumped over the line – whereupon they kept com-ing.

========

Stunned denizens of the hoodoo hamlet couldn't believe their eyes. The trap their top dogs (and cats) set for the Headworld's top gods had instead sprung on the trappers, them.

They weren't about to famously win anything. They were about to die feebly.

****

12: Ring-Gotten Getaway

Antheal 30, 5476 YD – The Garden of Earthy Delights, Coast of Corona

First, though, the vast majority panicked, started screaming and scattering willy-nilly, hither and yon. Some simply froze, remained rooted as if in mid-stride, too terrified to even try to flee their fates. A few, notably Herta Heartthrob and Tatty Tom's decapitator, stood their ground defiantly: in Deadnunk's case with both feet firmly planted to either side of the resultantly headless body.

Another didn't stand his ground so much as made his next move, between-space. That would be the cupid, the two aspects of him, dutiful devil and devouring demon, their putto-putative or possible father to rescue in both cases. He wasn't running away, though. Neither was he flying or even flapping away, not yet. He had a goal in mind. It wasn't a soccer goal. It was the prohibitive ball – said cathead.

One other sat his throne – high in the sky atop the already diminishing mushroom cloud.

========

In a manner of speaking Lazareme's *'who else'* amounted to a living ringot. Like his silver-haired, verging on white-as-light sister, he could hold onto devils that, unaware of the extent of his deviant talents, sought to occupy him. As with Janna vis-à-vis Rastha Aragon (the Skinless Rasp), he could also control them. Could probably do so only one at a time, but he could do it whether or not he or she (or it) still had his or her (or its) power focus. That actually made the, to devils, truly terrible twins one up on ringots.

With respect to whether he could control his *'possessor'* should he send him or her into another sentient shell – which Morgan Abyss could with those the Thanatoids and/or their allies stuck in the ringots the Legendarian brought to her up in Cabalarkon all those centuries ago – now was hardly the time to experiment. Minus Faustus Vladuca inside him (the Fop to Lazareme and his Unities), he'd do a Melusine Master with a morgue, as opposed to Morg, difference. He'd plummet to his indubitable death straightaway.

He could still absorb Brainrock-Gypsium – or at least extract the miraculous substance from those who shouldn't have it, such as all those resultantly desultory devils now reduced to whimpering last gasp mumble-jumble out there, beyond the suddenly retreating periphery. (What Godstuff he dare not hold himself, due to an appreciable fear of supersaturate poisoning, he could still store in his throne or else suspend as if droplets in the atmosphere of his protectorate.)

Thus, when he spotted the faux sun god (his half-father externally and his full-father internally) racing toward him on his splendid Pegasus, borrowed bow with an already notched arrow ready to let fly, he hesitated nary a sentimental whit. Opening his third eye even wider he loosed the Fop's eyefire, willing the weapon's Brainrock into himself, or his throne if he couldn't handle it, and the Great God into the heavens – as a star alongside that of Fata Fortuna and all the other Lazaremists who shone up there once blue day became black night.

Worked too; sort of ... Sure enough Lazareme was abruptly disarmed. But he didn't appear fazed in the slightest – just booted his white-winged charger even harder in the beastly belly, hastening it, him on it, upwards all the more furiously fast.

Whoa, what was he doing with one of Tvasitar Smithmonger's devil-specific talismans to start with? Great Gods didn't need anything Anvil the Artificer manufactured over on Sedon's Peak. That was why they shunned the Promethean god-devil's gift of the three Male Objects circa 2000 YD. They could do whatever their offspring eventually learned how to do without any suchlike props or fetishes through which to focus their therefore always impressive power.

It was too late for Sraddha-Vladuca to entertain regrets or second thoughts. What was done was done. Having only faint hopes of reconciliation he nevertheless cried: "Mercy, Great Googly-Woogly!"

========

His father tasked Chaos with securing Tatty Tom's body. He'd also tasked his despicable brother with disposing of the once out of shape, as the Legendarian, but now again fit-looking swordsman. (Fit for a mobile cadaver, that is. Then again the Glorious Dead formerly of Valhalla Prime – who hailed from the Ghostlands, before the idiotic Atomic Twins rendered them uninhabitable, but these days called New Valhalla, the Bloodlands of Sedon's Inner Nose, home – were just as dead. Valhallans nonetheless remained formidable fighters.)

The latter, Quidnunc Tethys, had straddled the former, the decapitated remains of the shape-shifting charlatan in tigerish togs. Not far from Deadnunk, already roaring at him for doing in her lover of howsoever many decades, vituperated Herta Heartthrob. That meant all three Unities were keying in on essentially the same space. Such a cataclysmic collision to come wasn't an invitation for disaster. It was a recipe for ruination, perhaps of the whole world.

By virtue of being first on his psychopomp, Chaos was also first off the mark. Already well ahead of his siblings, he wasn't about to slow down, not even to avoid that panic-stricken, contagion-carrying Outer Earth boy darting in front of him. Then he was a different sort of first off – unhorsed by a grossly oversized, airborne dachshund named Drang.

Since Drang simultaneously bundled over Abe's sickly psycho, Dire was safely out of harm's way (non-capitalized) before he truly realized he'd been in danger. Moments later, once Bosco caught and held onto the boy, that realization didn't so much dawn on him as it deadened him, froze him to the spot the same as Bosco had been until he prevented the non-Quid-kid rollicking about helter-skelter aimlessly.

Indeed, about the only thing about Dire not frozen were his streaming tears. As delighted as he still was about having this big boy and dog adventure of theirs, the youngster wasn't too sure what to make of Drang's newly elongated shape. As for his dog's third eye, well, he didn't even want to think about that. What he wanted to think about, he sniffed dolefully, was his mom. He was finally missing her, sorely.

Speaking of which, sorely, if wishes were horses, with wings, it behoved him belatedly to be careful what he wished for because, looking over there, he spotted her riding one right at him. So did Bosco, though he didn't perceive Dire's mother, Barbara born Holper. He reckoned the ebon psychopomp's rider was his as yet un-requited beloved, Aleyt Goyaerts van den Meerveen.

Both were now in Harm's way (capitalized).

========

At just that moment, Thrygragos Lazareme and his pterippus of a bleached palomino vanished exactly the same as his on loan talisman had. A delayed reaction? Had to be. Feeling correspondingly stronger and ever so much more confident, Shreds breathed far easier. Tremble devazurkind! He was Deviant Dand Sraddha, the dauntlessly depilated devil-dispatcher. He truly did edge toward omnipotent in his own protectorate.

So much for the big cheese, time for the spaghetti siblings.

========

So, what happens to tee-tees rendered tailless, for purposes of hair-plugs (for male Legendarians), scholastic studies (for librarians, Illuminaries or Ant Nightingales) and/or, once in a while, commercial sales (provided tail-reading collectors or their acquisitive agents were in the vicinity with Godbucks burning holes in their vestments)?

In terms of the majority, the luckiest of the hence only briefly tailless rodents simply scamper away, new tails to grow and they with more tales to tell. Unfortunately for the wondrous species (particularly on the Outer Earth, where they've been extinct for millennia), tee-tees also make for fine feasting – not so amazingly, they taste like rabbit. So that accounts for those eaten.

Then there are the chiropteran tee-tees. Pointed to as proof tee-tees are a type of demon, they too re-grow tales to tell. Since theirs are in the form of wings (not tails) bigger than those of vampire bats, whom they resemble in more ways than just nominally, they literature-literally could be read like an open book (albeit one with only four pages, one on either side of their two wings). Unlike ordinary tee-tees, who might be considered agathodaemons, chiropteran tee-tees are day-biters, rendering them clear-cut cacodemons (as in deep-dipshit do-bladder-badders, to fay-say some, in keeping with the present company).

Herta Heartthrob shared with her devic template attributes not so much in a *'godhood is in the eye of the beholder'* fashion as in a complementary *'beauty is'* manner. While any man, and most gods, got shaky knees, not to mention embarrassing bulges, in Harmony's presence, virtually any demon, and most forever fickle faeries, got just as involuntarily jelly-like weak and/or love-struck lumpy around Herta. They'd do anything she wanted; they'd also do, unbidden, anything they hoped would impress her.

Although undoubtedly animals, because they were psychopomps psychoswans may also at least partially be yet another form of demon. Their usual riders, the Valkyrie Choosers of the Slain – the so-called swan maidens who to this day picked the Valhallan Glorious Dead – were definitely Hellions; had to be in order to ride the arguable agathodaemons. That made them demon familiars, and vice versa, if not always successful demon-tamers.

Since the days of Zalman Somata's renowned ancestor Helena Somata, Kanin City's Master of Weir both before and for a few years immediately after Thrygragon, Hellions and Utopians often found themselves sharing the same Hate-Sedon agenda. (Indeed, Mel's Zal was descended in a straight line from Helena's son George, or Georgie, and his wife Ute, who like her mother Volsanga had been a Valkyrie.)

Chiropteran tee-tees were the quickest to Herta's defence. Psycho-swans followed. These last arrived mostly via the Weird yet strangely, excepting fowl fleas and suchlike nits, without passengers. Together they slowed her and her coal-black psychopomp down such that just about every eat-anything demon in close proximity to them got a chance to pounce, claws bared and teeth gnashing.

And there were a ravenous clutch of them. Unless it was a ravening murder of them since non-demonic crows and ravens, who adhered to Hellions like hounds to huntsmen, flocked and squawked not far behind the earthborn omnivores. (As for the Valkyries themselves, the psycho-swans' riders were likely keeping a discreet eye on proceedings. Being witches in large measure beholden to the three male Apocalyptics, notably War, for employment, they wouldn't want to be seen taking sides, so they were probably cloaked somewhere in nearby between-space.)

Harmony knew she was attractive. But a demon-magnet? This was getting ridiculous. Worse, it was becoming unbecoming, insulting, utterly inappropriate. It was no longer just starting to piss her off, it was pissing her off severely. Generally a do-gooder she had a history, or her-story, of becoming a do-badder when Necessity, by any name, compelled.

Abe never thought to add wings to the Harmony husk mainly because he'd buried their significance subliminally. Wings on her were anything apart from a nice touch.

They were an indicator of impending devastation.

========

Lord Order got Sparky, his human nickname, from both his lightning blade and the azuras he sired on almost any number of invariably willing Master Devas from all three tribes. Sparking azuras, by definition, gave off sparks. Sparks made them visible, which most azuras weren't except, ever so faintly, to those with heightened eyesight.

Had he thought of it beforehand he might have brought a mob of them with him. They were particularly helpful when it came to possessing and thereafter controlling low-watt animals, which psycho-swans had to be to a decent degree. He hadn't. Didn't need to – his stick was a monster.

The sparks it, his lightning blade, gave off were *protozurs*: pre-seminal azuras, as the humourless Librarian (Biblio Drek) might have it. That aspect of his stick was hardly unique amongst devils, even male devils. One of his most frequent mates prior to Sedon moving her as-good-as protectorate east to west, from one coast to another, was Lazareme's Venus, Mariamne then Dawnstar, Krepusyl nowadays Evenstar.

Her power focus was called a holy water sprinkler not just because it resembled a spiked mace. It sprinkled protozurs (non pre-seminal ones in her case). Like his, they were even more ineffectual than their regular azuras. They couldn't animate dead things, would have been worthless in terms of activating homos (homunculi), and only marginally useful when it came to pacifying wild animals. What they would do, once absorbed, was make those that absorbed them much more favourably inclined towards, depending on whose they were, him or her.

Evenstar's did tend to temper faerie wilfulness, though, thereby causing them to act much less ornery or obstreperous around sentient worshippers, potential or practising, so maybe a spray of his would too. Then again, despite the mishaps already afflicting his fellow Unities, no one had as yet even dared try to obstruct him. In other words, why bother? Besides, the swans hadn't gone for him any more than the vampiric day-biters had.

That allowed him to reach Deadnunk (ex-Quill Quidnunc) before either of his immediate siblings – reach him, sword slashing, and pass him, minus contact. Yajur reined in his roan (unless it was a bay). His blade bore no trace of blood, yet he'd consciously attempted to swipe off, not swipe at, Quid's deadhead. He couldn't have missed. He never missed. Quid hadn't ducked and Sangazur-animated corpses couldn't become intangible.

"Come along, hotshot," Deadnunk goaded, turning toward the Unity as the frenzied mayhem occurring all around them prudently, if counter-intuitively, shrank farther and farther away from them. Even Herta Heartthrob had backed off, gravitating toward Harmony and the demonic deputation so distressing the female Unity.

"If you won't dismount and fight fairly then at least have the courtesy to kill me again quickly. You didn't even come close to connecting that last go."

"What do you know?" puzzled Yajur from the space of a few psychopomplengths. He couldn't help but admire, howsoever begrudgingly, his foe's brashness. "You can teach a dead dog new tricks after all. Who taught you how to cast illusions? Unless a devil possesses you … But, no, that can't be. No devil would have the nerve to stand against me."

"Neither devil nor illusionist am I. Nor wizard, nor magician either, though I do admit to having artistic pretensions. I might not be the man you killed anymore but here's a hint: I could have won all those championships without you inside me. You do know that, don't you?"

Yajur shrugged. "So you're a Jordy who never got a chance to become a Quit Quill kid again. Hooray for you. Me, I'm Lord Order, about to become a triple-timing Quid Killer."

Confused he may be, but he wasn't going to waste any more brain cells on this wretched excuse for an enigma. Lightning worked on Tomcat once. Come to think of it, lightning worked on Master Morgan Abyss, too, not long thereafter. Lightning worked on anyone alive, terminally. Lightning bolts would toast ex-Quidnunc unto charcoal, if perhaps not dust, where he stood.

Lightning he generated. Make that should have charcoaled Deadnunk. He couldn't have missed again. Appeared to stand then.

"Congratulations on becoming Lord Loser, the Unity of Futility. I could do this all day and you'd be none the wiser. You're not who I owe for the first time, but I've decidedly delicious competition for her, so you'll have to do. Tell you what, let's make this a meaningful exercise, one I could actually win and you could actually lose.

"I heard tell your scrumptious but spiteful sister got rid of Strife on Sedon's Peak fifteen hundred years ago. Let me draw us both there. We'll duel. I'll chop you into the stuck pig you've always been, minus the '*up*' side. Then I'll melt you and your undeserved so-called Sword of Righteousness out of existence. Deal?"

The Legendarian could not draw anyone conscious anywhere without his or her permission. Even someone like Lord Yajur, who was indeed so stuck up he sometimes thought the world revolved around him, had to have recollected that. He did, perplexity perforce unravelled. "You've the quill!" he exclaimed. "You painted the blue."

"Argh!"

========

Drang had gone for his throat. Unlike odious Ordure when it came to Deadnunk, the devil-transformed, yet still non-hellhound didn't miss any more than he was about to let go. Dire relaxed moderately, allowing his nevertheless trepidatious benefactor, Bosco, to chance a glance backward, toward the unscattered few now huddled together, in what amounted to a crowd of the irrationally curious, on the outskirts of the hoodoo hamlet proper.

Without really knowing why, his artist's attention riveted on Dire's favourite, Jordan 'Squiggly' Tethys, and Twisted Tommy, the Roman Catholic Inquisitor that so terrified him. They weren't too far away from each other when something flashed from the former to the latter. It wasn't a smile, though it did seem to be smiling.

Did the hateful cleric now have a panpipe hanging from around his neck instead of a gruesomely gothic crucifix?

"God, no!" suddenly shrieked the boy.

========

Debrained daemons solidified devils, had done since circa 2000 YD, true. But be-brained demons, should they catch them napping, devoured them. That didn't mean they digested them. Chaos was just one of many devils to induce indigestion and thereby escape pre-excremental elimination (for example, by detonating Lady Lust's denim demon, from the inside, on or around Imbolc Day 4824/5).

Once you had a body, though, no matter how daemonic it might be, being eaten alive hurt. Plus, they slobbered caustic, not to mention smelly, stomach acid.

Harmony was far different from most third generational Master Devas in that she was bodily mostly Brainrock; an almost completely cathonic rather than chthonic individual. That should not make her indigestible, just very hard to keep down. Yet it did in the sense that she gave them gas. That gas was blue, as in air was all she left behind besides her ebony psycho.

Too bad about her, unless it was a him – she hadn't had a chance to determine its sex. As deadly as they were pretty, the swans took to her (or him) hungrily as well as, perhaps, jealously.

========

The bloodcurdling shriek of unmitigated anguish came from the right. It was both male and at once recognizable. Was Deadnunk over there too?

========

"About time you figured it out, Sparky." The voice was female, but it wasn't that of Pusan Wanderlust. Who then?

The non-Argh-air where it appeared Deadnunk was straddling Tatty Tom's decapitated remnants remained unaltered save for the fact the Dead Thing's lips stopped moving and his running-off-at-the-mouth commentary accordingly ceased. Simultaneously the actual Argh-air over there to his right, where her voice came from, shimmered as if a scrim or screen of ordinariness was dropping. Which it did.

That answered that then. The voice had only been vaguely familiar to him at first but he recognized the fish-faced Zodiacal Illuminaries called Pyçonja Volant the moment he saw her in the fishy flesh. He'd had the dubious pleasure of sharing her waterbed many centuries earlier when he grew gills and went on an unscheduled swim-about through the Headworld's undersea realms.

Pyçonja was the Piscines' mother goddess. Since she was born in the Head's Inner Ocean of Akadan, the mass-murderous Master of Cabalarkon so often on not just Yajur's mind of late, Morgan Abyss, probably grew up worshipping her. (Reputedly Fish-Face wasn't the Melusine's devic half-mother. General wisdom prevailing at the time had her as Fata Fortuna, hence the off-chance the Death's Head Hellion became a howsoever short-lived Quill Tethys after being jolted out of her lady buggy on Samhain 4825.)

Products of Old Eden's to this day despised science (from long before the Sedonshem landed on the then Whole Earth), there were all sorts of Piscines. Many, though hardly all, were amphibious. Some were froglike, with smooth moist skin, but most were scaly. If you could get over the webbed fingers and toes, the gills behind the ears and the shark-sharp teeth, the Melusine Master, Yajur recalled, looked almost human. Not so Pyçonja. She didn't just have shark-sharp teeth. In her present form she might have passed for a two-legged shark.

Except for the rare amatory excursion into their territory, Lord Yajur never had much in the way of dealings with Byronics after he achieved independent solidity circa 2000 YD. That said, her power focus was another reason he recognized her so comparatively easily. He kept scars from it as a reminder to stay away from her in the future. It was also why Deadnunk more like squalled than squealed so horribly.

A fisher's gaffe, right that minute it was hooked into his midsection. Which probably also explained why the erstwhile headsman's decapitating sword had turned back into a quill. (Especially for non-devils, the concentration required to maintain talismans in irregular shapes tended to falter when being disembowelled.)

As for how he'd painted not just an insubstantial, yet moving picture in the air, one that could both turn and talk, well, Deadnunk had had a couple of years to experiment with what was originally brother Rumour's talisman. That didn't count the nearly twenty years he spent as the then latest Legendarian. Plus, he'd been a bright lad, pre-beer.

He'd also been in the company of presumably pureblood Utopians from the Weirdom of Cabalarkon. Yajur had noticed them interspersed with the hoodoo hamlet's inhabitants. With or without eye-staves, alabastrine women accompanying too tall stringbeans of both the opposite colour and the opposite sex were hard to mistake. And didn't they still have this thing Weirdomites called cinema? Kanin City had theatres commonly called just that, so Cabalarkon might yet have fully functional motion pictures complete with sound.

Pyçonja Volant had wafted out of Tomcat's neck stump, hardened herself and her power focus, snagged the latter into the former Quill Tethys from below, then hauled herself to her feet even as she levered Deadnunk to his knees, dying anew. Warily eyeing the Unity, she tore out her barbed gaffe unnecessarily viciously, spilling even more of the Dead Thing's guts in the process. Making it glow all the telltale more, she redirected its gore-dripping hook downwards.

"That fucker, when it had a head, ate me," she warned Yajur off. "Harmony's forever lover or not, he doesn't get to do it again." The increased glow said it all. She was about to do to that fucker's headless corpse exactly what Deadnunk threatened to do, albeit with Rumour's then still transformed quill. (Even on old Weir, where they were first named, Gypsium had always been Solidium's counterforce.)

"Can't let you do that, darling," Yajur, returning the favour, cautioned her.

Father Lazareme charged his most hated sibling with preserving said remains but he'd also charged him with finishing off Quid's yet ambulatory dot-ditto. Tatty Tom's body had already partially sunk into the ground – bones and all, demons tended to do that sort of dust-to-dust stuff; hence why they, like fucking faeries, never left fossils of themselves behind.

Plainly oblivious to the genuinely earth-shattering importance of their Head-world-saving mission, depraved brother Abe was over there playfully wrestling with what? An oversized dachshund by the looks of things. Daddy would not be pleased with Chaos but in many respects they were birds of a feather.

Best he not be doubly displeased with Order lest he tighten his tether even more.

========

"Look out!" hollered APM, Pyçonja's much older, still cyclopean sister. Fish-Face had not been the only one eaten. She'd just been the only one wholly disgorged as yet.

Even with just the one eye, and it only momentarily raised from a prayerful downcast, APM could see better than most devils. Her bellow had nothing to do with Yajur's caution of seconds earlier, though. Grotesquely distended, the Harmony husk loomed leeringly over the Zodiacal. Her daemonic admirers having beaten her to the female Unity and her by now thoroughly munched psycho, Herta Heartthrob had returned her attention to salvaging her own forever lover, Harmony's dick-dildo as not just fays would say.

Perhaps also reasoning that, after due thought and culinary consideration, any devil would sate as well as the one Tomcat promised her such a long time ago, she seemed manifestly intent upon repeating his indulgence with the same meal, albeit this time without Nanapollo Dobury's shrink-wrap mucilage.

Either that or, not being overly endowed with snapping synapses, going through Fish-Face was just the quickest way to get to Tom's body.

========

"Don't hurt my pal, Mr Monster." This admonition, shouted from a safe distance, came from Dire. That Bosco still held onto him might have emboldened the boy because it was aimed at Unholy Abaddon, who was indeed in monstrous mode, though some of his (non-azura) sparklers had gone out.

Chaos clambered to his feet, dachshund-Drang attached to his throat and as determined as ever to rip it out. "Me, boy? What about your damn dog hurting me?" His trident wasn't a pitchfork and Drang wasn't a metaphoric bale of hay but, as Dire had correctly apprehended, both situations could change in a millisecond.

"Look out!"

Although it wasn't his voice, this came from a different dog, the *'Domini canes'* or *'Hound of the Lord'* (in Sedon Speak, not Latin). The once-tonsured Dominican known to those in the hoodoo hamlet as Twisted Tommy, but to Bosco (though not Dire) also as Tomas de Torquemada, was holding high a by now almost imperceptibly glowing, self-consecrated crucifix as if it would ward off evil.

(Which it might, if devils were evil and not three-eyed extraterrestrials more correctly known as Master Devas, aka the Shining Ones.)

========

"Cupid cocksucker!" Pusan Wanderlust raked into their psyches as the three-eyed putto came out of the Weird, snatched up Tatty Tom's cut-off cat's head and vanished back between-space. "I'm going after the little peckerhead. Someone grab the body." (In addition to Goat, folks often called Pusan both Trailblazer and Wayfarer. The latter because she was a Wayfarer in the Wild Weird; the former because she could track anyone through it.)

She vanished, leaving Krepusyl, gorgeous in grey, behind. "Look up there," she yelled.

Many did both – looked then yelled, mostly happily. Cheering quickly became almost as widespread, at least on the damper and hence more mist-miserable side of the divide.

========

One who didn't do either was the Harmony husk, the target of the Spaniard's alarum. Somehow the Outer Earth Inquisitor had looked into the Weird (which was also called the Grey, especially here in the Grey Lady's Grey Land of Twilight) and perceived Herta's certain doom approaching at breathtaking as well as breakneck speed.

Only highborn devils, the occasional deviant, extremely well-trained practitioners of the arcane arts (aka witchcrafts) like Anthean Nightingales, Hellion or Korant sister superiors, and a few wizards in their long gone heyday (mostly prior to circa 2000 YD) had that knack. It wasn't an ability one would expect someone who'd only arrived on the Inner Earth relatively recently to possess. Ergo, perhaps, just that – possession.

Even if the Harmony husk had heard it, she had no time to heed it. The Female Fury about to burn out of the nowhere that was the everywhere of Samsara, the Universal Substance, didn't want to hurt Herta. She wanted to annihilate her.

The hellish Harpy she so resembled no more had names such as those given to the Classical Erinyes or Eumenides – Megaera (Vindication), Alecto (Harangue) or Tisiphone (Reprisal) – than she was altogether the Unity of Balance as well as

Panharmonium by then. She was, however, altogether Herta's nemesis (with and without a capital *'N'*).

Her clothing and skin was black and red and fiery orange instead of glowingly golden, butterscotch and/or transitorily dependent on the onlooker's expectations. Her chains still had the Plates of Justice on their end but now they were serrated like a shipwright's belt-driven buzzsaw in a stream-fed mill. As for the wings, well, they were almost never manifest. Fletched more so than feathered, they didn't just look like flexible, cut-anything razorblades, they probably were.

What had to be the Scum Demon's worst nightmare screeched out of the Grey and into the blue. Chaos's arbitrary aberration barely had time to register what must have seemed to her a demented distortion of her own reflection in a maddening mirror. If Harmony was beautiful in the eyes of whoever beheld her, her alter ego had to have appeared purely baleful for Herta Heartthrob at the moment of her last heartbeat.

All that ambient Brainrock leftover from Vladuca-Shreds failing to sequester the totality of so many devic power foci came in awfully handy – unless it was handily awful. Discharge resulted in daemonic disintegration. Disposal dictated next door. Nemesis, capitalized, had already reasoned that Herta would have less chance of re-forming in liquid than either on solid ground or, because her atomized *'speckles'* might cohere out of it, the gaseous blue.

She was probably right as well. Although there were sea-scads of aquatic demons, water was shared commons for them. Not so Herta, all wet, all wrecked, too bad, so sad.

Sedon's Human Eye, as the Gulf of Corona was oft-times described cartographically, experienced precipitation on a daily basis. Until then almost invariably atmospheric (as opposed to anthropomorphic) and for the most part fluid, it was no more conscious than it had any capacity whatsoever for sight. Nemesis had both.

The devic goddess of retributive justice was inexorable. She wouldn't – if not 100% couldn't – be stopped. And she didn't, not until the Stopstone abomination was altogether a dust cloud blowing out to sea; one facilitated by her as a chains-whirling tornado dervish à la Vayu Maelstrom (ever-changing Chimacra's absent brood brother, often worshipped as *'Hurican'* beyond the Dome), and thence dispersed.

Satisfied with her day's devastating deeds, Nemesis reverted. Once more harmoniously inclined, the again designated do-gooder began to air-stroll shoreward next-to-nonchalantly. Her self-made vortex not gone unnoticed on high, however. As if sensing it, she glanced that way. What was the crazy loon up to this time?

Accelerating her return accordingly, she teleparted worriedly: "Don't deflate the damn Dome, dad,"

He wasn't paying attention.

========

The dozens of little flutter-eyes coming out of the seaborne dust devil re-gathered around and as APM. All eyes restored, she was certainly grateful. All her eyes back, and front, not to mention top and bottom as well as internally, also made her, if possible, all the more observant. Did Twisted Tommy have a third eye? Could he have tooted on his upraised crucifix like a tin whistle, recorder or flute? Was he smiling fiendishly?

He felt her glare, returned it and, yes, he did smirk disquietingly, very much dissimilarly to the humble parish priest or simple country friar he comported himself as ever-so-cunningly if not always convincingly. Keys typically turned. This one twisted or torqued. APM completely forgot not so much 'what' as 'who' she was seeing.

For his part, still not blowing on anything, he gleaned it time to blow this scene.

========

Krepusyl was the first to notice Thrygragos Lazareme appear high in the sky. Alone, beaming brilliantly (if stereotypically for a sun god), and standing on nothing except the blue out of which he'd just emerged, not at all proverbially, he was clearly in usurpation mood. Below, cloudy was routing sunny as the Grey Land reclaimed itself.

Even if he-they hadn't as yet realized it himself-themselves, that indicated it was pretty much all over already for Shreds-Vladuca. As if just to prove what a good anarchist he and virtually all his devic offspring were, the Great God proceeded to boot, ever-so-emphatically, the cocky pretender/s off his-their Brainrock throne.

Not just bad weather soon followed.

"Incoming!" This came from Squiggly, one of many who, responsive to Krepusyl's cry, had looked up, albeit with only two eyes, no visible panpipe, and in a voice entirely his own. He was pointing. Then he had an extra finger – #6 Dextral – indicating precisely the same direction. He hadn't become deceased. He'd been bequeathed.

The incoming was Shreds-Vladuca cascading one body, but still three eyes, inexorably earthwards just as Lord Order fulfilled his father's order in terms of Deadnunk the ex-Quidnunc. This time he didn't miss. Charcoal followed. Wisely, Pyçonja chose to reward the Unities, first for Harmony's rescue of her and, second, for Yajur's forbearance in not doing a catasterizing Deadnunk (or Fata Fortuna) to her. Instead of atomizing Tomcat's remains, she hook-scooped them wholly out of the ground into which they'd been sinking.

"You," boomed the not-so-much-localized replacement god poised hundreds of feet above them. In all likelihood he hadn't damaged his foot booting the solitary twosome off their Brainrock throne but he had taken a load off his feet by sitting in it. "Get your butt up here."

Faustus Vladuca, who was partial to long dark sleeveless cloaks with red lining, must have thought the boom was for him and him alone. Fortunately, as if a psychic psychopomp (which it may have been), a white Pegasus appeared beneath Shreds-Vladuca just as the two-in-one deviant split back into a pair of distinct individuals.

Showing consideration for his about-to-be-former host's lack of airworthiness, the Black Godling slowed their joint descent such that Sraddha Somata, who was as fine a horse wrangler as he was an excellent athlete overall, could grab hold of the flying palomino by its mane as he dropped out of the devil. With Shreds safe, he turned his cape into wings and swooped upwards. He was mistaken about the boom being for him, however.

"Not you, Fop. The Byronic hotdog."

The overlong, cynocephalic two-thing plaguing Chaos unclamped its doggy jaws. From them, out of its mouth, extruded a huge, seemingly hollowed-out, vermicular tube. It was alive. It was the real devil, the one giving Drang its elongated shape and third eye. Camorva Freeflight, the Byronic after whom the month of Kamor (July in parts of the Outer Earth) was named, didn't have to obey the thundering command any more than Djerrid Ruin had earlier but, uncurling and thereafter spreading out her own moth-like wings, the lepidopterous lowborn did as boombade.

Lazareme spotted a small satchel or kibisis looped beside Sraddha's throne. After sitting down, thereby making the throne his own, he opened it. He wasn't at all surprised to discover it contained dozens of presumably Cabalarkon-manufactured ringots. That explained so much. Having already watched Harmony make a Maelstrom of herself, he had one of his Great Godly brainstorms. Experimentally, he funnelled some of his own surplus Brainrock into one of them. Whereupon, it doing exactly as expected, brainstorm became Plan Next.

A few commands later and Bosco suddenly had something else to paint.

========

The overcharging slimeball who acted as his sales agent would entitle it something typically trite before he sold it to the Church's purchasing agents. A Biblical profundity like 'Ascent of the Blessed' might work if he added some more angels and they didn't drop anyone. Plus, he was already thinking of a multi-panelled pastiche called 'Visions of Beyond the Pale' and this might do as a left or right middle frame.

Since they were anything except blessed, he mentally determined to use 'Ascent into the Empyrean' as a working title.

Spectacular view from up here.

========

"Now do you see why I came here, dad?" Chaos asked his father once Lazareme deemed done to his satisfaction everything immediately necessary to accomplish today.

"To cause chaos?"

"No, to sort it."

"Seems to me we all did that," said Yajur, who'd incinerated the remains of dead again Deadnunk, ex Quill, ex Quidnunc, just because it seemed the orderly thing to do.

"Seems to me dad did most of it," said Harmony.

"Except we're left with cleaning up the rest of the mess as usual," countered APM All-Eyes. She was only the second eldest Byronic there but, since she was at least momentarily more in favour with the Lazaremists than Chimaera Glimmenmare, she'd assumed the role of their tribe's spokesperson.

"Only in the sense you're to track down the outsiders left behind in your homelands," Lazareme provided, again. (It was bad enough when his own children talked back, unbidden, but dealing with members of the other two tribes was positively exasperating. Why didn't they just do as he said?) "After that you're to summon Harmony. She'll handle their repatriation."

"Why her?" complained the Planter, Zuvem Nergalis, the eldest Mithradite there.

"Because she is who she is and all the rest of you are who you are. She's just shown how well she functions in the air out there and I won't do it."

"Because its beer tastes terrible?" queried Chaos.

"That's most of it," Lazareme allowed, without elaborating. (It probably wasn't that he didn't trust the Byronics and Mithradites to keep the peace in his absence. It was more a matter of Chaos and Order not destroying the Hidden Headworld while trying to kill each other should he dare go away on a mercy mission.)

"She'll need Camorva," said Chimaera, striving manfully – or devilishly, put better – not to switch shapes. (Lazareme claimed he got headaches when seeking to speak to someone who changed his, her or its appearance minute by minute. Consequently, at the Great God their saviour's insistence he had taken on his most regular form, that of Centaur stallion. Now he just needed to retain it.)

"I'm a fast learner," provided Harmony. "Besides, Squiggly likes me."

========

In order to expel rather than exterminate all the contagion-carrying seekers after secrets in the hoodoo hamlet, Lazareme first expanded one of the Utopian ringots. In this he did the same as Morgan Abyss had all those centuries ago when she – must have been her – launched her between-space assaults, via remote-controlled empyrean vessels, on the Thanatoids' armies then mustering in the Upper Head in preparation for invading Cabalarkon.

He'd next gone a step further than Master Morg. He opened a circular gap in Cathonia, the Sedon Sphere, Cathonic Dome or, more properly, Zone thereof, to the Outer Earth. Thinking her perfect for the job, he had Camorva insert her front end, as if the needle of a syringe, in order to keep it open. When that didn't deflate the Dome, he had her widen her tubular body, at both ends, such that she could create a luminescent tunnel through the Dome to beyond it.

'Now make like a vacuum hose,' he'd instructed her, referring to a device still found in former Weirdoms, at least a couple of which remained in the subcontinent of Aka Godbad, the Byronics' undisputed territory. *'And suck up the nauseating nebbishes. Don't drop them from too high a height on the other side either. They might accuse us of murder if you did and I'd rather leave murdering to the monotheists.'*

Hence Chimaera thinking he'd need Camorva, he reminding them that she'd just shown she didn't, and Harmony herself mentioning how much Squiggles Tethys liked her.

========

"Who doesn't?" Lazareme countered sternly.

"True enough. Except I'm most of the reason why Squiggly's still Squiggly."

"You mean why he's still alive."

"And not the Legendarian, yes."

"That's one lesson you didn't learn quickly."

"Mel would've killed Quid if she hadn't gone into labour at just that minute."

"We were there, Harm. You're the one who wanted to pin the award on his chest."

"But I didn't know she'd rigged the end to go off."

"And devils can't lie," Lazareme concluded. "You're still doing penance."

"What am I missing?" The voice, though female, didn't come from Harmony.

"About time you got back, Goat. What's Envy doing here?"

Pusan Wanderlust stepped fully out of the Weird. The 3-eyed cupid who was indeed most commonly known to devils as Sinistral Envy was perched on her shoulder like a parrot. She'd turned the end of her shepherd's crook into a basket, like a lacrosse stick amongst the Iroquois of North America (again to use the Entities' terminology). It held Tomcat's deadhead.

"She rescued me," enthused the cupid, gleefully free of the devouring putto.

"I caught up to the little imp between-space." Pusan started to elaborate.

"She turned her crook's other end into a blowtorch and blasted him," Envy, sometimes called Cupidity, albeit mostly because he generally did appear as a cupid, to the point his power focus was a dinky bow, finished for her. "And, joy of boys, I got out."

"Then let's get to it," said Harmony, unable to disobey her father.

And they did.

========

Took themselves, all fifty of them, to Sedon's Peak. There, in the shadow of Anvil's Prometheum, Harmony tossed both parts of her demon lover into its Brainrock crater.

========

Drang on his tail rather than the other way around, Dire raced down the high hill from Nuremburg Castle to his home in the town. He'd have some explaining to do. Only, when his understandably shocked, yet absolutely delighted, parents quizzed him as to where he'd been all this time, he couldn't remember. And, even if could, Drang was incapable of answering.

That was true for Bosco and virtually every other seeker after secrets who came through the Dome that day, thanks to Camorva, and everyday subsequently, thanks to Harmony. They all got home, though, because they all could remember where they came from and gave Squiggly Tethys permission to draw them there.

Less than two months later, Harmony told Squiggles and Shreds – Lazareme having banished half-son Sraddha for his arrogance as much as for the effrontery of his attempt to cathonitize a Great God – that they could no longer track down any more Outer Earthlings on the inside. That meant they were welcome to do as they pleased from then on. She didn't give them the chance of returning to the Hidden Headworld, however.

Rather, she said she'd take Squiggly back but couldn't overrule her father, so Shreds would have to stay behind, which amounted to the same thing.

Best buddies to the bitter end those two.

========

Confident they'd soon lose memory of the Inner Earth without her constantly popping by to remind them of it, she didn't confiscate Rumour's quill. Perhaps she should have since Squiggly had become quite good with it. He'd learned, for example, to keep a splotch pad in which he retained drawings of where he sent folks to once Harmony brought them back outside.

One day, on a whim, he drew them both to visit Twisted Tommy. They were momentarily astonished to discover how well the tight-assed Inquisitor had learned to play a panpipe.

Then Squiggly was more like horrified when Rumour's quill vanished. Who'd died?

****

Janna Fangfingers

- Years of the Dome 5476-5495, 5980 -

Jim McPherson

A ***PHANTACEA*** **Mythos** Mini-Novel
published by James H McPherson

ISBN 978-0-9781342-7-3

1: Back Alley Preamble

"Bat attack, bat attack!"
So shrieked the rat with a long, squiggly tail.

========

Thanks in large measure to monotheistic religions, the demons, the monsters, the gods and the goddesses of antique mythologies have been trivialized, their worship proscribed and the entities themselves confined to another realm. This realm is known by various names. In some traditions it is called the *'Otherworld'*, in others *'Shadowland'*, and in certain places on the Outer Earth, including parts of modern day Tibet, it is known as the Inner Earth.

When he's beyond the Cathonic Dome – or Sedon Sphere, as it's just as correctly called – the legendary 30-Year Man often prefaces the stories he's about to tell with suchlike preliminary commentary. He then goes on to remark that there are many supernatural entities. He further makes a distinction between *'cathonic'*, or skyborn, and *'chthonic'*, or earthborn.

Count chthonic such familiar creatures of folklore as faeries, demons, werecreatures, vampires and zombies. Count cathonic the fallen angels or devils of the Bible. Because devils are described as fallen that implies they are extraterrestrial in origin, which in his estimation amounts to a tautology.

Dictionaries regularly have you believe that the Sanskrit word for god is *'deva'*. In actuality – in that ancient tongue, make that – the word simply means bright or shining one. Be that as it may, he opines, as part of the show, it's difficult to deny that it's the root for English words such as devil, deity, deviant, divine and diva, as well as the Indian honorific *'devi'*.

At least, he'll qualify, if too many in attendance have brought said pocket- or backpack-sized reference books to whatever gathering he's yapping at, it is according to better dictionaries – he, conveniently, having forgotten his at what passes for his home howsoever faraway from his present severely diminished circumstances. It's too big to cart around, don't you know, especially when you're living on the street like he is, poor boy. So please give generously.

He'll further note that the Latin word for God is *'Deus'*. He contends it's just a variation of *'dev'*. This appears self-evident, he'll add gratis, when you consider that in English the plural of *'dev'* would be *'devs'* and Imperial Romans wrote *'Deus'* as *'devs'*. Ipso facto, he babbles on, to state that today's devils were the gods and goddesses of pagan faiths is to restate the bleeding obvious.

Naturally, he only babbles in universally understood, pre-Babel Sedon-speak when he's telling stories out there. When he's recounting tales in here, there's no need to preface anything. Some of the gods and goddesses of antique mythologies might be in attendance. As for the demons and monsters, since they were more or less mortal their descendants might be there.

Although, being for the most part subtle matter shape-shifters, they could be there in one form or another; the forms they take rarely inspire puking. Nonetheless, he'd been doing a lot of that in the last few moments. Ergo, he must have exceeded his 30-beer daily limit last night. That happened, he generally got disgustingly drunk and despicably disorderly. That being the case, or six pack of six packs, well, Fata Fortuna, to spout some genuine Latin, always seemed to favour his survival.

One form or another also probably explained why he'd woken up in the rubbish heap behind the bar where he'd downed his last beer. He might have, over the incessant chatter and amplified din of the pub's inexcusably shrill rock music, started shouting a tale about a devil that didn't appreciate his or her story being shouted, let alone told. He couldn't remember.

He could remember how much he hated getting drunk. It approximated how much he hated coming back as his daughter or granddaughter. Hangovers hurt. So did giving birth. Neither hurt as much as getting killed, though, and third generational devils, who by Sedonic decree weren't allowed to kill lesser beings, didn't count killing him as murder.

They counted him as one of them, an immortal, one who couldn't be put away permanently.

========

The only thing chiropters had in common with helicopters, besides the fact the two words vaguely rhymed, was both could fly. Bats were no more basically blind, winged and mostly night-flying rats than they were rodents. Strictly speaking, while there were chiropteran tee-tees, ones whose wings allowed them to be read like open books (so long as you could decipher the squiggly lingo), regular tee-tees weren't rats either. They were rodents, though.

On the Outer Earth neither bats nor rats could be deemed sentient beings. That didn't necessarily hold true on the Inner Earth of Sedon's Head. Sooth said, which the better storytellers swore they always did, within reason, on the Hidden Headworld there were heaps, if perhaps not hillocks, of different sorts of sentient species. However, even though tee-tees could speak, no one declared them smarter than your everyday or every night average, wires-munching, household rat or belfry bat.

Indeed, most agreed the only reason they could speak was because they were low-grade demons and, intelligence-wise, most demons – be they harmless, sometimes even beneficent agathodaemons or genuinely nasty cacodemons – came in at or near the bottom of the Head's totem pole in terms of sentience. Contrarily, one phylum of demon could and sometimes did possess intelligence approaching the top of said totem pole, where also perched humans, Utopians and devils themselves.

Of course most of these last started out as a different species. The airborne bat pursuing the ground-bound tee-tee was one of them.

Clang! That was the sound the bat made when she swooped in for the kill and instead collided with a big, commercial garbage bin. Seeking howsoever short-lived safety in a back alley, the tee-tee had scampered underneath just that. Crash! That wasn't so much the sound it made as the reality of what happened when the enraged bloodsucker, next to instantaneously transformed, effortlessly flipped the dumpster and hurled it into the concrete wall of the nearest building.

The tee-tee squeaked a terrified yelp when the vampire, impossibly fast by ordinary human standards, impossibly clothed by any logical standards as well, snatched it up.

========

Short, at maybe 5'5 or 5'6, and with a noticeable beer belly, Jordan Q Tethys was a hard-living man evidently in his forties. A street person by choice, he claimed to prefer living outdoors. When he couldn't take over a squat or a cave or even an empty dumpster for himself, he'd sleep under cardboard boxes before paying for a room at an inn or boarding house.

Given what he could do, it wasn't that he couldn't readily acquire the where-withal to fork over for much better than merely decent accommodations. He also had plenty of patrons situated in very comfortable circumstances throughout the Head. Some of them were exceedingly well off. In that regard you couldn't ask for a richer or more generous fellow than Alpha Centauri, who generally resided right here, in Aka Godbad City.

However, Tethys didn't enjoy being beholding to others for much the same reason. Too often others wanted him to do what he could do for them. To live outside the law, he'd heard said as well as sung, in a variety of tongues, you must be honest.

No freeloader, in return for his pilsners, of which he drank copiously, and food, of which he ate as if every meal was his last, Tethys would tell a tale or two. When no one wanted to listen to his stories, he'd go into busker mode in order to earn his beer and eats. The trouble with that was, although he could play just about any instrument there was, and many there hadn't been for long centuries, he could no more sing than he could dance, except at the end of a rope.

Plus, he'd finally remembered, last night's past-last-call, heavy metal band did not feel like jamming with a flautist; especially not with a flautist who flaunted his deviancy. He really shouldn't have drawn his own personal amplifier and speaker system beneath his table. Either that or he should have first thought to draw himself with big pink hair.

He hadn't, which was another indication he'd surpassed his thirty beer limit. He didn't think he had anything to do with the state of his pre-selected townhouse, though. He did wonder how a normal-looking sewing needle could stick a note, along with a severed tee-tee tail, into a freshly painted and therefore non-rusty, metallic dumpster, however.

The note, he read, said: *'I want to see you.'* It was signed *'Janna'*. The *'j'* was in lower case. Always dot your *'eyes'*, he thought to himself. He looked closer at the dot. It was rendered like a disembodied eyeball. *'Oh, aren't you ever so clever, Janna?'* He was about to pluck the note off the garbage bin when he noticed the needle holding it on was glowing ever so faintly. *'Eye of the needle, Janna? Hmm. Me-thinks now you're going out of your way to be funny.'*

"Bat whack, bat whack," squealed a near-rat no longer with a long, squiggly tail.

It lay sputtering its life away across the alley from the overturned dumpster. Tethys was fond of tee-tees. He wasn't at all pleased to see one that looked as if it had been discarded like so much inconsequential trash. Someone must have just missed hitting the bin and really didn't give a good or bad gods-damn it was only three-quarters dead.

Without touching it any more than he'd touched the needle, he bent down to examine the sorry beastie. Most of its throat had been ripped out. 'Oh, that Janna,' he muttered to no one in particular, not even to the hoot-owl perched on a fire escape railing above the alley. For his part, the owl didn't bother hooting a hello.

Mercifully Tethys quickly made sure the tee-tee was four-quarters dead.

========

"Nice crate, Janna," Jordan Tethys said in all genuineness.

It was too. Properly fumigated, it would make for a splendid, even spacious shelter in a back alley somewhere.

========

At 27, married, with one child and another one rumoured to be on the way, Janna St Peche-Montressor remained one of those women about whom it could be said that, when she walked into a room, all eyes were instantly upon her. Cut-short dark hair, shapely, extremely fit and trim without being skinny, everything about her said athlete.

Very little about her said witch, however. Yet that was what she was: two very different sorts of witches, a love-loving Afrite and an Athenan War Witch. The latter was the main reason you didn't want to describe her as drop-dead gorgeous. She probably wouldn't dropkick you dead for it but she could, in the blink of an eye.

As for the former, Lovely Lady Afrites offered up their lovemaking to the goddess and, yes, some of them were fairly free with their favours. It was theirs to give, and yours to receive, but only if they chose to bestow it. You didn't want to whisper, as she passed, that you wouldn't kick her out of bed. You did; you probably wouldn't get out of bed for a month afterwards, let alone out of traction.

You didn't want to *'presume'* upon Lovely Ladies either. While very few were War Witches like St Peche-Montressor, for multiple centuries rape of an Afrite was punishable by castration in the subcontinent of Aka Godbad. That hadn't been the case since the overthrow of the imported, Bandradin aristocracy back in the Fifties and its supposedly democracy-espousing successor, Centauri Enterprises, established the Corporate State of Greater Godbad.

Nonetheless, that's why there remained in the Godbadian vernacular an ancient saying. It went: *'Old traditions die hard – or not!'*

========

He wasn't admiring her backside, though he made sure he was standing well back of her when he opened his mouth just in case she took it the wrong way. She did whirl.

Maybe she did so with malicious intent. Fortunately she smiled the moment she spotted him, 10-feet behind her in the newly built museum's foyer.
   Smiling was good; it certainly beat being knackered.

========

"Jordy! I see you got my message."

That was another thing about this Janna. You didn't want to merely think, as she passed by, that you wouldn't kick her out of bed. All eyes sometimes weren't just on her when she entered a room. Sometimes APM All-Eyes was within SPM and APM's ilk had more than five senses. They may even have had substantially more than five senses. (Then again, the way some of them acted it was more like they didn't have any sense whatsoever, especially not of the common garden snake variety.)

Antique Illuminaries of Weir, whose ancestors were pureblood Utopians and therefore originally extraterrestrial, named this particular, third generational Master Deva Aphropsyche Morningstar, hence APM. A third-born Byronic, the very devil-goddess to whom Lovely Lady Afrites offered up their lovemaking, she most often manifested herself in the form of a human-shaped woman composed entirely of eyeballs, hence All-Eyes.

"I had a dream I should come here. I hope that isn't the message you mean."

"I don't do dreams and neither does APM."

Dream was another Master Deva, a firstborn Mithradite: Phantast Thanatos, as well-travelled Illuminaries from centuries easily 2000 years bygone by now named him. Although officially unbound – at least in Godbadian territories – Athenan War Witches originally swore adherence to the devic Dream Weaver's triplet sister, Heat.

Whereas some disrespectful, as well as foolhardy, devils called her Hot Stuff, those selfsame Illuminaries named her Methandra, after Mediterranean Athena. Her still inviolate protectorate, Mythland, which she abandoned more than 1200 years ago, was once the jewel of Sedon's Crown.

(These days the Mithradite Dream was merely a relatively bright star in the night's sky. The brightest, the Moloch Sedon himself, did not appreciate bad dreams. They made for dreadful ideas and worse repercussions. So, after narrowly avoiding perhaps the worst consequence imaginable – namely the sinking of his precious Headworld – most of 2000 years earlier, he cathonitized Phantast and his allies in the ill-fated Crimson Conspiracy.

(While the vast majority of stars shining out of the Sedon Sphere were devils that directly caused the death of lesser beings, you shouldn't screw with the approaching almighty Eye-Mouth upstairs in the heavens. He didn't need an excuse to cathonitize, catasterize or ill-star, devils that annoyed him. And if he ill-starred an innocent devil, tough two-by-fours. He was beyond punishment. He had to be. No one could cathonitize him. He was Cathonia.)

Jordan *'Quill'* Tethys was white but his skin was richly tanned and prematurely lined, like old parchment. Regardless of his manifest humanity, many devils believed he was a devic suicide, Rumour of Lazareme. Furthermore, most of those believed he was driven to cutting out his third eye by this Phantast-Dream. He wasn't, he asserted. He was a deviant; albeit, he would allow, one with stacks of knacks.

Among them he included occasionally having weird dreams indicating precisely where he should draw himself to such that he'd be in position to accurately report on what occurred there and then. Tethys had had one of his occasional dreams a couple of nights ago, which was why he'd drawn himself to Aka Godbad City.

"But she could."

"Sure she could, if she knew or cared where you were. She's a devil. But I don't see why she'd bother. So long as you weren't in Cabalarkon she'd just go and visit you in person. I don't have the time or ability to do that. So, on the off chance you were in town, I sent a tee-tee to find you. You're their pied piper, aren't you? Attracting tee-tees is one of your whatnot stacked full of bric-a-brac knickknacks, isn't it? What message did you think I meant?"

Puke-spattered as they were – and lacking both the inclination and requisite coinage for a morning at the laundrette – he'd replaced last night's rain slicker, sweats and running shoes. He now wore a scruffy, checked jacket; an oft repaired, though seldom cleaned and therefore not-quite-white-anymore, woollen sweater; an open-necked tee shirt, blue jeans, socks and, despite the wet, chilly weather, sandals. However, he still wore his familiar, peaked, tweed cap, pin-cushioned as it was with feathers like an Irache war chief's headdress.

Multicoloured strands reminiscent of knotted rat-tails wormed out from underneath it. They were the severed tails of tee-tees. As if somehow akin to Incan quipus, Tethys could read their Braille-like nodes, ridges, gaps and depressions. Consequently, he could weave tales out of tee-tee tails. So could any devil and most witches, even ones like St Peche-Montressor, who weren't as thoroughly well trained as Antheans or Korants, the two main rivals for the title of Superior Sisterhood.

He doffed his trademark cap, indicating his latest acquisition. "I got this and I got the message that went with it. It said: *'I want to see you'*. Except, I'm thinking it's the other way around. Shall we go somewhere private?"

She didn't say anything about his thinning hair. Neither did she boot him where it wasn't thinning. Instead she frowned disapprovingly. "Don't be obtuse. Every tee-tee has two tales to tell. I meant the tee-tee itself, not its tail. I told it to tell you I wanted to see you here. Which it must have, otherwise why would you be here, right? I've something to show you. It's in that crate, not in private."

"Perhaps I should have said *'read'*, not *'said'*. The message I got was written on a strip of lined paper ripped out of an ordinary notepad. It was signed *'Janna'*, which I realize is the middle name of every Sraddhite woman over in Hadd. But its *'j'* was dotted with an eyeball, which is highly suggestive. It was attached to a metallic dumpster with a sewing needle. And, unless I'm more mistaken than usual, that's one of APM's more quirky calling cards."

Her frown of disapproval changed into one of concern. "You didn't touch it, did you?"

"Not the needle, just the tee-tee tail. I decided I'd be better off waiting until I had a friendly devil beside me. So I drew the needle into a lead box in my satchel, then I drew you, a friend indeed, as well as both in need and sometimes in deed, whereupon I drew myself to you. That's why I'm here, not what the tee-tee said."

"One of these days I'll get a simple yes or no out of you. And that's all you'll ever get out of me, make no mistake about that."

"Heaven forefend I dare dream such a Phantast-folly. More pertinently, heaven forefend I dare tell you about it. Put it this way, I get feelings. It's one of my bevy of bric-a-brac bents and some of them, you might be shocked to learn, aren't at all bent. The one I got first thing this morning told me that, if I touched the needle then, I wouldn't be here now – though where I would be, well, like I said, I never got that far.

"Lady Luck was on my side once again, it seems. So was the tee-tee itself. Its last words were *'bat whack, bat whack'*, which …"

Something in the nature of relief etched her lips. "As good as identifies the writer as the Janna every Sraddhite woman is named after, I got you. Where is it?"

"Someplace private," Tethys repeated, cap in hand. He tapped one of the feathers stuck in it. The quill glinted a split second, for their eyes only. It was why his initial was a *'q'*. "Last night I blundered big time showing off my deviancy in public. Mind you, that's probably another reason I'm not three nights away from turning in my grave and rising again. I didn't come to until after dawn."

"She'd do that to you? Weren't you once lovers?"

"I was her lover twice, father and son. Actually I was her lover thrice, now that I think about it, but the third time doesn't really count because she was possessed."

"By that other lady, the former Sinistral Lust?"

Tethys nodded confirmatively. "May her star shine forever brightly."

He must have told Janna the tale before. Or someone else had. He was hardly the only yarn-spinner around; just the only one who'd been a recurring deviant for coming up to two millennia. Unless, that is, her inner spirit self (as opposed to her inner soul-self) had been there then, which she may well have been. All three tribes had their own versions of Venus.

"At any crate, we haven't really seen eye to eye since."

"Can the crate cracks, Jordy. And save the eye jokes for APM."

"I thought I had."

"You thought wrong. She's busy beyond the Dome."

"Then I better dispose of it myself. No point inviting Janna Fangfingers to come through without a devil around to protect me, is there?"

"On the contrary, there would be at least two points; one at the end of each of her fangs. Let me call the Fatman first, before you do anything drastic. He might have a better idea."

"Damn it, Janna. I know almost everyone else does it, sometimes to his face, but must you call your father-in-law the Fatman?"

"Oh, I don't mind, Jordy," came a voice from behind them. "Not when it comes from my Janna. Sooth said, I don't mind anything that comes from my Janna, especially grandchildren."

Evidently calling would not be required. Evidently also Janna had seen him because he was smiling at their exchange not unlike a bloated Silenus in the entourage of Dionysus.

========

Alpha Centauri had a new wheelchair. Electronic, hence electric, and, hence also, silent running, what will Centauri Enterprises come up with next?

He'd find out soon enough.

****